THE DEVILS' DARLING

MARISSA FARRAR
S.R JONES

*All rights reserved. No portion of this book may be reproduced, copied, distributed or adapted in any way, with the exception of certain activities permitted by applicable copyright laws, such as brief quotations in the context of a review or academic work. For permission to publish,
distribute or otherwise reproduce this work, please contact the authors at* info@castleviewpress.com.

© Marissa Farrar and S.R. Jones 2024
Published by Castle View Press

Cover Model Photography by Wander Aguiar

Typography by Marissa Farrar
Edited by Lori Whitwam
Formatted by Silla Webb

Written by Marissa Farrar and S.R. Jones

Dedication

To all our dirty Duchesses...
We know your darkest fantasies and put them on the page, just for you.

This is a whychoose, dark, bully romance and as such contains scenes that are expected with the genre, including scenes of SA. For a full list, please check S.R. Jones' website at https://skyejonesauthor.com/trigger-warnings
Your mental health matters.

Come and join the Duchesses at Marissa and Skye's Facebook group, The Duchesses (Marissa Farrar and S.R. Jones). Be the first to hear news about the series, get your hands on exclusive swag giveaways, and hang out with the authors!

***

To read a spicy epilogue, which follows on eighteen months after this book ends, and join the authors' newsletter, follow this link ->>
https://dl.bookfunnel.com/xdoijeo6cg

Do NOT read until after you've finished this book as it contains spoilers! You have been warned!

One

Mackenzie

"Here, pretty kitty, kitty..."

The male voice is distant and muffled, but I can still pick up on its teasing, taunting tone.

I'm in the dark. I don't know how many hours have passed since I was brought here, but I'm still none the wiser about who's taken me. Could Paxton have hired some men? It's not his style, but that doesn't mean it isn't possible.

I've been curled up in a ball on the cold, metal floor of the cage these animals have put me in. A cage! Like I'm a dog. I push myself to sitting. My throat feels like I've swallowed broken glass from having screamed for so long, though it did no good. The chill has worked its way down to my bones, and every muscle aches. I'm grateful for my sweatpants but wish I'd worn something more on top than my tank top. My arms are bare and covered in goosebumps.

From somewhere above, a lock clicks open.

"Here, pretty kitty," the male voice taunts again.

I freeze, my breath solid in my lungs. The clink of metal on metal reaches my ears—the key to the door, perhaps?

Tink-tink-tink.

A door opens, except it's set up high in the wall. Light floods into the room, illuminating a wooden staircase that leads down to the concrete floor that my new home—this disgusting cage—is set upon. My eyes water at the sudden intrusion of light, and I turn my head, my hair falling over my face. It's still slightly damp from where I'd washed it at the spa, so I know I can't have been missing that long.

I'm sure I can still smell chlorine on my skin from my time in the pool with the guys. I'd showered, but it lingers. I inhale deeply, trying to take myself back to that happy place. What will they be thinking? From their point of view, I'll have just vanished. Will they believe I've simply run? It's not as though I don't have a history of doing just that. But things were good between us, finally. We each have our issues, but it felt like we'd managed to put them aside so we could be a unit. My heart aches with longing. I pray they don't think I've abandoned them.

I imagine them thinking I've taken too long in the changing rooms, of coming in and trying to find me. How long would it have taken them to realize I'm not there? I try to remember what happened to my phone. Did I drop it? If so, did whoever has snatched me pick it up? I wonder if my location can be traced, but then I remember it's only a burner. I've deliberately made myself untraceable.

I gulp back a sob.

Heavy, slow footsteps land on the stairs. They creak under the man's weight.

I force myself to take in my surroundings, blinking in the sudden glare. If I'm going to survive this, I need to know my enemy.

Slowly, my eyes grow used to the light, and I'm able to make out the person coming down the stairs. He's almost at the bottom now. A hood is pulled down over his face, holes cut out for the mouth and eyes, like a man about to rob a bank. He's big, thick with muscle, a t-shirt stretched across the bulk of his pectorals and biceps.

Who is this man? What did I do to deserve this? There

are others, too. I've heard their voices and footsteps coming from above.

He reaches the bottom of the stairs and draws to a halt. His gaze fixes on me, still shivering, sitting on the bottom of the cage. His eyes are pale—possibly blue, but in this light seem gray and cold, twin pieces of flint.

I tell myself it's good he's wearing a mask. He doesn't want me to see his face, which means he's worried about me describing him to someone. I can only hope that means they're not going to kill me and might even be planning to let me go at some point.

The hint of a smile touches his lips. "Hello, Kitty."

"Who are you?" I try to keep the tremble out of my voice and fail. "What do you want with me?"

"You're our little pet now."

He holds something up in one hand and gives it a little shake. That metallic clink sounds again—the noise I'd heard earlier. Is that a...collar? What the actual fuck?

In his other hand is a bowl. A food bowl? I remember spilling water and quickly glance around. There's a second bowl already in the cage with me. It's metallic and shiny, and sitting on the floor.

"I brought you something to eat, Kitty," he says. "I thought that was a good name for a *pussy* cat."

Not a dog. A cat.

The inflection on the word "pussy" leaves little to the imagination.

The collar is for me. He's actually going to put a fucking collar on me.

My future suddenly flashes before my eyes. Is that what I've been brought here for? They're going to collar me, and keep me in this cage, and what? Take turns fucking me, over and over?

My blood runs cold.

I can't let this happen, but it's not as though I have

much say in the matter. No, I have to be stronger than this. I must be smarter. I won't just let them take me.

The only thing I can see as a tiny light at the end of the tunnel is that at least I won't live long. Without my meds, my seizures will steadily get worse, and, so soon after the one that hospitalized me, I'll be dead within a matter of weeks, maybe less. But weeks of being repeatedly brutalized by whoever these men are is still too much.

My brain spins with thoughts, and I fight against my rising panic.

Down here, there's only me and him.

My hands aren't bound, and neither are my feet.

If he plans on putting that collar on me, he's going to have to open the cage door. I allow my gaze to slide past him, toward the staircase and the door that remains ajar at the top. What lies beyond the door? More men? Even if I manage to get past this one, will I be able to slip past the others?

One thing I know is I must try. I'm done with waiting for people to rescue me, relying on others to make things right. I need to take matters into my own hands.

The cage is big—tall enough to stand upright in. It's more like a kennel or maybe a bird aviary. Did they buy it specifically with the intention of keeping me, or was it already here? Could it be that I'm not the first girl to have ended up in this place? The possibility that Paxton has nothing to do with this, and I've just been unlucky enough to catch the attention of a bunch of raping, murdering psychopaths, is even more terrifying.

The collar has a metal ring looped around it. I understand what it's for—to chain me to something like I'm a goddamned animal. To hold me in place while they take me. Tears fill my eyes. *Fuck.*

"Come here, Kitty," the man growls. "Hold that pretty hair back for me so I can do this up. You have such a beautiful neck." His gaze drifts down. "Nice tits, too."

"Leave me alone."

"No chance."

He sets down the bowl, and my stomach turns. It's not easy to see what's in it, but it looks like some kind of minced meat. Will I ever be hungry enough to eat from that? Thirsty enough to drink from the bowl? My mouth and throat are already dry, but I haven't been able to bring myself to take that step. I will, though; I know I will, if I'm here long enough. I won't die of thirst or starvation just because of my pride.

He uses a key to open the gate of the cage.

I brace myself, every muscle tensed, my breath caught. My eyes are wide and fixed on the space the gate will leave once it's opened. I know I'll only get one chance at this, and if I time it wrong, I'll be fucked.

The man opens the gate then bends to pick up the bowl.

I take my moment and lunge for the opening, trying to get past him. For a split second, I think I'm going to make it, and my heart lifts in hope, but then his thick fingers wrap around my wrist, and he yanks me back so hard, my head snaps from the whiplash.

He swings me back inside, and I crash against the bars on the farthest side. Pain bursts through me as I slide to the floor on my back.

I let out a howl of misery.

"Where the fuck do you think you're going?"

He enters the cage fully and stands above me, staring down at me. His eyes contain a kind of wickedness I'd hoped to never come across.

I lift my hand to protect my face. "Please, leave me alone."

He jangles the collar at me. "Not until this is around your pretty neck. I've had orders from the boss."

The boss? Who is his boss?

"No!"

I flip myself to my stomach and push onto all fours, but he lifts a large, booted foot, and plants it in the middle of my back, stomping me back down again.

I cry out, pain radiating down my spine and out through my kidneys.

He lifts his foot across me, so he's straddling my back now. I know there's no point in trying to get up again, that he'll only stamp me down, so I reach out and try to commando crawl to get away from him.

He reaches down and fists my hair, pulling hard. He yanks my head back, like I'm a horse in a bridle, arching my neck and spine.

"That's better," he growls.

Using his other hand, he loops the collar around my neck, then he releases my hair and sweeps it out of the way so he can click the metal clasps of the collar into place.

Utterly broken, I let out a sob.

"There's no point in trying to take it off, Kitty. Only a key will unlock the clasp, and you don't have it." He chuckles. "Neither do I, for that matter. Only the boss will unlock it, and I can't see that happening any time soon."

With that, he leaves the cage and pulls the gate shut again, locking it behind him.

With a trembling hand, I reach up and finger the collar at my neck. I understand what this means. It's a sign of ownership.

I don't know who these men are, but I belong to them now.

THE DEVILS' DARLING

Two

Domenic

It's been hours since we realized Mackenzie was missing.

I keep going over everything that happened, analyzing every moment, wishing we'd done something differently. We should have insisted she come into the changing rooms with us, or one of us should have gone with her into the women's room. We'd known this asshole professor had it in for her, but we'd let down our guard.

I pray we don't live to regret it.

My father is calling in some favors with the local cops. He insists they'll have caught whatever vehicle was used to snatch Mackenzie on camera and be able to figure out who it belongs to and where they've gone. I appreciate his optimism, but I wonder how much of it is being put on for Mackenzie's mom. Lucia is beside herself, as we all are.

My brain keeps circling back around to the thought of that fucking professor having taken her. She'd stabbed him because he'd tried to assault her. She was only defending herself, but I bet he believed he was taking what was rightfully his. My fear is if he tried to do it once, and failed, probably try again. This time, he will make sure she can't defend herself. He'll be angry at her, too, and it will make him more dangerous.

The longer she's in his grip, the worse things will go for her.

We've retreated to the den, seeing it as a place of sanctuary, to regroup and get our heads together. The tension in the air is like nothing I've ever experienced before. I feel like our combined anxious energy is enough to blow the foundations out of the entire building.

Tino paces the room. "I can call people in. My family has contacts. They're basically military. They can swarm the whole area looking for her."

I wonder how my own father would take to having Valentino's men involved, but I'm not sure I care. I'll do whatever it takes to get Mackenzie back, unharmed.

"How long will it take for them to get here?"

He twists his lips. "Twenty-four hours. Maybe less."

My heart sinks. "It's too long." Then I give my head a shake. "But do it anyway."

Mackenzie could be anywhere by now. If the professor has taken her, he could have access to her old passport, if she had one, and have taken her out of the country. With every hour that passes, she could be farther and farther away from us. I feel sick at the thought.

The urge to cut myself takes hold. My fingers itch with the need to pick up a blade and press it to my skin. I want to feel physical pain instead of this utter anguish that is tearing me in two. It's like a hunger I need to sate, but I can't give in. My focus needs to be on Mackenzie.

I turn to Kirill, who sits with his hands clasped between his knees, his head hung. He's been quiet, and I know this is eating him up inside.

"What about your father, Kill?" I ask. "I know things aren't easy between you two right now, but would he help if you asked?"

Kirill lifts his blond head. "Fuck, I don't know. I'm not sure him focusing on our Duchess again is a good thing."

"Lesser of two evils," I say.

He presses his lips together and nods. "Let me think on it."

"Okay, but not for too long. She might not have much time."

The phone we found on the ground outside the spa beeps.

The three of us exchange a glance. Who would be messaging Mack's phone?

"It's probably Lola wanting an update," Tino says.

I release a breath and nod. He's right. Mackenzie's friend from back home will be worried about her as well. She knows we have Mack's phone, as we talked to her on it. It's only normal that she'd want to check in to find out what's happening. I'd given her my number in case she remembered anything important that the professor said to her, but she might have forgotten.

I pick up the phone and check the screen.

<*You'll see me soon, my love, whether you want to or not. Pax.*>

I almost drop the phone in shock as I stare down at the message, my heart thundering. I don't understand. If he's the one who's taken her, why would he message her phone? He must know she doesn't have it.

"What does Lola want?" Tino asks.

I continue to stare down at the phone, trying to piece together what this means. "It-it's not her."

Kirill gets to his feet and takes a couple of steps closer. "Who, then?"

"It says it's from Pax, which I assume to be Paxton, but…"

Tino frowns. "Paxton? As in the professor? What does

that mean?"

"I'm not sure. I mean, if he's taken her, he's already with her. Why would he tell her he's going to see her soon?"

"Maybe whoever has taken her works for him," Tino suggests. "Maybe the son of a bitch sent them ahead to snatch her, and they just haven't told him that she doesn't have her phone?"

But Kirill shakes his head. "Not possible. If they let her keep her phone, the professor would know she'd just use it to call for help. No, he'd have instructed them to destroy it. It means he can't know she's been taken."

Understanding sinks in, and I swallow hard. "So, that means the professor isn't the one who has her. Fuck."

Is this good news, or bad? I honestly don't know.

"What's the number on the phone?" Kirill asks.

Finally, I tear my gaze from the screen. "It's blocked. I wish it wasn't. I'd call the fucker back and tell him exactly what I think of him." Something else occurs to me. "If the professor says he's going to see Mack soon, then it means he must be close to Verona Falls."

Tino chews at the inside of his mouth, considering this. "How does he know where she is?"

I try to remember what Lola told us. "Something about finding her mom's car, and a branded pen. He obviously has his contacts, too."

"Shit, so we need to watch out for him as well? What if he finds her before we do?" Kirill tears his hand through his blond hair. "If he doesn't have her, who does?"

I don't even want to think about that. "There was always a possibility the professor wasn't behind her going missing," I say. "Mackenzie's mom had Mack's dad killed because he'd brought bad people into their lives—people who'd threatened Mack's safety. It was part of why Lucia got back in touch with my dad."

"Your dad knows who these people are, is that right?"

Kirill asks.

The planes of his face are sharp like glaciers, the blue of his eyes glinting. His fists are bunched at his sides.

I nod. "Yeah, he should. It would make sense. If they are part of our world, then they're aware of the university, so they'd know where to find her. Maybe they followed us to the spa?"

Tino presses his knuckles to his lips, still pacing. "But if her mom and your dad paid Mack's dad's debt, why would they still come after her?"

I take a breath. "Maybe they just took a liking to her? Decided they wanted her, no matter what."

"Fuck. This can't be happening. This. Cannot. Be. Happening." Tino lashes out, his fist connecting with the wall. Pieces of plasterboard crumble.

His knuckles are bruised and grazed. It doesn't help anything, but I know exactly how he feels. I'd tear down the entire building with my bare hands if I thought it would bring Mackenzie back again.

"We need her," he says quietly, his voice like distant thunder. "*I* need her. It's like someone has torn out a piece of my soul. I keep tormenting myself with what she might be going through. What if someone is hurting her?"

We both know what he means by "hurting." The thought of another man's mouth on her skin, or fingers or cock pushing inside her pussy while she cries and screams, rips me to shreds. I torture myself with the idea of another man's semen inside her, spilling down her throat or filling her womb. I feel sick at the idea.

No, it's too much.

"I never told her I loved her," Tino says.

I shake my head at him. "Stop it."

He doesn't. "None of us did. Why the fuck not? Why didn't we tell her every waking second? Because we do, don't we? We're obsessed with her. We need her. We *love* her."

His dark eyes are glassy with unshed tears.

I duck my head, suddenly ashamed of myself. "I don't know," I mutter.

But I *do* know. I hadn't wanted to make myself weak because of her. I hadn't wanted to be vulnerable. What a fucking idiot I've been.

"We'll tell her," I assure him. "The minute we get her back, we'll tell her we love her, okay? That she's everything to us. That we can't function in this world without her, and we'll give her everything she could ever dream of. That she's ours forever."

"We should have protected her, but we failed," Kirill says. "We let her down." He presses his lips into a line then scrubs his fingers across them. "She'll hate us now. This happened under our watch. How will she ever trust us to keep her safe again? That's what a man should do, keep his woman safe, and there's three of us, and we couldn't even do that. Maybe she'd have been better off with someone else."

Silence settles around us. *Will* she hate us? I don't even want to think about what kind of trauma she'll have been through if we ever get her back. Will she blame us for it?

"We'll make it up to her, okay?" I tell him. "We'll treat her like a fucking princess. We'll make her love us again, no matter what."

"And if she tells us to leave her alone?" Kirill says.

I shake my head at that. "No. She has us. We're hers, and she's ours. That's just the way it goes."

We take what's ours.

"We need to go and find my father." I hold up the phone. "He needs to see this. He needs to know who we're dealing with."

THE DEVILS' DARLING

Three
Mackenzie

They've locked me back in the dark.

Hours pass, and these men still have given me no clue as to why they've taken me. I've cried so much it feels like I've sobbed myself dry. My eyes are sore and scratching, my skin tight. I keep reminding myself I won't just give in, and I'll continue to fight, but I'm weary right down to my soul.

It must be nighttime now.

Exhausted, and with the adrenaline finally leaving my body, I have no other choice than to curl up and try to sleep. I pillow my head on my hands, but I have no blankets or mattress, and the chill from the metal floor continues to seep through my bones.

I don't think I'll sleep, but eventually I do, dozing in and out of a troubled slumber. Nightmares haunt me, but when I try to pull myself out of them, I am caught in one even worse than my imagination can come up with.

Even with the nightmares, sleep offers me a reprieve, and I clutch it with both hands. I miss the guys—and my mom, too—like a piece of my heart has been cut out. I'd give anything to have them with me, though I'd never want them to be trapped in this terrifying situation.

When I eventually wake again, I'm even more disoriented than before. Is it morning? The following day? Or is it still nighttime? If it's the following day, it'll be more than twelve hours since I'd been taken—perhaps even longer. Everyone will know I'm missing. It's a small comfort knowing the guys will do whatever they can to find me, and they'll be bound to bring my mom and Nataniele onboard as well. Despite what I might think of Nataniele, I do believe he genuinely cares about my mom, and he'll do whatever he can to keep her happy. I just pray that includes calling in whatever favors he can to find me.

My bladder aches, but I don't even have a bucket in here with me. I hope they'll at least let me use the bathroom soon. I'm thirsty, too, and my throat feels like I've gargled with gravel.

Finally, my thirst gets the better of me, and I crawl over to the bowl containing the water. My captors probably wanted me to leave it on the floor, and lower my face to it to drink, but I won't give them that pleasure. Instead, I pick up the bowl and tilt the cool rim to my lips. I'd spilled some of the water when I'd first been put in the cage, so only a little remains, but it's enough to wet my lips, throat, and tongue, and for that, I'm grateful.

I've been left the bowl of food as well, but there's no way I can eat. My stomach is in knots. I'm not sure I'll ever be able to eat again. Out of curiosity, I pick the bowl up and give it a sniff. It's not cat food, thank God, but cooked hamburger meat, I think. I've got no intention of tasting it, and I throw the bowl to one side in disgust. How can I trust these people not to have drugged it, anyway? I don't know who they are or what they want. Being drugged and locked in this cage would make me way too vulnerable.

Hopelessness and fear wash over me, and I try to push down the emotions.

I sit down, my back against the metal bars. I lift my hand and finger the collar around my neck.

Who is that man's boss, and why has he chosen me? I remember my mother telling me about the men who'd been making threats against me, why that was the reason she'd felt she'd had no other choice but to have my father killed so she could pay his debt and remove him from our lives forever. The pain I feel over knowing that happened is overwhelming. So much of my life has been a lie. What have I ever done to deserve this?

Though a part of me wants to give in and accept my fate, the other part wants to fight. I've been through so much already, I can't just give in. I want to live. I want to make it back to my men and see if we have a future together.

Maybe my attempt to escape didn't work the first time, but that doesn't mean I can't try again. Whoever has me clearly doesn't think I'm much of a threat, because they've left my hands and feet unbound. They've locked me in this cage, and they believe that is enough.

In my mind's eye, I picture the open door at the top of the stairs and the freedom that lies beyond.

My captor hadn't been distracted enough, that was all. I'd only had that split second while he bent to put down the bowl. I'd needed something bigger, something that would have disabled him, or kept him occupied for longer, and then I'd have made it.

I don't let myself think beyond getting out of the door or the people I might have to face.

I pick up the empty water bowl and bang it against the metal bars.

"Hey!" I yell up at the ceiling. "Hey, I need more water! I'm thirsty."

I crash metal against metal once more, vibrations running up my fingers and arm. To my surprise, making the noise reenergizes me. It's given me a voice. I yell and stamp and bang, certain those assholes above me can hear. I hope they're trying to do something that needs silence, and I'm being as annoying as hell.

I just need him to come back down here, to unlock the gate and leave the door open.

"I need water! I'm thirsty! Hey, you fucking assholes. You hear me? I'm thirsty."

I'm making myself even thirstier by shouting, but if I can get out of here, that won't matter.

With all the noise I've made without anyone trying to silence me, I wonder if it means I'm nowhere anyone else can hear me. They're clearly not worried about the neighbors hearing and asking questions. I must be somewhere remote.

Just as I'm about to run out of steam, the door at the top of the stairs opens.

"Jesus Fucking Christ. Would you shut the hell up? Who knew you'd be such a little brat."

It's him again, the man with the pale eyes.

"I'm thirsty. I spilled my water."

He shakes his head and makes his way back down the stairs. He comes to a halt at the gate of the cage.

It occurs to me that he can just reach through the bars and take the bowl from me. Shit. I need to do something more, so he'll open the gate.

"And it's cold in here." I deliberately shiver and rub at my bare arms. I hate that I'm about to do this, but I have no choice. I need to get him in here. "Look, my nipples are hard."

He snaps his face down to my chest.

Feeling sick, but doing it anyway, I cup my breasts over the top of my tank top and run my thumbs over my nipples. "I'm so cold. I need something to warm me up."

His eyes, fringed with equally pale lashes, go round, pale blue glittering behind the mask. "Is that right?"

"Maybe I need a big man to warm me up." I swallow

hard, aware of how wrong this could all go. "You want to touch them?"

All he's thinking with is his cock. He reaches into his back pocket to retrieve the key to the gate, fumbles it a little, and then manages to unlock it. He swings open the gate and enters. I take a step back, doing my best to draw him in.

"My nipples are very sensitive," I say. "I love them being sucked, too."

He hesitates. "The boss won't like me touching you."

I flutter my lashes. "No one needs to know."

That he'd actually believe I'd want him only attests to his egotism. I hate that I'm exposing myself to this asshole, but I don't have much going for me right now. I must use what I have. I pull down the front of my top, revealing most of my left breast, the pink areola peeping from behind the material.

He lets out a low growl and strides forward to bring himself in front of me. His hand finds my breast, and he yanks my top and my bra down, revealing it fully. My nipple puckers further as cold air hits it.

"Fuck," he groans. "You have amazing tits."

"Suck my nipples," I tell him. "Use your teeth. I like it rough."

He ducks his head, his hot, wet mouth finding my nipple. I hide my revulsion, my stomach balking, and I place my hands on both of his meaty shoulders and slam my knee up as hard as I can between his thighs. From his reaction, I know I've hit the bullseye. He sucks in a wheezy gasp of pain and folds in half.

I don't hesitate.

Yanking my top back into place, I dart past him, focused only on the open door. He reaches out to try to grab me as I pass, but his grip is weak, and I shake him off easily. Then I'm out of the cage and running to the stairs. I can hardly believe this has worked, but I'm not free yet.

My legs feel like they're made of lead, and I can't move fast enough. I hear him cursing behind me, but I think he's still inside the cage. I wish I'd been able to lock him in there—give him a taste of his own medicine—but I couldn't risk trying to find the key.

I scramble up the stairs, focusing only on the light at the top. I'm anticipating it slamming shut the moment I reach it, but it doesn't. I burst through the door and out into a hallway with wooden paneling. I look left and right, trying to work out which way to go, but there's no obvious way out. I pick left and run. At the end of the hallway, to the right, is a door. There's daylight on the other side. I crash into it, and yank at the handle.

My heart sinks. Fuck. It's locked.

A male voice comes from behind me. "Where do you think you're going?"

It's not the man from the cage, but I do know that voice.

I spin to face my captor.

"You," I gasp.

THE DEVILS' DARLING

Four

Tino

After we took the phone to Dom's father, we'd had little choice but to call it a night.

I hadn't wanted to retreat to my room, feeling it was like giving up, but what else could I do? It wasn't as though I'd have been any help, just driving aimlessly around the Adirondacks, shouting out Mackenzie's name.

There was one thing I *had* been able to do.

Before I attempted to sleep, I'd called my father. He hadn't picked up.

Instead, my sister had answered and told me that Papi was in a cartel meeting, and he would be back late. I messaged my father instead and begged for his help. I told him I had met a girl, and I wanted her to one day be my wife, and she'd been taken. I didn't tell him I shared her. He'd have sent his men here to kill me, not to help Kenzie.

With that done, I'd finally been able to sleep, though it hadn't been restful.

Now I've woken, groggy and heavy-headed.

My first thought is Mackenzie.

Immediately, I check my phone.

To my relief, during the night, my father has replied, stating he has sent us eight men in a private jet to help us track down Mackenzie and deal with whoever has taken her. They'll be landing at a local private airport within the next couple of hours. It would have taken them possibly twenty-four hours or longer to get here using scheduled flights, but this way, with the use of the jet, they will be here much sooner.

My father always has an army of around fifty on the compound, so the percentage he's sent me is quite considerable. I had expected he might send me two or three men, but this is more than I had hoped for.

I type back a simple reply.

<Thank you.>

He can be a hard ass, and at times I've disliked Papi intensely. However, he has always come through for me when I really needed it. His hardness wasn't because he didn't love me, or at least that's the way I view it, but because he wanted me to grow to be tough and strong. He might be misguided, and somewhat old fashioned, but, in his own way, he loves me. The fact that he's readily sent me these men, and for a woman he's never met, reinforces my belief that deep down he does care.

I sit and run my fingers through my hair, wincing as the strands rub over my busted knuckles. Picking a fight with the drywall wasn't my most intelligent moment, but I completely lost it. A small part of me that I don't like to examine too closely blames Dom for some of this. Kirill and I were much faster on board with trying to make Mackenzie ours. Dom still held on to that hard, dark lump of hatred in his heart for her mother, and it swayed his actions toward Kenzie.

Climbing out of bed, I wince. It's not only the pain in my hands, but the pain I feel elsewhere in my body, which seems to have surged back with a viciousness that takes my breath away. Perhaps it's because I'm stressed, or perhaps it's because I slept for shit and was tense all night, but either way, my body throbs with pain.

The anxiety is back, too. I bounce on the balls of my feet and shake out my hands, trying to rid myself of the nerves nipping at my skin. I grit my teeth and tell myself this is temporary. This pain will pass, and so will this sense of panic. It continues to claw through me, though, until it threatens to overwhelm me. Jesus Christ, I can't be about to have a panic attack. Not now.

When Dom feels like this, he has his cutting to help him cope. What do I have now? Kenzie is gone, and she was the only thing that made me feel better, other than the drugs. I can't fall back down that dark rabbit hole again. What use would I be to her if I let myself do that? I wouldn't be able to make strategic decisions. Out of the three of us, when my head is in the right place, I believe I'm the one who can make the best calculations. Kirill can be too hotheaded, and as for Dom, well, he's more than a little messed up.

He went to speak to his father last night, to ask for his help. Kirill said he'd messaged his father, too. Although what good that will do is questionable. Kirill's father is a flat-out psychopath. I feel sorry for Kirill having to grow up with that man's influence looming over him. I imagine it would be like being brought up by the devil himself. There aren't many people in this world who truly scare me, but Kirill's father is one of them.

Glancing at the bathroom, I imagine a cabinet full of lovely, calm-inducing medications.

I can't resort to taking the meds again, though, and Kenzie isn't here, but there is something that might make me feel better.

Guilt and sticky shame crawl all over me as I open my laptop. This is so twisted when she's missing, but right now it's the release I need. I'll go insane if I don't do something.

Bringing up the video, I watch as Mackenzie's perfect body fills the screen. Her tits are gorgeous, and then, onscreen, I turn her around, so the camera gets a perfect view of her firm, full ass. Her pussy is bare and on display, wet and ready. She's delectable, and I'm hard as fucking nails.

I push my boxers down, and, using my hand without the split knuckles, I grab my aching dick. I take it slowly at first, enjoying the show as I watch Kenzie onscreen from that first time we were together and I filmed her without her knowledge. But soon, I need the release far more than I need the tease. I increase my speed, my fist moving fast over my swollen length. I smear around the pre-cum at my head, using it as lube, and jerk myself harder.

My grip is almost painful, and I don't know if this is still a distraction or a form of punishment. I grunt, and my back bows as my orgasm hits me. I shoot jets of cum through my fingers and onto the bedspread, staring right at her flushed face on the screen as I do.

When my orgasm subsides and sanity rushes back in, I slam the laptop screen shut. I'm disgusted with myself. Jesus, what sort of a freak am I? I always thought of myself as the saner one out of the three of us, but I bet Kirill and Dom aren't jerking off to videos of Mackenzie while she's missing and in mortal danger.

I wipe my hands on a tissue from the box by the bed and head to the shower. I need to wash the cum and the shame away and get dressed. Today, she needs us, and we can't let her down.

Once I'm showered, I'll go find Dom and Kirill, and we can make a plan.

THE DEVILS' DARLING

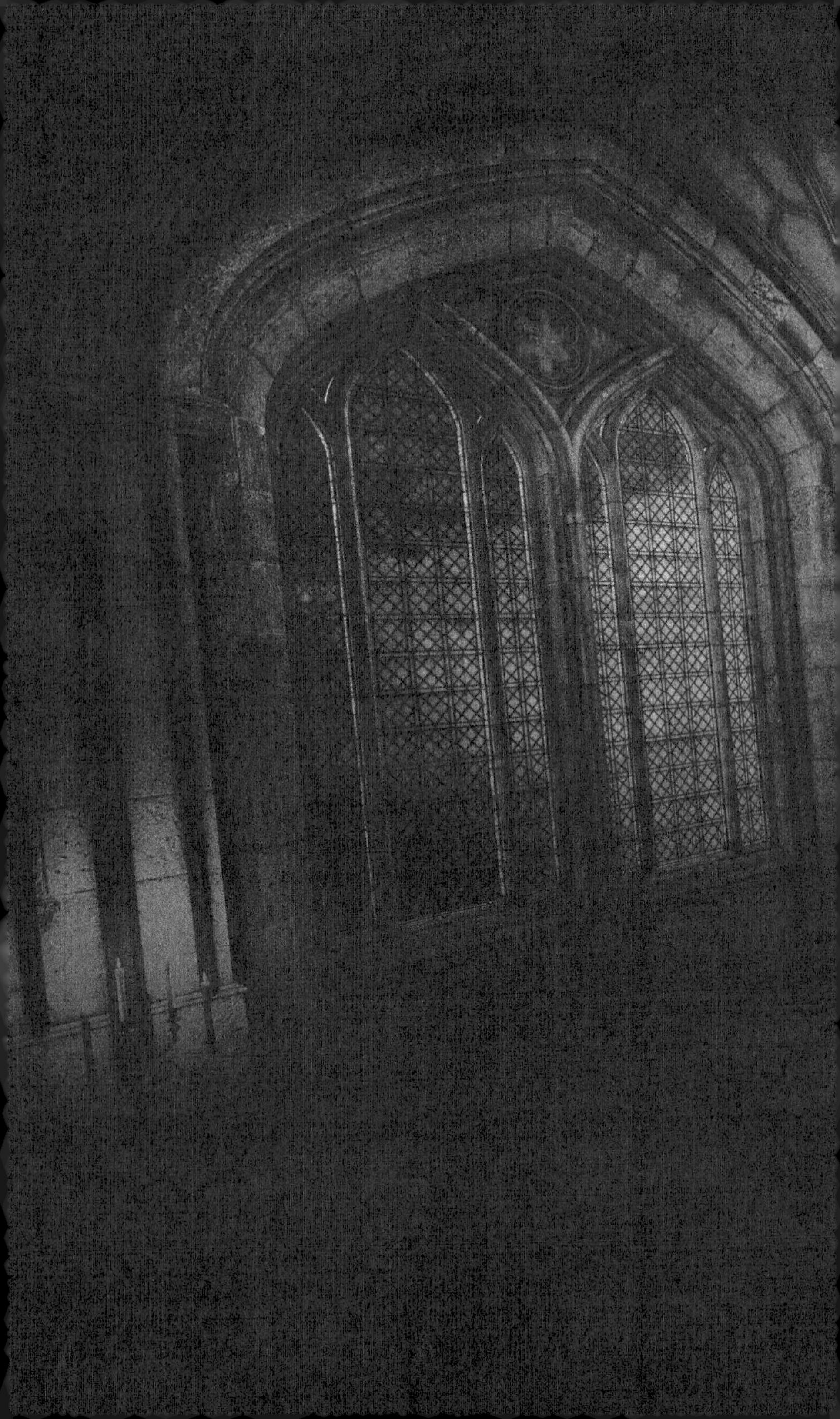

Five
Mackenzie

Standing at the locked door, daylight and freedom tantalizingly on the other side, I struggle to compute what I'm seeing. This can't be right. Deep down, I had assumed Paxton had taken me, or had paid some men to do his dirty work for him. At the very back of my mind, there was the fear that perhaps this was unrelated to anything, and I had been unlucky enough to have been grabbed by strangers intent on finding a girl. Any girl. Maybe I'd even considered the possibility of this being related to my father.

Never once had the man in front of me crossed my mind.

Six and a half feet of pure muscle stares me down. This man has a classically handsome face, but it's hard and savage. All the boyish charm his son still manages to retain has been battered out of this man and erased from his features. Short ash hair, olive skin, and striking blue eyes. He's the sort of man any woman over the age of thirty would fall on her knees for if he turned up to a blind date.

Unfortunately for me, this is no date. Even more unfortunately for me, below his handsome exterior beats the heart of a truly evil man. I know this because I saw what he did to his son.

What he did to Kirill.

"We meet again," Grigoriy Stepanov says. "You look even more beautiful now than you did the first time I saw you."

"Screw you." I sniff. "Kirill is never going to want anything to do with you ever again when he finds out what you've done."

I angrily brush the tears from my cheeks with the back of my hand. I don't want to give him the satisfaction of seeing me scared and upset.

He chuckles. "Oh, he'll find out. Don't you worry."

What does he mean by that? My heart lurches in fear for one of the men I love. Kirill's father might be the one responsible for taking me, but I still don't want Kirill involved. I want him to stay as far away from here as possible. Kirill's weakness is his father.

"Now, you seem to have escaped your cage, little kitten," he says. "How about we get you settled back in?"

Fear kicks in and overrides any sense of self-preservation. As he grabs me by the ring in the collar around my throat, his finger hooking into it, I whirl around and punch blindly in his direction. I can't face the cage again. It's too terrifying.

Small.

Cold.

Alone.

"No," I shout. "I won't go back there."

"Oh, but Kitten, it's your new home." Using the collar, he shakes me like a rag doll, and my teeth clatter together. "Stop struggling. I really wouldn't want to hurt you, now, would I? After all, this face is so pretty. So perfect. You will make such a good Russian wife."

"I'm not going to marry your son just because you say so," I spit back. "And if you think this is the way to make me do it, then you are even more insane than Kirill claims."

He laughs, and it's as cold and hard as the metal floor

of the cage. "How sweet of you. And how naive. You think I bring you all the way here just to make you marry my son? You have made it clear he is not good enough for you. I think you would like the real man, no?"

Oh, my God, he is literally a sociopath.

"You think I'm going to marry *you*?" I can't help the crazed laugh that escapes my lips. "Do you always use a cage as your favorite proposal tool?"

"No, Kitten, the cage is not for the proposal. The cage is for the breeding."

His words fill me with a cold, slithering sense of dread. It writhes inside me like a hundred snakes, and I struggle to breathe. It's like I'm choking on filthy mud, but the mud is his words and intentions.

"You will have a choice, of course." He shrugs casually. "I am a gentleman like this. You can either take me or my son."

"Your son isn't here," I point out.

"Not yet, he isn't. We will rectify that mistake."

What does he mean by that? Is Kirill coming here? A terrible thought occurs to me; what if Kirill knows about this? What if he's in on this plan? He'd said he wanted to marry me, hadn't he? Could he be working with his father to get what he wants?

No, I'm sure he wouldn't do this to me. Kirill has had some crazy moments, but deep down I believe he cares about me. He knows about my epilepsy and how dangerous it is for me to be without my meds. He wouldn't risk my health like this.

Grigoriy reaches out and catches me by the upper arm. "Come on, Kitten. Back to your cage."

Then he pauses, and his thumb rubs the inside of my arm. His eyes narrow, his lips thinning with displeasure. For a moment, I've got no idea what's going on, but then he yanks me closer.

"What is this?"

His thumb presses painfully into the spot on the inside of my arm, and it dawns on me that he's found my contraceptive implant.

"Wh-what?"

"This in your arm. This is an implant, no? To stop you having babies."

It's not as though I can deny it. "I'm too young to have children."

"That is bullshit. You are plenty old enough. You are a grown woman. Now I must deal with this."

A fresh shot of fear goes through me. What the hell does he mean by 'deal with this'?

"Come with me."

He keeps his hand clamped around my arm and drags me toward the stairs that run above the door for the basement. I try to pull back on him, but it's impossible. His strength is terrifying. It's as though a giant has hold of me.

I trip and stumble as he pulls me to the second floor, bashing my shins. Tears fill my eyes.

He pulls me into a bathroom and slams the door shut before locking it from the outside.

"Just making sure you don't try to run again," he says.

The bathroom is small, and his huge body blocks the way. There's no way I can get past him. He lets go of my arm and reaches one meaty fist to the mirrored medicine cabinet above the white porcelain sink. He swings the door open, and I catch my reflection in the mirror. Dark circles are beneath my eyes, and my skin is pale. I look like a petrified ghost version of myself.

"Aah, got it," he says and shuts the cabinet door again.

Pinched between his thumb and forefinger is the sliver of a single-edged razor blade.

He's going to cut the implant out of my arm.

I widen my eyes and shake my head. "No, please."

"This is going to happen, and if you fight and struggle, you'll only make things worse for yourself. I'd hate to nick an artery by accident."

I freeze, the image of me bleeding out on this bathroom floor filling my head. I don't want to die. I've fought for so long; I refuse to give up now. Unless someone has dealt with a chronic illness for most of their lives, they've got no idea how difficult it's been just to keep going some days. After my diagnosis, it had been so hard waking up in the mornings, knowing this was my life now. I'd grieved for the carefree girl I used to be before I had to constantly think about medications, and nutrition, and my stress levels, and grieved for the future I'd believed had been over.

I won't win against this man, not on a physical level.

Holding out my arm, I squeeze my eyes shut and turn my face away. "Just be quick."

I hear his smile in his tone. "Good girl."

The cold, sharp blade presses against my flesh, right at the base of the matchstick sized implant beneath my skin.

"Keep still," he tells me.

I can't help that I'm shaking. I swallow hard, and tears trickle down my cheeks. I brace myself for the pain.

When it comes, it's like fire or ice burning up my skin. I can't help it, I automatically try to pull away, but he clamps my arm tight. Hot blood flows down the inside of my bicep, pooling in the crook of my elbow. He produces a pair of tweezers, and I scream as he uses them to dig into my flesh, trying to get purchase on the tiny implant. He finally manages it and pulls, but there is resistance. A rush of heat floods over me, and I'm not sure if I'm going to be sick or pass out, or maybe both. The room spins around me. Fuck no, I can't have a seizure now. I just can't.

I remember my yoga breathing, and the sense of the room spinning fades.

"Got it," Grigoriy says, holding the implant up between

the twin points of the tweezers like he's caught some rare insect.

He tosses both items into the sink and then regards the blood running down my arm. "Better get you cleaned up."

I hold my arm out mutely as he finds wipes and a bandage. The way he patches me up is almost with tenderness and compassion, which goes completely against the way he's treated me so far. When he's done, he steps back to admire his handiwork.

"There. You are better."

I just nod, the pressure of the bandage and pain in my arm a constant reminder of how fucking insane this man is.

I'm also worried about what the change in hormones is going to do to my body. There might be a chance it'll bring on more seizures, especially as I don't have my meds. But a change in hormones will be the least of my worries if this man gets what he wants.

I know from warnings from my doctor that removal of the implant means I can get pregnant pretty much right away. Pregnancy isn't something I can take lightly, especially as my seizures aren't currently under control. The medications I take means a baby has a higher chance of having birth defects, and while some women might choose to stop taking them, if they haven't had a seizure for a year or two, I'm not in that position.

It's on the tip of my tongue to tell him the truth, but what will he do if he knows I'll not be the perfect Bratva wife and mother he wants for his son? He'll have no use for me then, and I highly doubt he'll just let me go. He'll probably decide to let his men have their fun with me—to use me and abuse me—and then one of them will kill me.

I can't let him know the truth.

"Now, let's get you back to your cage," he says.

My bladder aches. "Can I use the toilet first?"

He twists his lips, and for a moment, I think he's going

to refuse me, but then he nods. "Very well."

He turns his back on me, and I realize he's not going to leave. I'm too desperate to complain, and I pull my sweatpants and panties down, folding over on myself to try to hide my body from him, and relieve myself in a hot gush of urine.

He keeps his back to me, and I wipe, and flush, and rearrange my clothing as I stand. At the sound of the flush, he turns to face me.

"Done?" he asks.

"I'm just washing my hands," I mutter, keeping my head down.

They're sticky with blood, and do need washing, but mostly I'm thinking about that razor blade. He's just left it on the side of the sink, the sharp edge dark with my blood. It's not much of a weapon, but it's something. If I could just get my hands on it, I could use it to slash his goddamned throat.

I turn on the faucet and run my hands beneath the warm water. Diluted blood swirls against the white porcelain, and I angle my body to block his view.

Carefully, trying not to make any jerky movements that will alert him to my actions, I reach out to the blade, my fingertips touching the cool metal.

Grigoriy's hand slams down on top of mine, a fresh wave of pain hitting me.

"Do not get any stupid ideas, Kitten."

I let out a sob. That was my one chance, and it's gone.

He turns off the faucet for me then takes hold of the ring in the collar.

"Come."

He pulls me from the bathroom and back down the stairs to the first floor. He drags me so harshly that I trip and stumble. He doesn't try to hold me upright, but instead lets go so I fall hard on my knees. He kicks me, his shoe connecting with my ass, laughing as he does.

"That's it, little Kitten, crawl to the stairs. Make your way back to your cage."

A murderous rage fills me. I welcome it because it's so much better than the fear. If it's the last thing I do, I will get my revenge on this man. He doesn't know who I really am. Look what I did to the professor. He might be a terrifyingly huge Bratva leader, but he's still flesh and blood. And that means he can bleed.

I reach the stairs leading down to the basement, and he pulls me up by my hair, making me yelp. A second man appears in the doorway, a vicious-looking gun glinting in his hand. It's not the one who came down to collar and feed me in the cage. How many men are here?

"Do you need me, boss?" he asks.

"No, I think we can manage," Grigoriy says. "Can't we, little Kitten?"

"Get the fuck off me," I grit out.

He laughs. "Come on, my sweet pussy, let's go play. Maybe we can call Kirill and let him listen in."

I struggle, but it's no use. He pushes me down the stairs, and it takes all my focus not to fall and tumble down them. I'd probably break my head open if I did, so I try not to trip as he manhandles me roughly down to the bottom of the steps.

Instead of the collar this time, he takes hold of my wrist.

Grigoriy marches in front of me and pulls me behind him to the cage. He opens the door and throws me in, then slams it shut. I should step away, out of reach, but I don't. He reaches through the bars and grabs me at the last moment, one big, meaty hand wrapped around my neck.

With his other hand, he produces a large padlock from his pocket and yanks me close, so my face is pressed against the bars.

I realize what he's about to do, and terror shoots

through me.

"No, no, stop!"

He loops the hook of the padlock through the ring on the collar and quickly fastens it to the cage. The bars run vertically, but there are also three horizontal bars at equal spacing to strengthen them. He fastens me to a section in the middle, so I can neither slide the lock to the top or the bottom, preventing me from either lying down or standing straight.

Grigoriy stands back and admires his work. "That's better. No running now."

I let out a sob and claw at the collar and the lock. Already, the muscles of my lower back burn from the awkward position I'm in, and I sink to my knees to relieve the pressure. I look up at Grigoriy with intense hatred.

"Put your arms behind your back," he commands. "Let me see you push that chest out for me."

I ignore him, so he grabs my tank top and pulls me toward him, twisting the material in his fist.

"Fine," he snarls. "I'll just rip it down the front and free these nice tits."

And he does. He tears my top as easily as if it's made from tissue. He rips right down the middle until it floats around my sides in tatters, and then he pulls the remains from my body and tosses it away. It reveals my bra and the waistband of my sweatpants.

I try to cover myself with my hands, but he reaches between the bars and pushes them away.

"You've got the best tits I've seen in a long time. How about I take a closer look? After all, you're going to be feeding my heirs. Best make sure I think they're good enough."

He roughly pulls my bra down, and I cry out in dismay. I try to gather it against me, but he yanks it hard enough that the metal hooks at the back give, and he drags the straps down my arms, the material grazing my skin. His calloused hands grab my breasts, plumping them together and squeezing them upward for his perusal.

I hate the feel of his hands on me. I'm sick to my stomach and terrified, but I'm also utterly helpless, and that is the worst.

"Lovely," he breathes. "Fucking perfect tits. What a delicious little find you are. My son did well, but he failed to land the catch, as the Americans say."

I can't speak because I'm too terrified and traumatized. My words have dried up in my throat, and even my tears have run dry. I'm frozen. Held captive by fear.

He brushes his thumbs over my nipples, and I shudder in disgust. "Ah, you don't like that, Kitten? Wish it was my son?"

He drops to his knees, astonishingly graceful for a man so big. He licks his lips and pulls me right up against the cage until two metal bars frame one of my naked breasts. Then he ducks his head and sucks my nipple into his mouth.

My stupor breaks, and I reach through the bars to pound on his head and shoulders, trying to get his disgusting mouth off me, but it's like hitting rock. He suddenly sinks his teeth into the skin around the areola, and I scream in pain. I'm sure he'll have left teeth marks.

Satisfied, he releases me.

"Feisty," he observes. "This is good. We want fight in our women. The Bratva don't want meek and mild little mouses."

His English is wrong, but I don't correct him because we're too busy staring at one another. He with an odd mix of seething loathing and desire, and me with rage and terror.

"You have made me hard now," he says.

He cups his crotch, and I can't help but look at the powerful bulge there. Jesus, how big is he?

I think I'm going to find out because he unzips his pants and slowly reaches inside.

I'm frozen and horrified but unable to look away as he pulls his cock out and drops it in front of my face. He's only half hard, and he's hung like a fucking horse. Fear courses through me. If he uses that thing on me, he'll tear me apart. He's as thick as a beer can, and long, too.

"You like what you see, Kitten?" He smirks. "It is very big, the many women I've fucked tell me."

He's not wrong, but it's not big in a good way. It's freakishly big. No woman is going to look at it and think anything but *ouch*. I wonder how many of those women he claims to have fucked have spread their legs willingly.

"You're going to have to loosen your jaw, Kitten. You look tense, and if I shove my fat cock in your mouth right now, your jaw will break."

Do I beg? I doubt it will work. Cry? Plead? Bargain?

How do I get out of this?

Then a calmness washes over me. I can bite it off. I can bite the fucker so hard, he'll never procreate again. But if I do, he'll kill me. I need to understand that choosing that course of action is a death sentence. This is not a well-adjusted man.

He watches me, smirking, arrogant, and I hate him so fucking much. I won't let him rape me. I'll die stopping him. This man of all men doesn't get to have me that way, I loathe him far too much.

"Or we can call my son? What do you think to that?"

I shake my head. "No, leave him out of this."

Throwing Kirill into the mix will likely get him killed.

Grigoriy growls suddenly, all the vicious playfulness gone as he loses his temper spectacularly. I don't know what set him off, but he picks up a chair and smashes it on the floor with a bellow of rage. He looks almost comical, with his massive dick swinging about as he breaks the chair. Almost, but he's far too unhinged and terrifying for me to laugh.

He turns back to me and grabs my nape through the

cage. I scrabble at his forearm, using my nails, but it's useless.

I realize he's using his other hand to dial someone on his phone, and, after a moment, I hear Kirill's familiar voice greeting his father. Grigoriy has put him on speaker.

It's so comforting and intimate to hear him that I can't stop the desperate sob that escapes me.

Kirill recognizes me instantly.

"Mackenzie?" Kirill's voice is shocked. "Father? What the fuck have you done?"

"Son."

"What the fuck is going on?"

"I have your unwilling bride here. You seemed reluctant to marry her, too, so I thought I'd take matters into my own hands. I'd like another heir. I thought you and she could carry on our line, but I'm more than happy to breed her myself. I have the perfect cage for her here."

"Cage? What the fuck?" Kirill sounds dazed. As if he's just woken from a deep sleep.

"Yes. It's perfect for the little kitten. I'm going to fuck her, son, and I'll destroy her tight little pussy. I'll split her in two. Then I'll fill her with my cum and get her pregnant."

Kirill roars in anger, his voice echoing around the bare room. "I'll fucking kill you."

His father laughs. "Of course, you will. You'd have to come here first, though."

"Don't do it, Kirill," I shout. "Don't give him what he wants."

Grigoriy glances at me. "Come here, Kitten." He grabs my hair through the bars and tugs so hard I scream in agony.

"What are you doing to her?" Kirill demands over the phone.

"Nothing much," Grigoriy laughs, "just a little fun. Now, are you coming for her? Or do I need to shove my cock in her?"

"I swear to God –"

"Son, shut the fuck up and get here. Take down the coordinates of the cabin."

Grigoriy lists off a reel of numbers that mean nothing to me.

"Did you get that?" he checks.

"I wrote it down," Kirill bites back.

"Get your ass here, alone. If you bring anyone else, I'll gut her, and you'll find nothing but her entrails. I fucking mean it. I have cameras and drones, so don't think you can outsmart me."

Kirill makes a broken noise, a half sob, half growl of rage. "Hold on, Mack. I'm coming."

"Ah, how touching," his father laughs. "I told you that you two crazy kids were meant for one another. You'll thank me for this, son. One day."

"You touch her, and I swear to God..." Kirill threatens.

"Let Kirill know how excited you are to see him," Grigoriy orders. His massive hand grabs my breast again, and he squeezes so hard, I see stars.

I cry out, and Kirill roars again.

"I'm coming. Leave her alone. If you touch one hair on her head, I'll kill her myself, and then you."

He will kill me? *Kirill* will kill *me?* My head spins, and I fall backward, but the lock attached to the bars snags against the horizontal bar as I slide to the floor. The collar tightens around my throat, choking me, and I force my shaking legs to push back up into a kneeling position.

"You'll kill her?" Grigoriy sounds vaguely intrigued. "Why would you do that?"

"Because you ruin things, and I'd rather she was dead than having to live with the poison you put inside people. Keep your fucking hands off her until I get there."

His father laughs. "Son, sometimes you make me proud. But don't go thinking you can sneak a gun in here. If you kill her, you'll have to use your bare hands. You bring a gun, and

I'll shoot her in the head before you can get to where I am keeping her. No weapons. Don't fuck with me. If you do, I'll tie you up in the dark with her dead body and leave you for weeks. Until you fade away, too."

There's a choked sound of utter rage. "Don't fucking touch her. I'll be there, and I won't bring a gun."

Kirill hangs up, and I lean my head against the bars as I start to cry.

Hearing him talk about killing me has broken something inside me. Why do I keep convincing myself that the Devils are anything more than the depraved men I first came to know? If Grigoriy rapes me, will Kirill see me as damaged? Will he shoot me rather than have to look at me, knowing his father has been inside me?

He's clearly as deranged as his father, and not the man I thought he was at all.

Grigoriy puts his disgusting cock away and walks to a chair in the corner of the room. He sits back, his legs spread wide, and takes out a large knife from a sheath around his ankle. He proceeds to throw it up in the air, always catching it by the handle, not the blade.

"Now, little Kitten, we wait."

THE DEVILS' DARLING

Six

Kirill

I end the call, my entire body vibrating with rage.

I can't believe what he's done. The man who has haunted my entire life with his sick and twisted presence has gone too far this time. I never believed I could take his life, because to do so would mean coming up against the entirety of his organization. In recent years, though, that organization has changed. Some of his men have been lost to war, and others have been lost to my father's own carelessness. He sent them into fights they could never win, and in doing so, while he consolidated his power, he also devastated the number of men he had at his side.

The ramifications of what I want to do are huge, but I can't let him ruin Mackenzie's life as well as mine.

I hate myself for what I said about her. All I can imagine is her face, as she believes I would betray her. I would never do that, but I know my father only too well. If he believes I'll cry and beg, he's much more likely to keep pushing and pushing, doing ever more sick and twisted things. He might be clinically insane, but he's also predictable. After so many years in his orbit, I know how he operates. It means I understood immediately threatening to kill Mackenzie if he soiled her with his touch would actually make sense in his sick mind.

For some reason, he wants us to have a baby. I don't know what deranged thought process is fueling him, but that's the outcome he's focused on. If I let him think that touching Mackenzie means that will never happen, I do believe he'll leave her alone until I get there.

Guilt hits me. I should tell Tino and Dom, but I know if I do, they'll insist on coming with me. Or worse, they'll follow me. My father's threats are not empty.

If I don't go alone, he will kill Mackenzie.

I must do this by myself and somehow buy some time. There will be a way out of this for us both; I just need to figure it out. Hell, I really believe that if he thinks we're going to give him an heir and get married, my father will probably let us go. He'll think this is an amusing story about how we met. He'd probably tell it at our wedding, and everybody will think it's some sort of bad taste joke, but we would know it was the truth.

The sick and disgusting truth.

The legend within our family goes that my grandfather kidnapped my grandmother. They say he saw her at a dance, fell head over heels in lust, and when her family said no to his initial overtures, he decided to simply take her. He parked by the side of the road when he knew she'd be walking alone and waited until she passed by before throwing her in the back of his car and driving her to his home. She never saw her family again except for organized visits, where he had his entire armed guard on alert in case they tried to take her back.

If that's how his parents met, no wonder my father has a warped idea of what romance is.

I need to get Mackenzie out of there, and then, when she's safely back here, I'll do whatever it takes to put my sperm donor in the ground. He's lost all rights to call himself my father, and he's going to fucking pay for this.

I tear the paper from the notepad and shove it, crumpled, into the pocket of my jeans. I grab my phone and my wallet and push them into my pockets, too.

Before I leave, I pause. Should I take a gun? He said not to, but fuck, that leaves me and her exposed. I drop to the floor and reach under my bed, pulling out a lockbox. Inside it is a Glock 22. It's an American gun—one their police use—and I always figured if it was good enough for an American cop, it was good enough for me.

I hover with it in my hands, desperate to slide it into the back of my pants but knowing my father's men will search me the minute I arrive. Perhaps I can put it in the vehicle with me? Leave it where they won't find it? At least then I'll have access to it if we manage to escape. I decide that's what I will do. That way, I won't have it on me when I get searched, but I will have it close by. If we escape and we can reach the vehicle, we can get the gun, and it gives us more of a chance.

For now, I stuff it behind my waistband and cover it with my t-shirt. Opening the door, I poke my head out and make sure there is no one around.

I really don't need to run into Dom or Tino right now. They'll most certainly want to talk, and the minute I do, they're going to figure out there's something seriously wrong. Instead of walking down the hallway to the main stairs, I turn right and sneak down the back way, toward the service entrance.

Once I'm there, I slip into the kitchen and loiter around where the dishes are being stacked. Just beyond here is a door leading into a pantry.

I know on the wall of the pantry there's a set of keys, which belong to a truck that's always parked outside, unless it's on a run to fetch more vegetables and fresh produce, that is.

I wait, trying not to look suspicious, and hoping no one will question me, until the dishwashers have all gone to collect more plates to wash. When there's no one around, I slip into the small pantry space and grab the keys.

I press the latch on the door to the outside and open it. The bright sunshine of the day hits me as I step outside. It's disorienting after such a bizarre phone call.

The world somehow doesn't seem real. I shake my head and try to focus. The small truck is parked only a couple of meters away, and I jog to it, climbing in and starting the engine before I peel off down the drive.

No one will stop this vehicle at the gates because it comes and goes sometimes up to three times a day. Still, my hair stands out and the security guards will know me.

Crap, I hadn't thought of that. Slowing the vehicle to a crawl, I glance around and sigh in relief when I see the baseball cap on the seat next to me. Again, I thank God for seemingly being on my side right now.

I grab the baseball cap and pull it down tightly over my head. I tuck the strands of hair sticking out under the cap and pull it low over my brow. When I get to the security gates, I keep my head down and just jerk a brief nod at the guards.

If I lift my head and they see my nose ring, it might give me away. Luckily for me, the guards seem to be in a world of their own, and they wave me through without even looking.

I drive like a possessed man to get to the cabin where my father has taken Mackenzie. It's over an hour away, and I swear that hour is the longest of my life. It feels even longer when I'm forced to leave the main road and take a narrow mountain track, slowing my progress. The trees seem to close in around the truck—oak, maple, and birch, their leaves beginning their turn to oranges and reds—and every so often their branches hang so low that they screech across the roof of the vehicle like nails on a chalkboard.

With every second that passes, I torment myself with the thought of my father and Mackenzie. I have no doubt in my mind that he would take her against her will. The picture in my head of him holding her down and forcing her makes me want to pull the truck over and vomit onto the side of the road. How would she ever recover from that—physically and mentally? Our little doll would be broken, and now I realize just what stupid games we've been playing. We never truly meant to break her, not like that. Even Dom would never have wanted to see her hurt in such a way.

I wonder if the others have noticed I'm missing yet. What will they think? I'm fairly sure they'll piece things together quickly enough. They will know I've gone after our Duchess, and since I'm the one who's gone, I'm sure they will put two and two together and realize my father is the one behind all of this.

The road grows even narrower, and I bump and jolt inside the tin can of a truck, my knuckles white around the steering wheel. The gun presses against my lower back, where I've wedged it into my waistband, and I try to plan what my actions will be when I arrive. A part of me—the biggest part—wants to go in shooting. I want to kill every single motherfucker who has so much as looked at Mackenzie. But I hold myself back. If I start shooting, my father will hear the gunshots and decide to put a bullet in Mackenzie's head before I reach her.

It feels as though no matter what choice I make, I will lose.

And so will she.

I check my location and realize I'm close. I stop the truck, and, knowing it is for the best, I look around behind me. There are a few crates, and some have food in them—a perfect place for me to hide the gun. I clamber over the seat and stuff it down into a crate of oranges. Then I get back into the driver's seat and face forward, my hands on the wheel for a long moment as I brace myself for what is coming. My heart beats faster, and I force myself to slow my breathing. I can't go in there raging, as much as I want to. I need to be like *him*—cool, controlled, unemotional.

It's the only language he understands.

I get moving again, and finally, the dirt road opens. A clearing in the trees reveals a large, double story log cabin. I kill the engine, though I'm sure my approach will have been heard already. I sit behind the wheel for a moment, watching for movement, but there is none. That doesn't mean they aren't perfectly aware of my presence, however. I remember my father's threat of cameras and drones to make sure I came alone, but there's nothing obvious. Maybe he was bluffing.

I draw a shaky breath and open the driver's door. I climb out and look around the area, but there's no one around.

With no other choice, I approach the front door and bang on it with my fist.

It opens, and a man I don't recognize stands in the doorway. He must be one of my father's new additions.

"Arms out," he says.

He's going to search me, and I'm grateful I didn't try to get away with the gun.

He searches me thoroughly and steps back with a smirk. "Good boy."

My teeth clench, and for just a moment I wish I'd come in guns blazing.

Movement comes from behind him, and my gaze travels past this man's shoulder to land on Igor. That son of a bitch.

"It is okay, Rufus," Igor says. "I can take it from here."

Rufus and Igor switch places, and Rufus retreats deeper into the cabin and out of sight. I set my attention on Igor. This fucking bastard is the man I loathe more than anyone else, other than my father. I stare at him, hatred pumping through my veins with more ferocity than venom.

"Are you going to let me in," I spit, "or should I just wait here while you figure out a way to get your tongue even farther up my father's ass?"

Igor ignores my comment.

"You came," he says as if surprised. "Thought you'd be too scared, but then again, she is a prize piece of ass, and if your father shoved his frankly freakishly massive cock in her, he'd ruin her for a young man like yourself. He'd stretch her wide open, and you'd never satisfy her again, so I can see why you rushed."

There's a rock to the side of the door and it's out of Igor's eyeline. His leering grin makes me seethe and, without thinking, without letting my mind run through the consequences and acting purely on an autopilot of sheer hatred, I bend down and pick it up. Igor looks confused as I straighten. I smile at him and then swing my arm and smash the rock into his face.

He staggers back with a yell and clutches his face. Then he falls to the side, rolling to his left and groaning.

"You've had that coming for a long time." I spit on him in disgust. Fucking bastard. "I do wonder, too, how come you're so well acquainted with Daddy Dearest's cock. Does he shove it down your throat on the regular?"

The sound of a gun cocking to my side is no surprise. But I don't care. I wanted to show Igor how much I hated him, and I have. I didn't break Father's rules and shoot anyone, and I doubt he'll murder Mackenzie over me smashing up Igor's face.

I'm also fully convinced now that my father uses Igor for more than just security. I shudder, not wanting to imagine my father that way with anyone, never mind the man I hate so much.

It hits me then that I could end my father's life without raising a fist to him. If he really is doing something with Igor, and something about the way Igor looks at him and that last comment has clicked into place for me, then that would be enough for them to be killed in the patriarchal world they are from.

Could I get Tino to do some of his magic and find out if he can spy on my father? If I can make him think Mackenzie and I are going to do his bidding and buy us time, can I work with the other two to bring him down?

Now, though, I must appease that bastard by whatever means are necessary to get me and our Duchess out of here alive.

"Take me to my father," I say to Rufus.

He nods and jerks his gun toward a door at the end of the hallway. "Down the stairs."

I walk toward them, my heart pounding as I descend the stairs into the basement. My fucking father and his love of basements.

But my fear of the dark and small places is eclipsed by what greets me.

Mackenzie is on her knees, locked inside a large cage. She's naked from the waist up, collared, and chained by her throat to the bars. There's a bandage around her upper arm, and dark blood spots seep through the white.

My soul breaks in two.

I stare at her, and she looks up at me. All I see is despair. I hold her gaze, trying to show her with my eyes that I love her so fucking much.

Something else catches my eye. Inside the cage with her are two metal bowls.

The sight of them propels me back in time, to when I was a child and it was me in that cage. The impact on me is so strong, it's as though someone's just shot a syringe of adrenaline into my heart. The dank basement seems to pull away for a moment, and, for one crazy moment, I think I might pass the fuck out. I fight to control my breathing and regulate my heartbeat, and gradually I come back fully into the room.

I'm not a child anymore. I'm a grown man, and I need to handle my shit for Mackenzie's sake.

I want to go and cover her, but I can't show even a hint of weakness to my father. He'll kill me if I do, and then he'll fuck Mackenzie himself.

"Igor is indisposed," I say to Grigoriy as he regards me coldly.

The guard, Rufus, has also followed me down the stairs. He has his gun on Mack, not me.

My father raises an eyebrow. "You got here quickly. You really hate the idea of your old man touching your woman that much, huh?"

"Yes," I say simply. "She's mine, not yours."

"Fine." He jerks his chin. "Then fuck her. Make her have your child."

"She's on birth control," I say.

He gives a sly smile. "Not anymore."

So that's what the bandage is for. The son of a bitch cut out her implant. He's a fucking monster.

"It could still take weeks for her to get pregnant," I say incredulously. "People will be looking for us."

"Breed her, or I fucking will. Then you will marry her as soon as I can get a priest here. Once you and she are married, no one can put a stop to it, or do anything about it. It's the way things work in our world. You know that."

I stare at him in horror.

My father laughs. "Now, I see you think I am sick. Maybe I am, but not so sick I want to watch my son fuck his little kitten. I'll leave you with Rufus here, and Vadim."

I turn to see a second man has entered the room. Vadim is one of my father's most dangerous guards. His soul is pitch black and his anger management non-existent. When I was younger, I thought there was something supernatural about him because of the paleness of his eyes.

"If my son fails to mount his kitten," my father commands them both, "feel free to shoot him and let me know so I can do the job properly."

My father stands and slaps me on the back.

"Have fun, son. She's a gorgeous little pussy cat."

Then he leaves the basement, and I turn to face Mackenzie, dread balling in my stomach.

THE DEVILS' DARLING

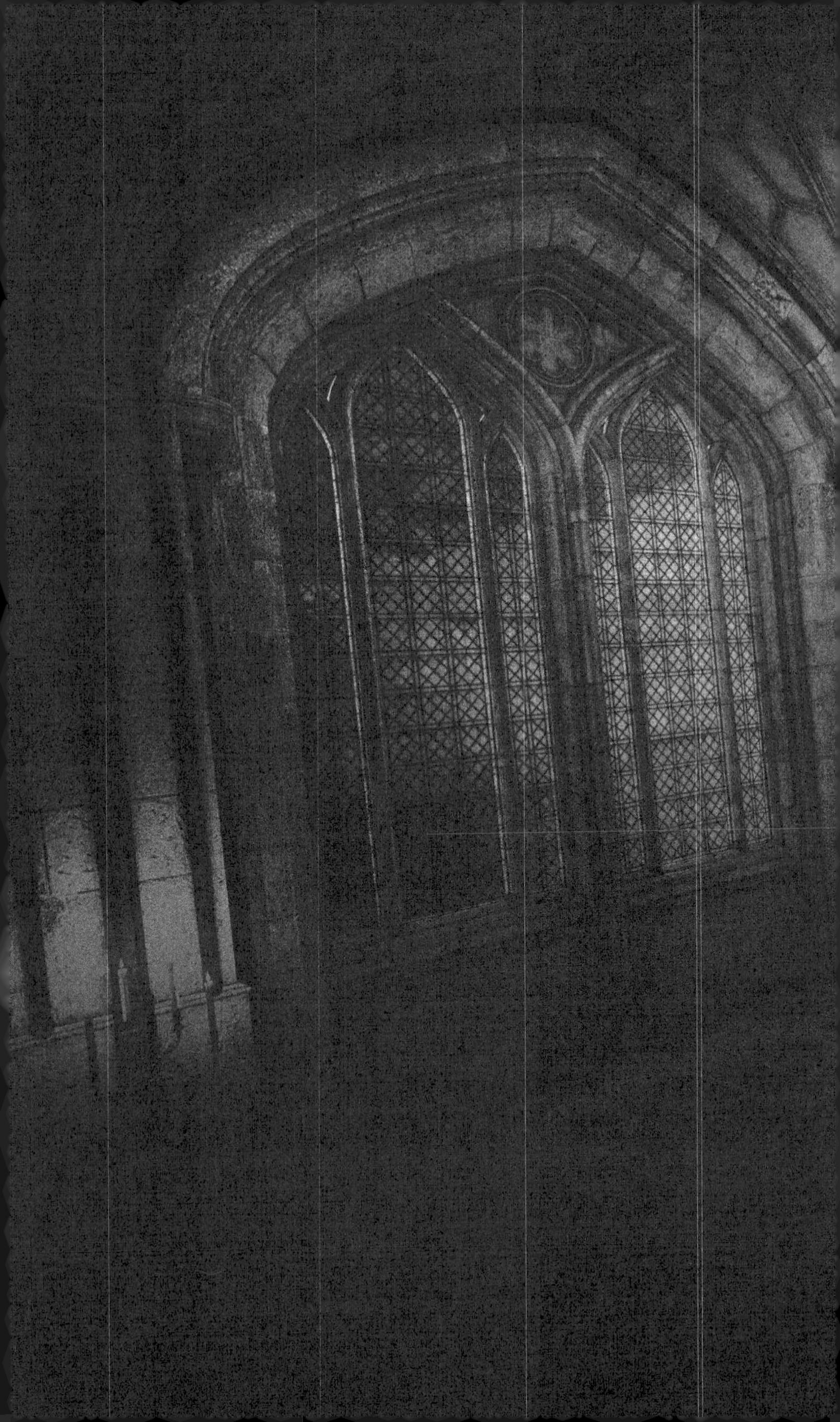

Seven

Mackenzie

I wrap my fingers around the bars and stare out at Kirill. Pale-Eyes jerks his gun at him. "Get in the cage."

Kirill shakes his head. "This is insane."

"You heard him," the other one says.

The men have forgone the masks now that I've seen Grigoriy's face. There's no point in keeping up the façade any longer.

"Fuck off, Rufus," Kirill snarls.

The one I now know to be called Rufus points at the cage. "In. Now. You really have no choice."

"Kirill," I sob, unsure of what I even want to say.

He stares at me, his blue eyes haunted in a way I've never seen before. Perhaps realizing he has no choice, his shoulders slump and he goes to the gate. It's not locked—what would be the point when I'm attached to the bars now?—and he steps inside.

With a whoop of glee, Pale-Eyes steps forward, slams the cage gate shut, and clicks the lock into place. Kirill is trapped.

Just like me.

Grigoriy won't leave his son in here, will he?

"*Kukla*," Kirill says quietly, stepping closer.

I break down, my head hung, tears streaming down my cheeks. I'm exposed and humiliated, and I'm terrified about what's going to happen. It must be approaching twenty-four hours since I last took my medication, and the thought of having a seizure in here is unbearable. What will Grigoriy think when he realizes I'm not the perfect little breeder he wants? There have been moments I've almost told him, but what would happen if I did? Would that make me useless, in his eyes, at least? I bet he's an ableist piece of shit because he's a disgusting human being. He's not going to be understanding. He comes across like a full-on, fascist fuckhead. If I had no use, would he decide to put a bullet in my head?

Kirill drops to his knees beside me and wraps his arms around me, using his body to shield me from the heated gazes of the two other men. He scoops me into him, as best he can with me in my current position, and buries his head to my shoulder.

He's trembling.

"Fuck, I'm so sorry, Mackenzie. I am so fucking sorry."

"It's not your fault," I say, but do I truly believe that? I can't claim that everything bad that's happened to me recently has been down to him and the others, but they've certainly played their part.

His hands go to the collar around my throat, and he tugs on the latch and the lock, but I know there's no way to undo it.

"Get on with this," Rufus says from outside of the cage. "We are looking forward to the show."

He ribs the man standing beside him—the one with the pale eyes—and they both laugh.

"She gave me a taste of those tits before," Pale-Eyes says. "I would like to fuck her too, but Mr. Stepanov will not allow it."

Rufus grabs his crotch. "I bet he will if his precious son fails. If you can't get it up, Kirill, we'll take over. We could take turns. Fill her up. Fuck her until she bleeds."

Kirill snaps to face them. "Shut the fuck up, both of you."

They howl with laughter. They're having a great time. Fucking pricks.

"At least unlock the collar," Kirill says. "I can't do it like this."

Pale-Eyes shakes his head. "Not happening. While she's locked to the cage, you're not going anywhere. The moment that lock comes undone, you'll try to take her out of here."

He's completely right.

"Besides," the other one sneers, "it's hotter with her half naked and chained like that. Women should be on their knees. Best place for them."

Kirill mutters something in Russian, which I take to be a curse.

Did he come armed? My thought of a gun makes me remember what Kirill had said about killing me. If he'd come armed, had a part of him believed he might use the weapon on me? What if he'd arrived to find his father raping me? Would he have put a bullet in my head before shooting his father? Would I have been that ruined for him? The thought makes me cry all over again.

"You said you were going to kill me," I say under my breath. "I heard you."

He shakes his head. "No, Duchess. You know I'd never hurt you. I only said it to make sure he didn't touch you."

I sniff and hiccup. "How do I know that?"

He takes hold of my chin. "Look at me. Look into my eyes. You *know* me. I love you. I'd kill myself before I harmed a single hair on your head. I should have protected you better. I should have seen this coming. I knew he was a fucking psychopath. I should have known he wouldn't just take me telling him no as an answer. This is on me. I'm so sorry, Duchess. I'm so fucking sorry."

He loves me.

Pale-Eyes cracks the gun against the side of the cage, and we both jump at the clang.

"Stop fucking talking. We want action."

A tear slips down my cheek.

"Fuck you," Kirill snaps. "I won't do it. Not with you two watching."

"You have no choice. Your father said so. We *will* watch. Make sure the job gets done."

Rufus sneers. "She will spread her legs for us when you are finished—show us the cum dripping from her cunt."

Kirill pulls me close. "Stay away from her, or I'll kill you myself. I fucking swear it."

They exchange a glance and laugh. They know his words are empty. What can he do? He's locked inside this fucking cage, too. Kirill is as helpless as I am.

We have no choice but to give them what they want.

"Just do it, Kirill," I say softly.

He jerks back. "What? No, not until they leave."

"It's only us. It's only sex. We've done it countless times before. Nothing has changed. We're still ourselves."

"We have an audience," he hisses.

The grinding of his teeth goes right down to my bones.

"Just imagine they're Dom and Tino. It's no different, not really."

We both know it is, but if this is going to happen, we need to lie to ourselves.

Pale-Eyes has grown bored. He marches over to us and puts the gun to my head, the metal circle of the barrel jamming against my scalp. I take a sharp breath and close my eyes.

"Get that away from her," Kirill growls. "*Now.*"

"Then fuck her, or should we get your father back down here? Let him take over?"

"It's okay, Kirill," I tell him. "I want you. I always want you." I can't let these men touch me, and I'll die before I let Kirill's father come near me with that thing between his legs. I can do this. It's not as if I don't always want Kirill.

I do.

The pressure of the barrel against my skull eases and then vanishes.

Kirill gives a throaty groan of desperation. "Not like this. I...fuck...I can't."

"Yes, you can," I encourage him. "Please. I need you."

"Fuck, *Kukla*."

Kirill must realize I'm right, and he drops his forehead to my shoulder. He's the one freaking out here, and I thought it would be me. He needs my strength now. He came for me, and I can't let that be for nothing. I want out of here, and the only way is to give his crazy father what *he* wants. I am convinced that Grigoriy Stepanov is insane enough to actually let us go if he thinks we're going to keep trying to make a baby and that we're married. I even find the strength to make a joke of it in an attempt to break through to Kirill.

"You made me come in front of the entire canteen. Don't go shy on me now."

He barks out a soft, surprised laugh, but it turns into something that sounds almost like a half-sob.

"Let's show these fuckers what real connection looks like," I say.

He'll have to take me in this position, with me on my knees. It means I'll be facing these two bastards, but there's nothing I can do about that. I'll close my eyes and pretend they're not there. Or picture them as Dom and Tino.

The thought creates a tingle between my thighs, and I find myself wet. Perhaps the sick things we've done in the past have primed me for this.

Yes, Dom and Tino watching Kirill fuck me—on my knees, my face and breasts pressed to the bars. That, I can work with.

I reach for him, take his hand, and draw it around my body to cup my bare breast. My nipple crinkles under his touch. I won't tell him how his father's mouth was on me, how his disgusting tongue laved me, how he exposed his huge cock to me. It won't help.

"Come here. Come closer. I missed you. I need you."

He shakes his head against me. "You don't understand. I can't do this. Not with them watching. Not with you like this."

"Just pretend it's your bed, and you've chained me to it. I know you like that. Remember the last time? I was in a similar position, wasn't I? When you used the hairbrush on me."

He's close enough that I feel his cock jump.

"Mackenzie," he groans, "don't."

I reach behind me and cup his dick over the top of his jeans and give him a squeeze. He grows harder.

"I'm wet for you. Feel me."

I move his hand from my breast, down across my stomach, and beneath the waistband of my sweatpants. He pushes his hand between my thighs and slides a finger along my slit, finding me wet and wanting.

He lets out a primal sound deep in his throat and curls his finger to push inside me. I gasp. Acting from a place of need and desperation, his other hand cups my breast, his fingers tweaking and rolling my nipple. He presses against me, on his knees as well, so the front of his body melds with the back of mine. I sense his urgency, how, in a matter of seconds, he's switched from refusal to need.

I've read about how when you're in a dangerous situation, sometimes adrenaline and other hormones can make you horny. Hell, look at all the baby booms in times of war. Maybe this is that effect, or perhaps we're just so primed for one another, we can't resist no matter what else is going on.

Either way, the fact that Kirill's body and desire have overridden his reticence and his morals is strangely hot.

"That's right," Pale-Eyes says, "now it's getting good."

The rasp of a zipper greets my ears, and I squeeze my eyes shut, not wanting to see these two men masturbating over us.

Kirill continues to thrust his fingers in and out of me as he kisses and bites my neck and shoulder. He grinds against my spine, showing me how hard he is.

"I want your cock," I tell him. "I want to feel you. I want your cum inside me. I don't give a fuck if these freaks are watching. I've been so alone and cold. I need to feel you."

It's actually a comfort having Kirill here with me. It's wrong I'm grateful for him being dragged into this hellhole, too, and being placed in danger now as well, but I *am* grateful. I'm less afraid with him here.

Kirill pulls down my sweatpants, and I push them off my feet. He doesn't remove my panties but yanks them to one side. It means I'm not completely naked, but as good as.

I twist my head as much as I can, and watch from the corner of my eye as he undoes his jeans and yanks them, together with his shorts, down his hips. His cock juts out from his body, thick and erect. His length is ridged with veins, the head smooth and darker in shade.

"That's right, fuck her," Rufus encourages. "I want to hear her come."

I reach behind me to stroke Kirill. "Ignore them," I tell him. "It's just us. Only us."

The position is awkward, with my face still pressed to the bars, but I do my best. He's rock hard now, and his breathing is harsh in my ear. Beneath that, I hear the whack of flesh on flesh, the beating of hands on cocks. I do my best to push them out of my mind.

"Fuck," Rufus groans. "I want a taste of that pussy so bad."

Pale-Eyes directs his question to Kirill. "Tell us how it feels to be inside her. Describe her. Is she tight and wet?"

Kirill ignores him and slips his fingers from my pussy. He replaces them with his cock, positioning himself at my opening from behind. He rubs himself in my wetness, groaning a little, then he dips inside me, just the tip, stretching me.

I push back on him. "Give it to me. I want you."

With a growl, he grabs my hips and then rams himself deep, shoving me against the bars.

He slams into me, hard and fast, as if he's wanting and needing this to be over. I am too, but also, I don't want it to end, as it is a respite from the terror. While I'm feeling Kirill in me, and the sharp, painful pleasure he is giving me, everything else fades.

The danger, the fucked-up-ness of this situation, all serve to heighten the arousal I'm feeling.

"Oh, God," I cry. "Oh, fuck."

One of his hands is between my thighs, his fingers working my clit. The other is on my breast, using it to hold me to him, so we're like one entity, unable to tell where one of us finishes and the other starts.

Heat and tension build, and the air is filled with the sounds of our heavy breathing. It's cold down here, but now our skin is damp with sweat. The way we're fucking is so raw, animalistic. Dirty, filthy rutting. I don't care. Despite everything, I find myself craving this connection. Being with him—and Dom and Tino, too—is when I feel the most alive. Maybe I'm addicted to them, or perhaps it's more than that, but I'll always want them.

Even in this fucked up situation.

I didn't believe I'd reach climax, not like this, with two

strangers watching, taking their own pleasure in the palms of their hands, but I can't fight the unmistakable rise of it inside me. My thighs and stomach muscles are taut, and I gasp and moan.

"Kirill...oh, God, Kirill."

Kirill keeps his face buried in my neck, as though he's hiding from the reality of what's happening and is losing himself in me instead. I look up, though, and can't help but stare at the two massive cocks, angry, hard, and the faces of the men twisted in pained desire. It's sick, and yet, I feel a kind of power. They want to be me and Kirill. They want what we have, but they never will get it.

"I'm going to come," I gasp. "Oh, fuck, I'm going to come."

"Jesus, Duchess."

"Don't stop. Oh, shit. Like that, yes, just like that." I stare at Rufus and my gaze is defiant as the pleasure builds. The man looks away, glancing down at the floor, his fist slowing for a moment.

Yes, you fucker, I think. This is what you can't deal with. Me being in control and taking what I want. They want a scared victim, and instead, I'm going to enjoy this moment.

Kirill angles himself perfectly, hitting the place inside me that tumbles me over the edge. For a few seconds, I forget men are watching, I forget we are captives, and give in completely to the utter bliss that courses through me. My pussy clenches around Kirill's cock, milking him for his cum. My fingers grip the bars as I hold on tight, needing the anchor against the intensity of the orgasm.

"Fuck, *Kukla*. I'm going to fill you up."

"Yes, yes," I gasp. "I want you."

He gives in with a groan, and I feel him pulse inside me, our heated wetness combining.

We slump together, both of us panting hard. My heart is racing.

Rufus steps forward, bringing himself right up to the bars.

His upper lip lifts in a curl of satisfaction, and he gives a grunt as he comes, hot seed spurting from his slit, and raining down on me and Kirill. The salty scent of semen fills my nostrils. Rufus's gaze holds mine now, triumphant as he thinks he's once more gained the upper hand, so I don't even let myself flinch.

But Kirill lets out a yell of dismay, and his hold on me tightens in anger. I put a soothing hand behind me. He can't get us killed. Not now. Not when we might actually get out of here if his dad is satisfied by this depraved spectacle.

"You son of a bitch," he growls. "You will pay for that."

Rufus only laughs.

Pale-Eyes steps forward. He hasn't come yet, his hugely erect cock still fisting in his hand. "Now spread those legs," he says. "The boss will want to know the job was done properly, and that wasn't all just an act."

Kirill tenses around me. "You think that was an act?"

"Pull your cock from her cunt and keep her panties to one side. I want to see the cum dripping out of her."

I squeeze my eyes shut. "You're fucked in the head."

"I'm just doing my job. Do it, and we'll leave and give you a good report to the boss."

"Do it," I murmur to Kirill.

Kirill edges away from me slightly and he slips from my body. Pale-Eyes works his cock faster, breath growing rapid. "Part your legs more," he rasps.

Not looking at him, I move my knees apart. Wetness trickles between my thighs.

"Fuck, yes," he groans, his movements becoming even faster, his gaze locked on my pussy. He curses in Russian and then comes, his hips bucking into his hand.

I turn my face away, disgusted, but I feel his cum hitting my hair and dripping down my cheek.

Kirill sits back on his heels, his head hung. I know he feels how I do now that the high has worn off—exposed, used, depraved. Neither of us looks at each other.

"We will tell your father you did what was required," the other man says. "And we will look forward to the next time." They've put their cocks away and are zipping themselves up as they gloat.

Both men turn and traipse back up the stairs.

His words echo in my ears...*next time.*

I actually find myself hoping that Grigoriy finds a priest because if I don't get out of here soon, I'm scared I'm going to get sick. Being married to Kirill isn't the worst thing ever. I've learned there are much worse things out there. If that's what it takes for us to escape, I'll gladly do it. I just want to be free of this dungeon. My hair and face are sticky, and I try to wipe at myself, but I can't get it off me. I am about to ask Kirill to use his t-shirt to help clean me up when the light clicks out.

Velvety thick darkness covers us, so dense it feels like it's pressing down on me, and Kirill lets out a soft moan.

The sound is strange, almost childlike.

What is wrong with him?

I reach for him in the dark and find him balled up. I try to pull him to me, but he's shaking like a leaf in the breeze.

Tears fill my eyes and spill over in the dark as I pray to God for a miracle.

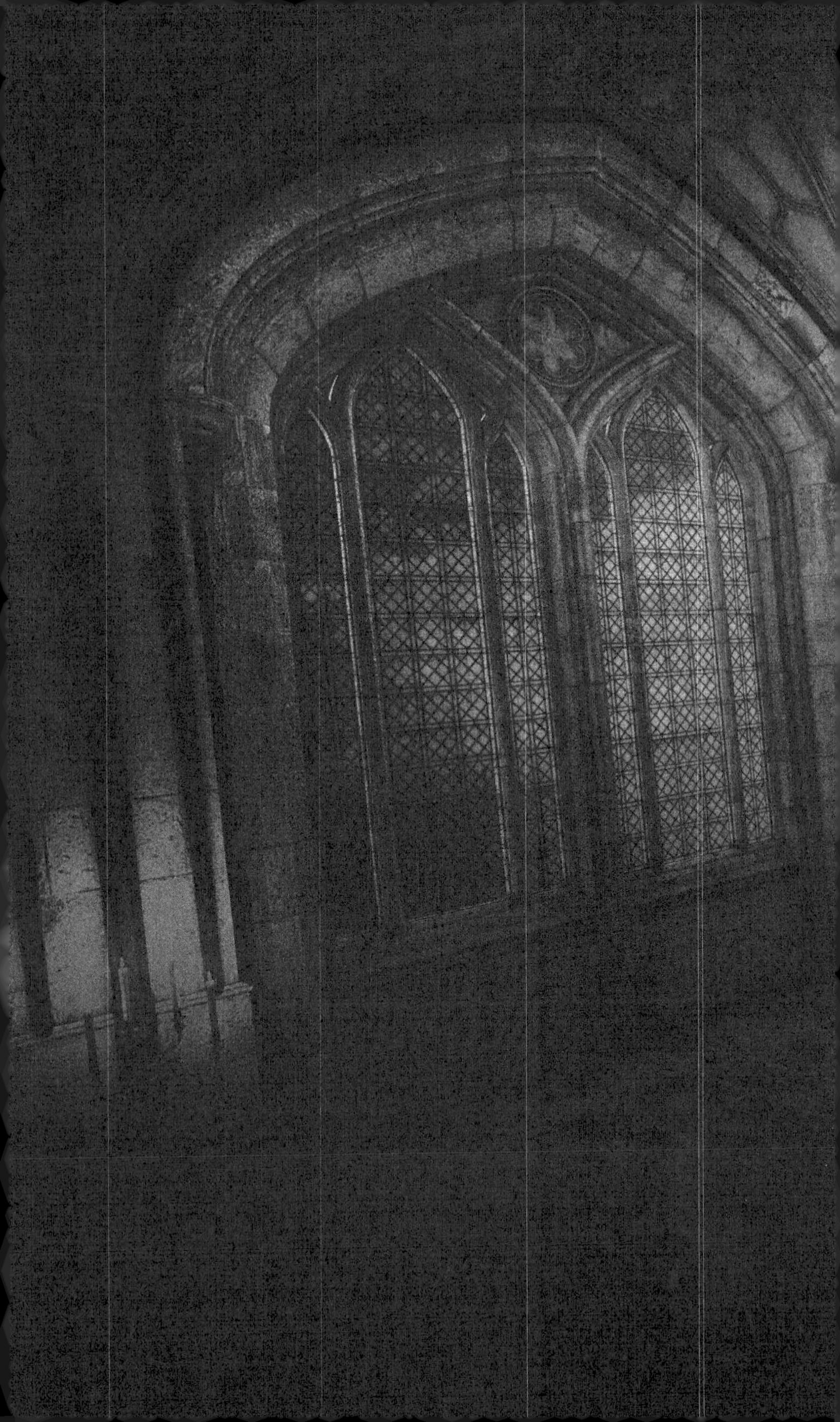

Eight
Domenic

My door opens and Tino bursts in.

I've not been up long, having slept for absolute shit. I've been trying to get my dad to use all the contacts at his disposal to find out who has Mackenzie. He thinks it might be the men who threatened her and her mom, and he's asked the police in his pocket to try to find out anything they can.

"Kill is gone," Tino announces. His eyes are wild. His hair is sticking up, too, and his tan skin looks wan and tired. He's clearly slept as well as I have.

I sit up. "What? Where?"

"I wish I knew. He's not in his room."

I frown. "Is his car gone, too?"

"No, it's still there." Tino paces the room, spearing his fingers through his thick, dark hair and yanking at the roots.

My mind is spinning. "What the fuck is going on? Has someone taken him, too?"

He pauses his pacing for a moment. "Not from inside the building. We'd know if someone was here who shouldn't be. The security is fucking tight, and more so now than usual."

This doesn't make sense. "So, he left voluntarily? What the fuck was he thinking?"

Tino draws a breath. "There's only one person I know who could make Kirill act in such a way, and that's his father."

My stomach plummets.

It all slides into place like a horrific jigsaw. The fact that Kirill's dad wanted him to marry our Duchess. The way Kirill is scared of him. The way his father looked at Mackenzie that day. As if he wanted her for himself. That utter bastard.

He's sick and twisted enough to do something like this and arrogant enough to believe he can get away with it. He's also a Machiavellian man who plots and plans, and his schemes are always bad news for everyone else.

"Fuck." I cup my hand over my mouth. "This is bad. I think Kirill's father is the one who has Mack."

Tino's white teeth dig into his lower lip. "I can't think of any reason Kirill would leave now if it wasn't connected to her, can you?"

"Fuck," I say again, digging my fingers into my scalp.

I want pain. *I need* pain. I crave it so badly; I want to scream with it. Kirill's father having Mackenzie is really bad fucking news. I'd have preferred it to be the professor, and that's saying something. Grigoriy is sick and twisted. He did depraved things to his own son, and he walked into our college like he owned it. He's not scared of my father, which puts us in a uniquely volatile situation.

"The men from my compound will be landing soon," Tino says. "I need to be there to meet them."

I nod. "Okay, good. The more people we have on our side, the better, especially if Kill's father is behind this. If he wants a war, he's got one."

I'm going to need to tell my father about these new developments. I hate constantly having to go to my dad for help, but he runs this place, and I don't have much choice.

He told me the cops are trying to pin down the vehicle that took Mackenzie. I'm aware the professor is also out there somewhere, trying to track her down. What if the son of a bitch has better luck than we do?

I go to Tino. I can see he's as tormented as I am. We almost lost him not so long ago, when his pain got too much, and the pills took over and he accidentally overdosed. I grab his forearm and yank him into me. I squeeze him hard and smack him on the back. "It'll be okay. We'll get her back."

He doesn't reply but gives a tight, curt nod against my shoulder.

We leave my room and part ways. He goes to meet his men, and I go to find my father and Lucia. My dad is going to be pissed when he finds out about Grigoriy Stepanov. They already had that run-in on campus when one of Girgoriy's men hit me. This is going to be the final nail in a coffin. What would a mafia war mean for the college?

I find him in his office.

He looks up, and I can tell from his eyes that he already knows there's been a development.

"The kitchen is saying one of their trucks is missing," he announces. "I checked the cameras and saw this."

He beckons me over so I can see his computer screen.

Sure enough, there is Kirill sitting behind the wheel of the vehicle. A baseball cap is pulled down over his face, but it's still clearly him. He's alone in the truck. Where the hell does he think he's going?

I clench my jaw. "I think his father might have taken Mackenzie. It's the only thing that makes sense."

For a moment there is silence, and then my father whirls around and punches the wall.

Ouch.

"That motherfucker," my father explodes. He's normally scarily in control. His power lies in not needing to make big displays of his anger or his might, but right now, he's a force of nature. "I'll fucking kill him. How dare he? This is a declaration of war against me, against the college. Against all the families here."

He's way angrier than I'd expected.

"If he took the daughter of my wife-to-be, what sort of message does that send to every other family sending their kid here?"

He's more concerned about his reputation and that of the college than he seems to be about Mack herself, but that's okay. I can use it and channel it to get what I want.

"It says we are weak, or at least it does if we don't get her back and take our revenge."

"Revenge?" he spits. "I'll fucking tear Grigoriy Stepanov limb from limb. I'll use his body to power the fucking furnace and his ash to feed the plants."

Jesus Christ. I stare at my father in awe. Of course I know he's a ruthless man, but I mostly only see the buttoned-up, control-freak side of him, not this raging anger.

He pulls himself together. "I will make sure we get information from police cameras and see if we have a direction on the truck."

I nod. "Thanks, Dad. It means a lot."

"You're all seeming a little bit rattled by this." He examines me, his gaze shrewd and too intense.

"Of course. She's one of us."

"A fellow student?"

I draw a breath. "Yes."

"Soon to be your stepsister—assuming you don't find another way to sabotage things." His gaze narrows.

I duck my head in shame. "I won't."

Fuck, where is this going?

"Is Tino in love with her?"

I jerk my chin back up. "What?"

"Tino. He seemed very upset."

"Um, no. I mean, no, it's not like that."

"Good, because she's going to be my stepdaughter soon, and your sister, and Tino isn't right for her."

Maybe I should be offended on Tino's behalf but I'm too grateful to realize my father doesn't seem to have any further suspicions about our relationship with Mackenzie.

"Or Kirill."

Those words make my blood run cold. He's leading up to something with this. I know how his mind works.

"She most certainly wouldn't be right for you." He stares at me hard. "That would be sick, especially considering she's to be your sister."

I swallow, unable to speak.

He smiles at me coldly. "I will do all I can to bring her back here, but once I get her home, I think she will be moving into this apartment with her mother and me. Where we can keep a close eye on her."

Shit. It's like the jail cell clanging shut. Even if we free her, if we stay here, we won't get to see her. I wonder how Mack will react to all of this. She won't like it. She's a grown woman, after all. They can't keep her under supervision like she's a child.

My hands are shaking, and I do my best to hide it.

My father continues, "You know, when I was young, my friends and I would do crazy things like sharing a woman." He shrugs as if he's talking about the weather.

I cannot believe my buttoned-up father is saying this.

"It was stupid kid stuff. Boys will be boys, right? Then one day it went wrong. Feelings got involved. There can only be one winner in that case." His all-seeing gaze is cutting through me like a damn laser, right to my fucking soul.

"Who was the winner?" I dare to ask.

He gives a slow smile. "I was."

I swallow. Does he mean my mother? Was my mother passed around between guys the way we do with Mackenzie?

"Mom?" I whisper.

"Christ, no. Not your mother. I couldn't marry a girl like that. I won her, and then I discarded her because she was used goods. We ruined that girl. Be a shame if anyone tried to do the same to Mackenzie. I am sure as her older brother, you'll do all you can to ensure that doesn't happen."

Blind anger surges in me. Even now, with Mackenzie missing, he's using events to twist things the way he wants them. Tino, Kirill, and I have all been fucked up and betrayed by our fathers in their sick rush for power and control.

It hits me then that Mackenzie was, too. Her dad was in debt and almost got her killed because of it. No wonder we have all bonded so well.

I stare at my father, my jaw working. "None of us is in love with her. We formed a support group. That's all."

"A support group?"

"Yeah, we call it the Cronus Club."

On that note, I leave him. His face is puzzled as I close the door. He'll get it, sooner or later, the fucker. Cronus was the Greek god who ate his own children so they wouldn't usurp him.

A support group for kids with evil fathers.

I laugh to myself as I stride down the corridor. I quickly sober, though. It is eventually going to come out about us and our Duchess. We can't let only one of us have her, so eventually the world *will* know. Until then, I'd rather my father not hide her away in his apartment with her mother, keeping her from us.

The thought keeps nagging at me that Kirill might have betrayed us somehow. What if he's not gone after Mackenzie to save her but to take her for himself? Even though we've said it is the four of us in this together, what if Kirill has relented to his father?

I want to see if his gun is gone. It will give me a clue as to his state of mind. If he's taken his gun, then he will be thinking he's going to have to use it. It means he's going there to fight, but if it's still here, then maybe not. Maybe he's gone there to give his father what he wants.

When I reach his room, I push open the door, which has been left half ajar, probably by Tino, and take a look around. There are clothes half spilling out of the closet like Kirill dressed in a rush. I kneel and search for his gun. It's gone.

So, he's armed, which makes me think he's going in there as an enemy to his father. It means he and Mackenzie are alone and up against Grigori Stepanov and his henchmen.

"Where the fuck did you go, Kirill, and why didn't you tell us?" I'm speaking to an empty room, but I still long for an answer.

If he's being a noble fuck and trying to protect us from harm, he's an idiot, and he's putting Duchess in even greater danger. We could have helped him get her back.

I idly wander to his desk and stare at a half-finished essay, but then my gaze catches on something else.

A notepad, with a half torn-off page, flutters in the breeze from the open window.

I lean over and stare at the piece of paper underneath the ripped top piece. There's a series of indentations on the paper. Writing, or rather, the impression of it.

I've seen the old pencil rubbing trick on ancient crime shows like Columbo, but I also know that doesn't work well and can ruin what you're trying to read.

The best bet is light and the correct angle to be able to see the message.

Kirill definitely wrote something on the paper on top of his notepad, ripped it off, and left this room. I need to see what's on it. I hold it up against the light, but that doesn't help. I turn on the desk lamp and angle it a ton of different ways, but I still can't read it.

Inspiration hits, and I grab my phone. With the flash on, I take a series of pictures at various angles, the flash of the light hitting the paper in diverse ways. I finally see it. A set of numbers.

I grab a pencil and paper on Kirill's desk and write them down. There's also a name, *Glenwood Drive.*

I know that. It's a long road that leads through the forest to a lake.

There are cabins near that lake.

I bet these coordinates lead to one of them.

With the information, I sit on Kirill's bed and plug the coordinates into maps on my phone. Sure enough, he's headed down that road because it leads to those coordinates. I bet that's where Grigoriy has Mackenzie. And Kirill now, too.

What the fuck is Grigoriy doing with them both?

I'm sure as psychotic as he is, Grigoriy won't kill his only son and heir. Kirill was never sure of that, but what better way to control him than make him think at any point he could be murdered? I've always thought Grigoriy was evil, but not as insane as he appears.

So, if we take murder out of the equation, why else would he take Mackenzie and demand Kirill come to him in the middle of nowhere?

What will he do out there that he couldn't do in a motel or nearer civilization?

Fuck. It doesn't bear thinking about.

If he takes them away, and they're trapped in Russia, we'll never get them back.

Shit. I glance at my watch, then I message Tino.

<How long?>

The reply takes a moment but then flashes onto my phone. *<Be with you in an hour.>*

Thank fuck.

We will need weapons when they get here. Plenty of them.

We're going to war.

THE DEVILS' DARLING

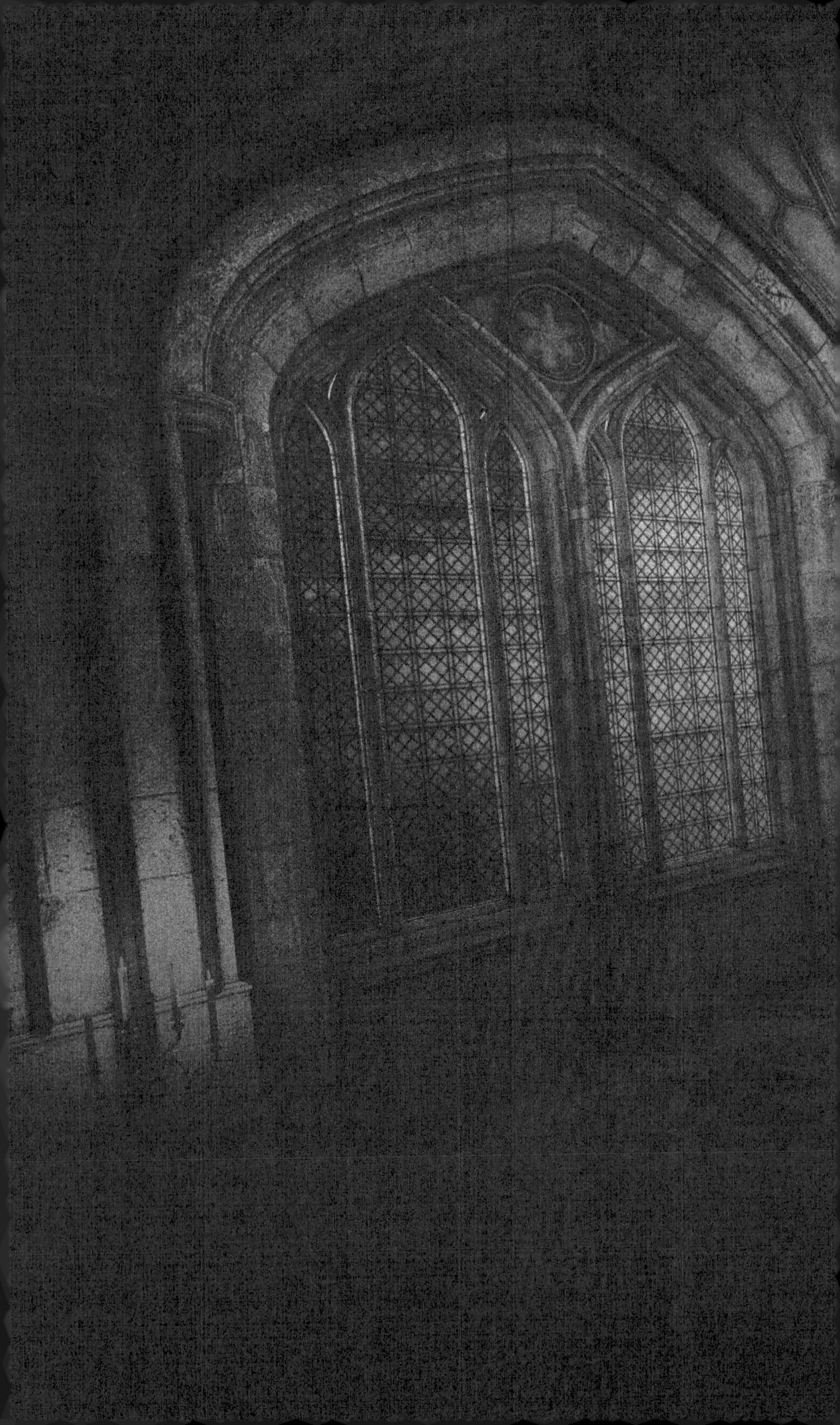

Nine

Tino

The men my father has sent me include two of his highest-ranking soldiers, Leon and Diego. Leon in particular is as deadly a motherfucker as I've ever met.

He looks at me, taking me in. "Good to see you, Mr. Martinez." He extends his hand to shake mine, his grip firm. "Your father says there's a situation here needs handling."

"Yes, someone has something of mine. I want to get her back."

"Her?" Diego's face splits into a wide grin. "You found yourself a woman?"

"Yes, I did." I don't tell them I share that woman with two other men. In my culture, that's a hanging offense. They'd as likely kill me as they would Stepanov and his men.

"Well, well, well, maybe there will be a wedding soon."

His words hit me deep. There won't be a wedding because how can she marry only one of us? I'd love to marry her and make her truly mine—to call her my wife—but she's not *mine*, she's *ours*, and there's no law where we can all marry her.

of fighting age. I grin when they unload the crates from the back of the private plane. This is a rarely used airstrip, and my father said he'd been given the promise of people looking the other way while we unloaded.

"There are some gifts from your father." Diego points to the crates. "He organized some vehicles, too, for us to transport these in."

"Let me guess, less cigars and brandy, and more guns and grenades?" I laugh, despite the situation.

"You guessed right."

I don't like my father. I'm not sure I ever will, but right now, in this moment, I'm fucking grateful to him.

As the men load up the two Land Rovers that are waiting courtesy of my father, engines idling, I glance around me, making sure no one is watching.

Then I place a call.

Dom answers immediately. "Yeah?"

"You're going to need to give your dad a head's up. We're coming in heavy. I need waving through security. We have a lot of weapons. Is he going to allow that?"

Nataniele would never allow anyone else onto his grounds armed to the teeth this way. By letting me in with these men and the weapons they've brought, he potentially puts himself and the school in harm's way. It means he trusts me.

I've basically got my own small militia unit now.

The power sends a tingling thrill down my spine. One day, everything my father owns will be mine. Not merely wealth, but enough men and firepower to take over a small nation. That's why my father never moved to America, and never let my mother take me and my sister back to her birth nation. Once you live here, you must start playing by their rules.

Nataniele's power is as much soft power as it is hard. It's as dependent on having the right senator in your pocket, and the right police chief reporting to you, as it is on the number of armed men working for you. I don't have the time or inclination for the schmoozing that entails.

This is how *my* family does things.

We kick down doors and go in guns blazing.

I suspect it's the kind of language Stepanov understands best.

My injuries are screaming at me today, and I can't be distracted. I discreetly pop a couple of pills. I tell myself it's different this time. I'll only take the Oxy until we've got our Duchess back. Then I'll stop. I just need to be on my A-game. I can't let her down, and if that means using the crutch of the pain meds just for a few days, so be it.

This isn't like before. I'm not using them to deal with emotional shit. This is purely pain relief, and I'm in control this time, not the pills.

"I'll talk to him and call you back in five." Dom hangs up.

When my phone buzzes, I pick up right away. "Yes?"

"He says come to the back entrance, the staff one Kirill left from. Drive into the parking lot on the other side of the stables. His men will greet you."

"Of course."

I could get bent out of shape about being made to use the staff entrance, the way I'm sure my father would in these circumstances, and start demanding my due respect, but this is about our Duchess, not about me. I wave Leon and Diego over.

"We need to take the Land Rovers in the back way. Nataniele, the dean, is going to have his men come and meet us there. They'll want to inspect the vehicles, so let them. This isn't about a dick swinging contest. This is about getting Mackenzie back alive. We need to work with Nataniele on this. I'll go ahead in my car, and you guys follow me."

"You're the boss," Leon says.

Those words make me feel the weight of the situation. This isn't a game and, if I fuck up, I could get Duchess or Kirill killed.

I'm sure Dom is feeling the same way.

We need to bring our friend home, and our Duchess, too. Then we need to go scorched earth. None of her enemies can be left alive, presenting a threat to her.

As the men get into the Land Rovers and I slide into the driver's seat of my car, I think about the future. In one way, the compound in Buenos Aires would be a safe place for our Duchess because she'd be surrounded by guards. In another, not so much, because there are always rival groups willing to risk everything to take it over.

Would anywhere be safe?

The college, maybe, but Dom isn't going to want to spend his life on campus with his dad breathing down his neck. And everyone would see we're a foursome at some point, and that would cause so much shit. Hell, if Dom's dad marries Lucia, we would have to leave, because no way would anyone accept him and Kenzie together.

Shit. This is all such a fucking mess.

I jiggle my leg and feel for the pill bottle in my pocket.

The reassurance of the smooth plastic calms me.

I can do this.

We can do this.

THE DEVILS' DARLING

Ten

Mackenzie

The reason Kirill is acting so strangely hits me.

It's the dark. Kirill is afraid of the dark.

The moment the lights went out, something changed. I thought things were already bad enough, but it's as though he's no longer himself.

He's panting like he's running a marathon, and he's on his feet, pacing. I wish I could see him, but the dark is like peering into black soup. I can sense his movement, though, the vibration of his steps through the metal floor, and the stirring of the air around us.

I can't reach him properly because of this fucking collar connecting me to the bars, but that doesn't stop me trying. I reach back, my shoulder straining, just trying to make contact with him. My heart is racing. I'm afraid of what he's going to do. It's like being caged with a wild animal, and when wild animals are trapped and afraid, they lash out.

"Fuck," he growls.

He smashes into something, and then he must have hold of the cage because it starts to shake violently as he

"Kirill," I cry. "My neck. Don't."

He doesn't stop. Shit. He's losing it. Fight or flight has kicked in.

"Got to get out of this cage." His voice is different. Animalistic. "I can't fucking breathe."

"You're going to break my neck." I scream the words at him.

The rattling stops, my terror getting through to him somehow and overriding his own fear.

"Please, come closer, I can't feel you, and I'm scared."

Verbalizing my own fear seems to make him calmer. I hear him crawling over to me.

He takes my hand, his thumb rubbing back and forth across the inside of my wrist. He's shaking violently.

"Kirill," I whisper. "What's the matter? What's wrong?"

There are so many things wrong, I don't know where to start, but this is something new. Something different.

I suddenly find myself wanting to protect him.

"The lights are out," he says, but I feel like he's only speaking to himself. "As long as they had left the lights on, I'd have been okay."

"You are okay. I'm here."

He lets out a bitter laugh, and it's as though he hasn't heard me at all.

"He knows that, though. He knows I hate the dark. He knows what he's doing. I fucking hate him. I'll never forgive him. No matter what. Not for this, and never for what he did to you."

He's clearly talking about his father, and I'm glad I didn't tell him exactly what Grigoriy did to me because I think Kirill would lose it completely.

"I'm here," I reassure him again. "I'm not going anywhere."

I almost laugh at that, but I don't. This situation is way too fucked up for any humor.

"Will they put the lights back on?"

He sounds like a child. A scared little boy, not the confident man I know. I can't lie to him. They've shut me in the dark a couple of times now, and there's no reason they won't do it again and again.

"We don't need the lights," I say. "We have each other. We're not alone. It's the same room, Kirill. We just can't see it. Nothing else has changed."

"It presses in on you. You can't breathe in it."

He's talking about the dark, and he's not wrong. It's so pitch black it's oppressive, but I can't give in to my own fear, because Kirill needs me right now.

"Talk to me," I say. "I've got you."

Kirill draws a shaky breath. "When I was a young boy, my father liked to lock me in small, dark places, sometimes for days at a time. He did it as a punishment, trying to make me be strong, but it had the opposite effect."

My heart breaks for him. How could any man treat his own son in such a way? I want to take his pain and absorb it, so it won't be able to hurt him anymore.

"You're strong, Kirill. Look at how you came to save me. A weak man wouldn't have done that."

"A strong man who is afraid of the dark?" He snorts at that. "I do not think so."

"A man who is brave enough to confront his fears makes him strong in my eyes."

I reach out, finding his face in the dark, and cup his cheek in my palm. He buries his face into my touch. His cheeks are wet, and I kiss his damp skin, tasting salt.

"Make love to me," I whisper.

He stills. "What?"

"They aren't here now. Use it as a distraction."

"No, it's what he wants. Us fucking all the time."

"Let me soothe you, then." I reach for his waist and trail my fingers down. He's not hard, but I cup him and squeeze him. "I want you."

As soon as I say it, I realize it's true. I might be trying to distract him, but it will distract me, too.

"*Kukla*," he breathes. "I don't think I can. Not in the dark."

"Yes, you can." Then I think of something. Kirill and his weird kink, which I find hot, too, these days.

"Those men are in my hair," I say. "I hate it. Let me make you come, and you can cover me in you, instead. Mark me as yours again."

"We all need to mark you," he growls, sounding scarily feral and unhinged. "When we get you back, we'll clean you and then mark you as ours. Our doll, not theirs."

It should be degrading for him to talk about me that way, but I find it strangely erotic. "Will you clean me up properly?" I ask.

"Yes, Kukla. I'll wash you and dry you. I'll cover you in that rose-scented lotion you like, and then brush your hair."

"Then what?" My words are breathy.

"Then we'll lay you down on a bed and we'll make you ours again."

He's hard now and straining under my hand. I rub him up and down, marveling at the size of him. I pause at the tip to swipe my thumb over his slit, finding him wet with precum, and he sucks in a sharp breath and shudders.

"How?" I ask, wanting to hear him.

It's as though my voice drives away whatever monsters might be lurking in the dark. He's stopped shaking now, and I know my attempt to calm him is working.

"Tino will come in your pussy, and Dom in your ass." He chuckles softly. "He loves your ass. Then I'll come all over your tits and your pussy. We'll be inside you and outside you and you'll be ours again."

"And you'll be mine," I say.

He gives a soft murmur of agreement, and I continue to

work him, feeling him growing harder.

"Come on me now," I beg. "I want your cum all over my face."

"I can't see your face," he says.

"Here," I take his hand and guide it to my cheek. "Wash those bastards away."

He pulls away from me slightly. "Fuck, Mackenzie, this feels wrong."

"No, it doesn't. It feels entirely right."

I lower my head as much as I can before the collar stops me. On my knees like this, my head bent, I feel like I'm praying.

"Stand," I say. "Then come on me."

"Fuck," he groans. "Jesus, Duchess, you'll be the death of us, I swear."

The sound of his cock fucking my fist in the dark is depraved and fucked up, but I love it. I reach up with my other hand to cup his balls, lightly tugging and squeezing as I masturbate him. He groans, and his hands find my hair, his fingers knotting in the strands. While I continue to move my hand up and down his cock, I let the other hand trail back, behind his balls to his perineum, where I apply pressure. He gives a groan, and his hips move, thrusting his cock as though it's my pussy he's fucking. Curious, and feeling experimental, I go back farther still, the tip of one finger trailing over his asshole.

"Ah, fuck, *Kukla*. What are you doing to me?"

"Distracting you, remember?" I purr.

I apply a little more pressure—not enough to penetrate him, but enough to make him think I might. He lets out a sound that's purely primal, and, for a second, I think he's going to yank out of my grip and spread my legs and fuck me hard, but instead he gasps.

"Christ, I'm going to come."

"Do it," I encourage him. "Come all over me. I love how

much you come for me, Kirill."

"Oh, fuck," he shouts.

Warmth hits me, splattering on my mouth, throat, and cheeks. I close my eyes just in time as a powerful spurt kisses my forehead. When he's finished, he's panting.

"I can't clean you up," he says, "but I covered up their filth."

"Yes, you did."

"I need to taste you."

He shuffles about, and I find myself propped up at an odd angle. I gasp as my panties are pulled to one side. He lies on his back on the floor, positioning himself beneath me. His hot mouth against me is a shock when I can't see a thing.

It's so silent and dark in this room that all I can do is *feel*.

He works me with his tongue, flicking my clit and groaning against me as if I'm the best thing he's ever tasted. I know he must be tasting himself, too—it's not been long since he came inside me. Lots of men would be disgusted at the thought of tasting themselves, but not him.

He grabs my hips, holding me in place as he sucks and licks and nibbles. I cling to the bars, grinding my pussy into his face.

My core has nothing to clamp down around, and he senses my needs.

Roughly, he pushes two fingers inside me and curls them to hit the fleshy pad of my G-spot. Guttural moans escape me, and I cry his name. Chasing my high, I'm barely aware of the words spilling from my lips.

"Oh, yes, Kirill, don't stop. I'm so close... more, give me more."

My climax builds, and I forget where I am. He's taking me away from the horrors of our situation, just as I did for him. Tension and heat build at my core, spreading outward, pleasure cascading over my skin.

I come in soft, powerful waves, and the tears come with it, too.

The release takes away some of the terror but only seems to enable the sadness.

Kirill slides out from under me. His big hands cup my cheeks and brush the tears away. "Please don't cry."

"I'm going to die here," I say. "Kirill, I can't stay kneeling like this. Everything hurts. If they don't take the collar off, I will end up fainting, or worse having a seizure, and then I'll choke."

"No, you won't. I'll fucking hold you up."

"I'm so exhausted." I close my eyes and press my forehead to the bars. It's not only choking I'm afraid of. It's been more than twenty-four hours since I last took any meds, and I don't know how much longer I'll last before a seizure hits.

In the dark, Kirill helps put my sweatpants back on, and then he goes to the bars.

"Hey," he shouts. "Hey, we need to talk to you. Fuckers, come down here. Hey."

He moves away from me, the loss of his heat adding another layer of despair.

He must have one of the bowls in his hands because he bangs the metal against the floor of the cage. "Hey, fuckers, come down here."

I grab hold of the bars and hold myself up, the sheer exhaustion washing over me, threatening to drag me under.

The sound of heavy booted feet at the door has me sobbing in gratitude.

The light flashes on, and I groan and slam my eyes shut against the glare. Gradually, I edge them open again, and I draw a breath of shock.

"Time to get ready." It's Grigoriy, and he's holding up a cheap-ass wedding dress. "The priest is here."

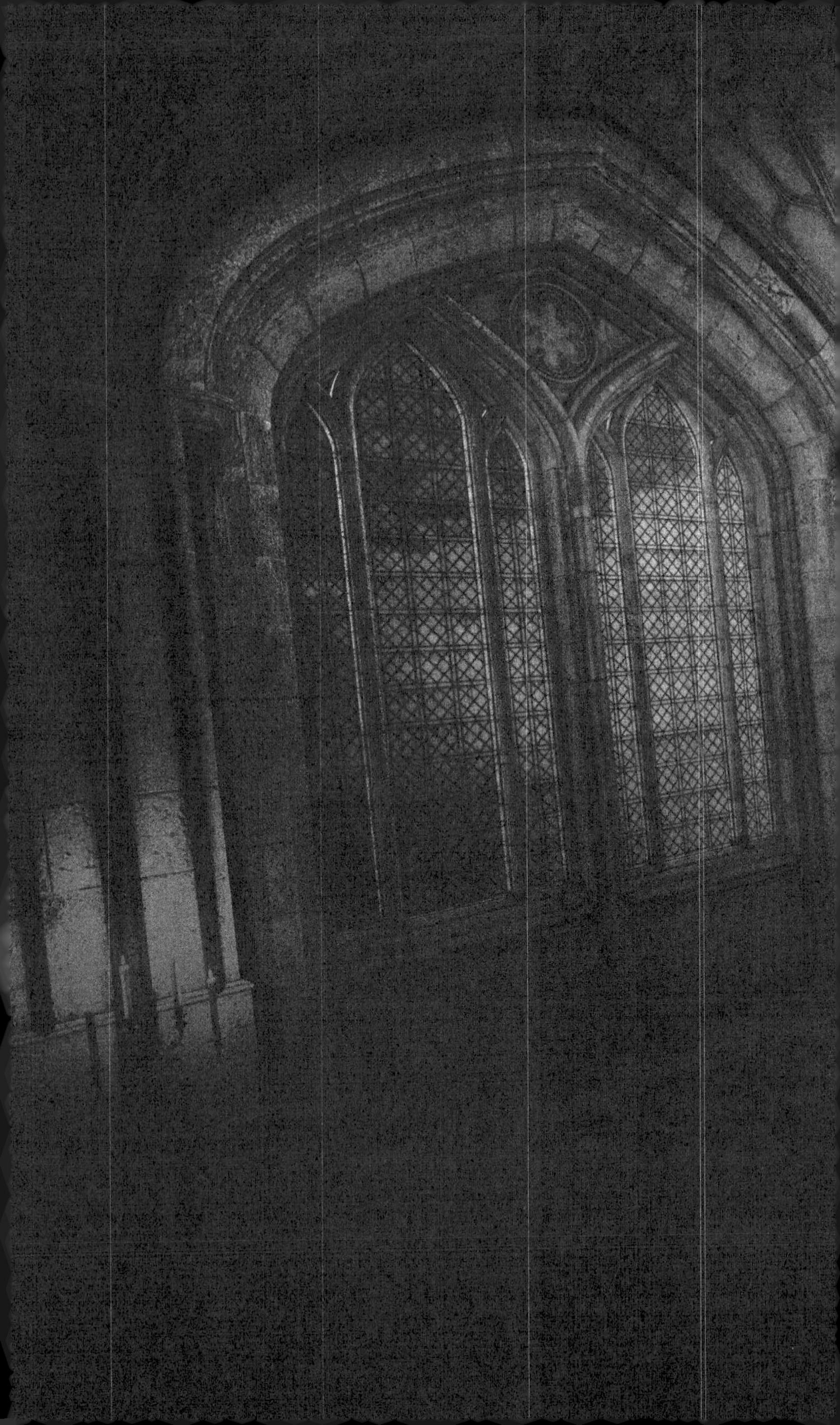

Eleven
Mackenzie

I swallow, hard, my eyes filling with tears.
He's actually going to make us do this.
My thoughts go to Dom and Tino. I think how angry they were when they found out Kirill had proposed. They thought he was trying to take me for himself. How will they react when they find out we're married? Will they see it as the end of us?

I tell myself that worse things could happen. Even if Kirill and I are married, we'll still be alive. We'll still be together. But my heart aches at the potential loss of the other two men in my life. This wasn't how it was supposed to go. It was meant to be the four of us against the world.

Another possibility occurs to me. If Grigoriy takes us both back to Russia once the wedding is done, we might never see them again.

My mind blurs, and I try to think of something to buy us some time.

"Please, let me use the bathroom first," I blurt. "You can't expect me to get married like this. I need to shower."

standing in a wedding dress, covered in the cum of multiple men, but, to my surprise, he nods.

"Very well, but the collar stays on."

He approaches the cage and takes a key from his back pocket.

I throw a subtle look to Kirill. If he lets me out of here, he'll have to undo the cage door. Maybe Kirill can use the moment to run.

But Grigoriy has predicted our action, and, together with the key, he produces a gun. "And don't try anything stupid."

Grigoriy uses the key to open the padlock, and I cry with relief to be able to get off my knees. I sink to my backside and stretch out my legs, rubbing at my poor kneecaps. They're red from the pressure. The backs of my thighs are also tight, and I've been fighting cramps in my calves and feet.

Grigoriy bangs on the bars. "Hurry up."

Slowly, I get to my feet and reach for Kirill. He takes my hand and pulls me in for a hug. I press my forehead to his chest, inhaling the familiar vanilla and spices scent of him.

"Let go of her," his father commands. "We are going now."

My heart beats faster, as it dawns on me that I'm about to be separated from Kirill.

I draw a breath, realizing my mistake. "Kirill can come with me."

Grigoriy huffs air from his nostrils. "No, he can't. Now, come here."

He opens the gate. Kirill's arms tighten around me, but I asked for this. I need to go.

"It'll be all right," I reassure him.

"Mackenzie, no."

He so rarely uses my full name. I squeeze his fingers and then release him and go to his father.

Grigoriy hooks his finger into the ring on the collar and

yanks me from the cage. Not wasting any time, he slams the gate shut again and locks his son back in.

"I'll supervise your showering," Grigoriy says.

I do my best to shake my head, despite the hold he has on me. "What? No."

Kirill realizes what this means and slams himself against the bars of the cage. "Keep your filthy eyes off her."

He only laughs.

Using the collar, he drags me up the stairs. I've got my sweatpants back on, but I'm still naked from the waist up. I try to use my arms to hide my breasts, but he moves with such long strides that I end up needing to hold them out to keep my balance. I sense the leery stares of the other men as I pass by. Maybe I shouldn't care anymore. They've already masturbated to Kirill and me fucking, and came on us, too. Worse, they made me spread my legs so they could see that Kirill came inside me, the depraved fuckers. What should I care that they get another eye-full of my tits?

I *do* care, though. Shame covers me in its sticky coat, but then I shrug it off. No, I won't be the one to feel shame here. They should. Rage boils through me, and that's a much more welcome emotion. How dared these men treat us like this? I hate Kirill's father more than anyone else—more, even, than Paxton, and I never thought I'd hate anyone more than him.

I'm dragged up the stairs and into the basic but clean bathroom. I can't see any sign of my blood or the discarded implant or the razor blade. Grigoriy still has my wedding dress in his other hand, and he steps into the bathroom with me and shuts the door behind him.

He releases his hold on my collar.

"What are you doing?" I say. "Get out."

"And leave you in here alone to try to escape or find a weapon? I think not."

"I'm not going to try to escape. Not while you've got

Kirill locked down there."

He eyes me curiously. "You would choose to remain here rather than escape alone?"

"Of course. I'm not leaving him."

It's as though I'm speaking another language to him.

"So, if I were to open the door, and tell you to run, you'd stay because of my son?"

I fold my arms over my breasts. "Yes. I'm not leaving without him."

"Some might say that is stupid, little Kitten."

Maybe I am being stupid, but I like that he doesn't understand why I am doing this. I don't believe for a second that he's just going to let me run—or, if he did, it would only be so he could chase me down like some kind of fucking sport. But now I'm playing with him, because he doesn't have any clue what it must be like to sacrifice yourself for another person. The very idea is utterly foreign to him.

"Some might, but others might say it is brave," I reply.

He laughs. "You misunderstand. I like this choice you make. It is brave, and loyal. I knew you'd make a strong Bratva wife. It is just perhaps over and above what I expected of you."

"It's not for you. It's for Kirill."

He angles his head. "You love him. You actually love my son."

His face lights up, and, for the first time, he looks vaguely human.

"Of course I do."

"Then you will make an excellent bride and mother, and I have done the right thing. You two just needed the push. I'm practically a saint."

He's smug in his self-praise, and I stare at him in loathing.

That is all women are in his world—wives and mothers. There to be fucked and bred, and to raise the children. I pity them, and I vow to not end up like them. God, imagine being trapped in a home with him always around like a dark, malign presence.

My bladder is aching, and I need to use the toilet. Just seeing it so close has only intensified the urge. "I need to pee."

"Then pee," he says with amusement.

"I'm not going to use the bathroom with you watching."

He shrugs. "Then do not urinate. It makes no difference to me."

I ball my fists, digging my nails into my palms. Trying to pretend he's not there, I yank down my sweatpants and filthy panties, and sink gratefully onto the toilet. For a second, I don't think I'm able to go, but then I relieve myself with a sigh and cover my face with my hands, my elbows on my knees.

I finish and lift my head to find Grigoriy still watching. Sick bastard.

I don't want to shower with him in the room, but I also feel disgusting. I'm basically naked already, and there is a thin white shower curtain I can hide behind. Without saying another word to him, I climb into the tub. The shower is positioned on the wall at one end. I'm still wearing my underwear, but I figure I'll take them off when I'm hidden behind the shower curtain. They could do with a wash, too. I contemplate what to do with them. I don't want to have to wear soaking wet panties, even if they are clean, but it didn't look as though the nasty wedding dress Grigoriy brought came with lingerie.

Maybe I'll just have to go without. What a classy bride I'll make—a cheap dress and no panties.

The faucet squeaks as I turn it, and there's a splutter and a gurgle from somewhere deep in the walls. Then water spurts from the showerhead. It's cold at first, and I suppress a shriek, but in a matter of seconds, it turns warm.

I stand beneath the shower and close my eyes. Water runs over my hair and face, washing away the men's semen. Quickly, I roll down my underwear and kick them to one side. I pick up the soap and use it on my hair and body. It's cheap and drying, but it's all I've got, and I'm grateful for it. It feels good to be clean again.

The shower curtain moves.

My eyes ping open.

Grigoriy stands there, staring. I gasp and grab the shower curtain, trying to cover my body, but he tears it from my grip.

"Don't worry, Kitten. I won't fuck you. It would confuse things not to know who the baby you'll soon be carrying belongs to. I just want to make sure you're doing what you're supposed to. All nice and clean?"

"Yes," I mutter, my head down.

"Good. Now get out and put on this dress. We have a wedding to attend."

THE DEVILS' DARLING

Twelve

Domenic

I go with my father to greet Valentino and his men.

They arrive in a convoy—two large SUVs, with Tino in his car leading the way. The college kitchen staff make themselves scarce, aware that trouble is brewing.

We do our best to stay out of view of the other residents of the college. People talk, and as the majority of the people here have ties to various mafia families around the world, we don't want them knowing our business.

It'll create suspicions of weaknesses, and we don't want that either.

I'm particularly conscious of the Vipers. Their missing third wheel is returning any day now, and that changes things. The French twins—Louis and Mattheo Laurant—are crazy fucks, but they have nothing on Zane. He's been away having surgery on his throat, but he'll be back soon and ready to rain terror over Verona Falls. Luckily, the three of them are in West House, so they don't have much to do with us, but we're still bound to bump into one another from time to time.

The vehicles all pull to a halt, and the engines cut off.

My father is on my left, and we share a glance. I sense he's braced for trouble, even though we're all on the same side.

The vehicle doors open, one after the other, and men with military short hair and olive skin climb out. Tino joins them, standing at their head like a commander.

"Thank you for coming," Nataniele says.

The men nod and dip their heads in deference to my father, which is good and makes me think this just might work.

"What's the plan? To move fast and hard?" my father asks.

"We have to be careful going in," Tino says. "We might have the coordinates, but that's all we know. We don't know how many men Grigoriy Stepanov has with him, or how well armed they are."

I agree. "We don't even know for sure this place is where either Kirill or Mackenzie are being kept. It could just be a meeting place, and they've moved on from there."

A lack of knowledge is a dangerous thing.

It's strange seeing Tino with his men. It's as though he's become someone else. I can see the man destined to take over the compound, and the surrounding city, on the outskirts of Buenos Aires.

He's at the head of his men, commanding them, and they clearly respect him.

It's as though something has shifted. It was only a matter of months ago that we were acting like kids at times, lording it around the college, messing with whatever girls we wanted and getting into fights. Now we've had to grow up, and we've done it *fast*.

Tino glances over his shoulder at his men. "Let's move in quickly but quietly. We suspect they're being held in a cabin at these coordinates. We'll surround the place, make sure there's nowhere they can run. If they are there with

Mackenzie and Kirill, and they move, we might not find them again. This could be our only chance."

"But we don't put their lives at risk," I add hurriedly. "That needs to be a priority. No risks."

"Right." Tino nods and echoes my words to his men. "No risks. They need to stay alive."

"Sir?" One of Tino's men steps forward. He's big, muscular, with a short buzz cut and hard eyes.

"Yes, Leon?"

"I've carried out extractions before, when I was in the military. Some of them were of VIPs, and the most important factor was bringing the victims out alive."

I regard him. "What would you suggest?"

"The weapons we brought with us contain a number of things like flashbangs."

"Flash-whats?" I ask, confused.

"Stun grenades," Leon supplies. "They make a lot of noise and produce a blinding light. We use them to disorientate people. The smoke helps, too. They won't be firing because they'll be stunned and then unable to see."

"Will the smoke affect Mackenzie and Kirill?"

"It might make them cough some. I'm not talking about poisonous gas, here."

"If you have the equipment for that, it sounds less risky than going in weapons blazing," I admit.

"We'll check out the lay of the land when we get there," Tino says, "and make a decision then, but we bring the weapons. We ought to make sure each man has a supply right now."

Nataniele nods. "Let's armor up."

Leon opens the back of the vehicles, and I stare at the number of crates. He flips the lids on them, one by one, revealing numerous weapons. It's like being a kid in a toy shop.

"Impressive," Nataniele says.

"Thank Mr. Rossi," Leon says, referring to Tino's father.

"I will be sure to once we're all back safe and sound," Nataniele says.

I pause at his words and then gesture for him to follow me off to one side. "You can't come," I say to my father.

He scoffs. "Excuse me? It sounded for a moment there like you were giving me an order on the grounds of my own fucking college."

"Dad." I drop the animosity and the formality that always simmers between us because in this I am right, and I need to make him see that. "If you come, you risk destroying all of this. You can't ever be found to have gone directly up against the Pakhan who sends his kid to your college. It will bring it all down. Your son, though? If he did it without your knowledge, what could you do?"

"I am not letting you go up against Grigoriy Stepanov alone."

I laugh. "I'm not alone. Tino's men are here."

"So, it's okay for *his* father to help but not me?"

"His father isn't directly here, is he? It's different. These men are working for Tino now. Plus, you can make sure Lucia is safe, and the college itself. We don't know what Grigoriy might do."

He pinches the bridge of his nose, but when he looks at me, I know he's seen sense.

"Don't come back to me dead." He swallows hard.

I think it's the most love he's ever shown me. "I'll try not to," I say.

The man called Leon clears his throat and raises his voice, addressing the rest of the men.

"Remember, this is an extraction, and the goal is to protect the lives of the hostages at all costs."

His words hit me hard.

The thought of either Mackenzie or Kirill being dead makes it harder to breathe. I'll fall apart if we lose them, and

I'm sure Tino will, too. Whatever progress we've made—no matter how small—since our Duchess came into our lives will be reversed ten-fold. The thought alone is enough to make me want to find a razor blade and carve the skin from my body.

This isn't just about her survival, or Kirill's. It's about the survival of all of us. We simply don't function without each other.

Once we're all tooled up with more weaponry than an army unit, we turn to each other.

"Let's move out," Tino calls.

The men bump fists and smack each other on the back, buoying each other up.

Tino leaves them for a moment to take me to one side.

"You holding up okay?" he asks.

I give a brief nod. "Yeah. You?"

He does the same, though his gaze flits to the left and then back again. "We'll get them back."

I grab his hand, and we pull each other in with mutual back pats of reassurance. Open emotion and affection isn't something that's easily shown to the same sex in our society, but we were never about following convention.

Tino leaves me to join his men.

My father has already arranged for our own vehicles to be ready. He's also managed to convince Lucia to stay behind. She didn't want to, but he doesn't wish to put her in harm's way. There are moments like this where I believe his love for her is real. Maybe I don't want to believe he'd put another woman above my mother, but who am I to tell him he's not allowed to move on? I might never learn why she was driving away from the college in the middle of the night, or why she lost control of the car like she did. It's a painful pill to swallow, but if I'm to move on with my life as well, I might have to force it down.

"Are you ready?" my father asks, his gaze full of concern.

I grit my teeth. "Yeah, I'm ready to show Grigoriy Stepanov that he fucked with the wrong people."

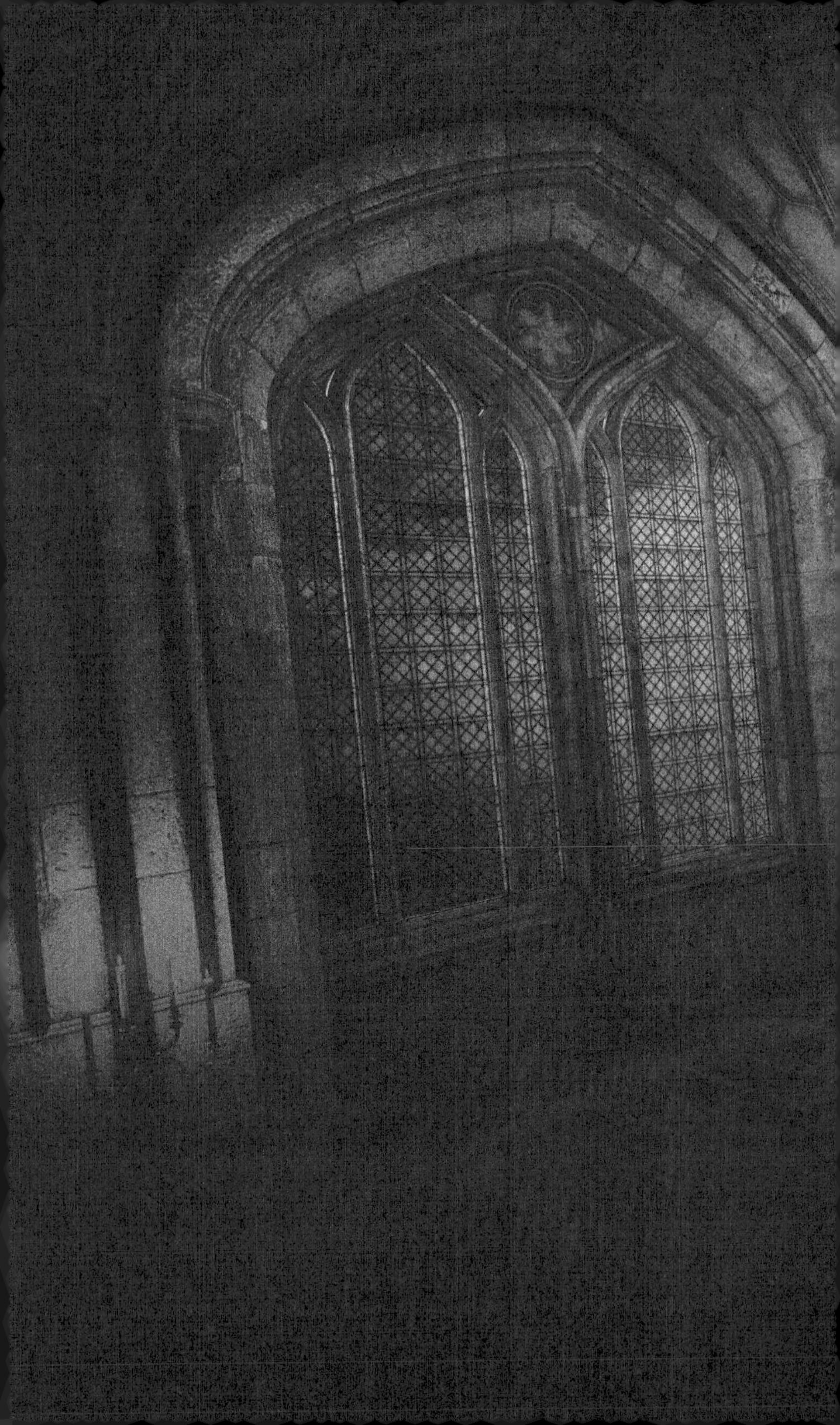

Thirteen
Kirill

All my raging and slamming myself against the bars has been for nothing. I'm still trapped in this fucking cage, while my father is upstairs with Mackenzie.

I squeeze my eyes shut, wanting to tear them from my own skull at the thought of what he might be doing with her. If he lays a hand on her, I swear I'll cut them from his arms. I hate even the thought of him seeing her naked, though I know he can do far worse.

At least they didn't shut the door at the top of the stairs and the lights have been left on. It's only a tiny glimmer of hope, but it's one to hold on to. It means she's coming back. We won't be kept in this fucking place forever. If my father wants this wedding to happen, then our circumstances will change.

I can't afford to be complacent, though.

What is it they say about lights at ends of tunnels? That sometimes they turn out to be trains.

Movement comes in the doorway and my father reappears with Mackenzie. She's still got that damned collar on, but now she's wearing a white dress. Her hair is wet and a shade darker than its usual honey blonde, and she seems uncomfortable, but not traumatized. Her blue eyes are wide and haunted, but she's not screaming and crying and trying to get away.

I take that as a positive sign that he hasn't hurt her.

Grigoriy hauls her back down the stairs. "What do you think of your new bride?"

He directs that question at me.

I hold my gaze on our Duchess. "She's beautiful. She's always beautiful."

She also doesn't deserve this. She should be a regular college student, hanging out with her friends, drinking coffee and complaining about her tutors. Instead, her tutor groomed her and abused her. She then had to run, and the poor girl ran right into our arms.

Now she's where she is because of us. Because of *me*.

She shouldn't be wearing a cheap-ass wedding dress, a collar around her neck, standing in a goddamned basement.

And she shouldn't be made to marry me.

Her chest hitches in a small sob.

"Did he touch you?" I have to ask.

I don't want to hear the answer, but I can't not know. If I want to be there for her, then I need to know everything, no matter how bad things get.

But she shakes her head, and I almost collapse with relief.

A male voice comes from the top of the stairs. "Go on, Father. Down the stairs. Everyone is waiting for you."

A short man in his sixties appears. He's clearly anxious, his expression troubled. When he takes the first couple of steps, I see why. Rufus is behind him with a gun aimed at his head.

Fuck. Are we seriously going to get married with a priest at gunpoint? Each time I think this can't possibly get more messed up, things step up a level.

Grigoriy moves away from Mackenzie and comes to the cage. He unlocks the gate, swings it open, and steps back.

"Come on, then. This is your big moment. Don't let me down, son."

I'm just grateful to be out of the cage. Though it wasn't like the bars stopped me seeing out, being free of them makes me weak with relief. Now, if only I can get us both out of this basement, but I guess it's going to take marrying Mackenzie to do that.

I'm not hesitant for my sake. I'd happily marry her tomorrow, but she's already told me, clear as day, that this isn't what she wants. I know she's worried about Dom and Tino, too, about what will happen to the four of us. She's right to be worried. They also made their feelings clear. The bruises Dom gave me when he found out I'd proposed have barely had the chance to fade.

My father's gaze drops down my body, and then back up to my face. "We should have gotten you a suit, but it's too late now. Come here. Stand beside your bride."

I do as I'm told, standing beside her, in front of the priest. She doesn't look at me, and I can't blame her. Don't young girls grow up with the idea of how they want their weddings to be? Don't they play dress-up, and imagine who their future husbands will be? If Mackenzie ever did that, I guarantee she never pictured things going like this. In a basement, with a terrified priest, and a collar around her neck.

I close my eyes and duck my head. Shame soaks through me, into my skin, penetrating my muscles, sinking right down to the bone.

What kind of man am I? I'd fucked her while she'd been cuffed to the bars by a collar, naked apart from her panties. I'd fucked her while two strange men were watching, and then they'd come over her, too.

How could I do that to her? I'm supposed to love her,

and instead of protecting her, I was the one who needed her comfort.

I want to punch myself in the side of the head, to throw myself against the bars of the cage until I break my bones. I'm a pathetic excuse of a man. How could I allow her to be desecrated like that, when she was already dripping with the cum of two other men, and she'd had my semen still leaking from between her thighs?

Those same men are down in the basement with us now. They stare at her with hungry eyes. She's a thing to them—a vessel to be used—and I treated her no differently.

But even as I'm thinking these things, my body reacts to her presence, blood flowing to my cock. Jesus Christ. When she was collared and on her knees, covered in cum, all I'd wanted to do was to grab her hair and thrust my cock into her mouth and fuck her face while tears flowed down her cheeks. I'd wanted to come down her throat, and fill her mouth, so she coughed and choked, and my cum trickled from the corners of her lips.

Realization hits me hard and fast. I'm the same as him. The same as the man I hate. Deep down, I share his sickness. In time, will I become him? If I do, I'm ruining her by marrying her.

"Let's begin," Grigoriy says to the priest.

My head snaps up. "No."

She's too good for this. She deserves so much better than me. Better than any of us.

"Kirill," she says, her voice breathy, "it's okay."

"No, it's not. None of this is fucking okay."

My father unholsters his weapon. "Do not push me, Kirill. I said you will marry your woman and give us an heir. You need to grow up and become a man."

"No," I say again.

Mackenzie's small hand slips into mine. I can't help but look at her. Tears shine in her eyes.

"Please, let's just do it," she begs. "We can figure everything else out after."

My heart hitches. A part of me wanted this—to have Mackenzie say she'd marry me—but I didn't plan for it to happen like this.

"Just begin," my father commands the priest.

"Errr...ummm..." the man stutters.

"Just do it!" Grigoriy roars, and we all jump in response. The priest begins to speak, but it's in Russian.

"In fucking English." My father looks like he's about to murder the priest. Surely to God, even he wouldn't go that far.

The priest begins the service again, this time in English. The service sounds real, but I can barely hear what he's saying over the rush of blood in my ears and my heart pounding. Mackenzie's hand is still in mine, and she squeezes my fingers, and I squeeze hers in return.

"—if anyone here has any reason why these two should not be married..." the priest continues.

I almost laugh at that. The man still has a gun pointed at his head. No one voices any concerns.

"Do we have the rings?" he asks, his eyes darting in one direction and then the other.

"Motherfucker," Grigoriy curses. "We forgot the fucking rings."

His men rush in. "Here, here. Use ours." Jewelry is pulled from fingers and handed over. They'll all be huge on Mackenzie, but I guess it's the least of her concerns.

Grigoriy nods at the priest. "Continue."

But, before he gets the chance, Igor appears at the top of the stairs and clears his throat. "Boss, there is a problem."

Grigoriy's eyes flare with anger at the interruption. "What is it, Igor?"

"We have company."

"Fuck. Just keep going. Say the words. Do you Mackenzie

take Kirill Stepanov..." My father has taken over, waving his hand in a circling motion to encourage the priest to keep going.

He does. "Do you Mackenzie—" He cuts off, clearly realizing he doesn't know Mack's surname.

"Kingsland," she fills in.

"Do you Mackenzie Kingsland take Kirill Stepanov to be your lawfully wedded husband?"

She presses her lips into a thin line and nods. "I do."

"And do you Kirill Stepanov take Mackenzie Kingsland to be your lawfully wedded wife?"

I open my mouth, but from somewhere outside comes the *pop-pop-pop* of gunfire. To anyone else, they might be mistaken for fireworks, or perhaps a car backfiring, but there's no doubt in my mind what they are. My heart lifts. Gunfire means someone else is here, and there's only one explanation I can think of.

Domenic and Valentino have found us.

"I do!" my father roars. "Say it! I do."

I open my mouth to speak, but there's a massive bang from upstairs and my words are lost to the noise and chaos.

THE DEVILS' DARLING

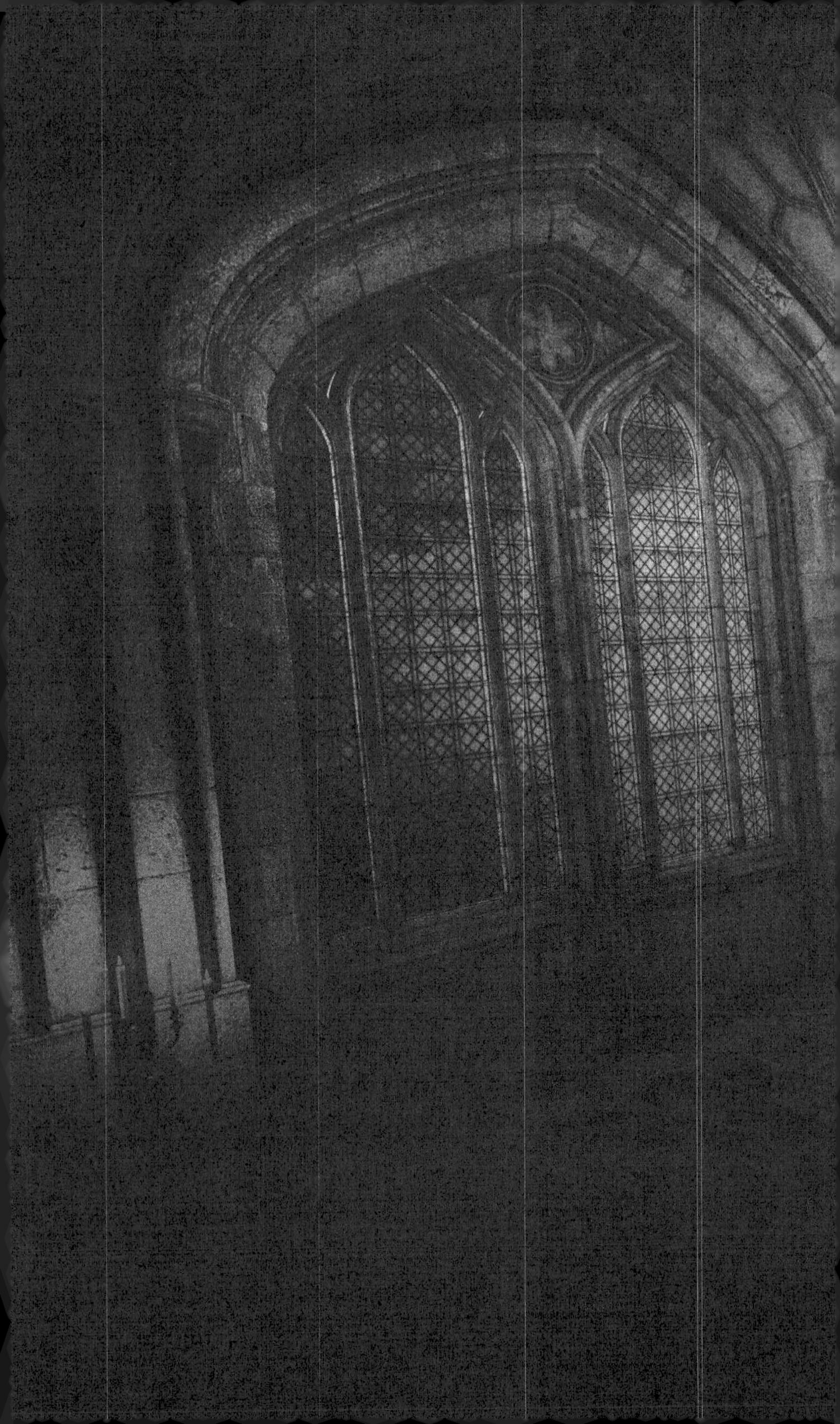

Fourteen

Tino

The plan for us to go in quietly and use flashbangs goes to shit.

We park the vehicles a short way from the cabins and approach quietly on foot, only to discover armed guards outside, patrolling the area. One of them is separate from the group, taking a piss, of all things.

He looks up, sees us, and, before we can put a bullet in him, using a silencer, he screams something in Russian.

Grigoriy's men run toward us, weapons raised. They indiscriminately fire off round after round, puncturing holes in the trees and splintering wood. Jesus Christ, they are not the best trained, but the volume of gunfire sends us scattering.

Diego pushes me back, urging me to take cover behind one of the trees, but I scramble to get around him. I am not going to cower in the background. All I care about is getting to Mackenzie and Kirill.

I glance over my shoulder, trying to get eyes on Dom. I spot him a short distance away, two of my men flanking him. He seems unharmed. He jerks his chin at me, acknowledging that we're both okay, and that we need to keep going. With every step, white spikes of agony jar up through my bad leg, but the pills I've taken make the pain seem distant.

Leon beckons with a curl of his fingers, and four of my father's men fan out and raise their weapons. They take out Grigoriy's men one by one. But one of the Russians gets a hit on one of our men. He goes down with a scream as his thigh bursts open like a watermelon.

"Fuck." I catch the eye of another of my father's men. "Stay with him," I command. "Bind up that leg." I won't leave one of these men here to bleed out.

With the Russian patrolmen taken care of, I storm toward the building, Dom by my side.

"Wait," Leon says as he races to catch up with me. "They'll know we're coming now, but we can still disorientate them."

I nod and put my arm out, holding Dom back with me. Leon reaches the door first, and he lifts his foot and kicks it open. He glances inside, ducks back out, and beckons the men, pointing toward the cabin. Two of our men pull the pins on the stun grenades and throw them inside.

The noise is loud enough to hurt my ears even out here. There's a blinding flash from inside, and it looks as if real grenades went off in there. Smoke billows out of the door and dissipates into the air.

Shit, will Mackenzie be injured by the blasts?

"Visual check showed me males only in that first room," Leon announces, as though he's heard my thoughts, and I breathe a sigh of relief.

Two men wait either side of the door, weapons raised. One cocks his fingers twice, and the men enter. Moments later, there's the strange low thud of silenced fire, and then Leon beckons us through. I enter the cabin. A couple of bodies are sprawled across the floor, blood slowly spreading in a circle beneath them.

Our men spread out, searching the place. Heavy feet clomp around overhead as they check the second floor. To my side is a cloakroom. It's empty.

Where the hell are Kenzie and Kirill? Then I see it, the door beneath the stairs. I pull it open and duck back as bullets whizz by my head. Trust Grigoriy to have them down there.

Fuck.

I need to distract him and his men, because I have no doubt he'll shoot Mackenzie rather than let her go with us. I wave at Leon and indicate the stairs. He pulls two of the stun grenades from the belt slung around his hips. I shake my head. We can't see down there, and if one of those things detonates right by Kenzie, it could still cause a hell of a lot of damage.

Leon purses his lips, but he nods and places them back on his belt.

"Give me one good reason not to shoot this cunt in the face."

The voice is unmistakable.

"Hello, Grigoriy," I say, trying to keep my voice calm. "We've killed your men, and we're armed. You're not getting out of that basement alive if you harm so much as a single hair on either of their heads."

He knows exactly who I'm talking about—Kirill and Mackenzie.

He shouts up his reply. "We're also armed, and if any of you try to come down here, we'll pick you off before your foot even hits the second step."

I grind my teeth and wish I could take a pill.

This is a standoff. How the hell are we going to play this without anyone getting hurt? I exchange a glance with Dom. His jaw is locked, and his eyes radiate concern. We need to get down there, no matter what. Even if it means putting ourselves in danger.

I call an offer back to Grigoriy. "If you don't hurt them, we will come down. Unarmed."

Maybe it's stupid to hand ourselves over to Grigoriy, but we'll still have our men upstairs. All I know is I want to be near Kenzie, to make sure she's all right, and check on Kirill, too.

Grigoriy laughs. "And why would you want to do that?"

"So we can talk. Let's find a way out of this without anyone getting hurt."

There's a pause as he considers this. "Very well. But if you bring weapons, we will shoot you."

"No weapons," I reassure him.

Dom is right beside me now. I glance at the stairs and then back at him. We both slowly lower our guns and place them on the floor, off to one side.

"I'll go with you," Leon says. Then he addresses Diego, keeping his voice low. "Pick our best marksman and get him ready for when all hell breaks loose."

Diego nods.

I edge to the top of the stairs, my heart in my mouth, bracing myself to receive a bullet. Fuck, if this goes wrong, we could get Mackenzie killed.

None comes, and I take the stairs carefully. They are not well lit. The light is behind us, meaning those at the bottom can see me clearly, but I can't see into the room.

I don't want to get shot before I can help Mackenzie, so I make sure to hold my hands above my head as I walk. The last thing I want is for someone to put a bullet in my head in a moment of panic. As I hit the bottom stair and finally adjust to see the room in front of me, my heart drops into my stomach.

Dom bumps into me, and I realize I've stopped walking.

The scene in front of me is like something out of a horror movie.

Kirill is ashen and standing next to Mackenzie, who is

wearing the most disgusting wedding dress I have ever seen. Her hair is damp and plastered to her head, and she's pale with bruises and a bandage on her arm.

In front of them is a priest, and behind them—oh, fuck me—behind them is a cage. I stare at the cage, at the dog bowls with filthy looking food and water in them, and then back at Kirill and Mackenzie.

The collar around her neck makes me want to vomit.

I take it all in and have to lock myself down, so I don't lose my fucking mind.

It's a wedding. We've interrupted a fucking wedding. Grigoriy got what he wanted all along. I wonder how far into the ceremony they've gotten.

Rage courses through me at nuclear levels. My gaze immediately flicks to Grigoriy. Did he put these marks on our doll?

How dare he hurt our Duchess?

I'm going to kill him with my bare hands if it's the last thing I do.

My arms are raised in the air, and so are Dom's, and my hands twitch with the desire to throttle Grigoriy until his last breath wheezes from him.

Leon takes the last few steps to enter the room. His arms are also held above his head.

"Who's this asshole?" Grigoriy asks.

"One of my men," I reply. "Like I said, there are more upstairs."

"How many more?"

"A couple of our men were hit," Leon says, "but there are ten left, and they're all armed. They're not going to let you walk out of here either. If we die, you die. You're as trapped as we are."

He's lied about the numbers, but it doesn't really matter. We *are* trapped in this room, because Mackenzie has a gun pointed at her head, which means until we somehow disarm these men, no one is getting rescued.

Grigory laughs, aware he's been lied to. "Yes, sure, of course that is the correct number of men, right?" He glances at Leon and then back at me and Dom. "I suppose I'm meant to be scared of this ragtag little band."

Igor is standing to one side, the weapon in his hand trained right on me. He lets out a strangely high-pitched giggle. Are they on fucking drugs? Shit, it wouldn't surprise me, and it makes them even less predictable.

I take stock of the room. There are two more men with guns. One of them has his weapon on Dom, but the other has his gun aimed right at the back of Mackenzie's head. I know it's enough to keep Kirill in place. My throat runs dry as a wave of sickness washes over me.

"Finish the vows and get this done," Grigoriy orders.

The priest is shaking so much that, when he begins to speak, his teeth chatter. It is clear he is not here of his own accord but is a pawn in Grigoriy's sick game.

I dare not even glance at Dom, and I'm completely unsure how we can stop this before the ceremony is complete. Any move we make is going to get Mackenzie shot. I look at her again, trying to communicate with my gaze how sorry I am that things turned out this way. It seems we came here so well armed for nothing. Because he's hidden away in this basement like the cowardly, filthy rat that he is, Grigoriy has made it impossible for us to do anything to save Mackenzie without risking getting her killed.

"I'm sorry, Duchess," I say.

I realize in this moment it seems hopeless, and I need her to know how I feel about her before I walk straight into Igor's weapon. One of us has to break this stalemate.

As if she realizes what I am going to do, her eyes fill with tears. "No," she whispers.

"I love you," I mouth.

Mackenzie jerks as if I shot her. She blinks rapidly and

sways a little on her feet. The priest has started speaking again, but all I can do is watch in horror as Mackenzie jerks twice more then falls to the floor. Kirill tries to catch her but misses. She hits hard, her head bouncing off the concrete.

She's rigid, and her hands curl into tight claws.

No. Fuck, no.

Her body jerks and her head snaps back as her throat and neck strain.

Kirill drops to his knees beside her.

"What the hell is she doing?" Grigoriy demands as if he can't fucking see what's happening. "Make it stop," he says to Kirill. "Make her fucking stop that."

"She can't control it, you fucking asshole," I seethe, already moving, no longer caring if they shoot me, just needing to be by her.

I fall to the same position as Kirill, only on the opposite side of Kenzie. We share a worried glance, neither of us daring to touch her. We're not trained for this, and we're both unsure what to do.

"She's having a seizure," Dom says. "She could die. Let us help her. She can't marry your son if she's dead, can she?"

"A seizure?" Grigoriy's face turns down in a disgusted sneer. He doesn't seem concerned at all for her well-being, only dismayed that she's having a seizure in the first place.

Igor takes a couple of steps back, lowering his weapon. "What is wrong with her? Is she sick? Could we catch it?"

Igor is freaking out. He even makes the sign of the cross. Grigoriy laughs. "She's not possessed Igor, just weak."

The fucking bastard. He really is a piece of shit.

Dom rushes toward us, and one of Grigoriy's men panics. A shot rings out, the loud boom in this small room enough to make my ears ring. His men aren't using silencers the way ours are, and it fucking hurts. I throw my body over Mackenzie's, as does Kirill, and a split second later Dom joins me, so we're all shielding her.

The men we've left upstairs must take the gunshot as their signal to get involved, as bullets rain down on us from above. They're shooting down the stairs, which means they can't see what the fuck they're shooting at properly. My heart pounds and my body tenses, and all I can think is that I don't want anyone I love to get shot.

"You fuckers," Grigoriy snarls.

Leon moves fast.

He flies at Grigoriy, smashing into him with his full body weight and taking him down to the ground. Both men grunt as they hit the floor. Leon grabs Grigoriy's wrist of the hand that's still holding the gun, lifts it, and drives it back down onto the hard concrete. Grigoriy keeps hold of the weapon, but Leon is on top and has the advantage. Leon repeats the process, and this time something cracks—most likely a couple of Grigoriy's fingers—and he drops the gun which clatters away. Leon's gaze flicks to the weapon, clearly trying to decide if it's worth going for it, but then thinks otherwise. If he lifts the pressure off Grigoriy now, the other man might get the advantage. Grigoriy is physically bigger than Leon, and most likely stronger.

Leon draws back his fist and viciously punches Grigoriy in the side of the head three times. Grigoriy tries to fight back, but he can't get a purchase on Leon, and his head rolls to the side as the final punch stuns him.

Bullets whizz by, the high-pitched sound terrifying when there are people I love in the line of those damn bullets. The gunfight continues, and it's a deadly stalemate unfolding. Blood blooms on the chest on one of Grigoriy's men, and he groans as he hits the ground like a sack of bricks. Igor is still returning fire, using the cage as protection—though it's not much. A yell of pain comes from the top of the stairs, and one of my men falls, slowly at first, and then all at once, toppling to the bottom.

Leon jumps to his feet, snatches Grigoriy's gun, and

points it right at Igor. Igor has been distracted by the gunfire from the staircase and doesn't see him coming until it's too late.

Leon jams the muzzle into Igor's temple. "Drop the weapon, or I'll shoot."

Grigoriy's other remaining man swings his gun in Leon's direction. I can see what's about to happen—he'll shoot Leon first. My gaze locks on the gun that had belonged to the man who'd taken the bullet in the chest, and I launch myself at it. I land on my side, skidding across the floor, white hot pain flashing up through my bad leg, but I get my hands on the gun. Without even thinking, I lift it and squeeze the trigger. The bullet finds its home in the man's shoulder, and he flies back, hitting the wall and sliding down. He's still alive, but he's also dropped his gun. I scramble back to my feet and kick it away.

Igor realizes he's fucked, and his weapon topples from his fingers. He puts both hands in the air, much like we'd done on our way down here.

"Okay, okay. Don't shoot."

I know how much Kirill hates this son of a bitch. If anyone's going to shoot him, it'll be my fellow Devil.

With them dealt with, I turn my attention back to Mackenzie.

The seizure seems to be easing off now, and I'm relieved it seems to be a small attack.

I glance over at Kirill, who is simply staring, his eyes almost blank, and his face as pale as death.

"How long since she's eaten or had a drink?" I demand.

He doesn't answer. He merely shakes his head, and I'm shocked when tears fill his eyes, and then, like a waterfall, spill over and stream silently down his face. Shit, he looks completely broken. What the hell happened in this basement?

I remember Kenzie's mother saying it was important to

keep her quiet, warm, and calm after a seizure. I can't help with the first or last one, but I can sure keep her warm. I pull my sweatshirt over my head and place it on her, covering her bare arms. Dom takes off his t-shirt, leaving him bare-chested, and now that the seizure has subsided, he gently lifts her head and places it underneath, cushioning her.

"I want that fucker kept alive." I point to Grigoriy, who Leon has now pulled to his feet.

Leon pulls a zip tie from his utility belt and quickly fastens Grigoriy's wrists behind his back before pushing him to his knees. Then he stoops and binds Grigoriy's ankles, ensuring he can't run.

"Igor, too," Dom says. "Tie him up as well. He's been involved with all Grigoriy's plans for years."

I nod. "The other one is still alive, but I don't think he's going to cause us harm any time soon."

The man in question has covered the bullet hole with his hand, applying pressure. He regards me with strange, pale eyes, and, even though he must be in a huge amount of pain, his lips curl in a sneer.

I don't know what his involvement was in all of this, but he's looking at me as though he knows something I don't.

A small voice comes from the corner of the basement, and I suddenly remember the priest. He'd managed to tuck himself away while all the fighting was happening and has come out of it unscathed.

"I was made to come here. I beg you, don't shoot me." The priest makes the sign of the cross.

"No one is shooting you, Priest," I say.

People are going to die today, but it won't be a man of the cloth.

THE DEVILS' DARLING

Fifteen

Mackenzie

I groan and sit up, strong hands helping me.

My head is pounding, but I'm okay. The seizure was a small one. In fact—and I feel guilty thinking this when I look at the frightened faces around me—it was almost a blessing that it happened. It was a mere blink of an eye compared to most of my seizures, but it was enough that it created a distraction.

It worked. Grigoriy, Igor, and Pale-Eyes are on their knees for us.

I don't merely want to kill Grigoriy Stepanov, I want to make him fucking suffer. I want to make him pay. He ruined Kirill, if the ghost of a man in front of me is anything to go by.

"I think we need to get you to a doctor," Dom says to me.

"I'm okay, really. I've had way worse."

"Your mom said you need to be kept quiet after."

"I'm okay, Dom, truly." Then, because I'm so happy he's here, I throw my arms around him and hug him.

One of the soldiers addresses Tino. "She seems awfully

keen on your friend." He juts his chin out at us hugging.

"They're family, Leon," Tino says smoothly.

The three captives are hauled to their feet and pushed to the far wall.

"Do you want us to shoot them in the knees for you?" the man Tino called Leon asks casually. "They'll live but be in screaming agony."

Tino's lips purse, but he shakes his head. "No, even that's too good for them."

Kirill walks over to his father and stares him deep in the eyes. "You're going to die now. I hope it was worth it, you disgusting piece of shit."

"You think you can kill me and take over?" Grigoriy spits back. "You'll be dead in a month. The sharks in Moscow will eat your entrails."

Kirill cocks his head. He's still pale—still eerily calm—but that blankness is receding. "Ah, that's touching. You think I want your shitty empire?"

Grigoriy frowns. "It's your birthright. What else will you do?"

"Not be you. That's enough for me. Oh, but I will do one thing."

"What?"

"Take my fucking watches back."

Of all the things Kirill has said to his father, this seems to offend him the most.

"The fuck you will!" Grigoriy yells, rearing back.

One of Tino's men is holding Grigoriy's arms, but the huge Russian lunges forward and headbutts Kirill right on the nose.

Blood splatters across Grigoriy's face as Kirill's nose crumbles. The crunch is horrific and turns my stomach, and I let out a scream, clamping my hands over my mouth. Before any of us get the chance to react, the bastard attacks again, smashing his forehead into Kirill's skull this time.

Kirill goes down hard.

"Fuck," Tino shouts.

He races to Kirill, and two of Tino's men bend to check him over.

"He's out cold, but he'll come around," one of the men examining Kirill says. "We need to get him laid down and quiet for when he does"

"How do you know?" I ask, trying not to cry.

"Combat medic in my previous life," he replies. "Can we take him out to the vehicles? I have a medical kit."

Dom glances at Tino, and they both nod. "Yes, it's probably best he doesn't see this next bit, anyway."

"You need checking over too, Miss," the ex-medic says.

"Not yet," I argue. I can't leave this room right now. Not until I've seen justice done.

"But Miss—"

I interrupt. "I promise when this is over, I'll let you thoroughly check me out. But I swear I am okay."

"She's good," Dom says, surprising me by taking my side.

Tino takes charge, addressing his men. "In fact, you all need to leave. Place two men outside the door and two at the top of the stairs, but give us some privacy." He jerks his chin at the priest still cowering in the corner. "And take him with you."

The priest holds his hands out in front of him. "Please, don't kill me. I won't say a word, I swear. I never wanted to be here. They made me, just the same way they made you. I know how to keep my mouth shut."

Tino takes his phone back out of his pocket and snaps a photograph of the cowering man. "Just know that if you ever say anything, we will find you."

"I won't, I won't." He does the sign of the cross again. "I swear."

"Okay. Leon, let him go."

Leon and Diego exchange worried looks, but they nod. It's clear they know how to take an order.

"Yes, sir," Leon says.

"Duchess, you sure you don't want to go with Kirill? This is about to get nasty."

Tino gives me the option of leaving again, but I shake my head. Resolute.

"I wouldn't miss it for the world," I say.

"What did they do to you?" Dom asks once we have the room.

Tino has a gun trained on the men, and Dom and I are watching the three of them.

"They made us—" I stop and swallow, and then try again. "They watched Kirill and me together. They ... they ... that one, he masturbated on us." I point to Pale-Eyes. "But he's the worst," I spit as I point at Grigoriy. "He's sick. He touched me. Made me do things. He showed me that disgusting thing between his legs and said he was going to make me suck it."

I hadn't realized I had started to cry until the dampness tickles my cheeks.

I wipe them away. He deserves only my anger, not my sorrow.

"You like forcing people?" Dom says to Grigoriy. "Like to watch?"

He looks at Tino.

"My friend here likes to watch, too, don't you, Tino?"

Tino nods and pulls his phone out of his pocket. "Yeah. I like to film it, too."

"Can you imagine one of your little movies, starring the head of the Stepanov Bratva with his men?"

Grigoriy snarls. "You fucking sick pieces of shit."

He tries to struggle but Tino's guy punches him in the gut, and Grigory doubles over.

"Takes one to know one." Dom shrugs.

He takes out a small but sharp-looking serrated knife and walks to Igor. "I am giving you two options. I cut your balls off, or you go over there to your boss and pull his pants down."

"What?" Igor's face is a picture of disgust.

"Pull his pants down and suck his cock until it's hard."

"It won't get hard because I am not fucking gay, you fucking piece of human trash," Grigoriy screams.

"Let's see, why don't we?"

Igor shakes his head, and Dom cuts a big, jagged tear in his trousers right by where his package is. Igor lets out a strangled cry.

"Next time, I'll slash at your cock the way I did your pants. I mean you could end up bleeding to death from your cock, or … you just give your boss a blow job and then we let you go. You're not the one we want. He is."

Igor swallows and stares at Grigoriy. He won't do it. He's too scared. Too terrified of Grigoriy. As if he realizes this, Dom slashes Igor's thigh, making him scream in terror, and then stabs it right into his underwear. Igor wails, and it's inhuman. Blood starts to ooze around the knife, and I have no idea exactly what part of his anatomy was hit.

"Best leave that in there because if I pull it out you might bleed to death, and your balls might empty their contents all over the floor, and no one needs to see that." Dom sneers.

Pale-Eyes retches.

Dom turns to him, his eyes blazing. "Guess it's your turn to find out whether you want to suck your boss's cock and leave alive, or bleed out here."

"I'll d-d-do it," Pale-Eyes stammers. "You're going to kill him, right?"

"Oh, yes. Painfully."

"Okay. Okay. Yeah, okay?" He's muttering as if talking to himself.

"What's your name?" Dom asks him.

"Vadim."

"Go and pull his pants down, Vadim."

Still on his knees, he shuffles over to Grigoriy, his head bent. His shirt is dark with blood from the bullet he's taken to the shoulder. He must be weak and dizzy, but he knows if he doesn't do this, the next bullet will finish him.

I'm sure the guys are going to call this off any minute. They're just scaring them. But when Vadim reaches Grigoriy, Dom walks up to Grigoriy and points a gun at the back of his head.

"Don't move," Dom says. Then he addresses the man on his knees. "Suck him like your life depends on it, because it does."

Grigoriy struggles and curses, and when Vadim pulls his pants down, taking his underwear with it, I understand why. He's ragingly hard, and Tino is filming.

This will destroy his legacy in the macho, patriarchal world of the Bratva.

His cock is massive, the head dark and swollen. Thick veins run up its length.

"Jesus fuck, did you pay to have that thing enhanced?" Dom laughs.

Some part of me can't let this happen. I hate Pale-Eyes—Vadim—for what he did to me, and Grigoriy, too. They all deserve to die, and I will pull the trigger myself, but doing this makes us as bad as them.

"No," I say. "Stop this."

But to my shock, Vadim ducks down and sucks half of Grigoriy's cock into his mouth. His lips are stretched around his huge girth, and his pale eyes go wide. He chokes and gags a little but doesn't pull back.

Grigoriy hisses, but his hips buck as he pushes farther in. Vadim gags again, and from the expression on Grigoriy's face, he likes it.

He moans, and Vadim does too. Jesus Christ, were they

all screwing each other or something?

Grigoriy grits his teeth and fucks Vadim's mouth harder. I imagine he'd grab Vadim's hair and hold him in place, if only his hands weren't tied behind his back.

"Are you getting this, Tino?" Dom asks.

He's lowered the gun now. If this is to look real, it won't work if Grigoriy is being held at gunpoint.

"I don't know if this is enough to ruin his legacy." Tino shrugs. "I think we should make Vadim here fuck Grigoriy in the ass."

"No, please," I beg. "This is enough. We've got what we need on camera. We've ruined them."

Dom and Tino exchange a glance, and Tino gives a tiny nod.

"Okay, you can stop now," Dom commands the two men.

But Grigoriy shakes his head, his hips continuing to thrust. His ass muscles are bunched tight, and he crowds Vadim back against the wall, so the other man has no chance of pulling away. He's weak and bleeding, and now Grigoriy is using him like a human fuck toy. The noises they're both making turns my stomach, and I'm sure Grigoriy is going to empty himself down Vadim's throat at any moment, if he doesn't choke Vadim with his cock first.

I don't want Grigoriy to have that pleasure. He doesn't deserve it.

"Stop!" I yell. "I said stop."

"Fuck off," Grigoriy snarls. His hips are pumping as if he's got no control of himself anymore. He's violent in his need.

With a couple of swift steps, I grab the gun from Tino, and he whirls around in shock. "Kenzie?"

"Turn the fucking camera off," Dom snaps.

Tino stops filming and puts his phone down. "What are you doing?" His tone is cautious, as well it might be.

I aim the gun at Grigoriy's head. "I told you to fucking stop."

Finally, his hips stop moving and he backs away. Vadim falls to one side, coughing and choking. I have no sympathy for the man. Serves him right. Grigoriy's disgusting thing is red and so swollen it looks painful. His hips give a little jerk and I realize he's still fucking, but just air. His cock leaks, and he groans. I stare at him in disgust. He's nothing but an animal.

My hands are shaking like crazy, but I keep the gun level.

"Okay, Duchess, you stopped it. We'll take it from here." Tino touches my wrist, but I jerk out of his touch.

"No." I step right up to Grigoriy, who still has his disgusting snake hanging out of his pants.

"You want to suck my cock, Kitten?" Grigory snarls. "It would look perfect shoved down your throat." He looks at me and laughs. "I know deep down you wanted me. Wanted a real man to fuck your holes. What a fucking waste."

He knows he's dead now no matter what, and he's lost all inhibitions.

"I wouldn't touch you if you were the last man left alive. I'd crawl through a tunnel of shit to get away from you. You're pathetic. Nothing." His cock deflates as I speak. "You're a pale imitation of a human being, and you lost it all. Everything. Most of all, you lost your son."

I step back, and with the gun steady now, I stare in his eyes. "When I pull this trigger, Tino will get a lovely photo of you with your pants down, your cock all pathetic and shriveled and that's what will be your legacy. That's what your men will see. You will be a joke. A seedy little punchline. And you deserve every damn minute of it."

I aim, close my eyes, breathe, and squeeze.

THE DEVILS' DARLING

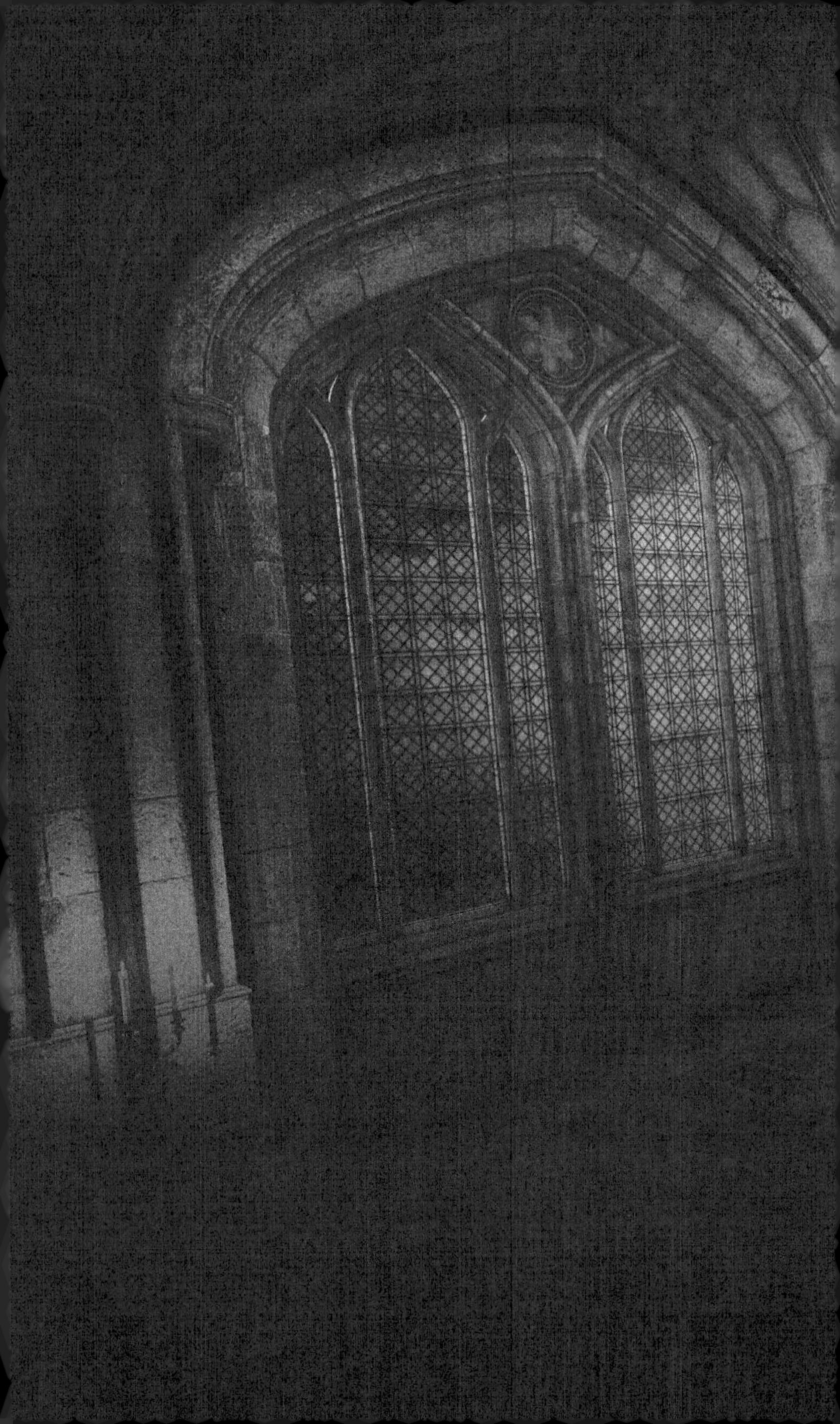

Sixteen

Domenic

Boom.

I jump even though I was waiting for it.

Fuck me, she did it. Our Duchess just shot the head off the Stepanov Bratva, one of the most feared men in the world.

He hits the wall behind him, a large chunk of his skull, brains, and blood splattering the brickwork, and slowly slides to the floor. He lands in a slump, his chin to chest, leaving a smear of more blood behind him.

The gun clatters from Mack's fingers, and she spins away from him and vomits onto the floor. I don't know if it's a result of what she's just done, the sight of all the gore, or because of the seizure she's only just had, but I go to her. I hold her hair out of the way and rub her back as she heaves. She's shaking all over.

"Oh, my God. I just killed Kirill's father. Oh, fuck. Oh, Christ."

"It's okay. Here. Sit down."

But she shakes her head. "No. I want to get out of here. I don't want to spend a single second longer than I have to in this place."

I glance over at Tino, who nods.

"Okay, let's get out of here."

My arm is around Mackenzie's waist, and I try to guide her, but she pulls back on me.

"No, wait," she says. "I know what I said, but there's one thing I need to do."

To my surprise, she slips out of my grip and goes back to Grigoriy's body. She crouches and does something that's hidden from my view, and then stands again.

"Okay?" I ask her.

She nods. "Let's get the fuck out of this hellhole."

I scoop up my t-shirt, and pull it down over her head, so it covers the top part of that hideous, and now blood-spattered, wedding dress. Tino picks up his sweatshirt and puts it back on too.

The gunshot has drawn Tino's men back down into the basement, clearly wanting to check we still have the upper hand.

Tino addresses Leon. "Take the two surviving assholes with you, and then torch the place—any vehicles you find, too."

Leon gives a curt nod. "Yes, sir."

He yanks Igor up by his shirt, and the man screams. I can't tell where the knife went when he was stabbed, but it hit some part of his junk if the slowly spreading patch of blood is anything to go by. He hobbles, and each step conjures a moaning, retching sound from his throat.

Leon shoves him again, pitiless and cold.

I can hardly believe it's over. Mackenzie and Kirill are safe, and Grigoriy is never going to hurt anyone again. I imagine the news reaching Russia, and the huge fucking impact it's going to have on their society, but that's not our problem. I expect there will be some people over there who will want to shake our hands. I just hope there are no other repercussions, but then there won't be as long as no one finds out what we did.

It means we'll have to be very careful that, if we do circulate those pictures of Grigoriy dead, naked, and flaccid, we don't let them be traced back to us in any way. No one can know we did this. Our Duchess can't be the further target of any of the Stepanov Bratva who might remain active in Russia.

It's the reason we can't let these two men live. It's clear from their eyes that they think they're getting away with it, though. They played their part. Mackenzie said the one with the weird pale eyes—Vadim—came on her, and that information alone makes me want to kill him.

As for Igor, well, Kirill gets to have the final say in that. The man has been a thorn in Kirill's side for as long as I've known him.

We leave the cabin, and head toward the vehicles.

Sunlight hits like disinfectant, washing off the grime of that cabin. Fuck, I'm glad to be out of there. Mackenzie is walking, but she leans on me the entire time. I glance over to Tino. He's noticeably limping, his face tight with pain. He must have hurt himself when he went for the gun.

As we near the vehicles, Vadim stumbles. The man guarding him holds him up, but Vadim's eyes roll back in his head. His face pales suddenly and alarmingly. His body slumps again, and this time the man lets go as Vadim hits the ground hard.

His guard bends over him and rolls him onto his front. He's pale, sweaty, and mumbling incoherent bullshit.

The medic who was treating Kirill jogs over and squats by Vadim. He looks him over. "He's lost a lot of blood and is in a lot of pain. He's probably also gone into shock."

"Is he going to die?" Mackenzie straightens, her arms wrapped around her waist as if hugging herself.

Her voice is hopeful. I glance at Tino, and his jaw

tightens.

"Without treatment," the medic says, "yes, probably, but it will take a long time. He might survive."

"You thinking of leaving him out here, Duchess?" Tino asks.

She purses her lips. "I was, but if he might survive, then no."

The medic confirms her fears. "If someone found him, got him medical help, then yes, he might still live."

"I don't want him to live," she whispers. "He did things to me... and to Kirill."

The thought of this man touching her makes me want to tear him limb from limb, to rip off his head and spit down his neck.

But Tino gets there before me.

"Duchess, your word is my command." Tino takes the gun he is holding and aims it at Vadim.

"Come on, baby. You don't need to watch," I say with my arm around her. "Let's get you checked out and see how Kirill is doing."

She nods, and I take her hand and lead her away. The shot rings out, and she flinches and draws a sharp breath but says nothing.

Igor is staring around him while Diego pushes him along, and I can tell he's thinking about making a run for it. He won't get very far, the fucking idiot. He's still got a knife sticking out of his balls. The sight brings on a wave of faintness, and I look away, but I keep my peripheral vision on him. Waiting for when he tries to make that move.

The door to one of the vehicles opens, and Kirill steps out. His nose is bloodied, and he's still ashen, but he isn't as checked out as he was. His eyes have something of his soul back in them.

"Hey, man," I greet him. Then, not sure of what the fuck I can say, I lower my gaze.

Mack said they did things to him. How bad? I'm not sure I want to know.

"Is he dead?" he asks.

I know he means his father.

"I'm sorry." Duchess sobs and throws her arms around him.

Kirill might be in shock, but his arms come around her automatically, and he nuzzles his face in her hair. "It's okay, *Kukla*. It's okay. He deserved it. It has to be this way."

She pulls away from him and reaches down the front of her dress. "I got something for you."

To my surprise, she produces a watch. It was the same one that had been on Grigoriy's wrist. Holy shit, that's what she was doing when she bent down to him. She took his watch to give to Kirill.

My jaw drops. She never fails to amaze me. Even when I think she's at her weakest moment, she pushes herself to do more, thinking of someone else rather than herself.

He squeezes the watch in his fist and then pockets it. "Thank you."

She gives a tiny nod, and they move together again. This time, Kirill lowers his forehead to hers, and they just stand that way, breathing each other in.

There's a connection between them now, a bond, and I can feel it. It makes me an utter asshole to be jealous of it, but I am. How can I begrudge them this? They only had each other to get through the absolute hell they were in, but I still find it hard to watch.

Will she always be bonded to him now in a way I can never match?

Igor suddenly makes his break for it. I let him go, enjoying letting him think he has a chance.

Leon raises his weapon, but I put my arm out and steady his. "Let him run for a while. False hope dying is a beautiful thing to witness."

Kirill releases Mack and storms away from us. He opens the rear doors of the truck he drove here and reaches inside. A moment later, he straightens with something in his hands.

I realize it's a gun.

Face hard and set, he follows Igor into the woods. The other man is stumbling, babbling, and crying. He's totally pathetic, and I can't believe this is the guy that terrorized so many people, including Kirill.

"Hey, Igor," Kirill shouts. "Get on your fucking knees and crawl to me, and I might let you live."

Igor stops. He turns slowly to Kirill, and I can see it. That flash of defiance, the strength that stopped him from sucking Grigoriy's cock, but then he flinches.

"This really hurts," he moans as he gestures to the mess that is his package. "I think I'm going to need surgery."

"Crawl," Kirill says again.

"You won't let me live." Igor laughs, and it breaks into a sob at the end.

"Then why did you try to run?"

"I don't fucking know. That stubborn will to survive?"

"Crawl to me," Kirill says, and it's almost soothing. Almost seductive.

"No."

"Fine." He raises the gun, and Igor shouts.

"Okay. Okay. Just, give me a second, this fucking hurts."

He clambers down onto his hands and knees and starts to crawl.

"Wiggle your butt like a good doggie," Kirill snarls.

Jesus Christ. I remind myself never to truly get on the wrong side of my friend.

Igor does as Kirill says and he wiggles his butt, sobbing in pain each time he does.

"That's perfect. Pant for me."

Igor looks up at Kirill, and a flash of pure hatred beams from his narrow-eyed gaze, but he does it. He pants like a fucking dog.

"Lift your front paws up like a good boy. Kneel up." Kirill laughs.

Igor does it. He raises up, hands in the air like paws, and Kirill smiles slowly.

"Good little doggy."

Then he pulls the trigger, the crack echoing through the trees. Birds burst from branches and take off into the sky. The bullet hits Igor right between the eyes. His mouth falls open as if in shock, but no sound comes out, and he falls to the ground.

Behind us, the crackle of flames grows increasingly louder. The cabin is burning. Good fucking riddance.

"Drag him to the cabin and burn him," I order the men. I turn to my friend. "Kirill, you did it," I say. "He's dead."

"I know. Don't fucking patronize me."

I swallow down my anger at his hostility because this is not the time or the place. I simply nod.

"Come on," I say quietly. "Let's go home."

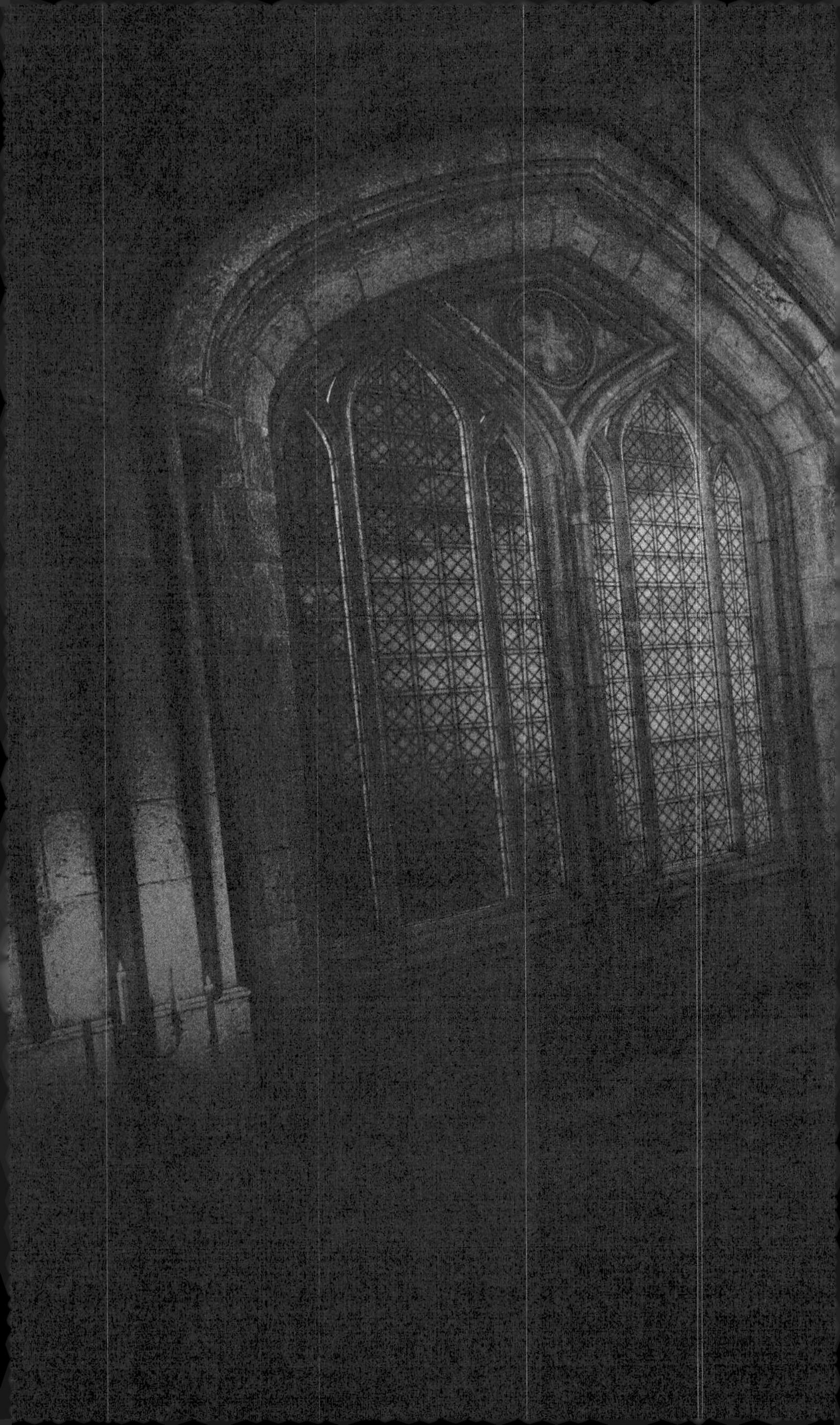

Seventeen
Mackenzie

I've killed a man.

For real this time.

I saw his brain explode all over a wall, and there's no way I'm mistaken.

I'm sitting in the back of one of the Range Rovers that was parked a short distance from the cabin. Tino is driving, and Kirill is in the passenger seat. Dom is beside me, holding my hand. He's still bare-chested because I'm wearing his shirt over this hideous wedding dress. I know it has spots of blood on it, but I'm trying not to look. Maybe I should have picked up my clothes and left the dress to burn with the cabin, but I hadn't even been thinking about what I was wearing. Besides, it would have meant going back in to retrieve my sweatpants, and I wasn't going to do that either.

I twist my body and peer out of the rear window. Through the trees, a curling cloud of thick smoke reaches into the blue sky. Someone will report the fire soon, but by the time the services reach it, there will be nothing of the cabin left. I hope it doesn't spread, but there's no wind today, so luck might be on our side, for that, at least.

Dom squeezes my fingers, and I turn back to face the front. There's no point in looking back now. It's done.

I stare at the part of Kirill's blond head that's visible on one side of the seat. He has his fingers pressed to his temple, his elbow resting on the door. It's as though the weight of the world is on his shoulders, even though we're free.

Does Kirill know I'm the one who shot his dad? I gave him the watch, but was that enough?

I can't bring myself to say the words, 'I shot your father.' Will he hate me for it? Resent me for not letting him pull the trigger? The man was an evil son of a bitch, but he was still Kirill's dad, and there's got to be a lot of complicated shit that goes with him being dead.

Who will take over his family name? Will Kirill be expected to return to Russia to step into his father's place? The thought of him leaving knots me up inside. We can't have gone through all of this only to end up apart.

This drive feels like the one I did with my mom when we left for Verona Falls. I'd been in shock then after Paxton tried to rape me and what I did to him. This is the same, except now I have my guys surrounding me, giving me their support, the way I will support them. Judging from his body language and his pale face, Kirill might need the buttress of *us*, this crazy but beautiful group, more than I do.

I still find myself going back to what my mom said to me in the car that day, how the only way I'd make it through this was by burying my emotions and trauma deep inside. Fake it until you make it, by keeping my chin lifted, and making my way through the world as if nothing has happened.

Only this time it's not the other students I'm hiding what happened from—it's her. I don't want my mom to find out what I went through in that cage. I don't want her to know I was degraded and assaulted. I can't stand to see the pity in her eyes, and, truthfully, the memory fills me with shame. The thought of going back over it all is too much.

I'm sure she and Nataniele will be desperate to know what happened at the cabin, but all they really need to be aware of is that Grigoriy and his men are dead, and we're safe.

I'm so exhausted that I drift off against Dom's shoulder. When I come awake again, it's to the stopping of the vehicle. I lift my head and see we're back at Verona Falls, except we're not at the grand front entrance, but instead around the back.

People are waiting for us.

I spot my mom standing next to Nataniele. Her hand is covering her mouth, and, as I open the door to climb out, she leaves Nataniele's side and rushes toward me.

"Oh, my God, Mackenzie."

My mom bursts into tears and hugs me tight. I find myself crying as well, burying my face against her shoulder.

"I thought you were dead," she cries, over and over. "I thought you were dead, I thought you were dead."

I untangle myself from her grip and wipe my face. "I'm not, Mom. I'm all right. I'm safe."

Twin lines appear between her brows as she takes me in. "What on Earth are you wearing?"

I shake my head. "It's a long story."

"It can go in the furnace," Dom says. "You'll never have to see that dress again."

"Why are you wearing a wedding dress?" Mum's voice is faint, and she pales. "Oh, God, Mackenzie what happened?"

"Mom, I'm okay, truly. I will explain, but please, not right now. I'm so tired."

"You're not married?" Nataniele asks, his tone suspicious.

That man is so close to guessing our secret.

"No," I say, "because your son and Tino made sure that didn't happen. I'm so grateful he's going to be my stepbrother." I add that last bit hoping it isn't too much and hoping it will throw Nataniele off the scent.

He merely gives a non-committal low hum and nods.

Thankfully, my mom doesn't press me further; she simply fusses some more. I don't want to have to explain to her how Kirill and I came only seconds away from being married. Or remotely get drawn into what happened in that damned basement.

She looks to Tino, and Dom, and Kirill. "Thank you for bringing my girl home safely. I don't know how I'll ever repay you."

Except I'm not her girl now. With everything that's happened since we came here, I've gradually felt those apron strings unravel. This is how it's supposed to be. I'm twenty years old. I shouldn't be dependent on my mother. It's normal for someone my age to want to form their own family, and I've chosen that family in the Devils.

One day, I'm going to have to tell her that, and I don't think it will go down well. Now is not the time, however. We've already got too much to deal with. We can do without that bombshell landing.

"She suffered a small seizure," Dom tells my mom.

Fresh concern fills her eyes. "Oh, sweetheart. How are you feeling?"

I lower my chin. "I need my meds, and I'm exhausted."

She clasps my shoulder. "Of course. Let's get you up to your room. You'll need something to eat and drink, too. And a shower."

She's not wrong, but I don't want her to be the one to be with me. "It's okay, Mom. The guys can take me. I need to talk to them about some stuff. I'll come and find you later. Is that all right?"

She drops her hand. "Oh. Okay."

My rebuke has hurt her feelings, but that's how it has to be now.

"Come," Nataniele says. "Let's leave them to sort

themselves out. We'll expect you later this evening." He addresses this to me and Dom. "We can talk then. Tino, thank your men for me."

When they leave, I release a long breath from between my lips.

"Actually," Kirill says, interrupting the moment and not meeting my eye when I turn to him, "I need to take a shower as well. I'll head back to my room and catch up with you later."

"We'll be in the den," Dom tells him.

"Kirill," I call after him, suddenly anxious.

He pauses and glances over his shoulder at me.

"Are you okay?" I ask. It feels like a feeble thing to say, but it's what I want to know. Of course he's not okay.

But he nods. "I will be."

Then he turns away and keeps going.

Tino has to see his men back to the airfield. I'm aware I probably wouldn't have made it out of this alive without them, and I take a moment to thank them for their help and say goodbye.

Seeing Valentino at the head of his men has made me reassess who he is. I can see the man he's going to become in the next ten years—strong, and powerful, and not to be fucked with. I hope he won't lose that playful side, though.

Dom doesn't leave my side for a second. I feel like if someone says so much as one wrong word to me, he'll beat the shit out of them. I had caught Nataniele narrowing his eyes at his son earlier, and I remind myself to tell Dom to chill.

I know it's not going to be easy. The last thing I feel is chilled. It's as though every cell in my body is trembling and jarring within me.

We watch Tino and his men leave, and then Dom and I go up to my room.

The first thing I do is go to the drawer in my nightstand

and take my meds. It's a huge relief. If I'd gone much longer without them, I'm sure the small seizure I'd had would have become a big one.

Dom goes into the bathroom and turns on the shower. Working carefully, as though I'm a fragile china doll that might break, he undresses me. He pulls his t-shirt up over my head, and then turns me around so he can undo the buttons on the back of my dress.

"Burn it," I tell him, stepping out of it and kicking it away.

He nods. "I will."

I'm naked now, but he doesn't touch me or look at me in that way. I stand under the water while he washes my hair and soaps down my body with strong, firm fingers. When I'm clean, I step out, and he wraps me in a towel then guides me to my bed. My hair is still damp, but I don't care. I'm too exhausted to think about blow-drying it now. We lie, side by side, and he folds me into his arms and holds me.

"Will Kirill be all right?" I mumble against his chest.

"Hush, don't worry about Kirill right now." He strokes my hair in a soothing pattern. "Just get some rest, and then we'll go and meet them in the den. You'll feel better after you nap."

I'm powerless against it. My eyelids are heavy, and my limbs seem to sink into the mattress.

"I'm frightened I'll dream of that place," I tell him, my voice already distant.

"If you do, I'll be right here. I'll always be here for you, to scare away your nightmares."

I believe him, too. "Thank you," I murmur.

His arms tighten around me. "I love you, Mack. I'm so fucking sorry for the things I did to you. I wish I could go back and change everything. I'd kill the man I was when you first came here for treating you the way I did. I love you so much."

I try to bring the words to my lips, but they fade away as I sink into oblivion.
I love you, too.

Eighteen

Kirill

I take my time under the shower.

It's surreal being back within the comfort and safety of the Verona Falls grounds. The place never truly felt like home to me, but now my room is the lap of luxury. Just having the hot running water of the shower and privacy is heaven. My nose throbs, and my entire body aches. I think it's from holding myself so tense for so long during the entire ordeal in that basement.

The gothic walls of this old building that sometimes used to be creepy now feel like a fortress. The high fences are my friend, not my jailor. The labyrinthian layout, so confusing to a new student, is now reassuringly hard to navigate for anyone breaking in.

My father is dead. It's huge. Momentous. It doesn't seem real. I know it must be, because I've got his blood-spattered watch, but I never saw his body. Maybe he saved me from that when he headbutted me in the face? It's hardly surprising that the last time he ever touched me was with anger and violence. It had been that way my whole life.

I don't know if I should be experiencing sorrow, anger,

joy, or relief. The scary thing is I feel nothing. I'm like a fucking block of ice inside.

It's why I've been standing under this hot water for so long; it's the only thing that reassures me I'm actually here, alive, still on this Earth. I've got the thermostat turned up to scalding, and I still can't get warm deep inside where it matters.

I bring Mackenzie to mind—I can always feel something for her—but instead there's still that awful, black hole of nothingness.

The guys are probably down in the den by now. It's been hours since we got back. I spent most of it sitting on the edge of my bed and staring into space, reliving the horror of it all. I keep replaying every moment, trying to work out if I could have done something different.

I need to contact my mother and sister, too, inform them Grigoriy is dead. It's not right that they'll find out from someone else. But the thought of speaking to them overwhelms me. I can't face it. I know that makes me a coward, but it all feels like too much. Will they take his death as good news—that they'll be free from his tyranny—or will they now be unprotected? What if, with my father gone, one of his enemies decides to step in and claim his daughter and widow for themselves?

I finally force myself out of the shower, dress, and run my fingers through my wet hair. What are the guys doing? Is Mackenzie okay?

I ought to go and be with them, even if all I want to do is ... what? What the fuck do I want to do? Damned if I know. Every time I close my eyes, it's not my father I think about, but instead how I acted when the lights had gone off. I'm so fucking ashamed of myself, it sickens me.

I'm not sure I can face them, but I can't hide forever.

Before I go, I pick up my cell phone and pull up my mother's number.

She answers within a couple of rings. "Kirill, is everything all right?" She speaks in Russian and sounds anxious, as though she's already gotten word that something has gone down.

"Mama, I have news for you." I speak in my mother tongue, too. "I need you to tell only my sister, okay? Otherwise, you must keep it to yourself. You can't let anyone know you found out this information from me."

"What is it, Kirill. What's happened?"

"It's Grigoriy," I say, unable to call him my father after what he's done. "He's dead."

She draws a sharp breath down the line. "You know this to be true?"

"It is true. I know for certain."

She lets out a sob, and I picture her standing with her hand over her mouth, trying to hide her emotions from anyone who might hear.

"Then we are free of him," she says. "Finally, we are free."

"I love you, Mama. Don't speak of this to anyone but my sister. And warn her to stay quiet. I can't have this coming back on me."

"I understand, son. You can trust me."

I do, too.

I end the call and blow out a lungful of air. I hope they'll be safe. I don't know what kind of repercussions will fall on them now that Grigoriy is gone.

Leaving my room, I find my way to the den as quickly as I can. I have a hoodie on, and I pull the hood up and tie it close so no one will recognize me. I keep my head down as I navigate the halls. I don't want to talk to anyone.

When I hit the den, I push open the door and take in the scene.

Mackenzie is lying between Tino's legs on the sofa. Her back is against his chest, and her legs are stretched out over

Dom. There's a film on, and Tino is caressing her hair.

It looks like such a pretty picture. If I interrupt, will I turn it into something bad?

"There you are," she says.

She pushes up as if to come and greet me, but I hold my hand out.

"Don't get up."

She falters. "Okay. Are you all right?"

"Yes, you?"

She nods, but our gazes catch, and they tell a different story. One of horrors seen and fucked up shit being done to us.

"I showered," she says softly. "It still doesn't feel as if I got them off me."

I nod but don't reply.

"I hate that they touched you." Tino's voice is dark and angry.

Dom lifts her foot to his mouth and kisses her toes. "I want to lick everywhere their hands were on you and make them disappear."

"You can," she says, but there's a hesitancy in her tone.

"Baby, you don't have to do anything but let us hold you," Dom says.

The pet name jars me. Since when does he call her baby? I take a seat and watch them.

"I think I want you to. I want their touch washed from me. By you." She glances around. "By all of you."

I blurt my thoughts. "It wasn't just their touch, though, was it *Kukla*? It was mine, too."

She frowns. "Kirill, I didn't mean it that way, and you know that."

I don't know anything anymore, but I don't answer.

Tino runs his hands up her sweater, lifting it until her beautiful breasts are revealed. She's not wearing a bra, and he trails his fingers over her nipples, and she shivers as they peak.

I'm hard already, but I don't move to join in. Every time I think about touching her, I see those men coming on us. On her. On me. I picture her cuffed by the throat to the bars while I fuck her and other men watch. I played my part in that. They made her show them her pussy so they could see my cum dripping from her—*my* cum.

I can't seem to do anything but sit here, watching.

Dom looks at me. "You want to come join the party?"

"Nah, I'm good. You know I like to watch."

It's true. Tino might be a voyeur who films things, but they know I like to go after them sometimes, and mark her with my cum. Dom nods, clearly buying what I said.

Tino pinches her nipples and pulls on them, elongating them, and when he lets go, they're tightened nubs. She moans, the sound going directly to my cock.

"You like that, huh?" Tino says. "Me playing with these gorgeous tits."

She nods. Her eyes are different, though. I can see she's struggling to ground herself in this room, with them. Her mind is going back to the basement the same way mine is. This is fucked up. Wrong.

They need to give her some time.

"You don't have to do this, *Kukla*," I say.

She looks at me. "I do, Kirill. I need this."

I get what she means. If she doesn't do this, she might never do it again. She needs to claim her pleasure back from them, from that fucking place. I should, too, but I simply can't.

I'm frozen, a statue watching the scene unfold in front of me. I'm hard, but intellectually, I'm distant, unaffected.

Tino keeps playing with her nipples until they are red and swollen. I bet they ache. I bet she'd like a warm mouth on them, to soothe them.

Dom must be thinking the same thing because he gently

moves Mackenzie's legs from him and crawls up her body. Tino holds her tits up, offering them to Dom. He bends his head and sucks a nipple into his mouth.

She gasps, and her eyes flutter closed. I can't read her emotions this way, with her eyes shut. So instead, I focus on her tits, and what Dom and Tino are doing to them.

Dom releases one nipple with a pop and moves to the next, leaving the one he's just suckled crinkling in the cool air.

Tino massages the sides of her tits, as Dom works her nipples until they are deep red and she's moaning and whimpering.

"You seem all hot and bothered, Duchess," Tino whispers in her ear. "Do you need some attention on your pussy?"

She nods, and Dom climbs off her. He helps her up and pulls her sweatshirt completely off, then he pulls her sweatpants and panties down.

When she's naked, Tino sits on the edge of the sofa and pulls her onto his lap, so her back is flush with his chest. He uses his knees to knock her legs apart.

Her pussy is exposed, glistening and puffy, and I lick my lips as if I'm going to be tasting it myself.

Dom drops to his knees, and Tino nudges Mackenzie's thighs farther apart, spreading her so wide that Dom groans. He crawls up to her and leans in close before he licks right over her clit. Mackenzie jumps like she's been shocked.

Dom worships her clit with his tongue, moving it around the edges and then flicking side to side. She's gasping and squirming on Tino's knee, but he's holding her still.

"Take it, Duchess, take it all," he orders. "We need you. Need to feel you. Touch you. Taste you."

She groans when Dom pushes a thick finger slowly inside her.

I close my eyes. I was inside her, and those fuckers were

watching it. They *checked* her after, to see my cum. I hate myself.

My fucking father did that.

He's dead. It hits me, and this time I feel something. I don't know what. My stomach drops like a rollercoaster.

He's dead.

My father is dead.

I wonder what happened. Who did it? How did he die? I should be happy. That fucker can't lock me in a room, in the dark, ever again. He can't do anything sick to my *Kukla*. So why do I feel so ... scared? I feel scared. Like the top just blew off my home and I'm completely exposed to the elements.

Mackenzie cries out, and I look up, wanting to be back in this room, not there, in that cabin.

Dom pumps two fingers in and out of her pussy, and Tino isn't holding her legs open anymore but is back to roughly playing with her tits.

She's like a pornographic vision, and I lean forward in my chair to see better.

"You want my cock?" Dom asks her.

"Yes." Her voice is breathy.

"What about mine?" Tino adds.

She turns her neck to look sideways at Tino. "I want both of you."

He takes her mouth in a hungry kiss. "It will be my pleasure."

Dom pulls his glistening fingers from her pussy and sucks them into his mouth.

He glances at Tino. "I think our Duchess is ready for us."

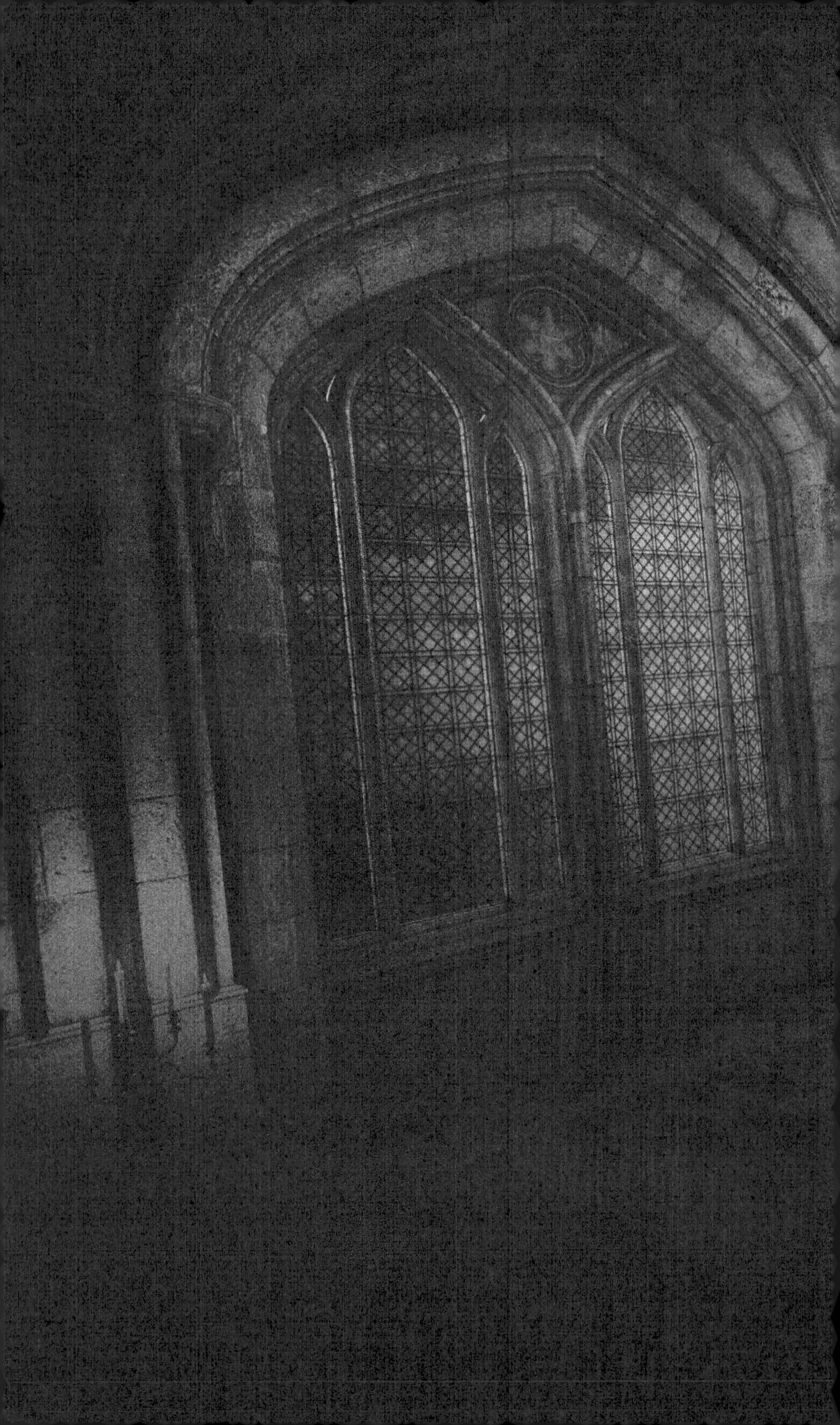

Nineteen

Tino

I have an idea, but I'm not sure how it's going to go down.

"Think you can take both of us at the same time?" I ask her. "Both of us in one hole?"

She stiffens slightly in my grip. "I—I'm not sure."

"We'll go slow and use plenty of lube, get you good and stretched first."

"I've never done anything like that before." Her eyes are wide.

"I know, sweet girl, but we'll take care of you. Right, D?"

I catch his eye, and he nods. It'll mean our cocks will be pressed right up against each other, that we'll be bathed in each other's cum, but we'll be surrounded by Mackenzie's pussy while we do.

I rub my hand across the tattoos that run up the side of my neck, massaging the muscles there. I'm all fucking knotted up after being in that basement, and I can't even imagine what sort of shit Kenzie and Kirill went through. Kirill, in particular, seems haunted.

I saw my men back to the small private airport, made

sure they got onboard safely. Not all of them did, however. We lost a couple of men back there, and I'll forever feel responsible. I know my father will make sure their families are well compensated and looked after, but no amount of money will bring back a loved one.

Mackenzie is naked and sitting on my lap. I take hold of her shoulders and kiss the side of her neck. My fingers scrape the bandage on her upper arm.

"What's this?" I ask.

She draws a breath. "Oh, shit. I completely forgot."

"About what?"

Her gaze flicks over to Kirill, and then back to me. "Grigoriy cut out my birth control implant."

My eyebrows lift. "He did what?" If he wasn't already dead, I'd kill the son of a bitch all over again.

"He wanted Kirill to get me pregnant."

I glance over at our friend. "And might he have?"

She nods. "It's possible, yes. The implant stops working almost the moment it's removed."

My hand slides around her waist to cup her stomach. "So there might be life inside you already. And if there isn't, us fucking you now, with no protection, might fill your belly with a baby."

The thought makes me even harder. I picture Kenzie with her stomach swollen and rounded with one of our babies, her tits huge and heavy, her nipples fat and sensitive. I jam myself against her ass, rocking my hips to create pressure.

"I don't care," she blurts recklessly. "I just want to feel you inside me. I want your cum. Skin on skin. It's important."

I thumb her lower lip. "We'll give you whatever you want."

"Thank you," she whispers. "I want you to wipe away every memory of those men."

"Forget those assholes. They're nothing. Less than

nothing. You're ours, and this pussy is ours. They never even existed."

I slide my hand from her stomach, down between her legs, and push my fingers inside her. She's already wet from Dom playing with her, but we need to make her wetter if she's going to take both of us.

"Get the lube," I tell Dom.

He nods and gets to his feet, and returns with the small bottle.

First, I use only two fingers, working her slowly, and then I nod to Dom, who adds lube to my hand. I push in a third finger, stretching her.

Her back arches against my chest. "Oh, God. Oh, fuck."

"We're only getting started. If you want to stop, just say so."

In any other circumstances, I probably wouldn't have given her that out, but she's been through so much. She needs to know we'll take care of her, and that we have her well-being at heart.

We owe her so fucking much. So many apologies. Years of making how we've treated her—how every fucking man in her life has treated her—up to her. And I'm determined to do it, too. I'll spend the rest of my life making it up to her.

"D, we need you here," I tell my friend.

He understands what I'm saying. He kneels back between her legs and pushes a finger next to mine, edging inside her as well, so now she has both our fingers inside her. She whimpers and moans, her body shaking, and I think it's the hottest thing I've ever seen.

I kiss the side of her neck again, biting and sucking. She's close, I can feel it, but we can't let her come yet.

"Add a fifth, D," I instruct. "Stretch her wide open. I want to see her gaping."

He does, his gaze fixed on her pussy. I wish I had his view, but I can see enough, and I can feel his fingers next to mine. We're not pumping in and out of her, as we would if we were just using a finger or two. No, this is about stretching her wide enough to take us both.

Kenzie shudders and mewls, her hips bucking to encourage us to fuck her. I'm so hard, I'm surprised I don't come in my jeans like a horny teenager.

"Calm down, Duchess," I tell her. "Just roll with this."

"I just...I can't...oh, God."

She can't even form a complete sentence.

"One more finger, D." Then she'll have six fingers inside her, and I'll know she can take us.

Dom changes the angle of his hand to push another finger in next to mine. Kenzie squeals and arches her body, but I use my free hand to clamp her against me. Dom ducks his head to suck on her clit, and I feel her pussy clenching around us.

"I think she's ready," I say.

We both slip our fingers from her body. Her pussy is wet and squelching—primed to take us.

Dom helps her to her feet, though her legs tremble, and we both quickly strip. I sit back down on the couch, facing into the middle, and Dom sits opposite me.

I'm taller than Dom, so I grab his legs and pull them over my thighs, so he's almost straddling me. The position brings us face to face, but more than that, it brings our cocks so they stand erect between us. Our balls press together, hot and soft. It's a strange sensation, but we're not doing this because it turns each other on—though I have to admit it's hot as fuck. No, this is for Mackenzie, so she can feel both of us inside her pussy at once.

Dom's cock is big, but mine is bigger, plus I have the addition of the Jacob's ladder piercing running down the length.

I can tell Dom's curious.

"It's okay. You can touch it," I tell him.

He does, too, running his thumb between us, over the barbell. My dick jumps at the contact and a little precum leaks from the slit.

Mackenzie's eyes are wide, her lips plump and parted.

"Want to suck us, Duchess?" I ask.

She nods and drops to her knees on the floor beside the couch. Using both hands, she holds us together, so our cocks are pressed tight. She goes to town, moving between us, licking and sucking, running her tongue up and down our lengths. Dom's balls tighten and contract against mine, and I shuffle a little lower, enjoying the sensation of her mouth on my dick, and Dom's balls pressed flush against mine.

My gaze flicks over to Kirill. He's still sitting there, just watching. I don't know how the fuck he can stop himself from joining in, but he's a grown man. He'll do what he wants.

Dom puts a hand on Kenzie's shoulder. "You have to stop, or I'll come."

"Yeah, it's time," I agree. "We want to be inside you."

She licks her lower lip nervously. "Can I really take both of you?"

I nod. "Slowly, yes. You're on top, so you control the pace."

We get the lube back out, and I use it to smother my cock, and then I rub some over Dom's. He sucks in a breath and clenches his teeth as my hand slides down his length and then smears more lube over the head. Then I wrap my hand around both our bases, holding us together.

"Ready, Duchess?"

I know her pussy is wide and gaping from our fingers, and she's dripping wet, too.

"You can do this," I tell her. "Breathe deep."

She swings her leg over our joined cocks and settles her pussy above us. She's facing me, so I get her mouth and tits, and Dom gets her ass. He's always been more of an ass man. I'm sure when she's settled on us fully he'll play with that hole with his fingers as well.

"Can you feel my piercings, D?" I ask my friend.

"Yeah, fuck. Shit, they feel good."

Kenzie uses her hand to hold the heads of our cocks together. She wiggles that sweet little ass and spreads her legs wider. It's slippery, and wet, and I think one of us is going to slide right out of her grasp before she can take us, but then her pussy stretches wide enough, and both our cockheads enter her.

THE DEVILS' DARLING

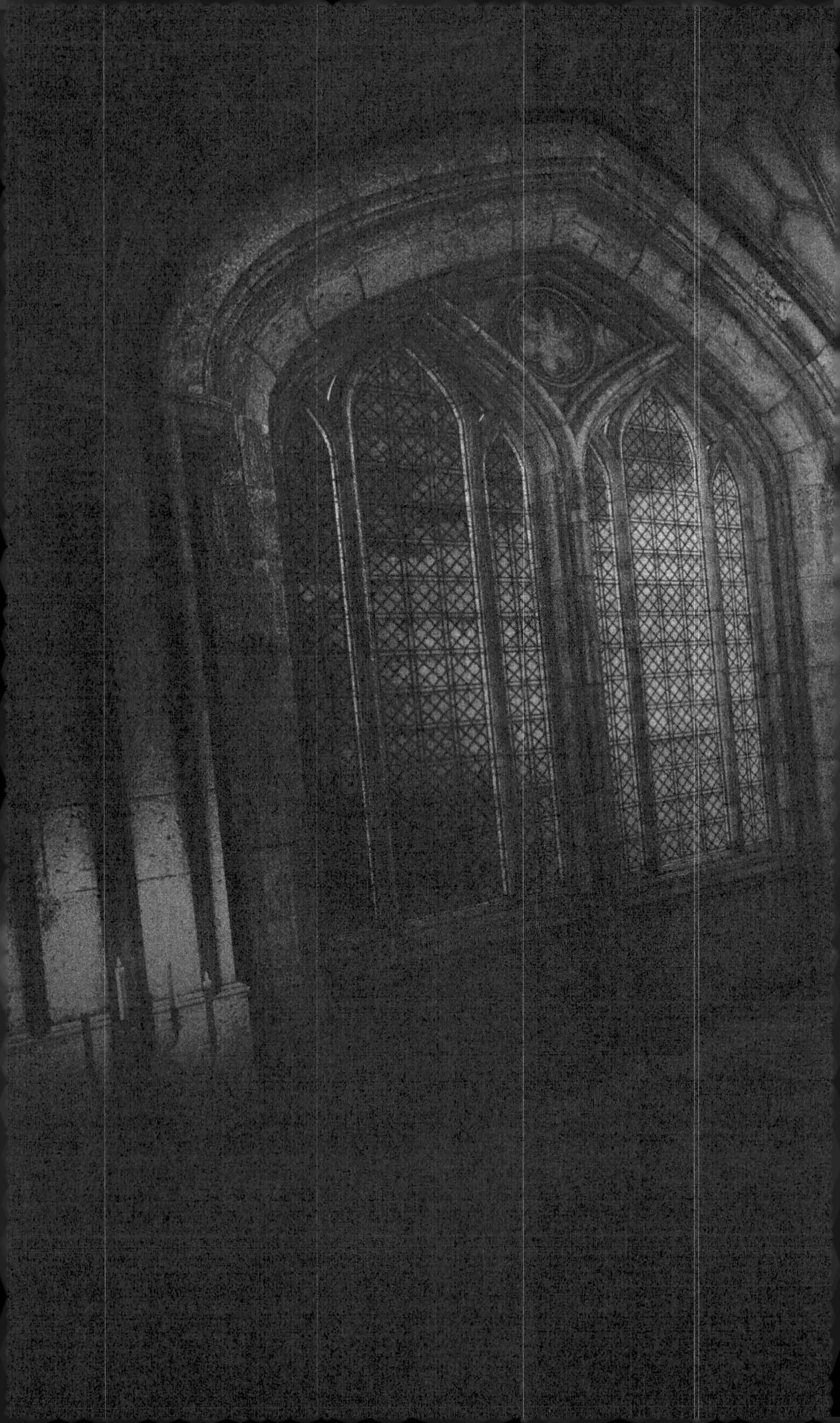

Twenty
Mackenzie

Oh, God.

It burns for a few seconds, and I squeeze my eyes shut, willing away the pain. I'm breathing fast. I have one hand on Tino's solid shoulder to hold myself up, and my thighs are shaking.

"I can't," I blurt, opening my eyes again.

Tino locks his gaze with mine. "Breathe, Duchess. You can do this. I know you can. You're so good at taking us. Your pussy is made for us."

Then his thumb finds my clit, and he applies pressure. I moan, and my hips move almost involuntarily, pressing down on them, taking them deeper.

Having their cocks pressed together, knowing they can feel each other, is so fucking hot, I think I might lose my mind. I'd loved going down on them both, licking one dick and then the other, holding them both together with my hands. Now my pussy is wrapped around them, and when they climax, they're going to bathe each other in cum.

I sink lower still, and Dom gives a primal growl behind me. I twist my upper torso, and he cups my cheek with one hand and kisses my mouth. Our kiss is urgent and needy, all tongues and bruised lips, but it's what we need.

I can't believe I have both of them inside me. As my body grows used to them, I sink right down to the hilt. I've never felt so full before, and I'm surprised they haven't split me in two.

"Oh, fuck, that's right, Duchess," Tino gasps. "We're right inside you now. Both of us. Your pussy is so fucking perfect."

I turn my face from Dom's kisses to catch sight of Kirill sitting there. He's watching intently, but he's not touching himself. I can see the outline of his erection beneath his jeans, though. Having him watching only serves to turn me on more, if such a thing is even possible.

I don't move for a moment, just remain seated on them both, memorizing the feel of them inside me like this. Their cocks twitch, and I can feel it, but, perhaps even hotter than that is the knowledge that they can feel each other, too.

"God, baby. You're so good," Tino praises me. "You're so fucking perfect. I hope you know that."

As slowly as possible, I start to move. I use Tino's shoulders as support and gradually bring myself up again. I don't dare go too high, as I don't want to risk either of them slipping out. The sensation is intense, and my eyes slip shut again, needing to focus. Tino continues to rub my clit, and Dom grabs my ass, spreading my cheeks, perhaps for a better view. Then his thumb finds my asshole, and he applies pressure, the same way Tino is doing to my clit.

My pussy clamps around their cocks, pleasure coiling tighter in my lower belly and deep between my thighs. I move a little faster, rocking on them. My breathing grows ragged, and my nipples are as hard as bullets. With the help of Dom's hand on my ass, guiding me up and down, I increase my pace. I know I won't last long. I'm so close already, just climbing and reaching, desperate now to reach my peak.

My breaths turn to cries, and now we're all working together, a combined three-way of need and lust and animalistic desire. The scent of sex and sweat and the sweetness of the lube fills the air, overwhelming my senses.

"I'm gonna come," Dom growls from between clenched teeth. "I can't hold much longer."

"Ah, fuck. Me, too," Tino replies.

I barely hear them. I'm so caught up now, I don't give a fuck if they're going to come or not. I'm right on the precipice, and it's only going to take seconds before I spiral down the other side.

It hits me, my orgasm exploding through my body. Heat and pleasure rush through me like no other high I've ever experienced. My skin prickles as every nerve ending is set alight. My eyes roll, and my toes curl, and it's as though my brain loses connection with my body and sends me somewhere higher.

My pussy clamps down around them both, rippling and pulsing, and, almost at the exact same moment, my two men give in to it, too. The noises and curses exploding from their lips is enough alone to get an X-rating. I feel them coming inside me, the hot gush of cum from two cocks. It'll be dripping out of me for days.

With their cocks still twitching, they slump against me—Tino to my front, Dom at my back. I feel their hearts racing, just as mine is. Our skin is damp with sweat.

As they grow softer inside me, the pressure on my poor pussy eases. I'm not sure I'm going to be able to walk properly for at least a couple of days.

I can't help myself. I giggle. "We're about to make one hell of a mess of this couch."

From across the room, Kirill says, "Hold still."

He goes and grabs a towel for us. He hands it to me, and, as he does, I grab his wrist.

"Hey, are you okay?" I ask him.

He nods. "Yeah, I just wanted to watch."

With the other two Devils still inside me, I pull him closer and kiss him on the mouth. "I love you," I tell him. "Never forget that."

THE DEVILS' DARLING

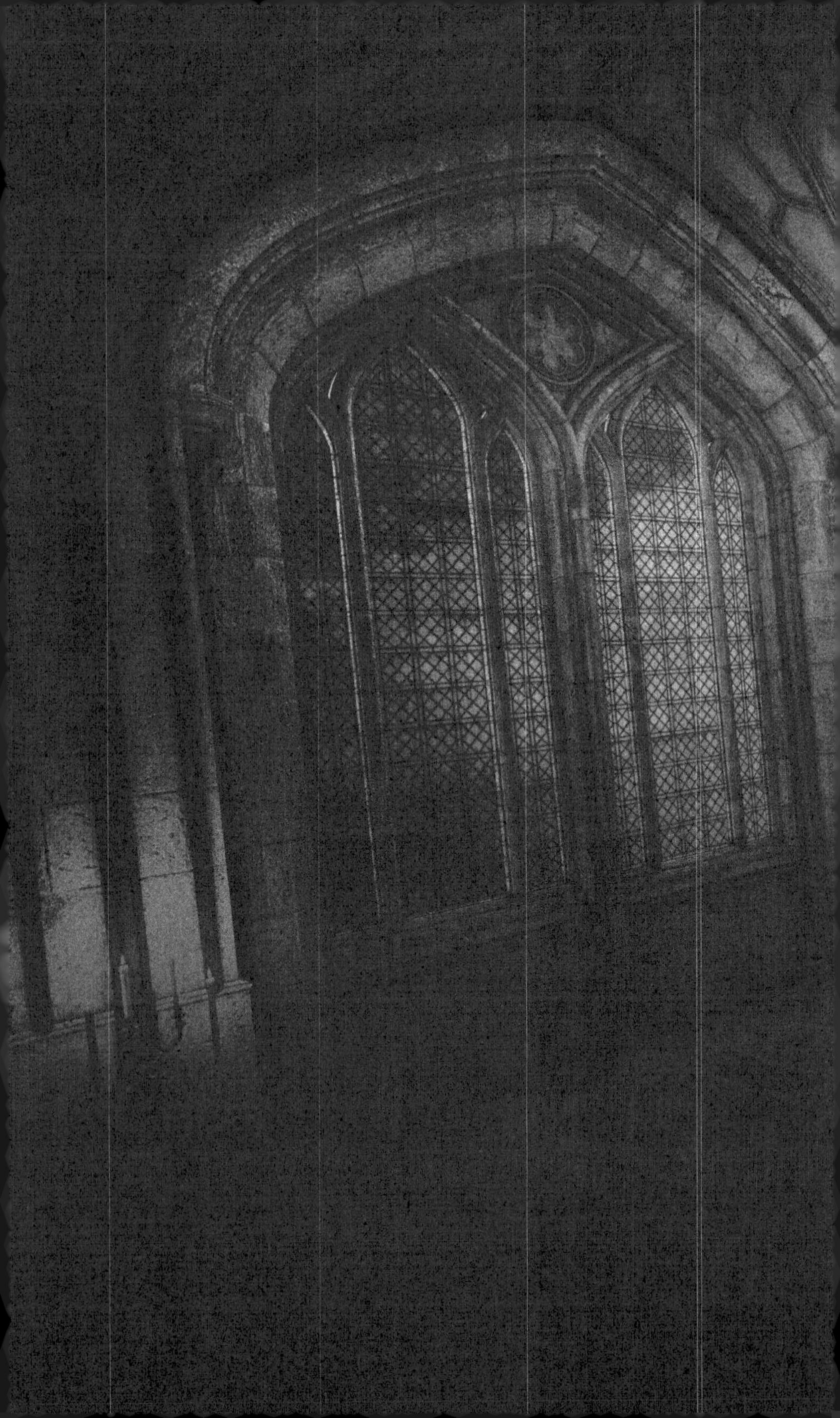

Twenty-One
Kirill

I stay where I am, focused on Mackenzie's poor, swollen, red pussy. Dom slides out first, and then Tino, followed by a rush of their mixed cum.

Mackenzie's pussy lips are still parted, and she's so engorged, it makes my dick almost come without being touched. She scoots over the men and sits on the towel and then shocks the shit out of me when she leans back against the tangled mess that is Dom and Tino and lifts her legs in the air. Her knees are pressed together, so her pussy is presented squeezed between her legs, all puffy and leaking milky cum.

She's fucking perfect—all my wet dreams in one hot package.

"Do you want to add your contribution?" She whispers the question.

I do want to. More than anything. She's a beautifully obscene picture, and I want to come all over her peachy pussy. I can't, though.

The tension builds in me. The sense of there being someone watching us, even though there isn't. The way those men looked at her pussy the exact same way I am now, but without her consent.

I rake my fingers through my hair. "Fuck. I need to go."

"What?" She puts her feet down on the towel so she's now just hugging her knees. "Kirill, what's wrong?"

"Nothing. I just want some space. I just lost my fucking father, and you guys are playing sex games."

Shit. I don't mean that. I don't begrudge them. Or at least, I don't begrudge her. The other two, I don't know what I'm feeling right now.

Mackenzie's face falls, and I hate myself a little. "Don't, *Kukla*. It's okay. I love you, but I need some time to myself."

She nods. "Okay. But will you... can I see you tomorrow?" Her voice is small.

"Yes, tomorrow."

"Kirill," Dom says, but I ignore him as I walk out of the room.

I am so hard, I'm going to burst. My head is all fucked up. The stuff they did to us in that basement turned me on, but I hated it. Yet my mind goes back to it, and how amazing it felt to fuck her there, with the heightened adrenaline of the situation.

I feel as if I'm going to scream, or break something, or murder someone, so I go straight to my room.

The minute I'm in there, I'm pushing my pants and briefs down and grabbing my cock like a crazed person. I'm so hard I hiss in shock when I get hold of it. Fuck. I've never been this sensitized.

One hand is on my cock, the other bracing myself against the wall next to my bed. I work myself hard and fast, my teeth gritted, my ass muscles bunched and tight. The room is filled with the whacking of my hand on my dick. I masturbate faster, my bicep burning and bulging. I know I won't last long. I've been desperate to come the entire time I'd been watching our doll with Dom and Tino. I didn't even know I had the sort of self-control it took to stop me joining in with them.

Even as I chase my orgasm, my head races with thoughts I can't seem to control or understand. Mackenzie full of Dom and Tino. Mackenzie, showing me her pussy like that. Mackenzie showing it to those men and how I hated it. Yet now, the thought is making me hot in the sickest, darkest way.

My climax rises through me, tightening my balls and condensing in my cock. I give in to it with a shout.

Milky cum sprays the wall as I climax so hard I see stars.

Collapsing onto my bed, I am horrified to see I'm still half hard, and still horny. Am I turning into my father?

He was famous for fucking for hours. A child should never know this about their parents, but I heard the girls he kept around in his clubs talking sometimes when I visited him there. One of them said to another girl about how Grigoriy had fucked her twice and come twice and then immediately fucked her friend's face and come again, all over her chin.

I'd been about fifteen at the time and weirded out to hear them talk about him that way. It made me sick. Now here I am, coming over the thought of what happened in that basement and ready to go again.

Do I have his sickness in me? His spirit? Maybe, when he died, a part of his soul entered me? Like a fucking possession.

I turn to face the opposite wall to the one splattered with my cum and close my eyes. Right now, in this moment, I feel nothing but shadows eating away at me.

My disgusting hard cock eventually gets the message, and I zip my pants and curl into a ball as I let the darkness take me.

***

Banging at the door jerks me out of a nightmare-filled slumber.

"Open up, Kill."

It's Dom. I really don't want to see him right now. He bangs again, though.

"One minute," I shout.

I push up off the bed and pull the door open.

Dom storms in, the usual whirlwind mix of charisma and asshole that he always is. Then he proceeds to shock the shit out of me when he grabs me and pulls me into a hug.

The door is open, and I hear a soft snigger. "*Touching.*"

I look right into the blue eyes of one of the Vipers—though I couldn't say which one. The twins are completely identical. Dom lets go of me, turns to him, and gives him the finger before kicking my door closed.

"You okay?" he asks. Then he rubs his hair. "That was a dumb question. Clearly not. I just want you to know, I'm here for you, man. If you want to talk. Or if you just want someone to sit in here while you lose your shit. I can do that, too."

I nod. "Appreciated, but I don't even know what I'm feeling."

Dom sits on the bed, staring at the wall. His face morphs into a confused frown and then a look of disgust. "Eww, dude, you been doing some interior decorating?"

I follow his line of sight to discover the evidence of my earlier activities still painting the wall. I jump up, my face burning, and grab a towel. I wipe it off angrily.

"If that's all?" I say to Dom, my back to him.

I'm embarrassed and defensive.

"Are you done?"

His voice isn't confident anymore. In fact, if I didn't know better, I'd say he's scared.

"With what?" I turn to face him.

"This? *Us*? Duchess offered you her pretty pussy on a silver platter, and you turned her down and came up here to pebbledash your walls with cum."

Shame coats me, and I've felt more than enough of that the past few days. "Dom, fuck off out of my room."

"No."

"I'll make you."

He stands and walks right up to me. "I'd rather you beat me to a pulp than give me this silent treatment."

I'm about to tell him again that my dad just died, but he holds his hands up and pre-empts me.

"I get that your dad died, but that's not all this is about. It's about her. Mackenzie. What gives?"

I sigh. "Dom, I did things to her. Things they made us do. Things I fucking *enjoyed*. Things I also hated. How can it be both?"

He shakes his head. "I don't know. Did she want you to do those things?"

I give a bitter laugh. "She said so, but we had no choice. They made us do it."

His brow furrows. "Think of it this way, though. If you hadn't been there, she'd have been all alone in that experience. If she said she wanted it, maybe, in time, you can turn it into something less horrific. I won't say beautiful, 'cause I realize it could never be that, but maybe you can be grateful you were there together? Without you, she might not have survived."

I consider his words, twisting my lips. Maybe he has a point, and things would have been a hell of a lot fucking worse for her if she'd been alone. But also, if I didn't exist, she'd never have gone through any of it in the first place. If I'd never come into her life, she'd still be unharmed.

Dom pauses and wrings his hands together. I can tell there's something else he's not saying.

"What?" I press him. "What is it?"

"When we were down in that basement, after you'd been knocked unconscious, Tino filmed some—" He cuts himself off and clears his throat. "Some compromising footage of your dad and his men."

I raise my eyebrows. "You what?"

"We thought we could use it to ruin him, if we needed to. My question is, we can still release it, destroy his legacy and reputation, but that's up to you. What do you want us to do with it?"

Maybe ruining his reputation would be the right way to go, but I can't face any more hatred in this world.

"Delete it," I say. "It's enough that he's dead, and he died while believing his reputation would be ruined. If we release it, we're just as bad as he is."

Dom reaches out and pats my shoulder. "I thought you might say that. I'll make sure Tino deletes everything. I'll leave you in peace now, but I'm truly sorry about your dad. I can't imagine the head fuck it must be. I really am here if you want to talk."

I bite the inside of my cheek, relishing the pain. I deserve it.

"Thanks, dude."

When he leaves, I collapse on the bed, feet on the floor, head in my hands. And then, finally, the tears really come.

Chapter Twenty-Two
Dominic

I don't head to my room, but back down to the den where Mack is waiting. She turns to me when I enter, snuggled up on the sofa with Tino, and asks me where her phone is.

"I've got it," I say. "I kept it for you."

I remove her cell from the desk drawer where I had placed it for safe keeping when we went to bring her and Kirill home and hand it to her.

"Thanks," she says. "I want to message Lola and let her know I'm okay."

"Of course. *Are* you okay, Duchess? Do you want anything?"

She shakes her head and moves her feet for me to curl up on the sofa with her.

"I'll have to go soon," she says. "I need to talk to my mom. I don't want her and your dad getting themselves all worked up. I can't face it. I'm so tired." She yawns, hiding her mouth prettily behind the back of her hand.

I watch her as she keys in her passcode—a code I know from when I was spying on her. She seems to be doing surprisingly well. Better than I'd have expected or hoped. I thought Kirill would come back stoic, and Duchess would be a mess. Not that both of them being a mess would have been an issue. They would be well within their rights to go to pieces, but it still makes me think about how much crap she's been through.

I've underestimated her.

Not just once, but repeatedly. The entire fucking time I've known her, in fact. Duchess is resilient, and it's about time we gave her credit for it.

She swipes the screen and then pauses. The blood

rushes from her face, and I freeze.

Fuck.

Fuck, fuck, *fuck*.

The message. That damn message from the professor. I want to hit my fists against my head and beat my brains out for being such an asshole.

I forgot to tell her about it. To prepare her for it. Everything has been so crazy.

She glances up at me, and her eyes are wide, scared, but dry. "So now I've got this maniac to contend with, too? Does the universe hate me?"

"*We've* got him to contend with, baby," I say.

"He's not getting within fifty yards of you." Tino tucks a strand of hair behind her ear.

"So long as he's out there, he's a risk to me," she says softly. "I should have finished the job right the first time."

Pride swells in my chest. Our girl is going to be a fearsome enemy and a great mafia queen.

But who gets to be the king?

Do we have to name just one, or can we do things in a new way?

The fact is, she's all of ours and we are all hers, and if the world doesn't accept it? So what? We hardly live by the normal rules. Our parents might not accept it, either. We're all adults, though. We can do what we want.

I lift one of her feet to my lips and kiss her toes. "You're ours now. I'd like to see that asshole try something."

I slide my mouth over one of her toes and suck on it. Mackenzie giggles and squirms, but there's a smile back on her face again.

Tino's hands drift down to cup her breasts, and he kisses the side of her neck. "Yes, you're all ours." He lightly nips at her skin with his teeth. "Your mouth is ours, your pussy is ours, and these gorgeous tits are ours, too."

She's dressed herself in a pair of sweatpants and a

camisole top while I was talking to Kirill. She keeps a few clothes down here in our den. Just a few pieces. A toothbrush too. I like it. Makes me feel like she's really a part of us.

"Tino, I've got to go," she says sleepily.

She doesn't move, though, and he slips her tits out of her top, her nipples peaking in the cool air. He pinches them, pulling and elongating the dusky pink nubs, and she lets out a tiny groan of arousal.

I smirk and move to her next toe, sucking it into my mouth like it's a tiny cock and I'm giving it a blowjob, using my tongue to swirl around the tip. She giggles, but then she stiffens. Her eyes go round, and a small squeak of horror escapes her lips.

My head swivels to follow the line of her sight and oh, fuck. My heart goes into double time.

Standing in the doorway, looking as if he's about to start breathing actual hellfire, is my father.

"What the actual *fuck*?"

That's when I know I'm in a world of shit. He shouts the phrase, and it goes against everything he pretends to be. My father has spent years developing the kind of cool, collected front that he shows to the world. It's an act he rarely drops. His accent even comes out now, and instead of sounding like an Ivy League dean, he sounds like what he is. A man who would kill you and dump your body in the river for the fishes.

"Mackenzie, your mother wants to see you."

She doesn't move. She's so horrified that she's frozen.

"Now," my father roars. "Move your fucking ass, and put your tits away."

Yeah, he's lost it. He's no longer Nataniele the smooth dean, but he's Nate, the brawler who will cut your dick off for looking at him the wrong way.

"Domenic, I need to speak to you, too. Get upstairs to our rooms now," he rages.

Am I about to become a eunuch?

I shoot Tino a look but grab my wallet and cell and follow my father. Mackenzie is right behind me, and I fight the urge to reach back and take her hand. The last thing she needs is the wrath of my father right now. I want to protect her, but I also don't want to make things worse.

He stalks through the school like the fucker who owns the place that he is, and with every step, his mask shifts firmly back into place. By the time he reaches his rooms, you'd never believe he'd let me and Tino see the thug underneath the icy, cultured exterior. He's like a shapeshifter, and now he's taken his ultimate form, the one he wants the world to see.

When he opens the door to the suite he shares with Lucia, he speaks to her in the same controlled, cold way he often reserves for me.

"My darling, would you please take your daughter to her room for your talk? I would like some space with my son."

Lucia hesitates. "We could go into the bedroom here."

"No," he snaps. "Go to her room, now, please."

She frowns and, for a moment, mutinous anger crosses her features, but then she schools them.

"Don't look so sad, step-mommy-to-be. At least you got a *please*." I sneer at her.

The crack is hard and swift. My head whips to the side as my father's palm makes contact with my cheek.

Mackenzie gasps, and I turn to her, knowing what is coming.

"Leave, now."

Christ, I sound just like the fucker I hate. But I don't want her witnessing this. She's seen enough violence recently.

"You and I need to talk later, Lucia," Nataniele says.

"Of course."

She almost bows at him as she scurries out of the room. God, how did someone as magnificent as Duchess come from such a craven woman?

Then again, what choice does Lucia have? She must do all my father demands because he's the one in charge here, not her. He holds all the cards, and quite literally, holds her and Mackenzie's lives in his hands.

That needs to change. But how?

I turn back to him, and he's calmly rolling up his sleeves. My muscles bunch, not in preparation for a fight—I won't do that—but to prepare for the pain.

It comes in a swift blow to my stomach. I bend double, winded, and try to suck in air.

"Nice. Going for the places people can't see this time, are we?" I laugh as I force myself upright.

His uppercut to my jaw disabuses me of that idea. My head rocks back, and I clutch the spot where his fist connected. I tongue the inside of my mouth, checking for loose teeth.

"You lied, you little fuck," he rages. "You told me she was nothing but your sister-to-be."

Another smack. I don't try to defend myself because better he takes it out on me with his fists than trying to banish Duchess and her mom or something else insane. Although, I do believe, insofar as my father is capable of it, that he loves Lucia. He at least loves the *idea* of her. Her beauty and grace. He likes having all of that on his arm.

Grunting, he piles his fist into my side, and I stagger and fall. Holy shit. Blinding pain has me shaking with the intensity of it. I think the bastard hit my already damaged ribs. Nothing new there, then.

With an arm wrapped protectively around my side, I straighten and stare at him.

"Don't go killing the heir now. Or this will all be for nothing." I wave my free hand around as if to indicate the entire college. I wince in pain at the action.

"It's sick. We will be a laughingstock." His expression

changes and he regards me, head tilted to one side. "Is that what gets you off, son? The sickness of it all? You want her exactly because she's going to be your sister? Like sucking your little stepsister's perky tits, do you?"

"Oh, you noticed them, then? So, you're sick, too."

He sneers at me. "Not in the way you are. I'm not weak. Do you suck your boyfriend Tino's cock?"

I laugh at that pathetic attempt. "No more than you did with the men you shared with."

Now he's the one laughing, except there's no humor in his tone. "We didn't share them at the *same time*. Is that Russian freak in on this, too. Is that why you and Tino were so desperate to rescue her? Because Grigoriy would have given her solely to Kirill?"

He's looking at me with such rage that his nostrils are flared like he's running a marathon.

"It's not sordid like you're trying to make out it is," I argue.

"It's fucking sick and twisted, and the whole world will know you suck your sister's tits and your friends' cocks, and then you'll be shunned for life."

"She's not my fucking sister," I shout, finally losing my temper. "And it's not fucking illegal to marry a stepsibling in most states."

His face turns puce. I've never seen him that color. "Marry her? Fucking *marry her*! No, never."

"Why not? You're marrying the mother, and you brought her here when my mother was barely cold in her grave, you bastard."

He clenches his fists, and I brace, but there's a knock at the door.

"For the love of Christ, Lucia."

"It's Jeremiah Pickman," a deep voice says.

He's a math tutor here at the college.

"For our appointment. You asked me to meet you here?"

"Fuck," Father whispers under his breath. "Yes, of course. One moment." He says this more loudly. Then he addresses me in a hiss. "Go into the fucking bedroom and don't come out until I tell you to. This conversation is not over."

He pushes me roughly in the direction of the bedroom, and I stumble, dazed and reeling down the corridor.

When I enter the room that used to be my parents', I still get that awful jolt to the stomach when I see Lucia's things. I used to want her gone as soon as I saw them, but now I know that means losing our Duchess, too, and that can't happen.

I pace in the bedroom, the door closed behind me. Will I have to do as Kirill has and kill my own father like something out of a Shakespearean tragedy if I want to be with Duchess?

The closet door is open, Lucia's clothes where my mother's once were. I'm drawn to them even though they make me sick. I put one to my nose and inhale, but the perfume is all wrong. It's not the floral scent my mother used to wear, but something musky.

I move away, my stomach like a block of ice at the sense of loss.

My father's side is as anal as it's always been. I pull out his sock drawer and smirk at the rolled up, color coded Hermes socks. Fucking asshole.

The ties are next, and I resist the urge to throw them all over the room like silk streamers.

Then his cufflinks. What a fucking peacock. So many of them.

I pull out his handkerchief drawer and can't believe one man can own so many pocket squares. As I'm pushing the drawer back in, it catches on something. I frown and pull it farther out and see in one of the very back slots, instead of a handkerchief, there's a folded piece of thick paper.

Three words are visible. Three words that make my

throat run dry because they are in the familiar, sloping hand of my mother.

Fingers shaking, I reach for the paper and unfold it. My eyes scan the page, and I sit heavily on the bed behind me as I read.

THE DEVILS' DARLING

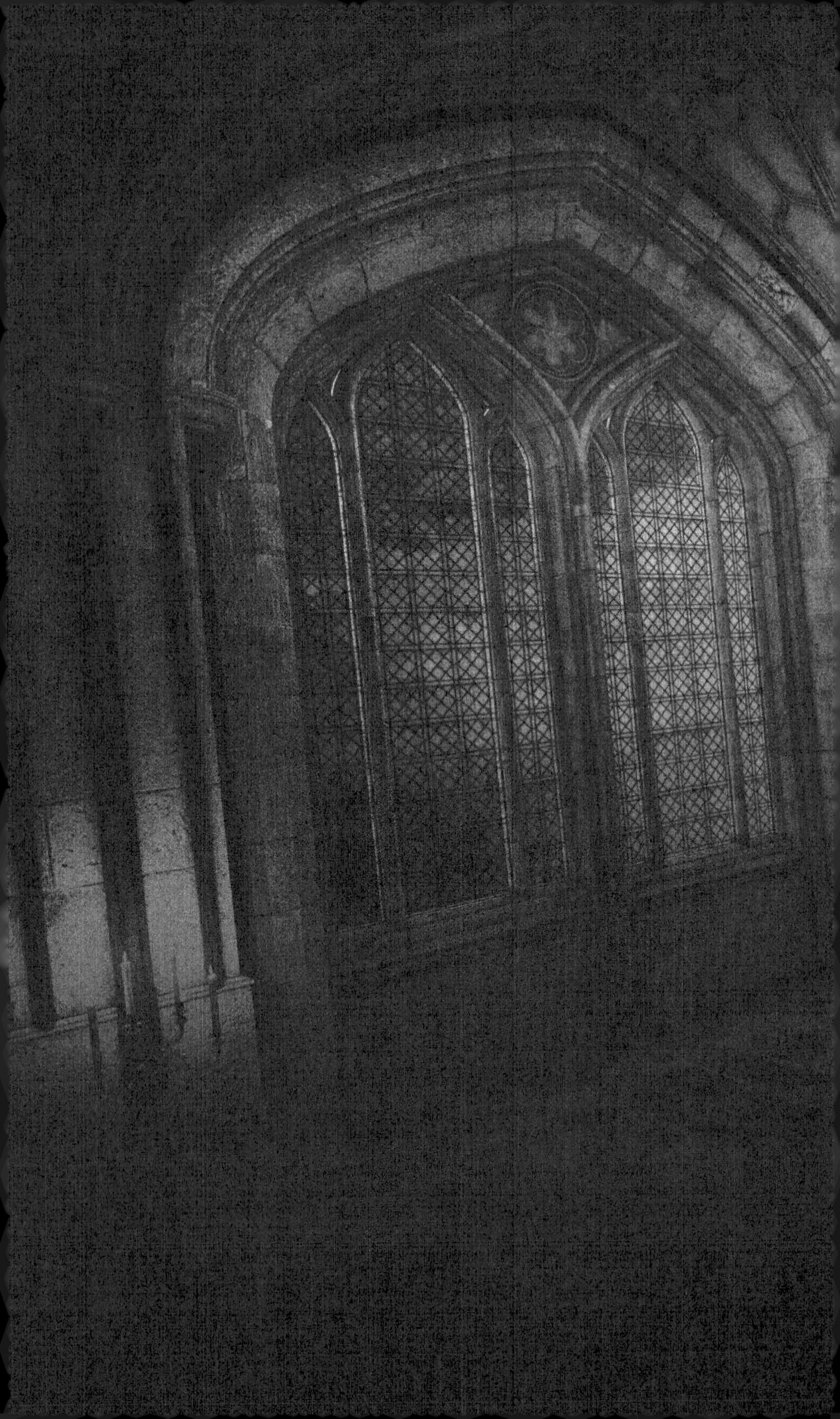

Twenty-Three

Mackenzie

I stand in my bedroom with my mother. Her expression is creased in concern, but her shoulders are rigid.

"What the hell is going on, Mackenzie? It's like every time I dare take my eye off you, something else blows up. Why is Nataniele so angry?"

There's no point in not telling her. She's going to find out anyway. A rush of heat floods over me at the prospect of telling her the truth. I should be proud of my three men, not ashamed, and I hate that she's making me feel this way.

"Nataniele discovered I'm in a relationship with Domenic."

Her eyebrows lift. "You're *what*?"

But I'm not finished. "And Valentino... and Kirill."

She blinks several times, trying to take it in. "I-I don't understand."

"I'm with all of them, Mom. All three of them."

"Together?"

"Yes, together. We love each other. It's not just a fling. We're serious about each other."

I can literally see her brain trying to compute how that

works.

"So...are the boys *together,* too?" she asks.

I shake my head. "No, not like that. They're friends, but they do love each other. Just more in a brotherly kind of way."

I'm not sure mentioning brothers is the right way to go, but I'm not sure how else to explain it.

"*Domenic* is going to be your brother."

I sigh and try not to roll my eyes. "Hardly. We're both adults, and you and Nataniele aren't even married yet."

She clenches her teeth. "We would have been."

She's got no standing on that. Maybe the Devils ruined the wedding, but they were only able to do that because of the actions she took.

"And we still will be," she adds.

"That's not my problem, Mom."

Her jaw drops at my dismissal. "Think about Nataniele! How's this going to look for him? His son sleeping with his stepsister, and her being shared around by his friends." She pauses and shakes her head. "Christ, Mackenzie. Can you even hear how that sounds? I've never wanted to repress your sexuality growing up, but I thought I'd taught you right from wrong."

I stare at her, anger bubbling inside me. "Can you even hear yourself? Right from wrong? This coming from the woman who ordered my dad's murder? And as for Nataniele—I couldn't give a flying fuck what he thinks. I don't owe him anything."

"Yes, you do. You owe him your life here. What would we have done if we hadn't had him to clear up your mess?"

"Well, I'd have known Paxton was alive a lot sooner than I did, that's for sure. I wouldn't have woken up every morning believing I'd killed a man."

Of course, now I actually *have* killed a man—Kirill's father—but she doesn't know that.

She shakes her head. "It's like you're just out looking for trouble, Mackenzie. First with the professor, and now these men…"

"What are you saying? That I'm asking for it? Is that it? That I've brought this upon myself? That's not very fucking P.C. of you, is it, Mom?"

"You can watch your language when you're talking to me. I don't appreciate being sworn at."

I suppress an eye roll. "I'm not swearing at you. And I'm not going to stop my relationships with any of them, either, so you can get that thought out of your head. I love them, and they love me."

She scoffs. "They're just saying what you want to hear so they can get into your panties."

The words hit hard, and she's making me feel cheap, but I don't let them take hold and sink deep because I don't believe that for one second. She has no idea how difficult it is for any of them to admit they have feelings for another person. They'd never say they loved someone if they didn't mean it. They each had walls built so high, I never thought someone could get over them, but I have. They've let me in, and I refuse to believe it's all just an act.

I'm resolute. "You're wrong. We have something special."

She drags her hand through her hair and then covers her face, shaking her head. "My God, I thought your time with Professor Kassell might have taught you to be a little more suspicious of men, but instead it's like you've become even dumber."

How can she say that? I understand that I've dropped a true bombshell on her, but sometimes she says the most hurtful things. She's been worse since she's been with Nataniele, as if some of him is rubbing off on her.

Tears fill my eyes. "I'm not dumb, Mom."

"Well, it most likely won't be your choice, anyway.

There's no way Nataniele is going to allow this kind of thing going on beneath his roof."

I fold my arms across my chest. "Then we'll leave."

She scoffs. "And go where? You're just kids."

"No, we're not. We're all in our twenties. We're adults, and we can do as we please."

For the first time, I see doubt in her eyes. She's always had such control over my life. I used to think we were so close—like best friends, or even sisters—but now I wonder if a part of her liked that I was so dependent on her. Maybe she liked that I was sick and that I needed her. Has she made me this way?

"You can't stand it, can you, Mom? That I've found people who want to support me? You wanted to be the only person in my life I needed. You couldn't even stand Dad being in my life, so you had him killed." I know as soon as those words are out, I can never take them back, but it's not as if she's not said terrible things to me, too.

I have the awful thought that Nataniele might go the same route—but for different ends. Perhaps he'll be so horrified at the thought of the four of us and the shame he imagines it will bring that he'll get rid of Tino and Kirill so they're not part of this. The situation would be less horrifying, I suppose, if it was just Dom and me. But then I remember that still won't change the fact that Dom and I will one day be stepbrother and stepsister. Plus, Nataniele has witnessed the might of Tino's army for himself. He'd be a fool to bring that kind of wrath down on his head.

No, the only thing that will work is if Nataniele somehow convinces Dom not to see me anymore.

How will he do that? Through violence and fear. It's the only way. I'm one hundred percent sure Dom won't give me up voluntarily.

"How can you say that?" Mom cries.

A tear spills down my cheek. "I need you to leave now."

This is too painful, and I can't do it anymore. Not right now. I need to be able to think clearly, and she's making me feel like trash.

She purses her lips and stares me down. "Not until you promise me that you're not going to see those boys anymore."

"They're not boys, Mom, they're men, and you're going to be waiting a very long time, because that's never happening."

It's like we're breaking apart all over again. First Kirill is acting strangely with us—unsurprisingly, considering what happened—and now this? Maybe she's right and we have no future, but even if that is the case, I'll keep fighting for us, right to the very end.

"I mean it, Mom. Go. And you can tell Nataniele that what I do in my personal life is none of his business. I'm not frightened of him."

She opens her mouth to protest, but I point at the door. "Now."

For once, she takes me seriously. Shaking her head, she leaves my room.

I cover my face with my hands and gulp back a sob. I need to hold it together. Nataniele is going to come down hard on Dom, and Dom's going to need our support.

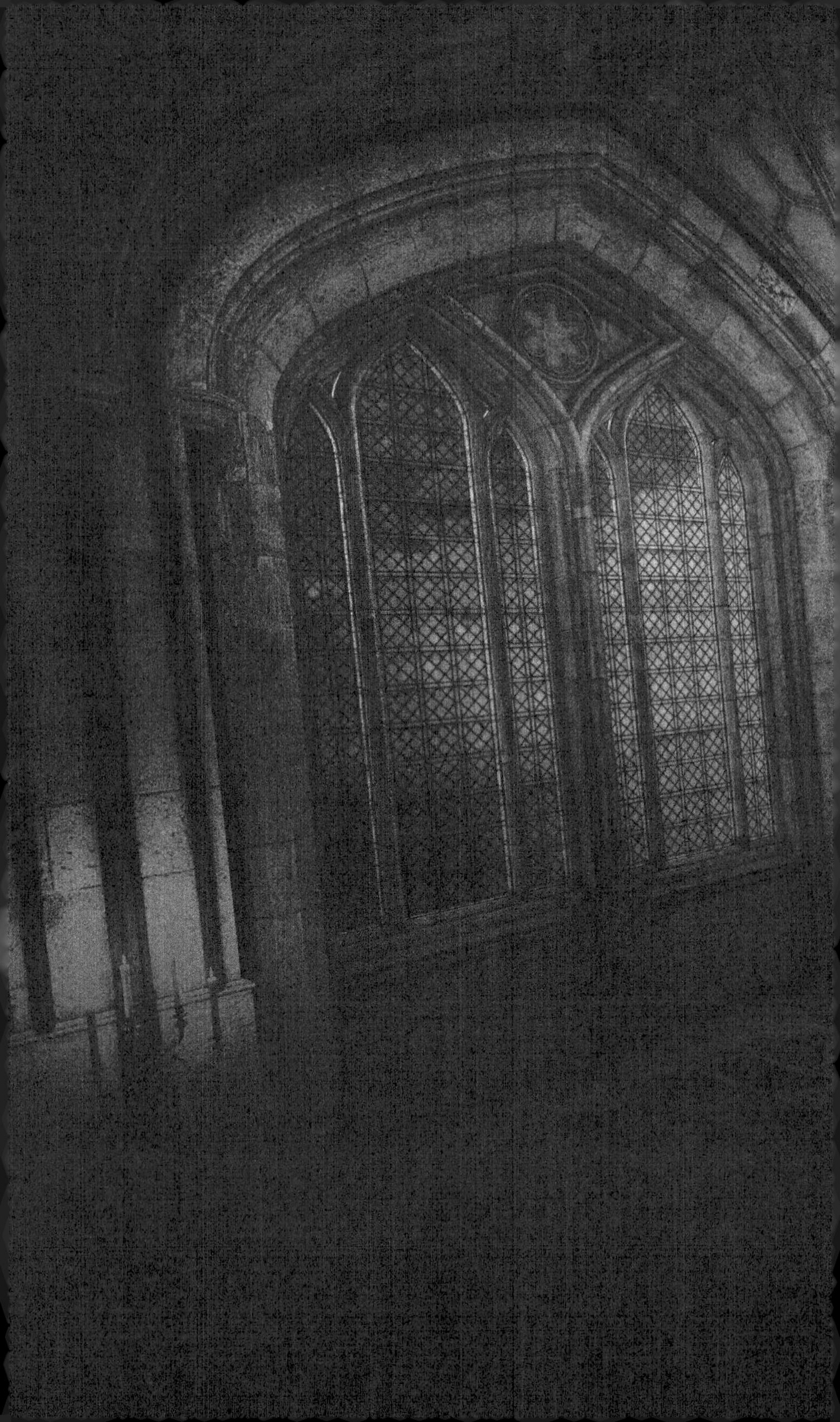

Twenty-Four
Mackenzie

As soon as I'm sure my mom is no longer in the corridor outside my room, I slip out and hurry through Verona Falls' stone hallways until I reach Kirill's room.

I pause outside the door, and knock on it, hard. "Kirill, I need to talk to you," I call through the wood.

It occurs to me that he might not be in, but then movement comes from inside, followed by the click of the lock, and the door opens.

I wince at the sight of his face. His poor nose is still swollen across the bridge, and dark bruises are beneath his eyes.

"What are you doing here, Mackenzie?"

I don't allow him the chance to shut the door on me again, but instead slip past him, into his room. He lets out a sigh and softly shuts the door. I'm glad he hasn't told me to get out.

"I need to talk to you. Nataniele knows about the four of us. He's threatened Dom."

He doesn't respond and he still won't meet my gaze, but I notice his eyes are bloodshot as though he's been crying.

"Please, Kirill. You're the only one who truly understands what I went through in that place. I need you on my side. Nataniele is going to try to break us apart, and we need to be stronger than ever. It's the only way we're going to survive."

"What if we're already broken?"

I widen my eyes at him and reach for his hand. "What? No! How can you say that?"

Pain is etched across his handsome face. "I don't even know how you can stand to be in the same room as me after what I did."

I blink, not understanding what he means. "After what you did? What—coming to my rescue?"

He scoffs laughter. "I never did that."

"Yes, you did. You could have left me there, with *him*, but you didn't. You came, even though you knew he would put you through hell, too. You had a gun in that truck you took. I saw it. You shot that other motherfucker with it."

"None of that matters."

"Of course it matters! It matters more than anything. If you hadn't come, Grigoriy would have raped me. He told me himself. He was going to rape me and impregnant me and take me off to Russia for himself. You stopped him."

"No, I gave him what he wanted. It's not the same thing."

"You didn't have any choice. Neither of us did. Is that what you're beating yourself up about?"

He grinds his teeth so loudly I can hear it.

"I'm sick, *Kukla*. Fucked in the head. I'm just like *him*."

I can't believe he thinks this of himself. "You're nothing like him."

"I enjoyed it. When I was fucking you with those men watching, and you were cuffed to the bars, and then they desecrated you."

I reach up and cup my hand to his cheek. "And then you made it all better again."

"No, I didn't. I cried in the dark like a fucking baby." He yanks himself from my grip, swings around, and punches the wall. A dent is left in the plasterboard, and he cups one bruised hand with the other.

I soften my tone. "It's okay to be vulnerable, Kirill. We've all done things we're not proud of. It makes us human."

I take a breath. I need to tell him. He needs to know I'm not perfect either, that he has a far worse reason to hate me than the reason he's beating himself up for. I don't think there will ever be a right time, but it doesn't feel good carrying this piece of information and not knowing how he's going to react to it. If we're all going to fall apart, we might as well do it with one huge explosion.

I force the words from my lips. "It was me."

He glances over at me with a frown. "What was you?"

"I was the one who pulled the trigger. I killed your dad, Kirill."

He freezes. "You what?"

My blood runs cold, and my heart practically stops. How did I think he was going to take this news?

"I couldn't let him get away with it. I just couldn't. If there was any chance he got to walk out of there, he'd never leave us alone. We'd never find peace again." I draw a shuddery breath. "I'm sorry."

But instead of turning from me, he reaches for me and takes my hand.

"Jesus, do not be sorry. It should have been me. I should not have put that on you as well. Now you have to carry the guilt with you."

I shake my head. "The only guilt I have is around you and fearing you'll be upset with me."

"I'm not upset with you, *Kukla*. Never." He cups my face, presses his forehead to mine. "I love you so much. I wanted to be able to protect you, but instead I feel like I contributed to your degradation. I hate myself for that. I want to lock you up in a safe box somewhere so nothing can ever hurt you again."

"Getting hurt is a part of living. It's how we get up again afterward that matters. I'm just happy you're not angry with me for what I did." I sigh. "I know it must hurt and that it will make you look at me differently. How can it not?"

He shakes his head against mine. "I won't lie, it's all a headfuck. But he was evil. And he wasn't going to stop. If anyone was going to do it, I'm glad it was you. He hurt you, too."

There are so many things stacked against us right now. It feels almost hopeless, as if we were naïve idiots thinking this could work, and it is slowly breaking down around us.

I still don't know how we're going to fix the Nataniele issue, but in that moment, I don't give a shit about him. All I care about is reconnecting with Kirill. At least this is one part of our broken whole I can try to mend.

"Come back to me," I whisper.

"I'm here, *Kukla*."

"Not fully. Not in mind and heart and soul."

I lift my head, and my lips find his, and it's soft and gentle. A jarring juxtaposition against what happened in that tawdry space of his father's.

Suddenly, I know what we need.

"Will you do something for me?" I ask.

"What?"

"Make love to me."

His gaze holds mine as uncertainty haunts the ice-blue of his eyes.

"Please?" I'm not averse to begging to get what I want.

He swallows hard, his Adam's apple bobbing, but he nods. "For you, anything."

THE DEVILS' DARLING

Twenty-Five

Kirill

She doesn't understand what she's asking. I'm not the kind of man who makes love. I fuck, hard and nasty. For her, though, I will change everything about who I am. I brush the hair back from her face, exposing her high cheekbones. I look at her, *really* look at her, drinking in how beautiful she is.

Not only beautiful, but brave too.

If she is brave enough to survive what happened in that basement and not blame me, I'm brave enough to do this for her.

If she is brave enough to kill my father, the man who haunted my nightmares, then I can step up for her right now.

I duck my head and take her lips in another soft, warm kiss. She tastes faintly of cinnamon, and a soft groan escapes me as we deepen the kiss.

My hands sweep down her arms and back up again to rest at the base of her throat. I caress the side of her neck and up to her nape as I add a swirl of my tongue into the kiss. Her arms wrap around my neck, and she presses herself tightly against me.

There is a part of me that is scared I won't be able to do this. That my body will let me down. The shame I keep feeling is overwhelming, but as her warmth seeps into me, my body begins to respond.

She breaks off the kiss and steps back, licking her lips. I frown, confused for a moment. Her smile lights up her face, and she begins to slowly undress.

It's not a striptease—she's slowly unwrapping herself for me in an open and honest way, letting her clothes fall to the floor until she's completely naked. Once she's undressed, she stands in front of me, her arms down by her side, and her palms facing outward. It's as if she's saying, *here I am, look at me. See me.*

"I see you," I say.

"This is all for you, and I include my heart in that."

Something inside me snaps, and a wave of emotion rolls over me. I find myself growing hard, but more than that, I feel an upsurge of love for her. In two strides, I'm in front of her, and I swoop her into my arms to carry her to the bed. I place her gently on the mattress, and then, not taking my eyes off her beautiful form for one second, I undress myself, too.

Once I'm naked, I climb onto the bed and over her body. I kiss her forehead, her cheeks, her nose, and then make tiny butterfly kisses across her mouth. I trail my kisses down her chin and the long column of her neck.

When I reach her chest, instead of going immediately for her tits, I kiss across her collarbone, and then down into the dip between her breasts. Her flat stomach is warm, and as I work my way down it, she lets out a soft giggle.

"That tickles," she says.

I blow a raspberry on her belly, and her laugh is rich and free. The sound is happy, and it fills this room that was so haunted by sadness mere moments ago with joy.

Part of me knows we shouldn't be doing this. Not

really. Not when we did it without the other two back in the basement, and also in my room with the hairbrush.

I pause and look up at her. "Do you think they'll mind?"

"Not if it brings you back to us," she says.

Us, not *me*. If it brings you back to *us*.

I smile at her, at her words, and kiss across to her hip bone, giving a tiny bite there and then licking it better.

When I reach between her legs, I ignore her pussy and work my way down her right leg until I reach her foot. I kiss each perfect toe, and then do the same back up her left leg. She tastes delicious. Her skin is as soft as velvet and as smooth as silk. I relish the feel of her against my lips as I work my way back to that place between her legs, where she's already glistening with arousal for me.

I part her folds and gently lick her. I want to make her come, but I also want this first one to be gentle. I keep the flicks of my tongue light, and when she starts to whimper and moan, I slowly push my tongue inside her, groaning at the taste of her.

A dark part of me—that sick, wild part—tries to break free in this moment, but I ruthlessly push it back down.

As she breaks and comes around me, I keep gently working her with my tongue until she falls back against the bed, panting like she's just run up two flights of stairs.

Lazily, I kiss my way up her body until I reach her face, which I take in my hands. For a long beat, we simply stare at one another, and then I'm kissing her again and she's kissing me right back. Her arms snake around me, and her legs too, and I don't know where I end and she begins.

She hitches her hips upward, and I pause. "Are you sore?"

I'm aware that she had both Dom and Tino inside her at the same time, and I don't want to hurt her.

"A little," she admits, "but I know you'll be gentle."

She *knows* I will, and that means everything to me. She

still trusts me, even after what I did. I press down, then I'm inside her, her wet heat enveloping me. I lick and suck at the side of her neck, nibbling the delicate shell of her ear, as I move in and out of her.

Her muscles grip me, and even though this is slow and lazy, she's still clamping deliciously around me.

Scenes from that basement push their way back into my mind, but I refuse them entry.

This is why I am not like my father. He would never have been capable of this. The way he treated my mother was never with tenderness or compassion. Everything about him was hard, vicious, and cruel.

I can be those things if needs be. I will be them for our Duchess if she needs protecting, and will be them for my friends. However, I will not show those tendencies toward Mackenzie, unless she wants me to, in bed.

Her pussy is soaking, and she grinds hard against me as we become more heated in our movements. I'm chasing that high, craving that moment I fall over the edge into bliss. Into *her*.

When it comes, the pleasure crashes over me in big, rolling waves.

Mackenzie gives a soft cry and pulses around me as she joins me, clinging tightly to me. I fill her with myself, and even when I'm finished, I still keep moving inside her. I slide in and out, relishing the sensation of her wetness and my seed mingling together.

For a crazy moment, I let myself fantasize that I get her pregnant like my father wanted. That I am the one who puts a baby inside her.

If I did have a baby with her, if we all did, we'd need to step up to the plate and be much better fathers than we ever had for ourselves. We'd need to vow to break that generational curse together.

I just hope I can be man enough to do that for her.

THE DEVILS' DARLING

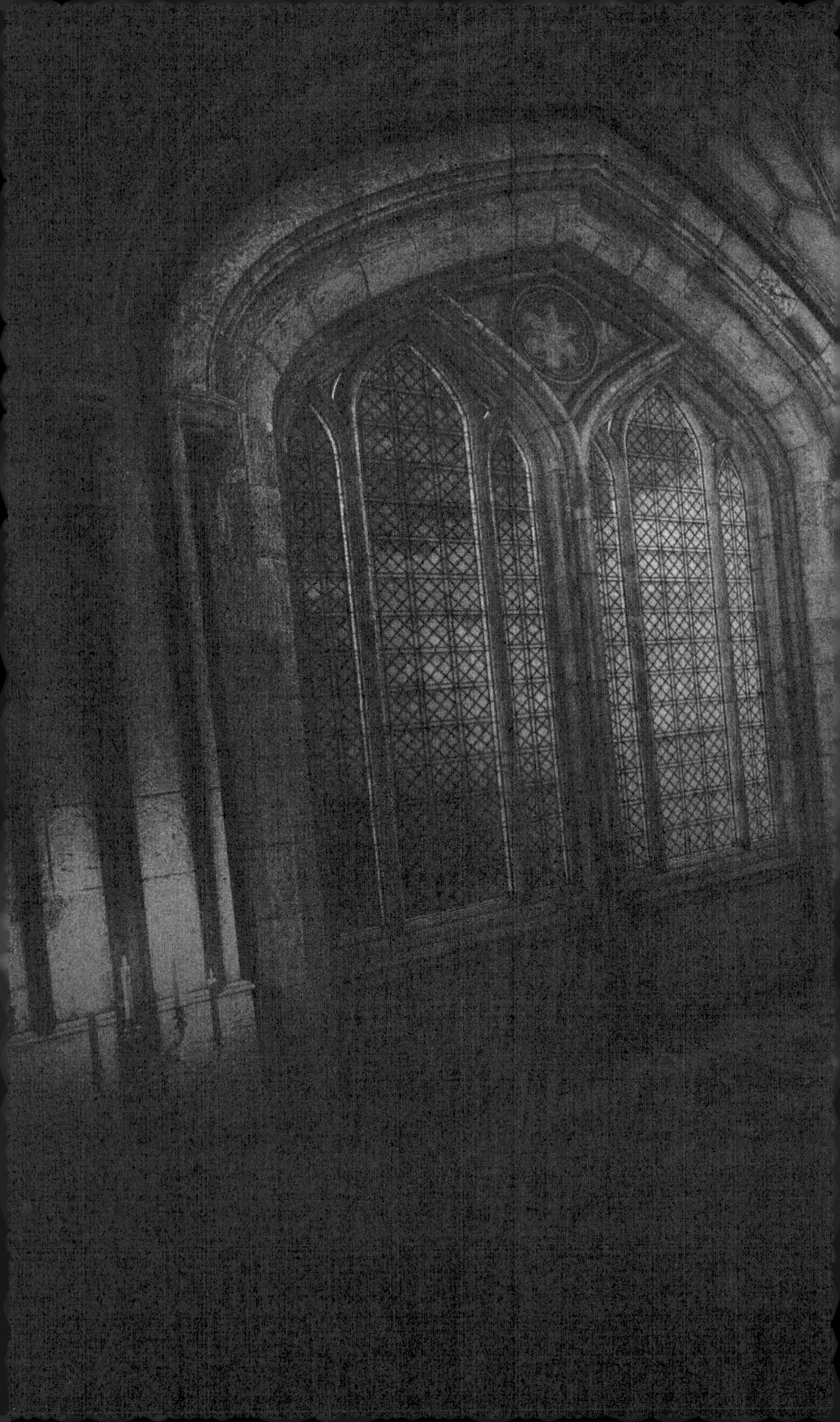

Twenty-Six

Tino

I'm pacing the den, unsure what the hell to do with myself. Mackenzie has been taken to her mother, Dom is with his dad, and Kirill is still lost in whatever fucked up world he's ended up in since the cabin. They've all been gone a long time, and I'm getting worried.

I've taken a couple of Oxy. My leg was throbbing again, especially after landing on it badly in the cabin, and I needed to take the edge off my anxiety about Nataniele catching us like that. It was fucking humiliating to have him order us about like we were stupid little kids. I hate he saw Kenzie all exposed, especially after what Kirill's fucked-up father did to her.

I'm filled with guilt about taking the pills, but I promise myself I'll stop again, just as soon as all this shit settles down. I can do it. I did it before, right? And I'm not addicted this time. It's purely for the pain and the recent situation. Not a need. Not the way it was before.

Footsteps come from outside, and Mackenzie and Kirill burst back into the room. They're holding hands, and Mackenzie glows as if she's taken an afternoon at the spa. I might have been jealous before, but now I take it as a good sign. We need Kirill back on board and for Kenzie to be happy. For that to happen, I truly believe she needs all three of us.

"Hey, have you two seen Dom?" I ask them.

Kenzie shakes her head. "Not yet. He was still with his dad, last I knew. I bet he's getting so much shit. I did. My mom was horrible to me, but she doesn't understand. None of them do, so we have to show them."

There's a determination in the set of her chin and a new sense of calmness to her, as if she's seen how bad the world can be, and a little bit of parental disapproval can't hurt now.

"We need to create a united front." She nods as if agreeing with herself. "It's the only way Nataniele and my mom are going to understand what we are—*who* we are. That we're serious about each other, and a bunch of threats isn't going to change anything. We're adults now. We get to choose who we're with, not them."

"What are you saying?" I ask. "That we need to go to Nataniele's quarters?"

"Yes, all of us, together. Let him know we're not to be messed with."

She straightens her shoulders, and I realize I'm so fucking proud of her. The three of us were nothing before she came along—just a bunch of kids screwing around. She's made men of us all.

"I agree," Kirill says. "We stand beside each other. Always."

There seems to be some of the old light back in his eyes. I'm glad. I miss my old friend—the one who loves to dance and who'll start a fight in an empty room. I've missed his fire.

I take a step forward. "Okay, let's do this."

Kenzie and Kirill spin on their heels, and together we leave.

But, to my surprise, we meet Dom in the corridor, heading toward us.

"What's up, D?" I ask. "Everything all right?"

"We were just coming to find you," Mackenzie says.

"Dad was distracted, so I got out of there. I went for a walk outside to clear my head." He seems shaken, and he's paler than usual. His hair is all messed up as if he's been raking his hand through it repeatedly.

He thrusts a piece of paper in our direction.

"Look what I found."

I frown. "What is it?"

"A letter my mom wrote to my dad the night she died, saying that she was leaving him. It says she overheard him telling another woman on the phone he loved her, and she couldn't live like this anymore."

"Fuck," I curse. "Does it say who the other woman was?"

Dom cocks an eyebrow. "No, but I can take a damned good guess."

"My mom," Mackenzie says.

He smiles wryly. "Unless he's got a third woman on the go, yeah, I'd say so." Dom closes his eyes briefly. "The letter also says she'd planned to send for me later, if I wanted to leave, too. She didn't want me to grow up like him."

"Have you spoken to your father about the letter?" Mackenzie asks.

He shakes his head. "Not yet. I'm still not sure what it means. It doesn't prove anything, does it?"

"Doesn't it?" She gives him a sympathetic smile. "It sounds to me like she left voluntarily, that she was upset, and it was the middle of the night. Maybe she was crying, and she misjudged the road."

Dom lowers the letter and knots one hand in his hair. "Fuck, I don't know what to think."

"It's definitely your mom's handwriting?" Kirill asks.

"Yeah, it is."

"So you know she *did* want to leave," Mackenzie points out.

Dom sucks air over his teeth. "But what if he didn't let her? What if instead of letting her leave, he drove her off that bridge? Maybe he thought if he couldn't have her, then no one would?"

"You're going to have to talk to him, dude," Kirill says. "If you want to know the truth, you need to ask him. Your dad isn't exactly a saint, but compared to some men, he's not all bad."

Dom twists his lips as though he doesn't quite believe that, but Kirill's got a point.

"My *papi* is the same," I add. "He's a hard man, but he's not evil, not in the way Grigoriy was." I grimace. "Sorry, Kill."

Kirill shrugs. "No, you are right."

Dom lets out a breath. "I wish she'd come to me that night and told me what her plans were. Maybe I'd have gone with her, and she'd still be alive today."

"Would you really have gone?" I ask. "Would you have given up your life here to go with her?"

Dom scrubs his hand over his eyes. "Fuck. Honestly, no, probably not. I'd have been partying, or pissed that she'd woken me, if I'd been sleeping. I'd most likely have told her she was mistaken, that she overheard Dad wrong, and she was overreacting."

I offer him a smile of sympathy. "I know it's not what you want to hear, D, but you wouldn't have been able to change what happened. It was an accident, and if you'd gone, you might be dead now, too." I know that's harsh, but it's the truth.

Mackenzie puts her hand on his bicep. "You need to talk to your dad, let him explain it to you. At least give him the chance to try."

He bites the inside of his lip. "Can I trust him to tell me

the truth?"

"Your mom has already told you the truth in that letter," she says. "Let him tell his point of view, and then maybe it's time to make peace with what happened to her. You can't grieve unless you find peace."

I stare at her, proud of how strong she's become. God, we all owe her such a debt of gratitude for giving us chance after chance. When I think of all the times we nearly blew it, I want to punch myself in the face.

Dom holds Mackenzie's gaze and blows out a long breath. "You're right. Fuck. I'm going to go talk to my father."

Twenty-Seven

Domenic

"Where the fuck did you go?" my dad says when I return to his quarters. "I wasn't done with you."

I don't know why, but this letter has changed something. I'm no longer afraid of him. My mom chose to leave him. She walked out on him. She'd planned on forging her own path, without him. And if she had the guts to do that, so can I.

I hold out the sheet of paper. "I found this letter."

He pales and reaches for it. "That's not yours. What the fuck? Were you going through my things?"

His face turns red—a sure sign of his building rage—but I ignore it and remain calm.

"Why didn't you ever show this to me before?" I demand to know.

"It wasn't for you. It was a letter she wrote for me."

I wave the letter at him. "Mom talks about me in it. Don't you think I deserved to know she wanted me to join her?"

"Why? What would be the point? She died. It wasn't as though that would ever be possible."

"How can you be so fucking cold? She was my *mother*!"

My voice is raised, and it cracks slightly.

He drops his head, the fight suddenly gone out of him. "I loved her, too." His voice is gruff, like mine.

I narrow my eyes. He's putting this on. Pretending. He has to be. This bastard isn't capable of love. He wants Lucia because she's a pretty object to have on his arm, nothing more or less.

"Liar! It says she overheard you on the phone to another woman. I assume that woman was Lucia, and then surprise, surprise, Mom dies under mysterious circumstances, and then the other woman turns up at Verona Falls."

His head snaps up, his eyes blazing. "I didn't have anything to do with your mother's death, if that's what you're implying."

I bite my lower lip and force myself to speak. We've never spoken about mom's death properly—not really. I've certainly never let him know what's really been on my mind. "What else am I supposed to think?"

"It was a terrible, tragic accident, that's all. Don't you think I've beaten myself up over the way she died? I treated her appallingly, and she didn't deserve that. I wish she'd never overheard me that night, or that I'd stopped her from leaving, but wishing something doesn't change it. No matter what you think, I loved her!"

"How can you say you loved Mom when you were acting like that?"

"I loved them both." He pauses and then adds, "I still do."

For a split second, I'm about to throw all that back at him in rage. How dare he love a woman other than my mother? But then I hesitate.

I realize something profound. "What if they'd both agreed to be with you? What would you have done then?"

His eyes narrow. "I'd have been a very happy man, of course, but that was never going to happen. Your mother never wanted to share. She was extremely jealous."

"But you'd have been happy if she'd said she would?"

"Of course. Any man would be happy with that situation."

"Then why can't you understand our situation with Mackenzie? We all love her. She loves each of us, equally. It's the same situation, except ours is an amicable one, and it won't end in someone dying."

His mouth opens and closes. "She's your stepsister."

I hold my ground. "No, she isn't. You and Lucia don't need to marry. The police aren't looking for Mackenzie. She doesn't need a new identity, and neither does Lucia. This can work, Dad. Don't let anyone else die because you're being stubborn. It's pretty fucking simple. Just let us be happy."

"You expect me to stop my marriage for your little poly experiment?"

I sigh and pinch my nose. "Dad, we want to be together, and it's either that or we'll leave. You can't control everything. This is one of those things." I suck in air and say what I've been dreading. "If you want me to be a part of your life going forward, you have to do this. You lost my mother. Do you want to lose me too?"

He hesitates, and for the first time, I see a chink in his armor. He knows I have a point, and he's considering my proposition.

I push the advantage. "You and Lucia can be very happy as you are. I think Lucia will agree to this because she knows it means we are all with her daughter and can keep her safe. There are still men out there after them both. One day we might find them, but we may not. If we don't, what better way to ensure her safety than being with us?"

He shakes his head, and his mouth is set in a hard line, but eventually he gives a deep sigh. "I'm not going to say I'll support what you're doing, but you are all adults. The best I can do is turn a blind eye, but if I do, you have to give Lucia a chance, too."

I press my lips together and stick my hand out to him. "Deal."

He lets out another sigh but clamps his hand against mine. We shake once.

"Don't make me regret that, Domenic."

"I won't."

THE DEVILS' DARLING

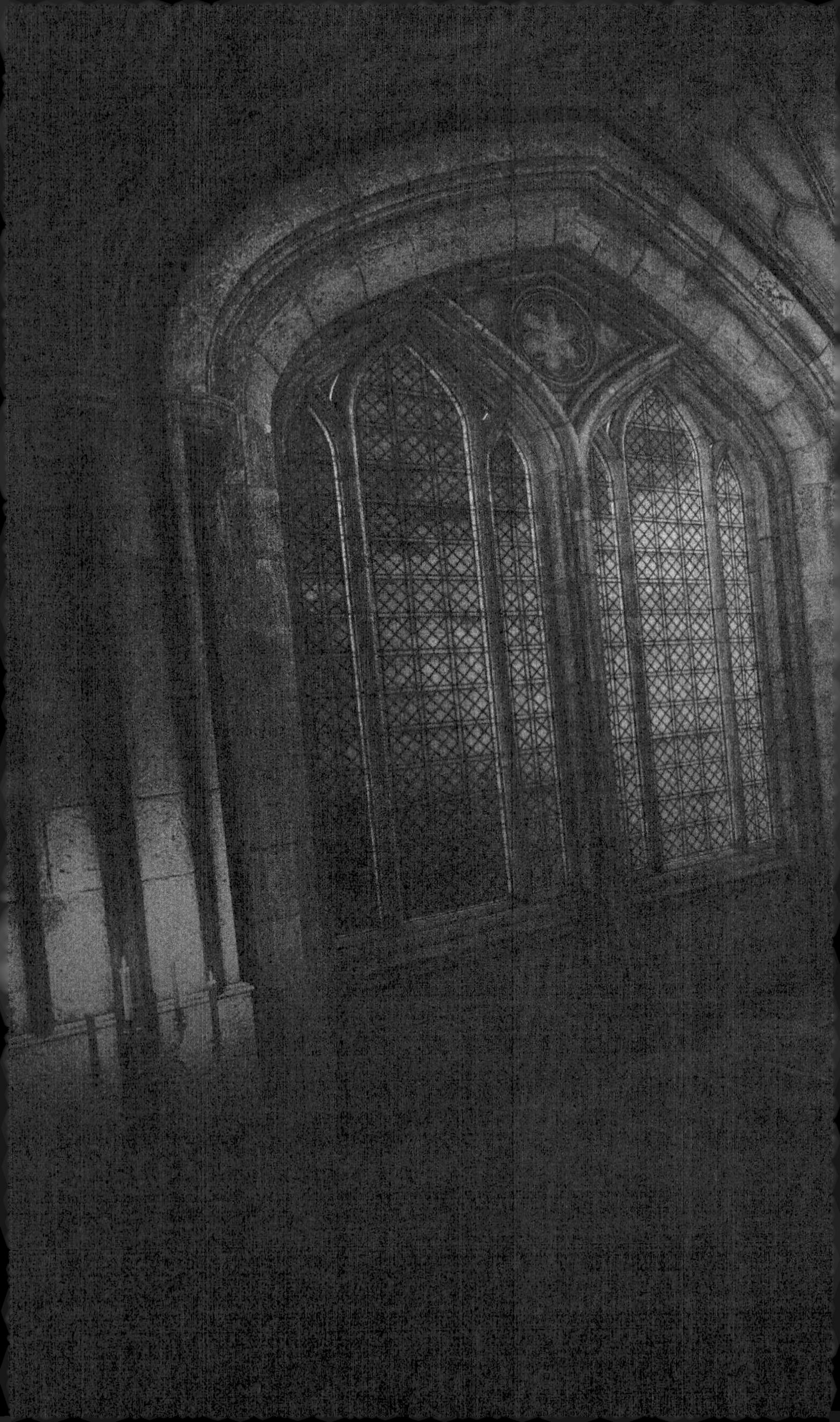

Twenty-Eight
Mackenzie

The sun beats down, and a happy atmosphere fills the air. For once in my life, I don't feel like a misfit, and I'm feeling kind of happy, too. It's strange to have this little fizzing of joy inside me after all that's happened, but the sun is shining and fun is afoot, and I'm with my men.

It's been a few days now since Dom's confrontation with his father, and things finally seem to be on an even keel. I know Mom and Nataniele aren't happy about our relationships, but, other than the occasional disapproving look, they haven't brought it up again.

I haven't had any more creepy messages from Paxton either, which is a relief. I was tempted to destroy my SIM and get a new phone, but there's also the part of me that wants to keep track of him. Lola has promised she'll get in touch if she hears he's returned home, but so far there's been nothing. I hope he's crawled into a hole somewhere and he'll stay there for the rest of his life. After dealing with the likes of Grigoriy and his men, Paxton now seems like nothing more than a pathetic irritation. I'm not sure why I allowed him so much of my headspace.

"Hey, girl." Camile plops down beside me on the blanket.

I smile over at her. "Hey."

We're on a slope, overlooking the sports field. The four houses of Verona Falls University are playing each other in a baseball game, and, right now, Dom seems to have hit a home run. He's only seconds away from home base, and I start to clap and cheer. Tino, who's on the other side of me, whistles, and Kirill, who is also playing, jumps up and down on the field.

The crowds are slowly gathering, and apparently, from what I've been told, as the afternoon progresses, things will only get increasingly fun and rowdy.

"It's the one day all the different factions take a break from trying to beat one another up," Camile says with a giggle. "Our version of the famous soccer match on Christmas Eve during the First World War."

"What soccer match?" Tino asks. His fingers idly brush up and down my bare arm.

The sun warms me, and I tilt my head up and smile.

"There was a Christmas truce in 1914," Camile says, "and the German and British soldiers met in no man's land and exchanged gifts and played soccer."

"Wow." Tino's fingers trail along my wrist and then back up, slowly, sending a delicious tremor down my spine. "That's pretty cool."

"Not if they all killed one another after," I say. "It's really sad."

I stare out at the field and watch the game, though I'm not really interested in the result. I'm not a big sports fan and don't really understand the rules of baseball. Still, it's nice to soak up the atmosphere and see everyone enjoying themselves. Most people are dressed in light, summer clothing, despite it being fall, or sports gear, and there are games of more seasonally appropriate things like apple bobbing off to one side.

I'm sitting with my legs tucked to one side of me, and I pull at the short skirt of my sundress, trying not to expose too much thigh. I've kicked off my white sneakers and socks, preferring to have the soft, green grass underfoot instead.

I close my eyes and let my thoughts drift.

Something in the air changes, and I open my eyes, almost expecting to discover the sun has darted behind a heavy thundercloud. A murmur, a ripple of something like excitement, surfs the crowd like a wave. The chatter approaches us, rumbling like a storm, and I turn my head, frowning.

Walking right in front of the field where the game is being played are three tall, dark-haired figures.

I watch them and recognize two of them. Matteo and Louis, who everyone refers to as the Vipers. I don't recognize the guy with them, though. Hell, this guy is huge. He's taller than the twins—and even taller than Kirill. It's not only his height that makes him big, but the way he's bulked with muscle, filling out the long dark coat he really doesn't need in this weather. He even has a scarf wrapped around his thick throat.

"Holy shit," Camile exclaims.

Tino blows out a low breath. "He's back."

"Who? Who is he?" I ask, confused.

The three men have turned and are headed up the hill, right toward us, although they aren't looking our way.

"*Insane* Zane," Camile whispers.

I snort loudly and regret it when a few heads turn my way. "Camile, that's not very politically correct, or kind toward mental health issues," I admonish.

"That's his fucking nickname," Tino mutters, "and it's well deserved because he's one unhinged dude."

My God, if one of *my* men thinks this Zane character is unhinged, he must be bad. I look at the new arrival and, as I do, his head swivels my way.

He's wearing sunglasses, so I can't see his eyes, but I feel his gaze on me. It's branding me everywhere it touches with a freezer-burn of fear.

Shit. I don't like the feeling of him looking at me at all.

His gaze leaves me, his head turning to the right when someone yells to him, calling his name, and I heave a huge sigh of relief.

"Jesus, he's creepy," I say to Camile, my voice low.

"He's dangerous," she says. "I'd avoid him, and all of them."

"The way you do?" I ask, disliking the way she sometimes tells me how to live my life while doing the exact opposite herself.

"Trust me, Mackenzie, I do avoid them as much as I can. I know what you saw in the hall, but it's not what you think."

"What was it, then?"

She sighs. "They want a new victim, and they were trying me on for size, but Mattheo is known for having expensive tastes, so I'm clearly not what he wanted."

"What do you mean, he has expensive tastes?" I ask, wondering what that's got to do with Camile.

"He likes fine wine, and dining, and fucking classical music—shit like that. That's why everyone calls him Saint."

I frown, not understanding. "What's Saint got to do with anything?"

"Saint Laurant?" She shrugs. "It's spelled differently, but it's basically cause that's his surname and he wouldn't be seen dead in anything other than designer clothes." She gives a cold laugh. "I'm too common for him. I'm definitely not the kind of woman he'd want on his arm at the opera."

"You're not common, Camile," I say.

"If it keeps them away from me, I don't care. Besides, they also didn't get the reaction they wanted, so in the end, they left me alone."

"What reaction do they want?" I ask.

"Fear," Tino says. "They drink it up like vampires drink blood."

I shiver a little at his words, but they make me think back. I turn to him. "I don't think they're that different from you guys, then."

"What?" His eyes widen. "Seriously?"

"Oh, yeah. You liked to scare me half to death when we first met."

He grins, all sexy and boyish. For a moment, it makes him look a few years younger than he is.

"Nah," he says. "That was just a bit of mild teasing."

I raise my brows, but he shrugs. "Just fucking with you, Duchess." Then he leans in close and whispers in my ear. "I'm fucking with you because I can't be fucking you right now, and this is like foreplay for me."

The nip to my ear has a tiny squeak escaping me, and Camile shoots Tino a disgruntled glance.

"I'm going to get something to eat and drink. Do you ladies want anything?" Tino asks.

"Just a Coke, please." I grin.

"Dr Pepper for me, please," Camile says.

Tino nods at us and jogs down the hill.

Camile gives me her full attention. "So ... you look happy."

I can't help it; a grin splits my face. "I am. For today, at least. Things aren't easy."

"In what way? If those Devils are hurting you, I swear, babe, I'll deal with them."

I giggle. "Thanks for offering, but no, it's not. It's ... there's so much to say. Can I tell you another time?"

She nods. "Sure."

"Well, if it isn't Camile and her little friend."

I jump at the voice and look up to see one of the twins

sneering down at us. His brother is not with him, but the new arrival, Zane, is right by his side.

"Piss off, Lex," Camile snaps.

Lex must be a nickname for Louis. I have no idea how she knows which is which. They seem identical to me, with their thick black hair and blue eyes. He has a small mole on his neck, and I wonder if that's the difference between him and his brother.

I'm shocked to hear Camile speak to him in this way, and my eyes widen, but she gives him the finger and turns to face me. Deliberately ignoring him, she starts to talk to me about our plans for the evening. I struggle to concentrate on what she's saying because my peripheral vision catches Zane hunkering down next to us.

His huge form seems to block out the sun, and he removes his sunglasses to reveal strange colored eyes—green with a hint of amber around the edges. He stares right at us both, and I shift uncomfortably.

Camile turns to him, but this time her feistiness seems to have deserted her. "What do you want?"

The huge man says nothing but continues to stare. I don't understand what's happening here.

"Zane," the twin says, "stop being freaky. You'll scare the new girl." Louis laughs, and it's deep and depraved.

Zane cocks his head to one side and observes me like a bird of prey watching a field mouse. Then, without turning around, he signs something to Louis.

A deep voice from my right startles me.

"She's called Mackenzie."

Tino hands me my drink and stares down at Zane.

"And she's with the Devils," he adds.

Zane nods once. Then he stands, glances over at Tino, shrugs, and strolls away.

What the fuck?

"Is he deaf?" I ask Camile.

"No, not deaf, but he can't speak."

"Why not?"

"Cat got his tongue," Tino drawls as he sits back down beside me, passing the Dr Pepper to Camile.

I nudge him in the side and shake my head, but I'm smiling at his goofiness.

"He was cut across the throat, they say," Camile explains. "It damaged his larynx, and he's just had another surgery to try to fix things, which is where he's been all semester, but he still can't speak."

"How long hasn't he been speaking?"

She shrugs. "As long as I've been here."

"Wow. So, he knows sign language?" That makes me think he's been unable to speak for a long time.

"Some, and him and the other two Vipers have made some up, too. It's like their own weird, little language." She shivers. "They all give me the damn creeps. He also carries a pencil and pad with him, and writes shit on that, and he uses his phone, too."

Kirill strolls up the hill toward us. The injuries his father gave him are starting to heal now, though they're still obvious. He's smiling as he approaches, and although melancholy lingers in his blue eyes, he seems as determined as I am to enjoy the day.

Does he feel like I did when I lost my dad, as if part of the roof blew off my house? It's a strange and scary feeling. One that leaves you unmoored and lost. Familiar places suddenly seem new, and the world can recede as if locked behind a glass wall you just can't break through.

"If you guys will excuse me, I'm just going to pop to the ladies' room." Camile giggles and hops to her feet, brushing down the back of her dress to dislodge any dried grass.

I laugh at her posh turn of phrase, and Kirill sinks down next to me, taking her spot.

"How are you doing?" I ask.

"Good," he says. "Better now that I'm next to you."

"Barf," Tino mutters.

"It's called romance," Kirill says. "You ought to try it sometime."

"I don't need romance," Tino responds smartly. "I've got my monster dick."

I have just taken a swig of my drink, and I snort and choke.

"Holy hell, try not to kill the Duchess." Dom jogs up to us and glares at Tino and Kirill. "We're supposed to be keeping her safe, guys, not causing death by soda."

He turns his back and drops to the ground directly in front of me, positioning himself between my thighs. With his back to me, he grabs my bare legs and hooks them on either side of his thighs, then leans into me, his hands on my feet. Tino drapes an arm around my shoulder, and Kirill plays with a strand of my hair.

They're claiming me in front of the entire school.

Everyone can see us together, and I'm proud to be with them. This moment is us going official on some level.

"Everyone can see," I whisper.

"Let them, Duchess," Dom says. "Our parents know. What more do we have to hide?"

He turns, tosses me a wink, and runs his hand higher up my leg. His touch is amazing, and I find myself letting out a sigh of pleasure. My legs are already on either side of his thighs, and my panties would be on display, if it wasn't for Dom's body blocking the way. Tino leans in and kisses my neck. I tilt my head to one side, giving him better access. His tongue darts out, leaving a trail of goosebumps in its wake.

"I'm not getting left out this time," Kirill growls, edging closer.

He leans in to kiss me, and his hand slides between my thighs.

My body is already alight with arousal, my nipples

crinkling, and heat gathering at my core. We're surrounded by people, but no one can really see what's going on. Encompassed by all three men, I doubt I'm even visible, unless someone had a drone hovering above us. It still turns me on, knowing someone might see us, though. What is it with me and sex out in the open? It's a kink I never knew I had until I met the Devils.

Kirill pushes my panties to one side, then his finger slides up and down my pussy.

"Already wet," he says as he breaks the kiss. "Dirty little slut. Are you a slut for us, Mackenzie? Taking it out in the open like this."

His mouth claims mine again, and I gasp and nod frantically against him. I'll be whatever they want me to be.

He rubs my clit, and Tino's hand finds my breast. Tino continues to kiss and suck my neck, as his fingers pinch my nipple through my sundress. Dom lifts my left foot to his mouth, and wet heat encloses my toes. It's ticklish at first, but the ticklishness quickly fades when Kirill slides a finger inside me.

"Oh, God," I gasp, my hips lifting, but his other hand covers my mouth.

"Shh, our little slut has to be quiet while we make her come, or everyone is going to know what we are doing to her."

I stare into his blue eyes, even as his finger slides in and out of me. "Are you going to be quiet?" he asks. "Or do we have to expose this pretty pussy to the whole school?"

I nod franticly.

He replaces his hand with his mouth and kisses me again. "Good girl."

"My turn," Tino says.

Kirill slides his finger from me and brings it to his mouth. He sucks off my arousal, keeping eye contact with me the whole time. It's so fucking hot, I think I might explode.

But then Tino pushes a finger inside me, and I snap my attention to him. Dom is still kissing and licking my toes—he's always had a thing about my feet. I remember when he bought me those fuck-me pumps. Hadn't he wanted me to stand on him in them?

Tino's thumb presses on my clit as he finger fucks me. I know I'm going to come soon. The attention of all these men, out here in the open, is too much. I curl into myself, pressing my forehead to Dom's solid back. Kirill takes my hand and places it over his shorts, so I can feel his hardness, letting me know he wants me.

I climax hard and almost silently, shuddering and shaking between them. My whimpers are soft, and my body stiffens and arches. My pussy pulses around Tino's finger.

"Good girl," Tino says. "Now we're taking you down to the den so we can take turns fucking you."

Tino pulls my skirt back around my thighs, and Dom stands.

He leans down, and I think he's going to help me to my feet, as my legs are still shaky, but then he ducks down and hauls me up. In a second, my feet leave the ground, and I find myself thrown over his shoulder.

"Dom!" I squeal, perfectly aware that in my short dress, my panties—which are soaked—are on display. I'm glad I'm not wearing a thong, or my ass would be on display to the entire school right now.

But he slaps the back of my thigh with a flat palm, the crack sounding across the field, and I squeal again.

"You're coming with us, Duchess."

My face is so hot, I think I might spontaneously combust. I simultaneously want to kill him and fuck him. People are noticing, and I hear ripples of laughter. I'm fully aware that Dom's handprint is showing as red marks on my white thigh.

"You are so dead," I warn him.

He only chuckles and keeps walking. I sense everyone watching, and I'm relieved when we enter the building and vanish from view. Dom still doesn't put me down, though, and instead carries me through the much darker, cooler hallways. Kirill and Valentino flank him. Before long, we're in the den, and Dom throws me onto the couch like I weigh nothing.

I try to leap back up, but he pushes me down. Valentino and Kirill move in closer, so all three of them are crowded around me.

Dom purses his lips and shakes his head. "Uh-uh, Duchess. You're not going anywhere."

"You won't get away—" I start.

He drops to his knees in front of me, yanks me toward him so I'm half-off the couch, and pushes my legs apart. In a swift movement, he rolls my panties down, tossing them away, and then covers my pussy with his mouth. My threat dies on my lips as he plunges his tongue inside me.

"Oh, fuck," I groan.

Kirill moves behind the couch, and his fingers cup my chin. He tilts my head back, and then ducks down to kiss me. I arch my hips up as Dom swirls his tongue around my clit. I'm still so sensitive from them fingering me in the field, and now I'm flying on a whole new level. Dom slides two fingers back inside me as he continues to flick my clit with his tongue, and Kirill captures my cries in his mouth. It doesn't take long before I've slid halfway down the couch and I'm riding Dom's face—albeit horizontally.

"I'm gonna come," I gasp. "Oh, shit. Oh, yes."

But to my frustration, Tino interrupts.

"Don't let her come yet."

Dom immediately pulls away from me, and I give a cry of frustration. I reach between my thighs to finish myself off, but Kirill grabs both my hands, stopping me. I squirm with need.

"Let's play a game," Tino announces. "Mackenzie is blindfolded and bent over the couch, then we each get the chance to fuck her."

A murmur of agreement rises among the other two, but he holds up a finger to stop them.

"But we have one rule," he continues. "We each only get three thrusts before we have to pull out and let the next one go."

"Three?" I exclaim. "You'll never be able to get off with only three."

"Who won't?" Tino asks.

"Any of you!" Despite my frustration, I'm half laughing at the idea. They're going to end up fighting over fucking me.

"Okay, five thrusts," Tino relents, "but Kenzie doesn't know which of us it is, and whoever makes her come, wins."

"What if we come first?" Kirill asks.

"Then you lose."

Kirill grins. "Coming inside Mackenzie doesn't sound like a loss to me."

Dom chuckles. "But whoever comes inside her last will be fucking her with all the rest of our cum inside her too. Isn't that like your dream scenario, Kill?"

I'm going to be able to tell the difference between them—especially Tino with all his piercings—but I don't tell them that. Let them have their fun. Besides, the idea of each of them taking their turn with me is hot.

"I'm up for it," I say.

I reach a hand to Dom, and he pulls me up and spins me around so I'm bent over the couch. I'm already without my panties, so he just flips up the short skirt of my sundress so it rides over my hips. Tino has found a silk scarf from the drawer they've been slowly filling with lingerie and toys for us to play with down here. He covers my eyes with the silky cool material, the room around me vanishing, and ties it at the back of my head.

"Beautiful," he murmurs.

In the dark now, I spread my legs. I'm still wet and swollen from them fingering me, and now I feel wantonly exposed. The rustle of clothing being removed around me only heightens the unbearable tension. Then hands grip my hips, and a smooth cockhead nudges at my entrance. I curl my fingers into the sides of the coach and groan as the cock penetrates me and slides deeper. Not Tino, so either Dom or Kirill. I suspect it's Dom, as he likes to be the leader and will want to go first.

"You need to count," Tino says, somewhere over my shoulder, but not directly behind me—just as I'd expected.

A cock is embedded deep inside me now. Whoever it belongs to is holding still, making the most of their time.

"One," I exhale.

Oh, so slowly, they pull back out of me, almost to the point where they'd slip out completely if they went any farther, and, with equally maddening slowness, they slide back in again. Oh, fuck. My breathing grows ragged. God, that feels good.

"Two."

I know it's Dom for sure now. I recognize the woodsy scent he wears as he fucks me with another stroke.

But I don't want to spoil the game.

"Three."

He rams into me, driving the words from my tongue with each slam of his hips.

"Four. Five..."

"Times up, dude." Tino's voice.

Dom growls from behind me. "Dammit." He holds on tight, sinking himself as deep as he can go. His cock twitches inside me.

But then he pulls out, and I'm left bereft. But not for long. A different cockhead presses to my pussy, and I feel the coolness of the metal and the friction of the metal balls against my inside walls.

Tino.

He thrusts inside me. "One," I gasp. Just like with Dom, he holds still, taking his time, making the most of being inside me.

"Two...three...four..."

He fucks me with smooth, deep strokes.

"Ah, fuck, five."

I feel wanton and filthy, being used like this. I love every second of it.

He gives a groan of frustration, but he pulls out as they swap again, and someone else starts fucking me. It must be Kirill.

I count his pumps inside of me, and then they switch.

The three of them each started off slowly, but now their need is building. I'm blindfolded, but I can tell by the sounds around me that, when they're not inside me, they're touching themselves, keeping themselves hard for me, while not climaxing. It must be a tricky rope to walk.

Pressure is building inside me, and I want to come, but each time one of them pulls out of me, it breaks the path to my orgasm. They're not only edging themselves, but me, too. At this rate, we're all going to lose our minds before we climax.

I've stopped keeping track of whose cock is inside me. I no longer care. All I want is to be fucked, and fucked hard. I reach between my thighs, clamping my arm between my body and the couch cushions, to rub my clit.

"Ah, shit, I can't stop. I can't." It's Dom. He slams into me.

"You've got to stop, D," Tino says. "You've had your five strokes."

"Fuck you," he growls from between clenched teeth.

I chase my orgasm as he does the same. He lets out a roar and releases himself inside me, but I haven't quite reached my peak.

Tino is next, sliding deep. "Fuck, D. Your cum is all over my cock. I think I'm going to be next. Kill will like that."

It's almost sweet that they want to fill me up for Kirill. The noises that are filling the room are embarrassing, so wet and squelchy, but I don't think they care. Tino counts his strokes, and then Kirill slips inside me.

There's barely a pause now as they switch, one taking place of the other.

I'm lost in the heady eroticism of the moment. As my climax creeps closer, I completely lose track of who is inside me. It's all about cocks and hands and mouths, and I no longer care what belongs to whom.

The most powerful orgasm of my life hits me. I swear my brain disengages from my body for a few seconds, and I'm soaring on a whole other level. My pussy clamps around the cock filling me, pulsing and rippling. I shake and shudder, every muscle coiled and tight. It doesn't let go of me, but sends my pleasure cascading over me again and again.

It's only when I come down that I feel Tino releasing spurt after spurt inside me.

He high-fives Kirill while his cock is still inside me. "I won," he says. "I made Kenzie come."

I manage to gasp, "I think you all played your part in that."

Tino slips out of me, and hot fluid gushes down the inside of my thighs.

"Hold still, *Kukla*," Kirill says, placing his hand on my lower back to hold me in place.

He pushes the head of his cock so it's just the tip in my gaping pussy. He's swimming in cum, and then he masturbates until his breathing is ragged. When he's close, he thrusts forward, into my slippery heat. A jet of hot semen travels up through his cock, spilling inside me as well.

"Holy fuck," he curses. "That was intense."

I'm trembling all over, my muscles at the point of exhaustion.

"Come here, baby," Dom says, pulling me into his arms. "Now we get to clean you all up."

I let out a happy sigh and relax against him. This is my favorite part—when they all take care of me. The fucking is about them desiring me, but this is them showing their love.

THE DEVILS' DARLING

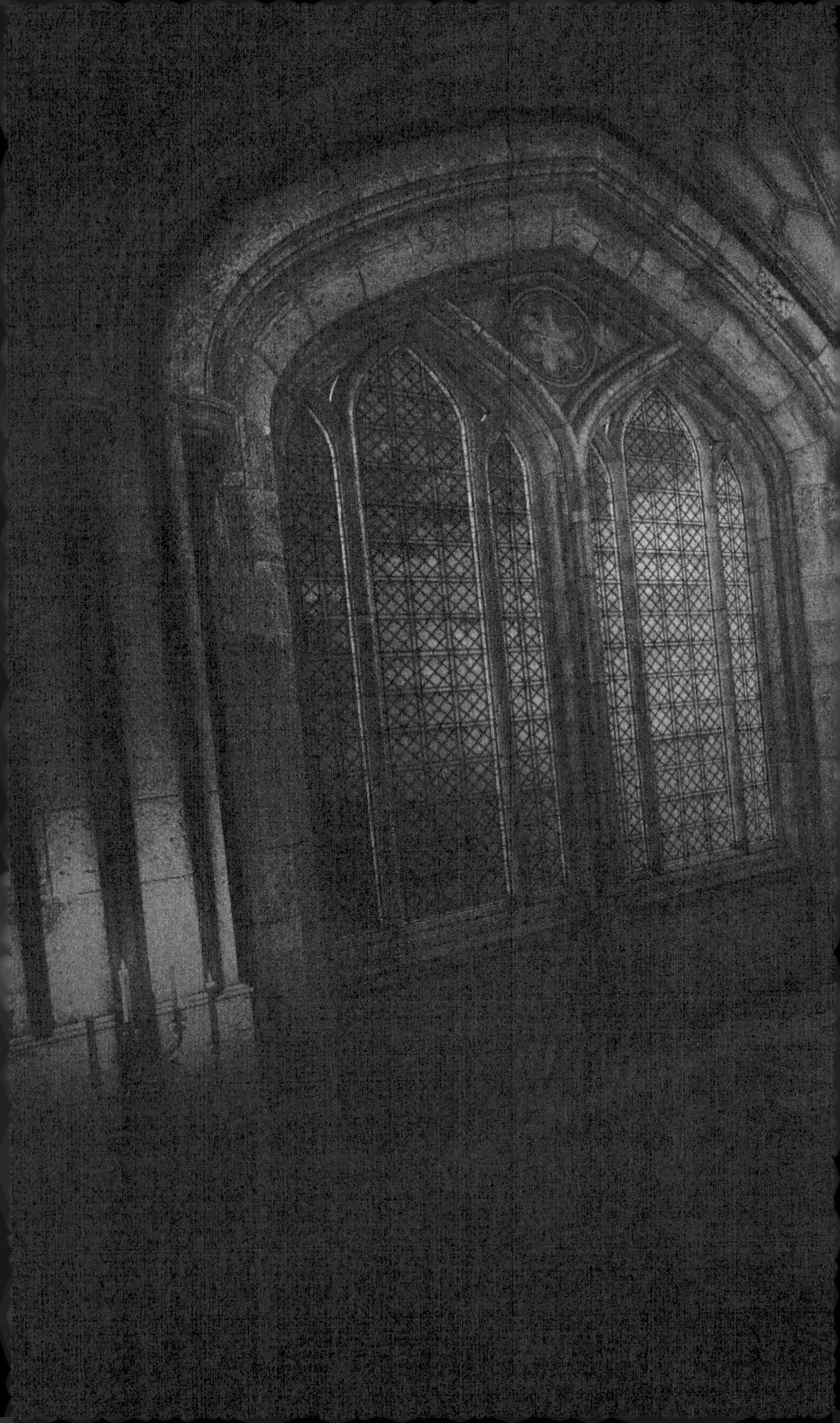

Twenty-Nine
Domenic

It's the day after the baseball game.

"Your birthday is coming up in a couple of weeks. What do you want to do for it?"

I'm in my father's living quarters while he plays at being a good dad. I appreciate that he's making an effort with me, but the whole thing makes me kind of uncomfortable. It's like he's trying too hard.

I shrug. "Nothing, really. It's no big deal."

"You're going to be twenty-two. You should make the most of it. Wait until you're my age, and then you can really start to say it's not a big deal."

"I just want to hang out with Mackenzie and the guys. Maybe we can go and grab something to eat in Arlington. Get away from this place for a few hours." I realize he's alone. "Where's Lucia?"

"She's gone to talk to the head of the kitchen. She thinks they need to mix things up a little. Apparently, we're not eating enough vegetables." He rolls his eyes at that.

It's childish, but I take a little pleasure from knowing that perhaps not everything is perfect between them. Serves him right if Lucia is nagging him about his diet. Not that he looks like he's overweight. He keeps himself fit.

His phone rings, and he answers it.

"What?" he barks down the line.

Aah, that's more like the man I know.

He listens for a moment, and then his expression tightens. "What? You're sure he's one of ours?" There's silence again, and then he says, "Okay, we'll be on alert."

"What's wrong?" I ask, stiffening.

"A man's body has been found on the side of the road just outside of the campus grounds. Looks like someone deliberately tried to hide it."

"How was he killed?"

"Strangulation, by the looks of the marks around his neck, but it's not like we've had time to do a fucking autopsy." He's snappish, but that's understandable, considering.

"Shit." I rub my fingers across my lips. "But we don't know who he is yet?"

"No, he's been stripped of his clothes, and doesn't have any ID on him."

"Why would someone strip him?"

"How the fuck should I know, Dom? I just found out about this seconds ago. I need to get to security and make sure we elevate the threat level and lock shit down if need be."

Immediately, my thoughts go to Mackenzie and the others. What are they doing right now? I think Kirill is in the gym, so I hope Mackenzie is hanging out with Tino somewhere. They need to know if something's going on.

I take my phone out of my pocket and call Tino first. He doesn't answer. "Fuck," I mutter to myself.

My dad has already stepped out of the room, but I can hear him barking orders to people. There is no world where a body being discovered doesn't mean bad news.

I try Mackenzie next, but, just like with Tino, the call

clicks to voicemail.

Damn it. If they're too busy to answer the phone, it probably means they're fucking. I'll kill them. Not because they're fucking, but because now I'm frightened for them, and they're too distracted by each other to ease my fears.

I try Kirill next.

He answers almost right away. "What's up?"

He's breathing hard, and there's the clank of weights being lifted in the background. Music plays tinnily.

"Do you know where Mackenzie and Tino are?"

"I think Mackenzie went to her room. She was going to do some yoga practice."

"And Tino?"

"No idea. Sorry. What's going on? You sound worried." Now he sounds worried too.

"I'm not sure, but the college is possibly going into lockdown. There's been a body found on the side of the road outside of the grounds."

"Shit. What does that mean?"

I glance toward the room my dad is in. "Not sure, but it's not good. I want to make sure everyone is safe. I'm with my dad now, and he's trying to find out what the fuck is going on."

"Okay, you keep your ear to the ground. I'll go and find Mackenzie."

"I can go. She's only a couple of doors down."

"No, you ought to stay by your dad's side so you can keep tabs on what the fuck is going on."

I growl a little under my breath but then sigh. He's right. "I suppose so."

"I'll make sure she's safe."

"And make sure Tino is, too," I add.

I don't know what any of this means, but I want to make sure the people I care about most in the world are safe.

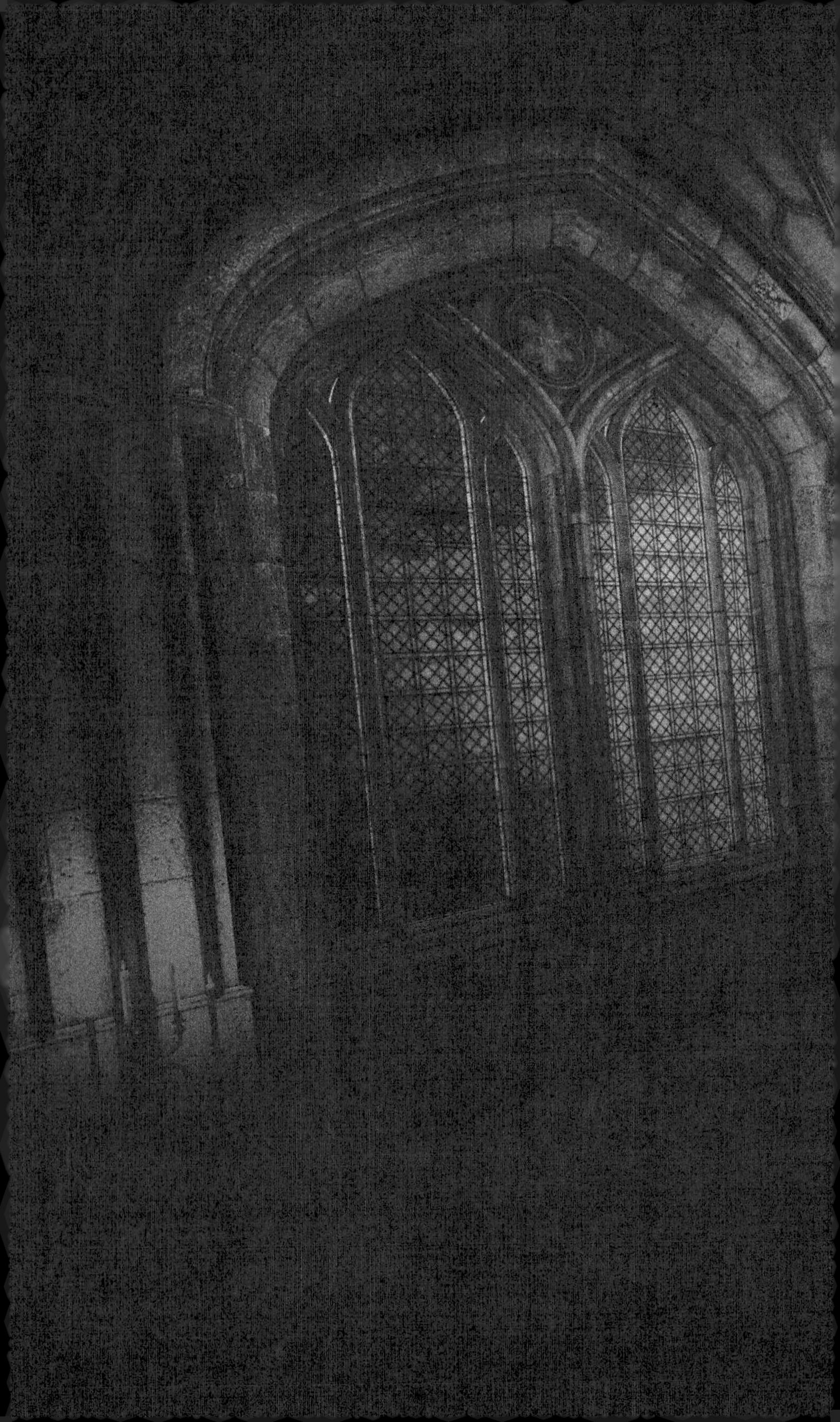

Thirty
Kirill

I return the weights and use a small towel to wipe the sweat away from the back of my neck. My muscles are burning, and I swing my arms and pull my shoulder blades together, trying to ease the tightness.

Should I be worried about what Dom's told me?

Maybe the body isn't even connected to the college. I admit, that would be surprising, but it's still possible.

Even if the body is connected to the college, it doesn't mean it's got anything to do with us four. There are plenty of people in this place who are just asking for trouble. I think of Insane Zane returning and wonder if the body has something to do with him. It wouldn't be the first time the discovery of a dead person has been linked to him. When that girl 'fell' from the tower last year, everyone looked in his direction.

I leave the gym and move at a fast jog through the university. Dom said the place is on lockdown, but there's no sign of fear or panic in anyone I pass. Everyone is acting normally. I assume it's only the security guards who've been told about the body. Nataniele wouldn't want to start a riot.

I try Mackenzie's cell phone, but it goes straight through

to voicemail. She often puts her phone on 'do not disturb' when she's doing yoga flows. She needs to focus. I try not to let it worry me that she's not answering, but after what we've both recently been through, it's hard not to let those tendrils of fear wind into my heart.

I reach her room and bang on the door. "Mackenzie? You in there?"

No response comes, so I knock again. She might still be practicing and is now cursing my interruption. I'm not getting any sense of there being life behind the door, though. Doesn't Domenic have a key? Maybe I ought to go ask him for it. I don't want to disturb him and his dad when they're coordinating things, but I need to get in her room.

One of the other members of South House walks down the hallway toward me.

"Hey, have you seen Mackenzie?" I ask her.

The girl frowns. "She was looking for her mom. I told her I saw Lucia heading to the kitchen, so she went off that way."

"Was she with Valentino?"

"No, she was alone."

"When was this?" I check, wanting all the details.

"Just now. Like literally five minutes ago."

"Okay, thanks."

I force myself to take a breath. Five minutes ago, she was fine. Nothing bad has happened to her—she's just gone to find her mom.

I keep trying to convince myself that this is no big deal, but every nerve ending is jangling on high alert. I won't rest until I have her with me and know she's safe.

My thoughts turn to the other Devils. Dom is with his dad, so I know he'll be protected, but where the fuck is Tino? Dom said he couldn't get hold of him either.

I turn from the door and follow the route Mackenzie has just taken, but I veer off when I get to the stairs. The back way is quicker, and if she set off a couple of minutes ago, she'll be at the kitchen soon.

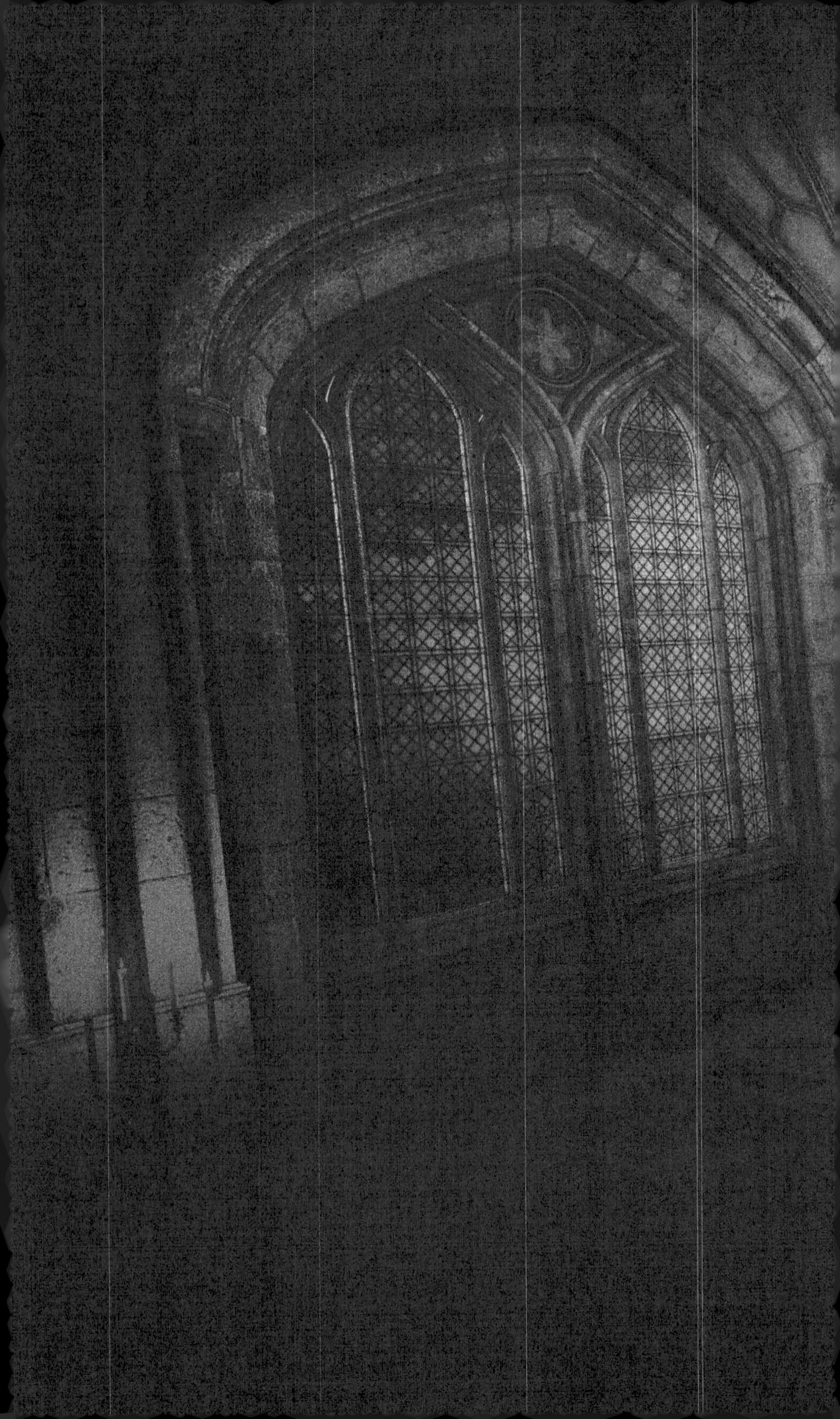

Thirty-One
Domenic

My father storms back into the room. "The body that was found is one of our drivers."

"Drivers? For what?"

"The delivery trucks."

I process this latest piece of information. "So, someone stopped one of our delivery trucks, killed the driver, and stole his uniform?"

I know we're both thinking the same thing—that whoever has done this has done it to gain access to the college. Shit.

"Do we know which truck he was driving?" I ask.

My father shakes his head. "Not yet, but I'm going down to the loading bay to see if we can figure out which one."

"What about security cameras?"

"It's not going to be much good to us if this son of a bitch is in a uniform, and it was far enough out of the college boundary not to be covered by their scope."

I remember the uniform involves a baseball cap that they're bound to have pulled down low over their face to avoid being recognized. Not that we'd know what any of the delivery drivers look like, anyway. We wouldn't know on the cameras if someone looked different than they should.

My phone rings, and I check the screen. It's Kirill.

"Yes?" I bark, aware I sound far too much like my dad.

"Apparently, Mackenzie was going down to the kitchen to find her mom," Kirill says. "I'm on my way down there now."

The kitchen. Potentially where this person would have entered.

"Let me know when you find her," I say and end the call.

I glance over at my dad. "Lucia and Mackenzie might both be down in the kitchen."

My fear is reflected in my father's eyes. He immediately swipes the screen of his cell phone and places it to his ear. He doesn't need any introducing, and I assume he's speaking to the head of the security team.

"If you see Lucia and her daughter, have them both brought up to our quarters right away." He pauses and then adds, "And don't let them give you an argument about it. Put them over your shoulder if you have to."

I almost smile at this, and I would have, if the situation weren't so serious. It's amusing that my dad is also aware that these are two women who don't appreciate being told what to do.

My phone buzzes again, and my heart jumps, hoping it's Mack. But it's Tino.

"What's up, D?" he asks, sounding way too casual. "I've had a couple of missed calls."

"Where are you? We have a possible security breach."

"Out for a run. What's going on?"

I fill him in on what we know so far.

"Fuck," he says. "I'll come inside via the back entrance, see if I can find Kenzie and her mom."

"Yes, good. Thanks. Bring them up to Nataniele's quarters if you find them."

"Will do."

I remind myself that whatever is going on might have nothing to do with Mackenzie, but I'll still feel better once I know she's safe.

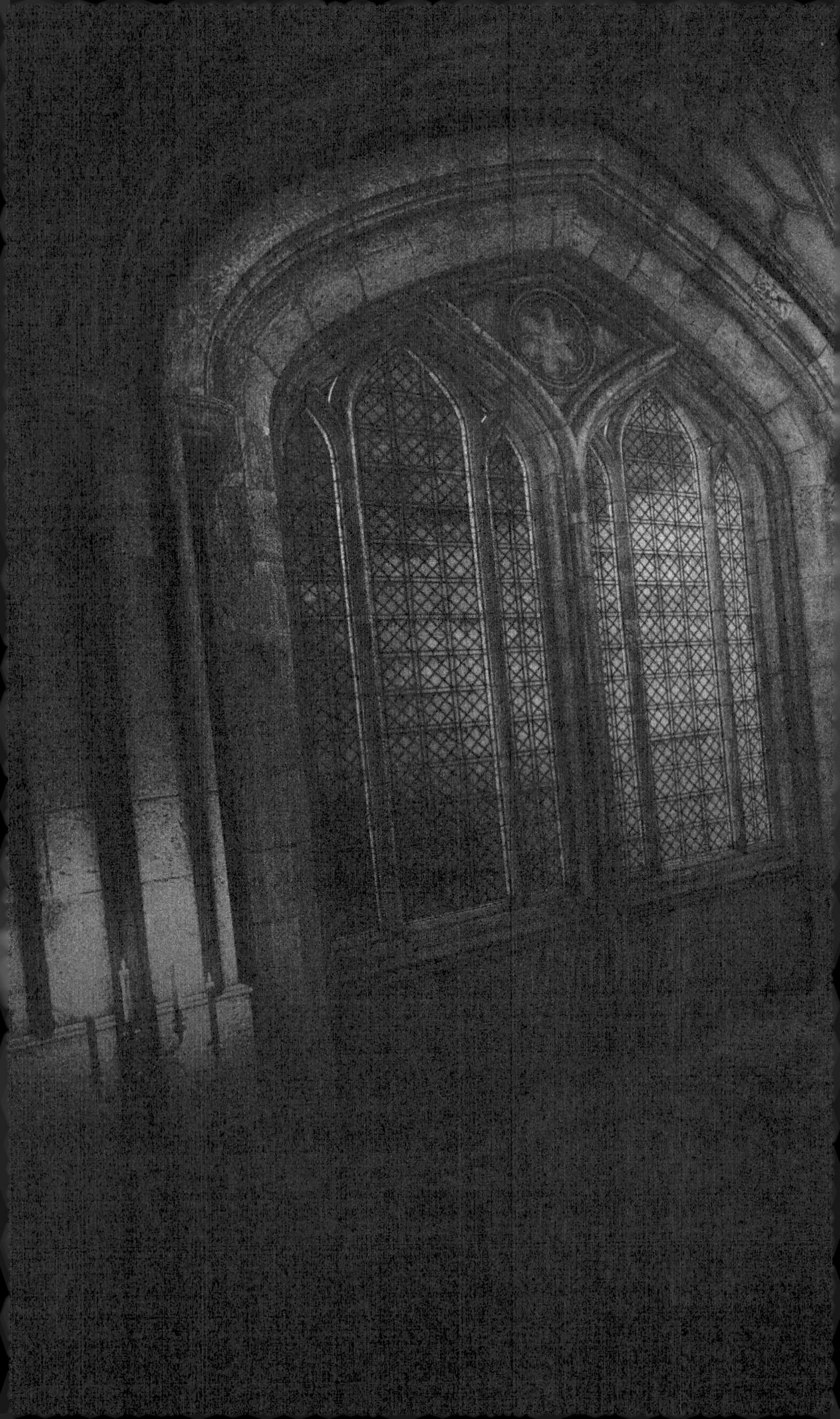

Thirty-Two

Mackenzie

Whenever I'm done with a really good yoga practice, I always feel like I'm on a bit of a high—like I've taken a muscle relaxant or had a deep tissue massage. I don't really want to be wandering through Verona Falls' hallways in search of my mom, instead of chilling on my bed, but I noticed my meds are low, and I'm going to need a refill soon. Everything medical is going through the clinic Nataniele runs, and I'm not one hundred percent sure how to access what I need. Maybe I should go and see him directly, but I'm still finding it kind of weird that he knows I'm sleeping with his son, and two of his son's friends, so I'd prefer to let my mom handle things. I sing quietly to myself as I navigate the hallways, a song stuck in my head.

My stomach gurgles, and I put my hand to my belly. I realize I'm starving, though it's only three in the afternoon, and nowhere near dinnertime yet. Maybe if I speak nicely to one of the kitchen staff, they'll let me rummage around in the refrigerator?

I find myself dreaming of a huge chicken salad baguette and a thick chocolate shake to finish it off. All this sex I've been having, combined with a new peace that's settled inside me, has given me one hell of an appetite.

I take the stairs to the first floor and exit into one of the corridors that leads to the kitchen.

Ahead of me is a delivery driver—I recognize the tan uniform and baseball cap.

What's he doing down this way? They don't normally come into the main body of the building.

He turns to face me, and I freeze, snatching a breath. For a split second, no part of me seems to work. It's like my feet are rooted to the floor, and the only thought in my head is *no-no-no-no*.

This is no delivery driver.

Paxton Kassel is standing in front of me. Everything slows as he reaches beneath his shirt and pulls out a gun. My eyes fill with tears of terror. No, it won't end like this. It can't. Not after everything we've been through. It's not fair. This cannot be happening. My hands are clammy and my breathing ragged, but I try to focus on survival and not let panic take over.

"Finally," he says. "Now I've got you."

But, as I turn to run, a deafening boom fills my ears. The blast hits me in the chest, throwing me backward, and I'm lost in a white limbo of utter disorientation.

THE DEVILS' DARLING

Thirty-Three

Tino

My ears ring, and debris rains down around me.
I have no idea what's happened. It feels like the world has ended. Fine dust coats my lips, and the world has receded to a fuzzy incompleteness. I'm completely disoriented. Am I dead? I can't move.

Trying to focus and make my scrambled awareness into something that resembles reality, I flail and come up short.

I can't quite remember where I was or what I was doing. All I'm conscious of is the ringing in my head, and the hardness of the floor beneath me.

I don't feel anything for a moment. I'm too stunned. Then I try to take a breath, and my lungs *burn*. Holy shit. What the hell? Coughing wracks me, and agony hits like a train, sending my senses reeling.

I hit my head when I was thrown, and sharp knives of pain stab into me, feeling as if they're lacerating my chest to my thigh. Christ, it's as if I'm being stabbed repeatedly. Have I broken something? Or have I been hit by whatever caused the noise? I blink my eyes open, but there's so much dust it's hard to see anything.

Beneath the ringing in my ears, I'm sure I can hear someone screaming. Another person is crying. Someone else shouts for help. A smoke alarm is sounding from somewhere in the building.

The kitchen. I was heading to the back kitchen entrance.

What's happened starts to take shape. There's been an explosion. Perhaps I could put it down to a gas leak or something, but knowing a man's body had been found shortly before the blast makes me believe this was fully intended. Some fucker has driven a bomb onto campus.

As the dust clears, I realize the external wall next to me is now a gaping hole. At least part of the reason I'm in so much pain is that the bricks and mortar that had made up the wall are now piled on top of the right half of my body. Fuck. What kind of damage has been done? I don't want to think about it, but I also know I can't just lie here. Where are the others? What was Kenzie doing when the blast happened?

That thought makes me face what I have to do. With superhuman strength and determination, I make myself move. I wrench my body, the way you do when trying to free yourself of a dream you're trapped in, and some of the rubble falls away from me.

I cry out in agony as I move again and reach to my right with my left arm, throwing the debris from me and trying to ignore the pain slicing into me with every movement. My body hurts, but it's my head that is pounding as if I have the hangover from hell, and every now and again zig-zags of lightning-like pain shoot over my skull. What the fuck?

I'm going to be screwed up again from this if I've been injured all over again, and I hope I can be as strong as I am now when the drugs call to me, whispering their lies of no pain and beautiful oblivion.

Christ, this throbbing in my head is beyond pain; it's all-consuming, making it hard to think of anything else.

Part of me wants to lie back down and let the darkness

take me so I don't have to face this, but I can't because I have to know Kenzie is safe.

Finally, I'm free of the heaviest of the shit piled on me, and I manage to sit. Blinking, I raise my hands to my face and wipe the dust from my eyes. I cough some more and then spit the foul, dry crap from my mouth.

"Tino?" The shout to my right has me turning my head to see Kirill barrel through the half-destroyed kitchen doors. He appears unharmed, though he's also covered in gray dust, and when he reaches me, he bends down and holds out his hand.

"Can you stand?"

"I can try."

"Try hard," he commands. "I just saw Mackenzie."

"What? Where?"

"From the window on the floor above. I was heading down to the kitchen, and I saw Paxton with her, and he was dragging her across the yard at the side to the converted stable blocks."

On the other side of the stable blocks is where the day staff park their cars. Is he planning on trying to drive straight through security at the gate? He could get himself and Mackenzie killed.

Shit. I have to stand. Grunting, I let Kirill drag me up as I ignore the screaming pain.

"Let's go get our girl," I say through gritted teeth.

Thirty-Four
Domenic

The boom is distant but distinct. The floor beneath my feet rumbles as if an earthquake hit, and books fall off shelves. A glass rolls from the table and smashes.

Something just fucking exploded.

I stare in shock at my father, but he's already moving.

He opens the safe and at the same time uses his other hand to place a call on his cell. "Lock it down. Everything. Students to the safe meeting point. Guards at every fucking entrance. Find out what the fuck is going on in my college." His words are snarled.

He's angry, but if I'm not mistaken, a little scared. That fact makes my stomach bottom out in dread.

Shit, I need to get out of here and find Mackenzie and my friends. This could be an all-out attack. What if it's the Bratva, vengeance for what we did in that cabin?

Would Kirill's father still have enough committed men to want to avenge his death? I'd have thought by now that his territory in Russia would be a mess as the remaining factions fought for superiority and to take over. Surely, they wouldn't have the resources or focus to not only figure out who was responsible for his death, but also take revenge. It's too much, too soon.

I pull my shoes on, fastening them hastily.

My phone buzzes, and I pick up immediately. Nataniele is pulling weapons from the safe and tossing them onto the bed. It looks like an arms convention in the room now.

"It's Paxton," Kirill growls down the line. "I'm with Tino now, but he's injured. Paxton has Mackenzie in the converted stables, across from the kitchen. I think he's heading for the staff parking lot."

"I'm on my way." I hang up and turn to face my father. "Dad, it's Paxton Kassell."

My father's face sets into a grim line of rage. "That motherfucker." He stuffs a handgun into the back of his jeans and pulls an automatic over his shoulder by the holster.

"He's got Mackenzie," I inform him.

Worry flickers across his face. "What about Lucia?"

"I'm sorry. I don't know. I've got to go."

"I'm coming." He takes a knife and sheathes it in the holster he'd strapped to his side moments earlier. He gestures at the weaponry laid out on the bed. "Take your pick, son."

I do. I select a pistol and a deadly looking knife.

We exit the door together and hit the hallway. I hide the weapons, not wanting Paxton to know I'm armed. I've already decided I'm happy to risk my life if it means saving Mackenzie.

I fucking owe her that much after what we put her through. What *I* put her through. If I'm being honest, Tino and Kirill softened up to her way before I did. Shame coats my mouth in its bitter taste. I swallow it down because now is not the time for self-indulgence.

Now is the time for me to do what is necessary to save her.

It's crazy to me that we live in a college where my father,

the fucking dean, is walking down the corridors openly armed.

The shouts of the security team, telling people to go to meeting point A, fill my ears. We all know where that is. The main gymnasium. We rehearse this shit once or twice a year, and we all have the emergency procedures in our welcome packs.

We reach the first floor, and I pass a window that gives me a view across the central courtyard toward the kitchen.

Or at least where the kitchen used to be.

Despite the urgency pushing at my back, I draw to an abrupt halt, the air punching from my lungs. I'd known it was going to be bad when I felt the walls tremble around me from the force of the explosion, but nothing had prepared me for this.

It's as though I'm looking out at a warzone.

"Oh, my God."

Thick dust still hangs in the air. People are helping each other from the rubble. There are bloodied faces, and both women and men crying. I catch sight of a pale arm poking out from beneath the rubble, but I've got no idea if there's even anyone on the end of it.

It's almost too terrible to comprehend. How can one person's actions suddenly change the course of all these people's lives? They were just getting on with their day, expecting things to be normal, and instead it's ended like this. A split second—a moment in time—and everything has changed.

"Dom!"

My father's snapped tone brings me back to focus.

"Sorry."

I tear my gaze away from the horrific scene and force my feet to move. My mind still lingers on what's happened, though.

Why did that fucker drive the van into the college and

only blow up that area? As soon as the question crosses my mind, the answer hits. *Distraction.* He wants Mack, and now we're all distracted and scared, running around like headless chickens, it gives him the chance to escape.

I call out to my father. "I know the instinct will be to have all the guards here, where they can defend us, but we need them on the exits and perimeter, too."

"Son, we can't cover the entirety of the grounds. The drones are up in the air and the dog handlers are patrolling. It's the best we can do."

I bet Paxton will aim for the woods. It's what I would do. There are trails wide enough to drive a car a fair way through, and, if he can get to the outer perimeter, it's his best chance of getting off the property with her.

We need to stop him before that can happen.

We keep going, passing frightened and confused students who are all being ushered to the meeting point. An alarm is blaring, and I wish someone would turn it off already—it's not as though we need it to know that everything has gone to shit.

I almost sag in relief when I spot Kirill and Tino in the ruins of the kitchen. Tino is glugging down water from a plastic bottle. He's covered in dust, and he winces when he moves toward me. Still, they're both here. Both alive.

"Where are they?" I demand. "Where are Paxton and Mackenzie?"

My father is distracted by the chaos going on around us. It's hard to ignore all the cries for help, but I have to if we're going to find her.

"I think we need to go after them alone," Tino says, keeping his voice low. He coughs and sips more water. "The security approaching with guns blazing could get her killed."

"Agreed," I say.

Kirill nods, and we hold one another's gaze for a long beat. We don't need to speak. We want the same thing—for

Mackenzie to make it out of this alive.

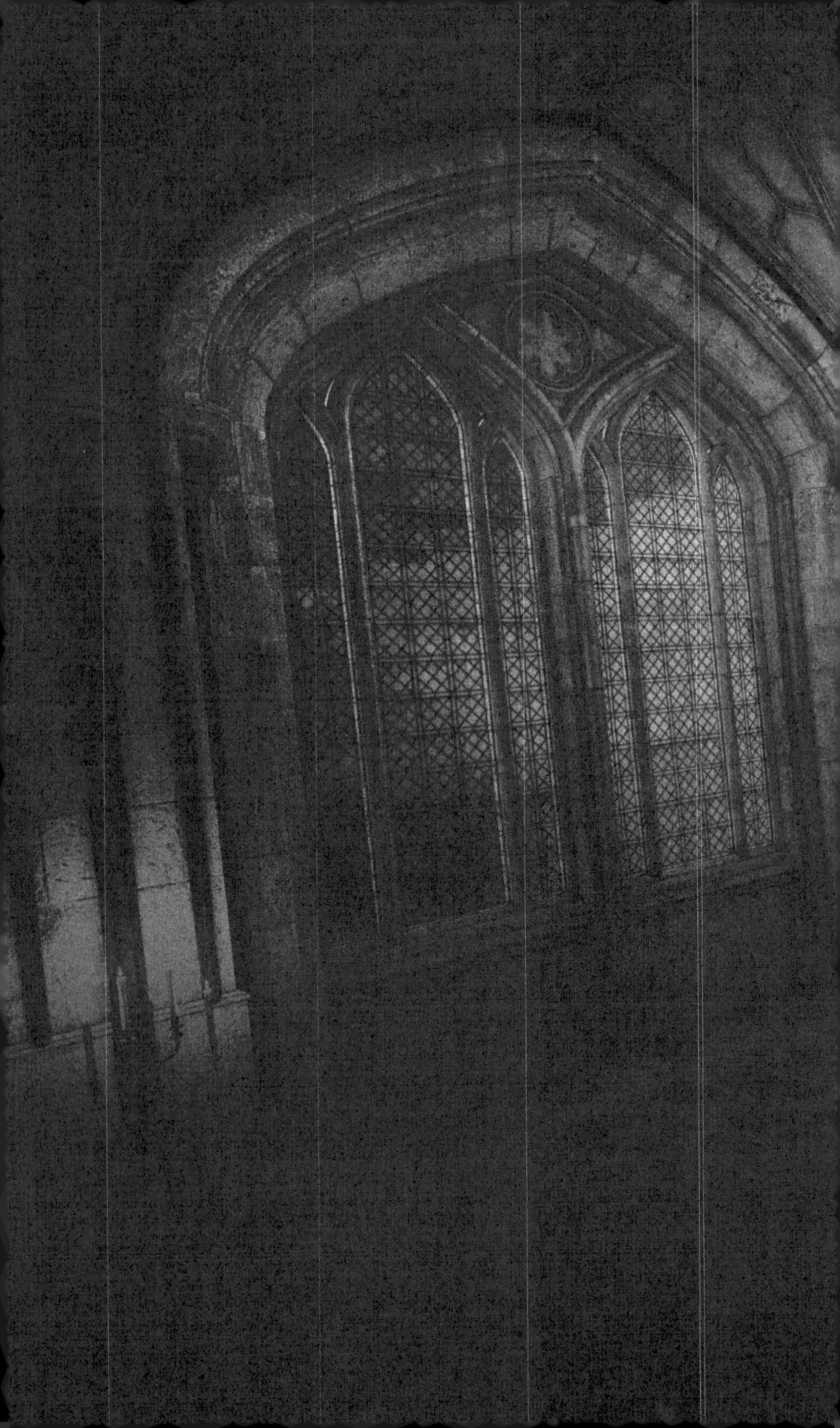

Thirty-Five
Mackenzie

The sharp point in my side reminds me not to fight. Not yet. I must choose my moment, but only when I have a chance of winning.

The moment the shock of the blast wore off, I was yanked to my feet and a deadly sharp blade was pressed against my waist. He still has the gun, but he's tucked it away. I can only assume he's decided a knife is a quieter way to kill me. If he fires a shot, he'll alert everyone to his location. Using the gun will be a last resort.

"Remember, if I push this in, I'll lacerate your liver, and you'll die in slow agony," Paxton hisses. "I don't want that. I want you with me. All you need to do, Mackenzie, for once in your fucking entitled life, is cooperate."

He thinks my life is entitled. I want to laugh at him, but I hold my thoughts inside. He's a madman. A verifiable maniac. He's just blown up a college, for fuck's sake. Not any college—a *mafia* college.

"You must know that if the guards get you, you're a dead man, right?" I slur my words slightly, my brain still struggling to catch up with everything. I'm punch drunk and a little dizzy from the blast.

He laughs. "I almost died recently. You might have heard about it. Some crazy cunt stabbed me."

I flinch at the hatred he puts into the words, but my gaze locks on the round scar on the side of his throat. It's still red and angry. He'll have that scar for life—a reminder of me every time he looks in the mirror.

No wonder he hates me.

"They say revenge is a dish best served cold, and mine, Mackenzie, my darling, is going to be like ice."

He's dragging me through the corridors, away from the half-destroyed kitchen. We reach the end, and he pushes through the side doors into a small courtyard that leads to the old stables.

I try to pull back, but he digs the knife in enough that I cry out with the pain. Wetness oozes against my t-shirt. *Oh, God, I'm bleeding.*

I put my hand down and bring it up shakily. My fingers are tipped with red.

"It's nothing," he scoffs. "A mere scratch. When I'm done with you, you'll be bleeding like that from every orifice, and then I'll leave you for dead."

I can't believe I ever thought of this man as handsome. I'd been obsessed with him once, studying every detail of his face, mesmerized by the unusual color of his gray-blue eyes. I'd dreamed of lacing my fingers through his thick auburn hair and had even 'borrowed' a t-shirt of his so I could sleep with his scent wrapped around me when we weren't together.

But he'd poisoned all of that, and now all I see is the evilness his beauty had disguised. A mask has been torn away. He doesn't care who he hurts, as long as he gets what he wants. All those poor people who'd been caught in the explosion were completely innocent in all of this.

"Paxton, please, stop this. I'm not worth losing it all over. You can go back home and resume your life. No one will know you're the one responsible for the bombing." I can't stop the bitter words that fall from my mouth next. "I'm sure you'll easily find some other young girl to hoodwink and make believe your lies."

His grip on my arm tightens, his fingers digging hard into my flesh. The blade makes itself known in my side again as he pushes that deadly tip just a tiny bit deeper.

"Shut your fucking smart mouth, bitch. I can't go back to my life because the shit storm you've caused meant people started talking, and you know what the internet is like these days. Some bitches from years back have crawled out of the woodwork, all accusing me of grooming them." He gives a bitter laugh. "They were adults, same as you. Can't groom adults—they were just weak."

I beg to differ. You can if you're in a position of power and they're young adults just starting out, but I hold my tongue this time. Getting the last word isn't worth losing my life over.

As we cross the courtyard and reach the double doors into the converted stable block that makes up the smaller gym, I glance up at the expanse of blue above my head. This might be my last chance to see the sky. If he kills me in there, or I get killed escaping, I don't want my last memories to be the sweaty, musty scent of the gym.

"Open the fucking doors." Paxton slides the blade along my side in a threat, and I do what he says, scrabbling with shaking fingers to grab the handles.

Once they're open, he pushes me through, and I stumble. But I take my chance because the knife is no longer in my side.

Pushing to my feet, I run. I race away from him, heading up the stairs. I have no idea what is up here. I recall Camile saying to me once that this space is pretty much unused these days. That doesn't matter, so long as there are things I can use as a weapon or places I can hide.

Heavy steps pound after me, but I grab a discarded chair from in front of the doors on the small landing and hurl it down at him with a scream. He staggers, swearing.

"You're fucking dead, bitch," he yells. "Fucking cunt."

I don't hang around to listen to any more, just barrel through the doors and race down the corridor. I see an empty classroom, but it's utterly deserted, nowhere to hide, and nothing to use to protect myself. Shit.

Heart pounding, I see the same through the second door. There's no rear staircase. Oh, God, I might have run myself into a dead end.

The final door I come to seems to lead to a deserted office, but there's still an old filing cabinet in there and a few pieces of furniture. I dash inside and try to push the filing cabinet in front of the door, but he's already here. He shoves it easily aside and stands in front of me, chest heaving.

He's staring at me, the bloody tipped knife in his hand, and a cold sense of dread washes over me.

But then he smiles. The maniac *smiles*. "You always were *almost* more trouble than you're worth," he says. "*Almost,* but not quite." His grin widens. "You're such an epic fuck that all the crap that comes with it makes the pain worthwhile. I am going to fuck that pussy raw when I get you home."

He backs me against the wall and pushes the knife against my throat. "Just one quick feel. I bet you're wet."

He shoves his fingers down my waistband and into my panties. I balk at the feel of his cold, hard fingers probing at me. My brain wants to check out, while my body wants to vomit. He pushes a finger inside me, and I whimper with dismay. Is this where he's going to rape me? I flush with heat, and then cold. I want to fight—to punch and kick and scream—but I'm frozen in place with the knife at my throat. The room swims around me as tears well, and I squeeze my eyes shut, blocking out my attacker's face.

He thrusts his fingers in and out of my pussy a couple of times, and I cry out with pain.

Paxton gives a growl of annoyance, and, to my surprise, pulls his fingers free of me, and slides his hand back out of my pants. I dare to open my eyes, only to find him frowning at me.

"You gone frigid on me, Mackenzie? You were always such a slut for it. Even when you said you weren't in the mood, this pussy would be dripping."

I hold his stare. "I don't find being threatened with death erotic, asshole."

"Oh, well, it's of no matter. I'll fuck you dry if that's the way it is going to be. It won't hurt me, but it *will* hurt you."

He caresses the artery in my neck with the knife. "Are you going to be a good girl now?" he demands. "No more games? If you try to run again. I'll disfigure this pretty face. Don't think I won't."

I nod and blink rapidly, trying to stop the tears from falling.

"Good girl. Let's go."

He pulls me out of the room, back along the corridor, and down the stairs. When we hit the small gym, he drags me across the space behind him, my shoes squeaking against the floor. I realize with a sick jolt that he's heading for the cars that are parked around the back of this outbuilding. No one will see us there. He can steal a car, put me in it, and try to get out of here.

He pulls the ballcap low on his head before he reaches into his back pocket. He takes out zip ties and makes quick work of tying my hands behind my back. The roll of gray tape he slaps over my mouth next is thick. It cuts off any noise I might make.

"It's not for long, darling, promise. Can't risk you alerting anyone to your presence as I try to get us out of here."

The place is under lockdown. No one is going to let him out. They'll search the car. Crap, they might shoot at the car, and then I could end up dead. If he puts me in the trunk and a stray bullet hits, it could kill me.

I pull back as he tugs me toward the door. He growls and throws me forward so hard I go down on my knees on the wooden floor. Pain slams through my joints, and a wave of sickness rushes over me. I swallow it down as best as I can because if I'm sick, I risk choking.

"There's a gap in the fence line that I've spent a long time making under the cover of darkness. It's through the woods." Paxton drags me up by my hair, and white shards of pain spear through my scalp. I scream against the thick tape, though the sound is muffled. "I can get us close in the car, but then you'll have to run. You slow me down on purpose and I'll carve my fucking initials in your face. Understood?"

I nod, and he laughs.

"Good girl. It's amazing how well behaved you can be, when truly incentivized."

He bursts out of the doors, dragging me with him, and stops.

Facing us, with no obvious weapon and his hands up in the air, is Kirill.

Thirty-Six
Kirill

I hold Paxton's gaze, even though I'm dying to look at Mackenzie and make sure she's unharmed. I can't take my eyes off this motherfucker for a second, though. I can see her in my peripheral vision, gagged, but standing on her own two feet. There's the glint of a knife digging into her side.

"Get out of my fucking way." Paxton pushes the knife farther into her ribs. "I'll gut her like a pig in front of you if you don't."

"You can't get out of here," I tell the son of a bitch. "There are drones up. Dogs who have your scent."

He laughs. "Nice try, but they don't have my scent."

"They do. When we knew you'd be a threat to Mackenzie, the college dean got his men to take a piece of your clothing from your apartment. The dogs have your scent. They'll rip you limb from limb if their handlers give the word."

"I'm taking a car, so no, they won't. Now, move aside."

"You can't drive out of here except by the main exit and entrance roads, and they're heavily armed," I say, keeping my tone level. "You have to go on foot some of the way. The dogs will catch you and tear you apart."

"Well, she'll be attacked, too." Paxton sneers. "So that's fine by me."

"No, she won't. They're highly trained. Why don't you just let her go? You can walk out of here if you do."

"*Sure,* I can." Paxton's words are loaded with sarcasm. "Who the fuck are you, anyway, to have any say in what happens to me?"

"He's one of the Devils," Tino says as he approaches from our left, also with his hands visible.

Dom isn't anywhere to be seen.

"Oooh, scary name. Am I supposed to cower in terror?" Paxton gives a shrill, overly loud laugh.

I wince at the sound because it isn't the sound of a well-adjusted man. He's unraveling. Already was when he drove a damn bomb onto the campus, but the longer this goes on, the worse he gets. That knife sticking in her side will only need a few millimeters more to end our Duchess.

"I'll drive you out of here myself," I say. "Right through the main gates."

"I don't think you get it. If I don't get to keep her, no one does."

I force a laugh. "She's not that special." The words stick in my throat, but I have to say them and try to get him to move away from her so I can take him down. "Plenty of fresh pussy out there."

"Yeah," Tino joins in. "What if we give you safe passage and throw some money into the equation, too?"

Paxton's gaze flicks between us. "She's special to me because she ruined my life. We're in a pact now, me and her. We either die together, or I ruin her fucking life in return. There can be no other outcome. Now I can see you're in love with her." He laughs at me when I start to shake my head. "Don't deny it, blondie. It's written all over your stupid face. I know if I push this knife deeper into her side, slicing through arteries as it goes and signing her death warrant, you'll kill me. Guess what? I. Don't. Fucking. Care. All I care about is making this cunt pay."

He pushes the knife a touch deeper, and Mackenzie sobs, the sound muffled and pitiful.

Loud buzzing comes from overhead, and a shadow falls on Paxton. He glances up, and, as he does, the knife in his hand lifts away from her side.

It's the moment I need. I take that split second of distraction and use it to throw myself into them, taking Mackenzie with me as I hit the ground.

"I've got you," I whisper to her.

I wrap her in my arms as the bullets start to fly.

Thirty-Seven

Domenic

The moment the drone distracts Paxton, I drop the controller. I rush toward him as Kirill takes Mack to the ground. Paxton is fast, though. He drops, rolls, and faces me. He has a gun held with both hands, and he pulls the trigger.

The crack of the gunshot is so loud it hurts my ears, and I feel the movement of air beside my cheek as the bullet passes dangerously close.

He misses, though, clearly not used to handling a gun, so he doesn't calibrate for the kick-back of the weapon when it fires.

Tino pulls his own gun from the waistband of his jeans and fires at Paxton, but he somehow misses, too. Fucking hell. That's not like him. But then I realize just how hurt he was in the blast. He's been pushing through for Mackenzie's sake, but he's barely standing.

Paxton goes to shoot again, but I'm already on top of him. I stomp on Paxton's wrist, forcing his hand to open, and kick the weapon out of his grip. It lands several yards away. He screams, his hand curling in on itself.

I draw the knife I had stashed in my waistband, covered

by my t-shirt.

I straddle him, my knees on his arms as he howls in outrage. He kicks and tries to throw me off, but I stay on him, riding him as if he's a bucking bronco. I raise my arm and bring the blade of the knife down hard into his shoulder. Metal punctures skin and flesh. He screams again, in agony, as I pull the blade free, and then stab his side, into his ribs.

I could kill him instantly by putting this blade straight through his heart, but I want this fucker to suffer.

Climbing off him, I turn to Tino. "Want a turn?"

He shakes his head, and I shrug and raise the knife again.

Kirill stands, his arm around Mackenzie.

I pause and look over at her. I'm aware I must look crazy. Knife in hand, sweating, blood all over me, but I want her permission.

In this moment, it's her decision whether this fucker lives or dies. If he lives, he'll be spending the rest of his life in a cell, but he will always be a danger to her, and I'd much rather he die. Even if I don't end him right now, I'm pretty sure my father will. The man has injured and killed some of our staff. No way will he be allowed to live.

No, he's ending up in a grave one way or another, but it's up to Mackenzie if I put him there.

It's not as if the police will go overboard looking for him, either. We can see to that.

She walks over to me and stares down at the professor.

"You know you said you were going to fuck me in every orifice until I bled? Well, now I'm going to let Dom make *you* bleed. I hope he takes his time and treats you like a pincushion. You're a sick man."

"Do you want to watch, my Duchess?" I ask her with a smile.

"No." She shakes her head. "I want to go and sit down. I'm dizzy."

"Come on." Kirill takes her hand and leads her away.

I raise the knife and bring it back down, relishing Paxton's bloodcurdling screams.

My mind goes far away as I stab him repeatedly and, eventually, a weight on my shoulder stops me. "He's gone, Dom. It's over."

I glance over my shoulder to see Tino with his hand on me.

"Come on. Let's get the wet work crew in," he says. "Call your dad. He can sort it."

I stand, shaky as fuck now that the adrenaline is wearing off.

"Where's Duchess?" I say.

"She's safe. She's with Kirill. Are you okay?" Tino looks worried.

"You're asking me? You're the one who declined to take a turn." I jerk my chin at the blood-covered, pulpy mess that is all that's left of Paxton. Christ, I really did lose it.

"I can't focus properly. My eyesight is blurry," Tino says.

Worry flickers through me. What the hell?

"Were you knocked out by the blast?"

"For a short period, yeah, I think so." He touches his head and winces.

"You've probably got a concussion. I wondered how the hell you managed to miss when you fired at him."

He looks down at the body. "Christ, Dom, remind me never to get on your wrong side."

I laugh at that, and he does too. He slings his arm over my shoulder and, both laughing, almost to the point of hysteria, we walk in the direction Kirill took Mackenzie.

"We nearly lost her again, Tino," I say as the laughter subsides.

"I know, but we didn't."

"There are still people out there who mean harm to

her and her mother. She's not going to be safe outside these walls."

"Then we don't let her leave." Tino turns to me and holds my gaze.

"Are you saying we all stay here forever?"

He shrugs. "I mean, forever is a long time, but there's no reason we need to leave as soon as we've graduated, is there? I have the compound, but I doubt our Duchess will want to live there. Kirill has nothing much left in the way of security to offer her now. You've got all this."

He waves an arm around.

I stare up at the gothic spires of the college looming over us. It's been a place I've known as home for a long time. I was home schooled within these walls and then started my degree education here. I always thought I'd be leaving soon, until a girl who looked like a doll and acted like a stuck-up aristocrat showed up here and turned my world upside down.

"We need to beef up security moving forward if we do decide to stay awhile. It's tight, but not tight enough if that fucker got in."

"I've been thinking about that," he says. "It will be costly, but what about biometric security for everyone? No one, not even food delivery, gets on the property unless they are in the database."

"I'll talk to my father."

Shit, are we really doing this? Staying here?

"We can't keep living in our rooms, though, so how about we move into the den?" Tino suggests.

It makes sense.

"I'll ask him about that, too. I'd like for us all to be together."

"Not the worst place in the world to stay," he says with a shrug. "I mean, it's all going to be yours one day, right?"

He's not wrong there.

THE DEVILS' DARLING

Thirty-Eight
Mackenzie

Kirill helps me back toward the main college building.

Paxton Kassell is finally dead. He can't hurt me anymore. But the destruction he's wreaked continues to play on as the survivors of the blast try to help those who've been injured.

The authorities will be here soon. Police, and firefighters, and paramedics. They'll take charge, or perhaps not. I'm not sure how much leeway Nataniele will give them and how much they will demand. This is no ordinary college, and while he can't keep the emergency services out when an attack this large has happened, I expect Nataniele will want control of it. He'll vet who comes in because having the place crawling with personnel who might gossip about what goes on here would be a disaster.

The cleanup alone will be arduous. Then we'll have to rebuild.

I could probably use a paramedic myself. The cut in my side isn't deep, but it's still bleeding and hurts like a bitch. I'm worried about Tino as well. He was obviously injured in the bombing, and he needs medical help, too.

As we get closer, I can still hear people crying for help.

My heart tightens in my chest. My God, those poor people.

I glance up to Kirill. "We should help."

He shakes his head. "No, you need to sit down. You said you were dizzy, and you're bleeding."

"I'm okay. I'd rather put myself to use. People need us, Kirill."

Tears mist my vision. These people are hurt because of *me*. Paxton would never have come if I weren't here, and everyone who'd been hurt or worse would still be going about their day. I can't believe how utterly crazy he clearly was and must have been the entire time I was seeing him, except I missed it. Only at the very end did I get a clue, and even then, I had no inkling he'd be the kind of person to commit an attack like this. Depending on how many people are dead and injured, a man I shared a bed with, let inside me, is a mass murderer. The thought makes me want to vomit.

How can I have gotten him so very wrong? I tell myself I was young and naïve, but my God, I'm barely older now, and what if I'm still the same, naïve girl, unable to judge character? I glance at Kirill, wondering what he'd do if he thought he was going to lose me. I have to start standing up for myself and what I believe in.

"I'm not leaving here without helping." I hold Kirill's gaze.

His expression tightens, and he's probably thinking about how Domenic will lose his shit at letting me back into this chaos, but he knows I'm right.

"Okay, but not for long. As soon as the authorities turn up, we leave them to it."

I nod once. "Deal."

But as we get toward what remains of the door, Nataniele appears. His shoulders are hunched, his head down. He sees me, and instead of being pleased I'm safe or even asking after his son, his features contort with pain.

He puts out a hand. "Mackenzie, stop. You can't go that

way."

I draw to a halt, Kirill's arm still around me. "Why not? I want to help."

"No, you don't need to. We've got it in hand."

"What are you talking about? I can hear people crying. If there's anything I can do..."

He snaps at me. "You can't. Okay? I already told you no."

But there's something about the stiffness of his expression and the shine of his eyes that alerts me. His eye contact is too intense. Something has happened—something terrible.

I suddenly remember my reason for coming down to the kitchen in the first place.

"Where's Mom?" I demand.

"Mackenzie, please..."

My tone rises in pitch. "Where is she? Is she hurt? Have you seen her?"

He closes his eyes briefly.

I shove past him. He tries to grab for me, but I shake him off.

"You're going to need to take care of your girlfriend," I hear him tell Kirill.

Kirill sounds worried. "Why? What's happened?"

But I barely hear him. I'm already in the middle of the remains of the kitchen, picking my way through the rubble and debris. My heart is beating so fast I think it might explode. I scan the twisted metal and crumbled stones, desperately hoping I'm wrong.

I draw to a halt and suck in a breath. When I release it again, it's with a cry of anguish.

"No!"

The scream tears from my lips, and I drop to my knees.

My mom's body is half buried beneath the rubble. Her blue eyes are glassy and unseeing. Blood trickles in rivulets from her ears and nostrils. Her face is impossibly pale. That goddamned dust clings to her eyelashes and settles on her skin.

The sounds peeling from my throat are raw and primal. "Mom? Mommy? No, please, you can't be gone."

I don't want to believe it. She can't be dead; she just can't be. There must be something we can do. My brain refuses to compute the possibility that this is real. I must be trapped in a nightmare, and any minute now I'm going to wake up.

But nothing changes.

"I need you," I sob. "I still need you."

Grief tears me in two. I desperately wish for some way I can go back in time and change what's happened, but that's impossible.

Paxton did this. But he did it because of me. Which makes my mother's death my fault. I'm a walking, talking angel of death, and all I attract is violence and chaos. Part of me wants to run away and hide forever, deep in some deserted forest where I won't be able to bring my toxicity to the world ever again.

I feel like all the strength has gone out of my body, my muscles have been drained of any power, my bones broken, my veins emptied of blood. I'm a shell of a person.

Hands try to hold me up, to offer me comfort, but I fight them off.

"No, leave me alone!"

It's Nataniele. "Mackenzie, you can't stay here. She's gone."

I fold in half, pressing my forehead to her chest, sheltering her with my body. I cry and scream and rock back and forth, utterly lost in my grief. I don't care about anyone or anything, only that I'm alone in the world now.

I touch her face and try to see any recognition in her eyes. Can I bring life back to her? Give her my own breath?

I would if I could.

Kirill's with Nataniele now, trying to help me up. "Come on, my love. Let us help you, please, Mackenzie."

But I ignore them both.

I scream and wail, as though my pain is a physical thing inside me that's trying to escape through my mouth. For a while, I think I genuinely lose it. My brain won't comprehend the reason for my grief, but my heart knows and is breaking.

Somewhere in the distance, I hear sirens.

I lost my dad, and now I've lost my mom too. I'm an orphan. What will happen to me now? The only reason I was ever tolerated here was because of my mom's relationship with Nataniele. Now she's gone, what will happen to me?

How had I left things with her? What were the final words I'd ever spoken to her? Had we fought? Had I told her I loved her? Did she know?

Our relationship had been fractious recently, more so than at any other time in our lives. We'd always been so close—more best friends than mother and daughter—but since coming to Verona Falls, things had been different. Revelations had been made, and I'd seen her in a different light—not one that I'd liked. But she'd still been my mom, and I'd loved her more than anything. I'd give anything to see her one last time, to tell her I loved her, and I was sorry for all the horrible things I might have said to her recently. I wished I hadn't caused her so many problems, and I'd made her life a little more peaceful.

If it hadn't been for my illness, we might never have found ourselves in any of this mess to begin with. If it hadn't been for my weakness and always searching for love and acceptance, I'd never have met Paxton, and Mom would be alive.

"The paramedics are here, Mackenzie," Nataniele says. "She can't stay here. They need to take her."

"No! Don't touch her! Don't touch her."

I know if they take her away, I'll never see her again.

He's got tears streaming down his face, and somehow, that makes everything even worse. That a tough guy like Nataniele is crying means it's real. She's not coming back. Nothing can change what's happened.

It's as though I've lost a part of me.

Dom is here now, though I have no idea when he arrived. He's covered in blood, but then so are lots of people after the explosion so no one asks where it's from.

Between Dom and Kirill, they pull me to my feet. My legs won't work, and I sag against them. They sandwich me between them, wrapping me in their bodies, trying to shield me from all the hurt and pain, but their efforts will never be enough. I'm distraught, crying and screaming against them. Their solid strength stops me from hurting myself, like they're trying to crush the anger and pain out of me.

A tiny part of me is aware that Tino isn't with them. He got hurt during the explosion, and paramedics are looking after him. I know I should check on him, to offer him some comfort, but I just don't have it in me. Dom and Kirill will look out for him. He's got his brothers, the other Devils. He doesn't need me as well.

All the fight goes out of me.

Dom bends slightly and scoops me up like I'm a child, holding me against his chest. I wrap my arms around his neck and bury my face in his shoulder. I don't even care if I get Paxton's blood on me. My cries have softened to sobbing now, and still the tears come.

"I can't leave her," I whisper.

"Trust me, baby," he says, "you don't want to see them carry her out of here. We can go and see her later, if you want, but for now, let's get you upstairs. Please."

"I don't want Mom to be alone," I sob.

"She won't be alone," Nataniele says. "I'll stay with her. Mackenzie, please, you look as white as a sheet, and you've been injured. Let the paramedics look at you, and I promise, I won't leave Lucia's side."

He bends down and takes her hand, his thumb brushing over her skin.

A new respect for this man blooms in me. "Okay," I whisper to Dom. "Okay."

The tears fall as I let him hold me to his chest.

"We'll get one of the paramedics to come up to the room," he says. "They can look you over up there."

He carries me away from the chaos and my mom's body, through the college, and up to our rooms.

We pass Nataniele's quarters, and the idea that my mom will never go into those rooms again enters my head and starts the tears flowing faster. I feel as if I'll never stop crying. Never smile again. Nothing seems real. This *can't* be real.

He lets us into my room—I don't even question why he has a key—and carries me over to the bed.

Kirill brings me a glass of water, and I sip at it shakily before pushing it away. I don't want it. I don't want anything other than to bring my mom back.

I curl onto my side and cry hopelessly into my pillow, until eventually a paramedic comes. I'm only distantly aware of him checking me over. I'm barely present as I go through the motions, allowing him to clean and dress my wound.

"I can give her something to help her sleep," I hear him say to Dom and Kirill.

"Yes, I think that will be a good idea," Dom replies.

They maneuver me again, this time to sit me up and get me to take some pills. I swallow them down like a good little puppet, and then lie back down. I just want them to leave me alone with my grief. I'm sure it will swallow me whole. That they'll come back one day to find I've just vanished, sunken into myself and become nothing, like an imploding star.

Thirty-Nine
Domenic

I'm worried about Mackenzie. It's been weeks now since her mom died, and she's barely gotten out of bed.

I'm worried about Valentino, too. Because of his injuries from the blast, he's been put on some pretty heavy meds. He's been sleeping more than usual, which is understandable, but even when he's awake, he's withdrawn.

They ended up taking him to the hospital for x-rays and scans. He has a fractured skull from the blast and a mild concussion. They said time will mend things for him, but he'll need analgesics while he's healing, and that's a worry.

He's withdrawn from us all, just adding to the rift that is slowly splitting us apart.

Kirill and I sit in the den, a somber mood hanging over us. We don't really know what to do with ourselves. Regular lessons have been cancelled because of the bombing and the investigation that followed. It's ironic that the attack on us wasn't from within our world, but, because of the college and the nature of the student body, it's caused a massive headache for my father and the other senior staff members when dealing with the authorities.

We were given work to do online, but none of us have bothered to do it. It's as though we're still shellshocked that something like this can have happened, and fearful of it happening again. Of course, I know it won't. I killed Paxton with my own hands, but, in our business, there's always going to be danger lurking around the corner.

I've been curling up in bed with Mackenzie at night, slipping into her room while she's sleeping and wrapping myself around her. I know she's been having nightmares about everything that's happened, and when her body tenses in my arms and she starts to whimper, I hold her tighter and stroke her hair until they ease.

I admit that being so close to her without anything physical happening between us has been hard. I have the bluest of balls that have only been kept at bay by watching the video footage I have of Mackenzie and looking at her dirty photographs, while masturbating like a teenager. Only a month ago, I'd probably have just fingered Mack while she slept and come in her panties, but I'm a changed man...well, maybe not changed, but slightly better adjusted.

Though the need to cut myself has been strong, I've been stronger. It's an addiction I've had to fight, and I've fought it for her. She needs me now, and I refuse to wallow in self-pity, as tempting as it is. Instead of giving in to a blade, I've taken myself out on a run, pounding the trails around the college.

It's not been easy, but it's worth it. She's my priority now.

Kirill sometimes sits with Mackenzie in the day, and I've heard them talking, their voices low and sad. They both have recently lost a parent, and they were both trapped down in that basement and went through hell, so, on those occasions, I leave them to talk, not wanting to interrupt. It's never for long, anyway, and when I ask Kirill if he feels there's been any breakthrough, he always shakes his head.

Mackenzie blames herself for everything that's happened, and nothing we do or say seems to get through to her.

"Fuck," Kirill suddenly says.

I jump at the curse.

"What?"

"I just remembered it's your birthday tomorrow."

"Oh, yeah." I shrug. "Not that it matters."

"Of course it matters, D. Why would it not?"

"You think Mackenzie and Tino are going to want to celebrate? Tino might, if I promise him a belly full of booze and drugs, but Mackenzie isn't going to be interested."

"She might be," he presses. "We should at least tell her. She probably doesn't know what day it is."

I scrub my hands over my face. "You just want an excuse to see her."

He pouts and adjusts his nose ring. "Maybe. And what's so wrong with that?"

He's right. There isn't anything wrong with it. "Just don't pressure her into partying, okay? She's got way more important things on her mind."

"Maybe she'll appreciate having a distraction."

I cock an eyebrow. "A distraction from her mom dying? I think it's going to take something a bit more important than me turning twenty-two."

My dad's been grieving, too, and I almost feel guilty about it. I'd doubted his feelings toward Lucia had been real, but they clearly were. The clean-up after the bombing and the investigations have kept him busy, but he's a shell of a man. He's lost two women he loved in the space of a year, and it's done a number on him. I keep putting myself in his place, imagining we'd lost Mackenzie instead of her mom, and find myself with unaccustomed sympathy toward him.

Kirill gets to his feet and puts his hand out to me to pull me up.

"Maybe," he says, "but sometimes it's good to have something that's just for fun."

I exhale and take his hand. It's warm and dry and solid, and he yanks me to my feet. Sometimes I forget how much Kirill has been through. His dad died recently as well, but it's different for him. Grigoriy was a bastard who tormented Kirill his entire life, and while I'm sure Kirill has mixed emotions about the man's death, I'm fairly sure one of those emotions is relief.

"Fine," I relent, "but if she's not interested, we don't push her, okay? I don't want her feeling bad because she doesn't want to celebrate my dumb-ass birthday."

"She will. She loves you," he reassures me.

I smack him on the shoulder. "Thanks, dude. She loves you, too."

He nods. "Yeah, she's just a little caught up in her own shit right now. We have to make sure she knows we're still here for her, whenever she's ready."

THE DEVILS' DARLING

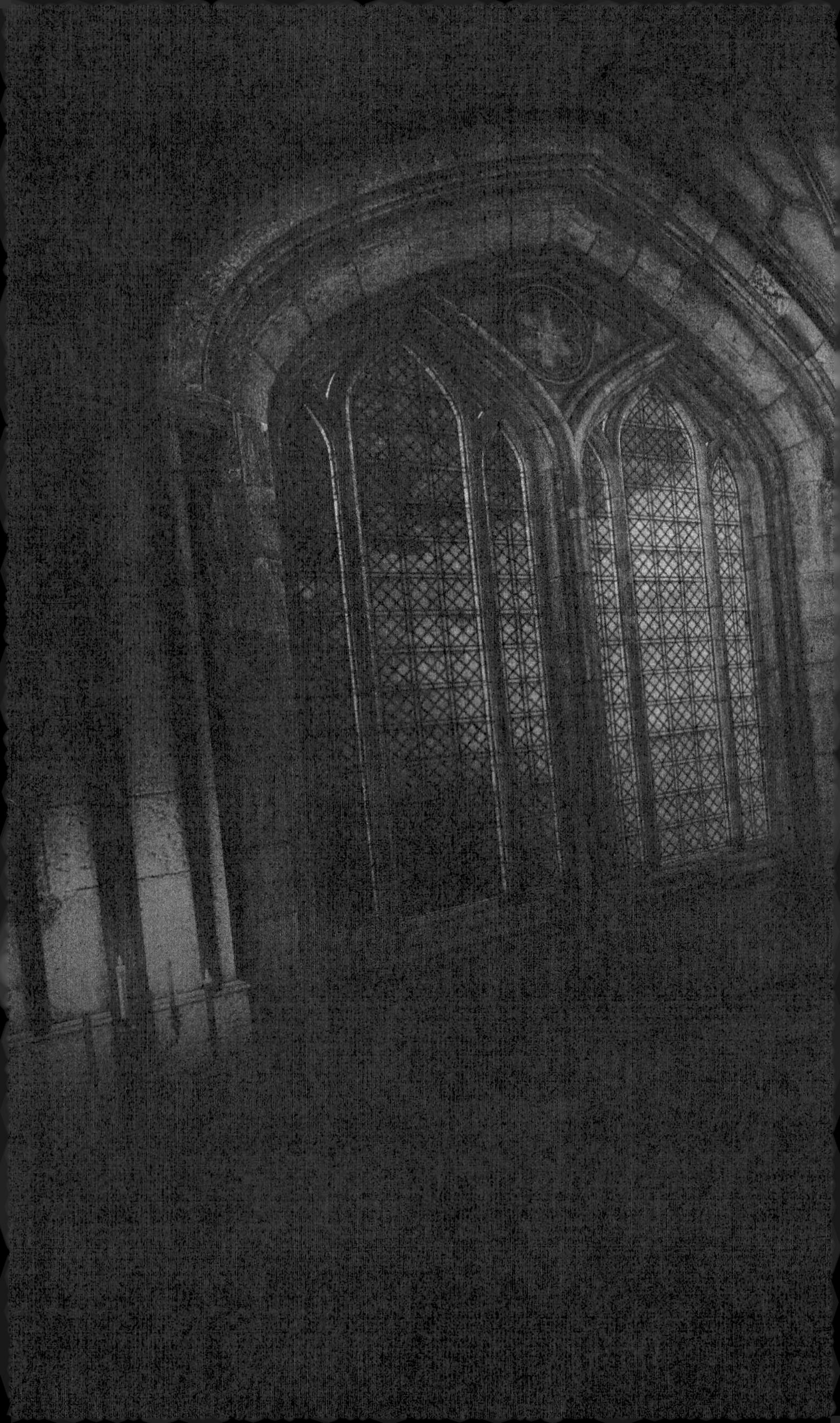

Forty
Mackenzie

I lose track of time. I lie in my bed, curled up on my side, crying against my pillow. I drift into sleep, still crying, and then when I wake and it all comes back to me, the tears start again.

Flashbacks haunt me. Seeing my mother in that pile of rubble. Or Nataniele taking her lifeless hand. Or, worst of all, the funeral. I was so out of it, medicated to get me through it. I had to pick music, and I don't know if I chose right. The church had been full of flowers because that's the only thing I was certain of. I wanted it to be beautiful for her. The way she was when she was alive.

I never knew it was possible to cry so much without eventually running dry.

The guys do their best to look after me, but I'm closed off from the world. They bring me food and drinks and help me sit up while they force tiny sips past my lips and morsels onto my tongue. They ensure I take my meds, too, though a part of me—the self-destructive side—doesn't want to. I want my physical body to break down in the same way my heart has. The only thing that stops me is knowing how hard my mom worked to keep my epilepsy at bay. My condition was the sole focus of her life for such a long time, and it's also at least partly why my parents ended up in so much debt. To give up now feels too much like I'm ignoring their sacrifice.

Camile has come to see me, too, but I can tell she's frustrated by my lack of interaction. She wants me to shake myself out of it and come to the bar and hang out, but it's the last thing I want. I've been on the phone to Lola, too, and told her what's happened. She knew my mom, so she was upset as well. She tried to convince me to return home, but how can I? There's nothing there for me now.

Sleep feels like my only escape, but I'm plagued with nightmares. All the terrible things I've gone through come back to haunt me—Paxton and Grigoriy and my dead parents. I dream my mom and dad are in cahoots with those two evil men, and my heart breaks over and over as they conspire to hurt me. I know Dom sneaks into my room at night to hold me, and though a part of me wants to be left alone, I also appreciate his presence. I think he knows what I need better than I do.

A knock comes at my door, and then it opens. For one crazy moment, I think I'm going to see my mom walking through, but then my brain does that thing where it reminds me she's gone, and my heart breaks all over again.

It's Dom and Kirill. I haven't seen much of Tino, and I'm feeling guilty about that too. He was hurt in the blast, and he's still recovering. I need to make more of an effort.

"Hey, how are you feeling?" Dom asks, heading over to the bed.

Kirill rounds the other side and perches on the edge.

I force a smile. "Same. How are you guys?"

"Missing you," Kirill says. "Missing Tino too. He's in his room almost as much as you are."

I wince as a fresh wave of guilt barrels through me. "Sorry," I mutter.

Dom takes my hand. "Don't be sorry. We understand. None of this is your fault."

Isn't it, though? If I'd never gotten involved with Paxton...

If I'd never gotten involved with Paxton, I'd most likely never have come here. I'd never have met the guys. But my mom would also still be alive. I know it's a futile thing, asking myself 'what if,' but I can't seem to stop myself. It tortures me.

"So," Kirill says, edging farther onto the bed, "it's Dom's birthday tomorrow. The old man is turning twenty-two."

I widen my eyes and turn to him. "It's your birthday? Already? Surely that can't be right."

Kirill responds. "Yeah, it's October now, *Kukla*. It's been weeks since it all happened."

I feel like I've been in a daze, or half-asleep—which I probably have. Shit. I become aware of how disgusting my bedsheets are, and that I can't remember the last time I washed my hair. The guys have been forcing me into the bath and washing it for me, but it's not the same as if I wash and style it myself. Plus, it's probably been a month since I last shaved my legs.

A month. Has it really been so long?

A worm of unease buries into my belly. There's something else, too. Something I'm missing.

"So, what are you planning?" I ask Dom. "You have to celebrate."

He shrugs. "Nothing much. I figured you and Tino wouldn't really be in the mood."

"How is Tino?" I ask. "I haven't seen as much of him."

Dom presses his lips together. "Honestly, I think he's struggling again. The doctors put him on some pretty strong meds."

My chest crumples at the thought of Tino struggling. "I haven't been there for him."

"It's okay," Kirill says. "He understands. You've been through a lot."

"So has he," I admit. "So have we all."

I realize how selfish I've been, withdrawing like this. I'm not the only one who's been in pain. They needed me, too, and all I've done is create another problem for them.

I sit up. "I'm sorry. I've been so hopeless."

Dom squeezes my hand. "You lost your mom. We understand."

I sniff and nod. "I think I'm going to take a shower and get changed, then I'll go to see Tino."

Dom and Kirill exchange a quick glance. I can tell they're trying to silently ask each other if this is a good idea or not.

"I'll be fine," I reassure them.

I will, too. For the first time, the fog of grief seems to be lifting.

"And then maybe we can think of something to do for Dom's birthday?" There's hope in Kirill's tone.

I nod. "Yeah, absolutely."

We've not been intimate for the longest time, and as I look at them, I feel the first stirring of anything approaching desire. Sex has been the last thing I've been in the mood for, and it can't have been easy for them abstaining for this long. I know how lucky I am to have found three supportive men who have all put their own needs to one side this past month to care for me.

Kirill gets to his feet. "We'll meet you in the den later."

I agree. "Let me get ready and I'll see you then."

They leave me with hugs and forehead kisses, and I force my legs out of bed. That it's been a month already still blows my mind. I had no idea so much time had passed.

In the shower, with hot water cascading over me, that other niggle I had at the back of my mind makes itself known.

A month.

An entire goddamn month.

Slowly, my hand trails down to my belly. I force myself to think. When did I have my last period? I'm sure I haven't had one since my mom died. But I've had the shock of what happened and everything else to deal with. Plus, I know I've lost weight from not eating properly, and I didn't really have any to lose in the first place.

The place on the inside of my arm where my implant had once resided has long since healed, but I find myself touching the scar there. Shit. It's perfectly possible, isn't it? That I'm pregnant? I have no idea how many times Dom and Kirill and Tino came inside me, but it was plenty enough to get me knocked up. We'd been reckless, but perhaps, on a subconscious level, it was because we'd all wanted this, too. We'd wanted something we could call our own.

My family has been torn away from me, leaving me adrift, but maybe now I could be making a new one.

My heart flutters with nervous excitement, and a warmth springs within me. Could I be pregnant? I've always told myself I wasn't ready to be a mom, but now I've lost my own mother, I discover my feelings have shifted. The idea of life inside me gives me an antidote to the pain of losing so many people. Maybe everyone will say we're too young, but if age can be measured by experiences, we're plenty old enough. We'd love this child with everything we have. We'd all had fucked up relationships with our parents, in one way or another, and I know we'll be determined to make sure we raise this baby right if I am carrying it.

Despite my mental reassurances, nervousness grips me.

Pregnancy isn't straightforward for me. I have my epilepsy to consider. I still need to take medication daily to control my seizures, and I have no idea if that medication can affect a developing baby. And what will happen after the baby is born? Will my condition affect how well I can be a parent?

My stomach twists and flips with all these considerations. I might be happy about the idea of becoming a parent, but this will be a high-risk pregnancy and I'm going to need a lot of medical care.

I'm also worried about what the guys will say to the news. Will they be happy? What if they say they're not ready to be fathers?

I shake the thought from my head. I don't think that's going to happen. Besides, I don't even know for sure that my suspicions are real. I haven't done a test or anything. I urgently need to get one.

I'll keep this news to myself until I know for sure.

THE DEVILS' DARLING

Forty-One
Tino

My head throbs.

Fuck me, it's bad enough struggling with historic injuries, but the pain in my head from the fracture only adds to it. Still, it's healing slowly, and I know full well that the time has come to cut the meds.

And yet, I haven't. I'm not taking them at dangerous levels like before, but I should have stopped by now.

I turn to the wall and close my eyes. I've been spending hours in my room, in bed. I know I should get myself moving. I know I should be reducing the painkillers now. I know Mackenzie needs me.

The more I *know* these things, the worse I feel, and the more tempting the bottle of pills becomes.

It's not purely for pain relief. I love the softened edges they bring. The way they make this too emotionally painful world all nice and fuzzy. The way they make me sleep, and sleep, *and sleep*.

I think I've lost weight. I know I've lost muscle mass. You can't sit around in your room all day, sleeping and watching crap on a tablet, and maintain the physique of an athlete. I'd be worried about getting fat, except I'm not eating much either.

I kind of wish I could slip away. Some days, I want to disappear into nothing. I'm so fucking *weak*. Kirill lost his father, after the man went certifiably insane and kidnapped Mackenzie. Mackenzie lost her mother. Dom lost his own mother not that long ago, and now his father is grieving and a shell of himself.

Out of all of us, I'm the one who should be strong. I ought to be stepping up and carrying the others through these horrific times, but instead I'm the weakest of us all.

The self-loathing fuels the pills, which fuel the self-loathing, and around and around I go. Stuck on this hellish merry-go-round.

At night, I add a little bourbon into the mix, and the warm and fuzzies hit even harder. I need to stop. I'm on a dangerous path, and the last time I followed it, I ended up in the hospital. I could have died. I don't understand why the fear of that happening again isn't enough, but it simply isn't. Some days, I feel as if there's nothing worth stopping for other than Duchess, and she's broken, too, now. She's closed herself off from us, and I've barely seen her.

The bang at my door makes me jump.

I ignore it. Kirill texted me earlier, saying he wants to go get some things for Dom's birthday and asking me to go with him. It's the last thing I want to do. Who gives a fuck about birthdays? Nothing much matters anymore.

The knock comes again, and I sigh. "Fuck off, Kirill. I'm not in the mood."

"It's me," a feminine voice calls through the wood.

My heart leaps.

Mackenzie.

I contemplate turning her away, too, but she sounds scared. Her voice is small and wavering.

My protective instincts kick in. My head thumps when

I force myself from horizontal to vertical, but it's not as bad as it was. Not bad enough for me to justify still taking the full amount of pain meds and washing them down with bourbon at night.

Mackenzie is pale when I open the door, and she's clutching a pharmacy bag in her hand. Fuck, is something wrong with her?

"Can I come in?" she asks.

"Yeah, of course."

She slips into the room and wraps me in a hug. I stiffen a little, not worthy of her affection when I've been so shit since her mother died.

Biting her lip, she eyes me warily. "Do you still love me, Tino?"

Her question hits me hard. "What? Of course. Jesus, Mackenzie, don't ever doubt that."

"Why are you avoiding us?"

I laugh and can't help the bitter edge. "I think that goes both ways."

Her lips tighten, and she flicks her gaze around the room, landing with unnerving focus on the pill bottle by my bed.

"How is your pain?" she asks.

My muscles tense, knowing she's asking because of the meds. "It's bad. Why?" I'm being defensive, but I can't help it.

"Because I am worried about you," she says softly.

"I'm fine. Focus on yourself."

"That's why I'm here. I'm scared, Tino. I was going to do this alone and then tell you all after, if I needed to, but I can't. You're the calmest. The one I trust the most to have my back with this. But … if you're not feeling up to this …."

"Are you sick?" I demand.

"No. Not sick, but um, I might … I might be pregnant."

I stare at her as the shock hits me. Then it's followed

by the desire to laugh at myself and my stupidity. Why the shock? We all knew this might be in the cards. In many ways, we encouraged it. Played with fire.

Now I might be about to get burned because I'm in no place to be a good father.

"Oh, my God." Mackenzie's expression takes on a tinge of horror as her mouth falls open. "You don't *want* this. You ... shit." She covers her face with her hand and shakes her head. "I made a mistake. I'm sorry I came to you, but you ... Forget it. I can sort this out myself."

Sort it out? What does she mean by that? Out of the fog of my self-pity, I get a grip and grab her arm as she tries to leave.

"No, Kenzie, don't go. It's not that at all, I'm just a bit screwed up, here, if I'm being honest."

Her gaze flicks back to the nightstand. "The pills?"

"Yeah." I clarify when I see the fear in her eyes get worse. "It's not like before. I'm not taking more than the allowed amount, but I've not cut down yet either, and I'm scared when I try I won't be able to."

"You must, Tino. You can do it. For me ... maybe for *us*."

She puts her hand on her stomach, and there's a protectiveness in the gesture that stirs something deep inside me.

"What do you need?" I ask.

"Wait while I do the test here? I'm scared that if I am pregnant this baby will be cursed."

"Cursed?" I stare at her in confusion. "Why would it be?".

"Because *I am*, Tino. I bring nothing but chaos and destruction everywhere I go."

Tears build in her eyes, but she blinks them back. I take her hand and squeeze it.

"Kenzie, that's not on you. It's not your fault life got so screwy. It was the people around you who failed you."

I realize there and then that I cannot be another of those people, no matter how bad I feel. "And you bring something else, too. Love. We all love you."

"You, too?"

"Absolutely, me too."

She bites her lower lip. "I'm frightened because of my epilepsy. What if my meds affect how the baby develops? What if it means I won't be able to be a good mom?"

"You'll be an amazing mom, and we'll make sure you have the best medical care, I swear it. Nothing will be too much."

She draws a shaky breath and nods.

"Come on," I say gently, "let's do this test and find out if we're going to be parents."

Her fingers feel so small in mine as I lead her to the bathroom. I'll never forget that, in this moment, she came to me, and I'll do whatever the hell it is I need to in order to step up if this test is positive.

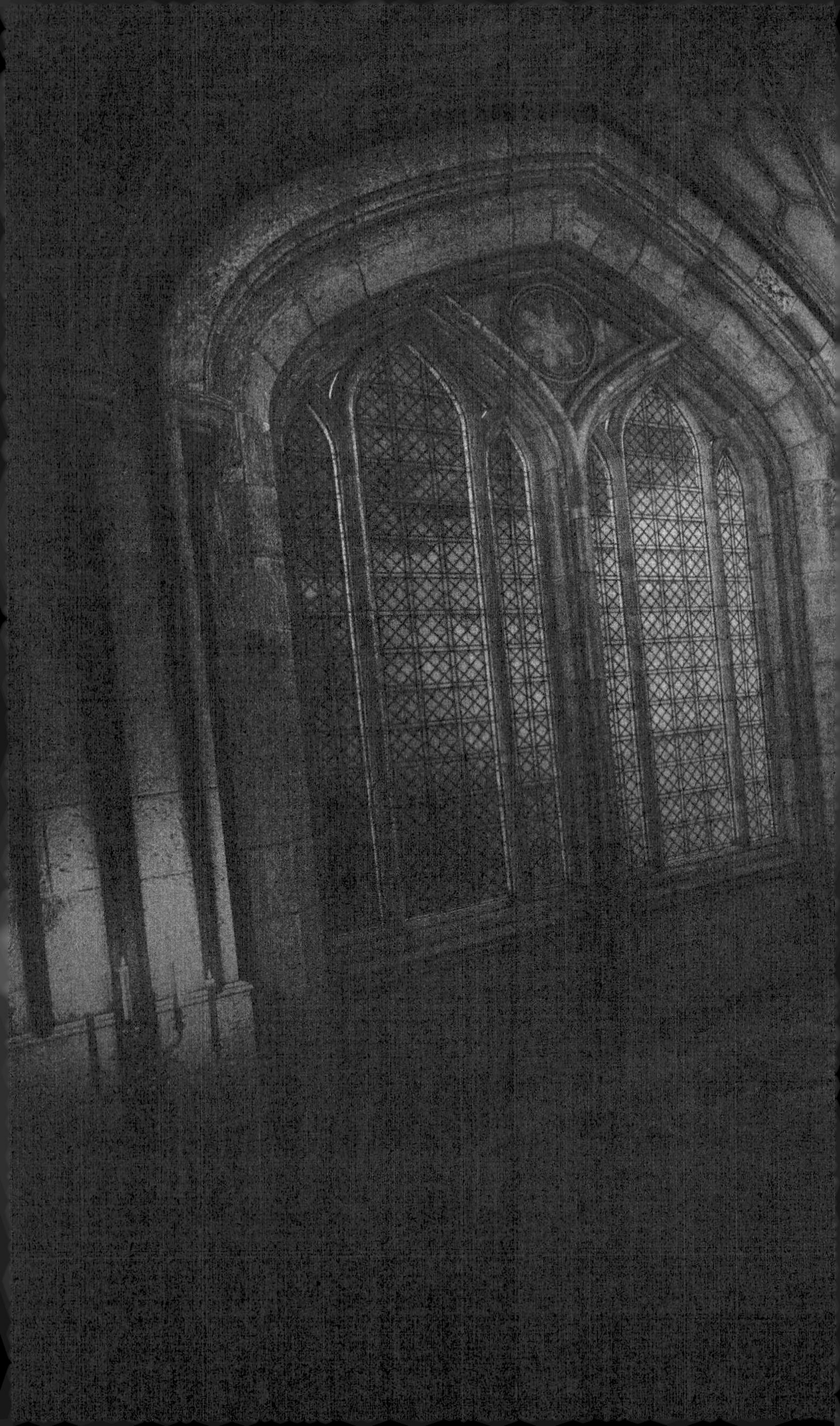

Forty-Two
Mackenzie

My hand shakes as I pull my zipper down. Tino is in the room with me, and I don't care. This man has had his cock inside me at the same time as his friend. I think I can deal with him seeing me pee.

Sitting on the seat, I unwrap the test. It trembles in my grip, and my heart races like it's trying to escape my chest. I don't think I've ever been so nervous in my entire life.

I read the instructions and then read them again, making sure I understand exactly what I'm supposed to do. I know it's basically just peeing on a stick, but I still want to get this right.

"You okay?" Tino asks.

I nod. "Yes, I'm doing it now."

He looks as nervous as I feel.

I hold the stick beneath me. The position is awkward, but I think it's in the right place. Now I just have to convince my bladder to let go. For a moment, I don't think it's going to happen, but then I relieve myself over the end of the stick.

When I'm done, I put the lid back on and place it on the vanity. Then I wipe and put my clothes back in order.

"How long do we wait?" Tino asks as I wash my hands.

"It says up to three minutes."

He nods and sets an alarm on his phone.

"This is going to be the longest three minutes of my life," I say.

I have two more tests in my bag if needed. These are the fancy new ones where you don't get the lines but get a screen that says *pregnant*.

"It's going to be fine," he reassures me. "Whatever the result is, everything will be okay."

I cover my face with my hands. "I feel sick. I can't look. I just can't. You're going to have to do it for me when the three minutes is up."

"I can do that."

I'm pacing in the small space, gnawing on my thumb nail, breathing too fast.

His voice is low and soft. "Kenzie, come here."

He reaches for me and pulls me into his arms, holding me tight. I bury my face in his chest and wrap my arms around him. I realize how much I've missed him—God, how I've missed him.

The alarm sounds, and we jump apart. It's time.

I blow out a shaky breath. "Oh, God. I don't think I can do this."

"I've got you," Tino says.

He picks up the test and stares at it. Adrenaline pumps through my veins, and my mouth is dry. Tears fill my eyes.

"Tino, what does it say?"

"Pregnant," Tino breathes, holding it out for me to see the word on the test. "Fuck, Mackenzie, you're pregnant."

I swallow hard and stare at the test as my hand automatically goes to my stomach. Tears spill down my cheeks. I have to do this alone, without my mom to guide me.

"Hey." Tino brushes the tears away. "It's going to be

okay. We'll be with you every step of the way."

"I don't know how to do this without her," I say.

He doesn't need to ask me who I mean.

"You can. *We* can. It's not you and this baby facing the world alone. It's you and the three of us raising this baby."

"We're all so young. What if some of you change your minds? Things do change." My fears rush to the surface, taking over. "I could end up alone. No family. No money."

The thought of being in that situation while going through a high-risk pregnancy is, frankly, terrifying, and I don't even want to think about what it would be like trying to raise a child by myself.

"You're not going to be alone, and the money side of the equation is easy enough to sort out. We all need to talk about this together, but you're our Duchess. We won't let you down."

He pulls me into a hug again, holding me so tight it's as though he's trying to squeeze my fears out of me. I cling to his t-shirt, burying my face into his chest, allowing him to be my strength.

When we step apart, he turns on his heel and marches into the bedroom. He returns with the pills and the bourbon. He proceeds to empty the meds bottle down the toilet.

"No more pills." Then he does the same with the bourbon. "No more booze. I will prove to you that I'm here for you."

I gently touch his face. "What about your pain?"

He shrugs. "It's getting better, and I can take Tylenol. You mean everything to me, and now so will this baby. It's scary, Mackenzie, but God, it's so miraculous, too. Don't you see that?"

I nod fiercely, not trusting myself to speak. A tight knot forms in my throat, and I'm sure if I try, I'll burst into tears.

His deep brown gaze holds mine. "So much loss," he says. "So much pain, but from that, a new life."

Part of me knows he is right, but also the fear is still there. It's such a mix of emotions. Fear, elation, excitement, guilt about my medical condition, and pain that my mom won't see her grandchild. Nor will my father. Grigoriy wanted this, and it's happened, but he lost his life trying to force it to happen his way and ensure the baby could only be Kirill's. The whole world tried to put us in a box and make us behave the way they saw fit, but we'll never fit in those neat boxes they want for us.

I put my hand on my stomach. I might still be an orphan, and an only child with no siblings, but soon, I'll have my baby and three amazing men. I will still grieve for my mom. There won't be a day I don't miss her, but maybe I can also start to look to the future, too.

"I'm scared to tell the others," I whisper. "What if they aren't happy? We don't even know who the father is."

Maybe it will be for the best if we never do, because that way they'll all be as important to this baby as each other. They look so different, though. If the baby shares his or her father's features rather than mine, it might be obvious.

Tino smiles, revealing a set of straight, white teeth. "Trust me, Duchess. This is going to be the best birthday present Dom has ever had."

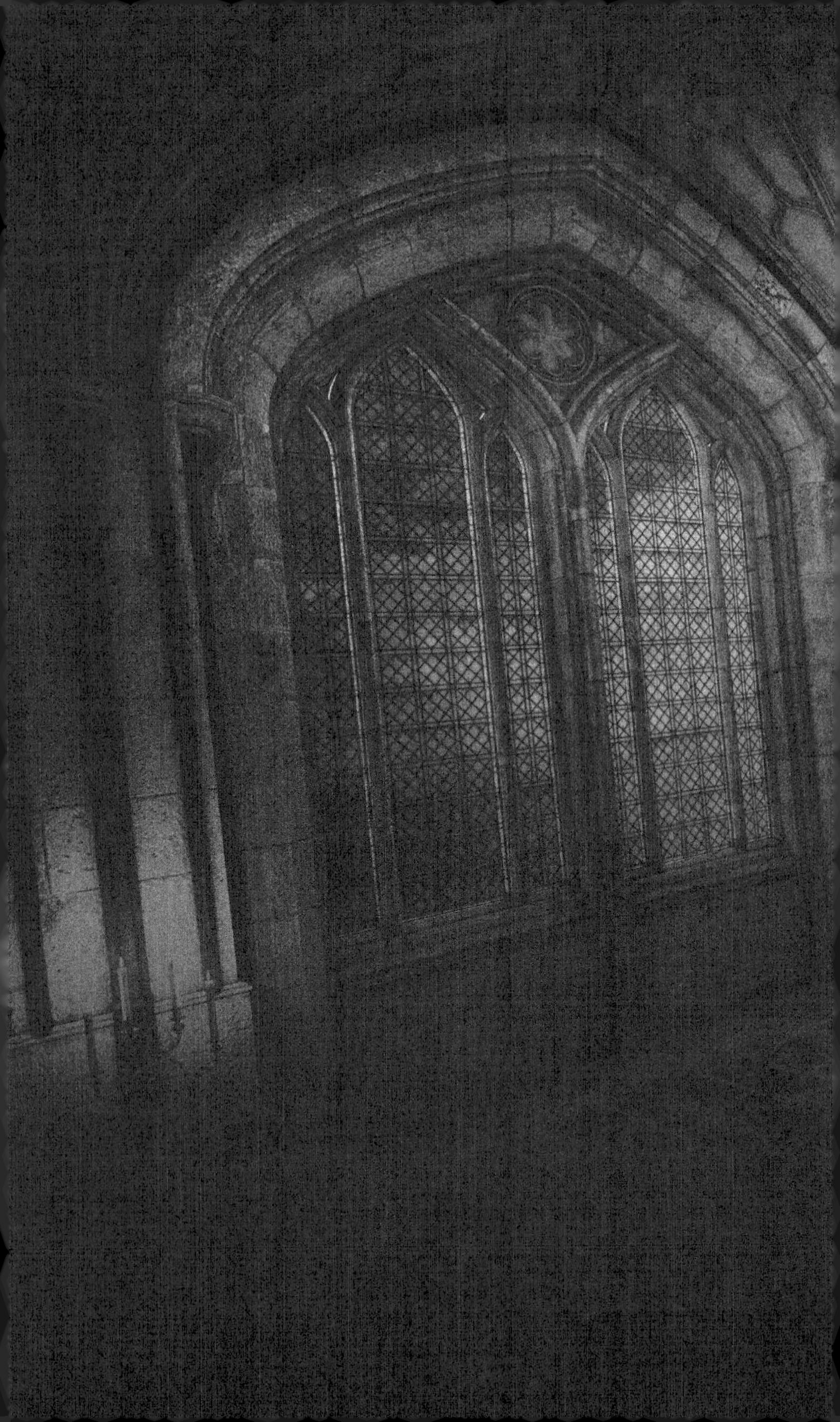

Forty-Three
Kirill

Something is going on, and I don't know what.
It's Dom's birthday.
Mackenzie and Tino have agreed to meet us in the den to celebrate Dom turning twenty-two. I'm pleased they're both out of bed, but they seem to be sharing some kind of secret, and it's bothering me that I don't know what it is. I keep catching them exchanging secretive little looks and smiles when they think we're not looking.

I wonder if it's something they've arranged as a birthday surprise, but I don't understand why they haven't included me. I don't appreciate being left out. Ever since I spent that time in the basement with my *Kukla*, we're closer than ever, and this is making me feel pushed out. I want to confront them, but I also don't want to send either of them back into a downward spiral. At least they are both smiling and happier than we've seen them in a long time.

We've got some gifts for Dom—a rare collector's watch, a one-of-a-kind engraved Jones Deluxe handgun, and a giant suctioned dildo, as a spoof. I'm sure he'll see the funny side. Mackenzie is hanging up a 'Happy Birthday' banner, as though Dom is turning two instead of twenty-two. I'm sure he'll be pleased she's made the effort, but Tino is hovering around her like she's a fragile piece of glass he's worried is going to break.

I know we've all been through a lot, but one thing I've learned is that Mackenzie is a hell of a lot stronger than we gave her credit for.

She turns her head in my direction and throws me a smile.

Fuck, she looks beautiful today. There's color back in her cheeks, and her golden blonde hair is clean and shiny. She's lost weight, and I miss her curves, but I'm sure she'll get them back now she's eating again. I've ordered a shit ton of food from the nearby town, since our kitchen isn't fully back up and running, and the table is laid out with pizza and chips and dips. Plus, there's a huge cupcake stand. Mackenzie has already snagged one of the chocolate cupcakes and wolfed it down. She got frosting on the corner of her mouth, and Tino wiped it off with his finger, and then bopped her on the nose, making her giggle.

I'm so fucking grateful that she seems to have come back to us. These past couple of months have been trying times, but the one thing we've all managed to do is stick together. I can't imagine where we would have ended up if we hadn't had each other to rely on.

The door cracks open, and we spin around as Dom enters.

"Happy birthday," we chorus.

Domenic pauses, drags his hand through his hair as he looks around, and then his face splits into a grin. "Fuck, guys, you didn't need to do this."

Mackenzie runs up to him. She launches herself at him, and he catches her, her legs hooking around his waist, and her arms around his neck. She kisses him hard.

"We wanted to," she says when she breaks the kiss.

"Happy birthday, baby."

He kisses her back and then sets her down.

"This looks amazing."

"We have food," she says, practically dancing over to the table to indicate the pizza.

Her energy is almost wild, like she's had five too many shots of espresso. Maybe it's all the sugar she's eaten, but my gut tells me it's something more.

He grins. "Awesome. I'm starving."

"Food first?" she asks. "Or gifts?"

"Definitely food."

Is it my imagination, or does her expression fall slightly? She catches Tino's eye, and he gives her a tiny nod. What the hell are these two up to?

We make short work of all the food between us. Dom and I have a beer, too, but Mackenzie and Tino both go without.

Mack claps her hands. "Gifts now!"

"Okay, okay." Dom laughs at her enthusiasm.

"What did your dad get you?" I ask.

Dom shrugs. "I think he forgot. It doesn't matter. It's not a big deal."

I can see it kind of is, though, and I feel bad for my friend.

We all sit and watch as he unwraps them. He thanks us for the watch and gun, and then unwraps the giant dildo and laughs. He holds it up and wiggles it up and down. "What am I supposed to do with this thing?"

Mackenzie throws him a cheeky wink. "I can think of a few things."

He arches his eyebrows. "Oh, yeah?"

The sexual tension simmers in the room. It's been too long, and we all know it. We hadn't wanted to push things, though—not with her still grieving and Tino with his head injury. My hand's been getting way too much use for the past couple of weeks.

Mackenzie shares that same secretive glance with Tino again.

"Actually," she says slowly, "there is one more gift."

She takes a breath, and it hits me that she's nervous. What's she got to be nervous about?

She continues, "I've got something else for you, and I really hope it's a good birthday present."

Dom looks as confused as I feel, and I'm glad I'm not the only one who has no idea what's going on. Tino does, though, I can tell from the tiny smile that tilts the corners of his lips. The son of a bitch. How did he get special insight?

"What is it?" Dom asks.

She licks her lower lip and then glances over at me too. "I guess you could say it's a present for all of you."

She pulls a small box from the back pocket of her pants. It's about the size of a box for a bracelet, and she hands it to Dom. He takes it with a confused smile, and then sets about removing the lid.

Dom freezes, his jaw dropping. He stares down into the box and slowly reaches in and plucks out the item it contains. He holds it up for the rest of us to see. It's a pregnancy test with the word 'pregnant' clearly showing.

I feel like my eyebrows just flew off my head and someone punched the air from my lungs.

For a moment, no one says anything, and then Dom stands and grabs Mackenzie. He kisses her mouth and swings her around, lifting her off her feet, before setting her back down again.

"Holy shit!" he cries. "You're pregnant? Seriously, you're pregnant?"

She laughs and nods. "Yes, I am!"

He squeezes her tight. "That's amazing."

I'm still stunned. "Are you serious? We're going to be dads?"

A flutter of worry goes through me. A dad. How do I even know how to be a father? It's not as though I ever had a good example of one. What if I don't know how to do this? I know one thing for sure, though—I'll never hurt my child. I'll never beat them and make them fear me. I'll never lock them up as a punishment. I'll be a safe place for them to come, and I'll protect them with every cell of my being.

"Yes, and I'm going to be a mom."

Her blue eyes fill with tears, but I can tell they're tears of happiness.

I glance over at Tino. He's grinning. He already knew, the fucker. That's what all their shared little smiles and glances were about.

"This is the best fucking news I've ever heard," Dom says.

"Is it?" she asks. "Are you sure?"

"Of course!"

She speaks with a warning in her tone. "It's not going to be easy. There's my epilepsy to consider. It will be a high-risk pregnancy."

"We'll get you the best consultant there is," Dom says. "We'll fly them in from New York, if we have to. Money is no problem."

But she hasn't finished. "Then there's the four of us, living here and raising a child. We have to do this together. That's non-negotiable for me."

"We'll make it work." Dom says, glancing over at the other two, who are nodding in agreement. "There's enough of us that we can look after a baby between us and still continue with our studies. And it's not as though we ever have to worry about money."

She bites her lip. "You all have to be good role models for this child. No more drinking and drugs for Tino..." Tino nods his agreement, and she turns to Dom. "And you can't keep self-harming, Dom. Our baby can't see his father hurting himself."

"I haven't cut myself for a long time," Dom says. "I've been fighting it, because I love you, and I want to be a better person for you, and for our child."

She smiles at that. "I'm so proud of you." She glances around at the rest of us. "Of all of you." Then she turns back to Domenic. "What do you think your dad is going to say?"

"I don't think he's going to be happy that someone is going to be calling him grandad—he'd argue that he's nowhere near old enough—but there's not much he can do about that."

She nods. "I mean, technically, we don't know who the father is, and I want to keep it that way. Do you think he'll see himself as the grandad of this baby with that in mind? Or do you think he'll demand we do a paternity test?"

Dom shakes his head. "He can demand, but I agree with you. If we are all in agreement, then this baby belongs to us all, and my father will have to accept that."

Tino nods. "Absolutely. We're all in it together, and this is the best way."

She glances over at me, the nerves back in her eyes again. "Kirill, you haven't said much. Do you have any doubts?"

I give my head a shake and get to my feet. I hold my arms out, and she falls into them. I hold her and kiss the top of her head, inhaling the scent of her shampoo.

"I'm happy," I tell her. "I'm in agreement, too, about the way you want to handle this. It was never really in any doubt that we'd all share this responsibility and the gift that it is." I pause, and then give her my truth. "I guess I'm just worried at the thought of having to step up and father a real, live human being. I haven't had much of a role model."

She tilts her chin up to look at me.

"You're not your father, Kirill. You're your own person. I don't believe for a second that any of the cruelty that existed inside him is inside you."

I press my lips together. "That's not true, *Kukla*. Look at how we treated you."

She smiles. "Yeah, you were complete assholes, but now you've got the rest of your lives to make it up to me." She takes my hand and places it over her belly. "To make it up to both of us."

"I will," I swear solemnly.

"We ought to go tell my father," Dom says. "He could do with something to look forward to in his life."

Mackenzie swallows nervously, but she nods. "Come on. Let's go let Nataniele know he's going to be a grandfather."

Forty-Four
Domenic

Nerves eat away at me as we approach the door to my father's living quarters. I truly have no idea how he will take this news. I'm praying inside, fervently, that he'll accept this child and us all raising it. The only way to keep Mackenzie and this baby truly safe is to raise him or her here.

If he doesn't, if he won't allow us to stay, we'll be in a vulnerable position.

I suppose we could always go and live on Tino's compound, but that's not what I want. I want to try, if it is possible, to repair my relationship with my father, and one day, I'd like for us to be the ones running this college. All of us. Not just me. Those are heavy conversations for a later date, though. Right now, I have to get through this announcement.

I knock on the door. Muffled footsteps thud behind it, and a moment later, the door swings open.

"Son," Nataniele says. "I was just coming to find you. Happy birthday."

He looks beyond me, and his gaze takes in my friends and Mackenzie.

"I see you're all here," he says. "That's good, because I want to discuss something that affects you all."

My stomach dips. Shit. Is this him deciding to read us the riot act about our relationship?

We all file into the apartment, and I turn to face my father. I know this is a defining moment for me. I must step out of his shadow now and stop letting him ride roughshod over me and what I want, and more importantly, what Mackenzie needs.

"We need to talk to you first, Dad," I say firmly. "We have something to tell you."

His gaze flicks between us. "Go on," he says, his words terse.

"I'm pregnant," Mackenzie blurts before I can say anything.

For a long beat, my father simply stares at her, but then, to my shock, his face breaks into a genuine, warm smile.

He nods and swallows, and, to even more shock on my part, I realize he's trying to blink away tears.

Eventually, he speaks. "That's wonderful news, Mackenzie. I'm sorry your mother didn't live to hear this news, but I know that baby will carry a part of her forward into this world, and as such, it's a miracle."

"You're not pissed?" I ask him.

"Three months ago, I would have been, I imagine. But so much has happened. I've reevaluated a lot." He clears his throat.

"We need to talk about where to raise the baby," Tino says.

My father's face darkens, and for the first time, I see a flicker of anger.

"Here, of course," he replies, as though there's any question in the matter.

"Really?" Mackenzie says as if she can't believe how easy this is. "You're okay with that?" She hesitates and bites her lower lip. "There is something else, something big, and you might not agree, but it's important to us."

My father nods, and I speak up, for her, and for all of us. "We're not going to find out who the father is."

Nataniele is silent, and it's as though we're all holding our breath, waiting for his response.

Finally, it comes.

"I mean," he says, "I understand why you might feel that way, but there could be legal implications. It might leave Mackenzie and the baby vulnerable."

"Not if we all name the baby as our next of kin," Tino says. "Not if we all give Mackenzie some money, now. Then she'll be safe in her own right, financially, at least."

Nataniele doesn't look exactly happy at this news, but he slowly gives another nod. "If that is what you all want, then I'll respect it. I might not agree, but these are your lives, and your child, so you must do this the way you wish."

To my surprise, Mackenzie walks up to my father and pulls him into a hug. "Thank you, Nataniele."

He hugs her back stiffly and then pulls away, his cheeks red at the show of affection.

"What about your...condition? You'll need extra monitoring throughout the pregnancy, won't you?"

She nods. "Yes, it'll be a high-risk pregnancy. I'm going to need extra medical care."

"We'll get you the best there is," he says.

"I already told her that," I add.

He turns to me. "I haven't given you your present yet. I think with this news, you'll find it is even more apt."

I wonder what the hell it could be. Money?

Nataniele clears his throat. "You can't all stay here living in separate rooms."

"I know. We had thought maybe the den," I begin.

He holds his hand up. "No, that's preposterous. There's no natural light down there, and it's no good for a baby.

These rooms would be much better."

I stare at him, not quite comprehending what he's saying. Does he mean he wants me and Mackenzie to move in here with him? I glance at Kirill and Tino. I don't think they'll go for that.

He continues, "There are rooms up in the attic where I can quite comfortably live. I already have a study up there, lots of my papers and books are there. It won't be a hardship to have the rooms nearby turned into a bedroom and living area for me." His expression grows serious. "These rooms are nothing but spaces full of sad memories for me now. First your mother, Dom, then Lucia. They need new life, and you will literally be giving them that. The four of you should have enough space."

I can't speak. For the first time in my life, I'm struck totally silent. This is beyond anything I had imagined. I'd thought he'd fight us on this and eventually, grudgingly, give in. The fact he's offering his space to us is amazing.

A strangled sob comes from my side, and I turn to see Mackenzie wiping her eyes.

"Oh, my God, Nataniele. Thank you, thank you, thank you." She goes in for another hug, and this time my father returns it a little less awkwardly. "You're going to make the best grandfather."

He groans. "Oh, my God, please. That makes me feel ancient."

She giggles, and soon we're all laughing.

This is the best birthday present I could have asked for.

THE DEVILS' DARLING

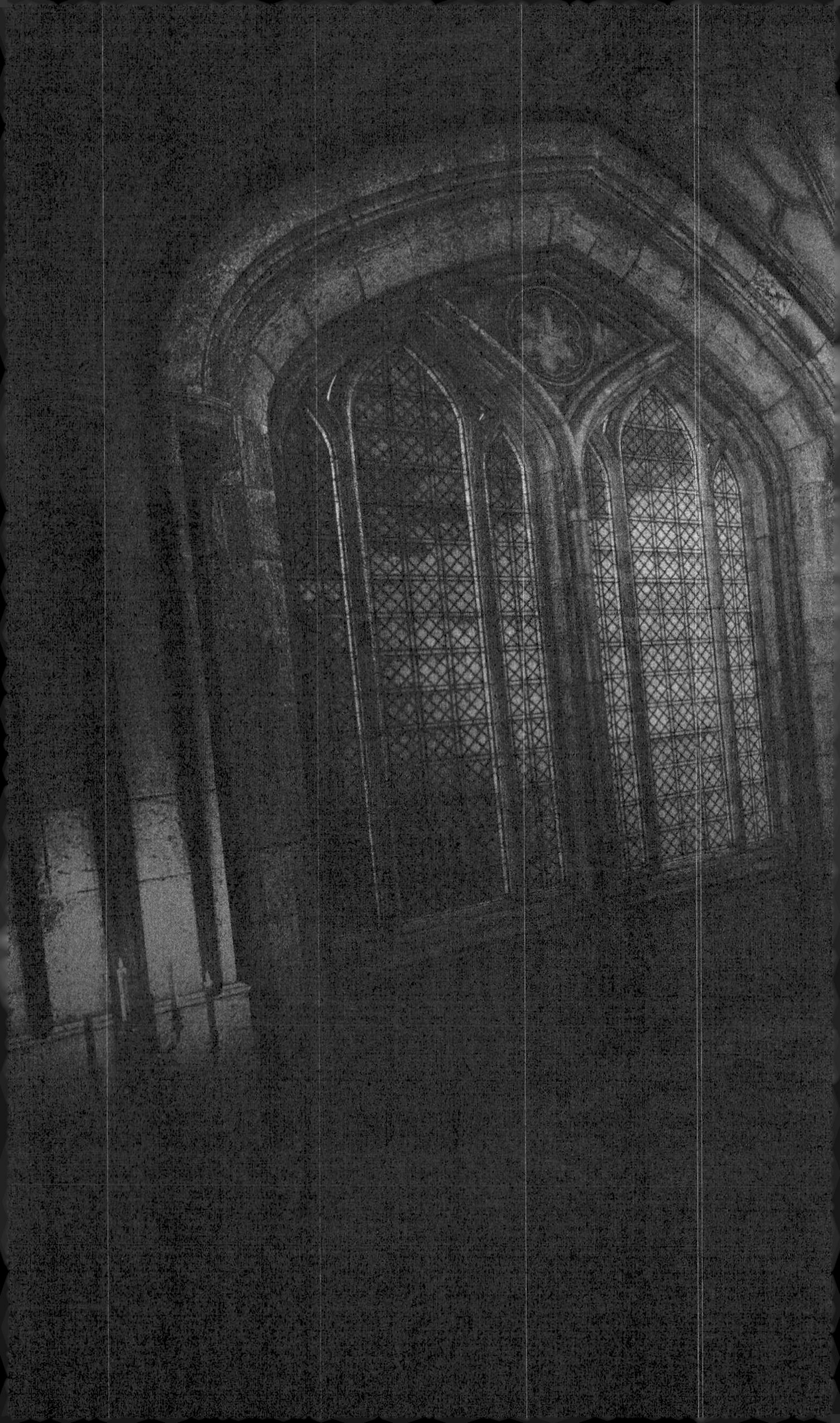

Forty-Five
Mackenzie

I haven't seen the guys properly in the last couple of days, and I am starting to wonder what is going on. I told them about the baby, and they seemed happy, but now they've been avoiding me. I tried to question Tino yesterday about this new distance, and he was all cagey.

Their absence is making me sick and panicky. I've already lost both my parents. The idea of bringing up a baby alone in this world is too terrifying to contemplate.

I check my phone for the gazillionth time, but there's nothing. No text, no calls. They haven't even come around to see me, and it's not like they don't know where my room is. Have they been talking behind my back, making different plans than the one they said to my face? Maybe I should take things into my own hands and track them down and demand to know what the fuck they're playing at, but my insecurities have raised their heads with full force.

The truth is that I'm petrified of hearing what they might say.

Staring at the ceiling, I try not to cry. When Nataniele offered us his living quarters, it seemed as if everything was going to be all right for once. I dared to hope ... to dream. I should have known better. Life has never been kind to me, so why would it start now?

Hand on my currently non-existent bump, I talk to the baby. "I need to stop the self-pity, huh? I'm going to be your momma, and I need to become brave and strong to do that. I want you to learn from me if you're a girl. I want you to not always have to rely on others. If you're a boy, I want to teach you respect for girls, and to be kind, not just fierce."

Will I find out at the scan what sex the baby is? Will the men want to know?

Thinking about them kicks the melancholy back in, but as I stew on their ignoring me, it turns to anger. How dare they? One of them is this kid's biological father, and if they're going to screw around like this, I'll take a paternity test and make damn well sure they pay their way.

Emotionally and mentally, I'm all over the place.

Elated one moment. Terrified the next. Angry, then sad. Do the hormones kick in this early? I need to read up on this, learn more about what to expect.

I pick up my tablet and scroll online stores for books about pregnancy. I pick three that look the most informative and order them.

My phone buzzes, and I glance at it, my heart pounding in anticipation. I groan out loud in disappointment when I see it's just a text from Camile.

I should be glad to hear from her, but I really wanted it to be one of the guys.

Hey, bestie. You need to get your ass down to the main lecture hall now. Major shit going down. Entire school has been called.

What the hell? My stomach flip-flops with anxiety. What now? Oh, God, could it be more security breaches?

As much as I don't want to leave my room, I can't ignore this. I hope it's nothing, and the school is just being overly cautious after what happened.

Throwing myself off the bed, I push my feet into some slides and check my hair in the mirror. I have to admit I'm not looking my best, and as much as I don't want to care, I also know if I see any of the Devils, I don't want to look like shit. I've always done my best to hide how I feel inside, and I won't stop now. I'm the Duchess, and I'll hold my head high, no matter what. I fluff my hair a little, add some gloss to my lips and a spray of perfume, and then set off to the lecture hall.

The biggest lecture hall doubles as an assembly room, too, as it has a stage and is also used for shows and other performances. I arrive and take a seat at the back. Everyone is here. I've never seen it this full.

Glancing at the front, I gasp. Dom, Tino, and Kirill are standing on the stage. What the fuck? Have they done something wrong?

My stomach twists with nerves, and I shake my head at myself. Of course they've done something wrong—at least in the eyes of the law. They've killed people, and so have I. Is that what all this is about? I'd been worried about bringing up a baby alone, but suddenly a different possibility hits me. What if the FBI are involved, and they're about to pull me onstage, too? I might have to give birth in prison and never get to see my baby.

Or maybe this is all the Devils' doing, and they've found some other way to humiliate me?

All the shit they've put me through in the past rushes back to me. The way they've repeatedly degraded me in front of others. What they did to me at my mother's wedding. Is this going to be the same?

Tears prick my eyes as a wave of intense fear washes over me. Surely, they wouldn't? Not after everything we've been through together. What if it was all a ruse, though? What if they don't feel anything for me, and this has all been a game?

No, that can't be true. Kirill most definitely couldn't have faked his fear and sadness in that basement. He was a mess.

What if Dom has decided he doesn't want me here again, though?

Camile walks up the central aisle, her gaze sweeping the seats.

"There you are." She reaches for me and takes my hand. "Come on."

"What? Where?"

Despite my fears, I allow her to lead me down toward the stage. At first, I let her, but as we near, I begin to pull back. The entire school is here. This is so scary. I can't get on that stage.

There's a deep-down part of me that believes the Devils won't do anything cruel to me now, because they're mine, and I am theirs, but there's a tiny voice that whispers I'm wrong. I'm a stupid girl who loved a murderer. A stupid girl who let three men claim her at once. A stupid girl who caused her own mother's death with her selfish actions.

"Camile, no," I whisper. "I can't. Don't do this."

But then we're at the stage, and Kirill hops down.

"Kirill?" I say, a question in my tone.

He grins at me and surprises me by kissing my mouth quickly. Then he lifts me with ease to place me on the stage, before he jumps back up himself.

Oh, shit. The lights of the hall are blinding, and I can't see the rest of the students' faces. Maybe it's for the best. My heart pounds, and my throat is dry. What the hell is going on?

"Everyone, thanks for coming," Dom says into the mic he's holding. "There's been a lot of rumors flying around about me and my friends, and Mackenzie, and we would like to clarify things and clear up those rumors."

Tino grabs the mic. "Some of you think she's with me, but she's not."

Oh, fuck, here we go. My stomach plummets.

Kirill takes it next. "Some of you have talked about her being with me, but she's not."

Dom takes the mic again. "She's with *all* of us."

I stare at him in shock. Did I hear him right? Has he just told the whole fucking school we're a foursome? Oh, my God, I'm going to be seen as such a slut.

Murmurs sweep around the auditorium. My face flares red, and I wish the stage would open up and swallow me.

"We love her." Dom's words silence the noise and chatter.

Holy shit.

I stare at him, my mouth half open in shock.

Kirill takes the mic. "But we treated her like shit at first, and we owe her an apology. We did terrible things to her, and we did it because we're idiots. Mostly Dom," he says with a chuckle as Dom tries to smack him but misses. "But me and Tino, too. We don't deserve you, Mackenzie," he says. "But if you can forgive us, we will spend our lives making it up to you. We will serve you as our perfect Duchess. I had something done for you."

He lifts his t-shirt, and there's new, raw ink on his pec. It's writing, but I can't read it as the script is unfamiliar.

"This says *Kukla*, in Russian," he explains. "You are right here, over my heart."

Then Dom lifts his t-shirt, and he has a set of teeth marks inked on his skin in the same place. What the fuck? I stare at it in shock.

"Your teeth marks on me, baby. Always."

The students whistle, and some clap.

"Hey," Tino says, grabbing the mic. "The best is last."

He lifts his t-shirt too, but then pulls his pants low on his narrow hips. The audience whoops and whistles, some encouraging him to reveal more. Low down on his groin, between those glorious V-Muscles on either side, is the word 'Duchess.'

"This is for you, sweet girl. I went for having you above my cock," he says with that patented, devastating grin of his, "though I was tempted to have your name on it, since it's all yours now."

Dom takes the mic again, and they close in together, facing me. As one, they all drop to one knee in front of me.

"Mackenzie," Dom says, "we know it can't be legally binding, but Verona Falls is a world within a world. A place of its own rules and customs. We want you to be our wife. We want you to belong to all three of us in the eyes of our community here. Do you say yes?"

Kirill produces a box from his pocket and passes it to Tino, who pops it open. Inside is a sparkling, massive solitaire.

From the audience, a female voice yells, "This is fucking bullshit," and there's a flurry of movement as the person the voice belongs to storms out. It barely registers that it's Verity who's left. I'm far too occupied to care about her.

I stare at the ring, and, with tears streaming down my cheeks, I nod.

"Yes," I shout. "Yes, yes, yes. All the yeses."

Camile hollers and whoops and jumps up and down clapping. Kirill takes the ring out of the box and places it on my finger, and Dom takes my hand and kisses the back of it.

My heart overflows with happiness.

"Did we make up for all the shit, Duchess?" Tino asks softly. "At least a little? It's only the start. We'll spend forever making it right."

"It's the best start I can imagine," I say happily.

"Free bar all night, on us, in the college pub," Dom shouts into the mic.

The students cheer and clap and begin to file out of the

hall, all ready to go and party.

"Thought we could maybe just go for one drink and then head back," Dom says. "Spend the night in the den, watching a movie?"

"And other stuff," Kirill adds.

I laugh. "And other stuff, of course. That sounds perfect."

We walk out together—me, flanked by my three men.

In the hallway, we see Zane. He's standing back, one leg bent at the knee, leaning against the wall. He stares at us as we walk by, and his gaze crawls all over me as his smirk tells me exactly what he thinks of me.

"What are you staring at, fucker?" Tino growls.

Zane doesn't answer or give any sort of response. He just keeps watching me, that smirk on his lips, and then we're gone, turning the corner.

The men are surrounding me, cocooning me and making me feel safe, and even though I'm nervous about facing all the students in the bar, I know I can do it with them at my side.

Forty-Six
Mackenzie

I'm feeling fat.

I know it's not fat, it's baby, but it doesn't change the way I feel. Three months have passed since I first discovered I'm pregnant, and I'm starting to show. My belly is still small, just a tiny bump if you look closely, but my boobs feel massive. My face is fuller, and I'm gaining weight around my hips too.

I've been under the best medical care with my new consultant, and she's reassured me every step of the way that everything is fine. I still feel guilty that I haven't been able to stop taking my meds while being pregnant, but that option simply isn't open to me. If my seizures had been under control for the last couple of years, I'd have considered it, but unfortunately, that's not the case.

I have had a couple of scans now, though, and everything is fine. We decided not to find out the sex of the baby. So few things are really a surprise these days, and we're looking forward to finding out when he or she is born.

Turning to the side, I put my hand over my belly. The massive solitaire on my ring finger glints in the mirror, and

I can't help but smile at it. I love looking at the ring and hearing the word 'wife' on each of the Devils' lips.

I push my belly out, imagining how I'll look five months from now, ready to pop. Giggling, I turn away and focus back on the task at hand.

I stare at the freshly made bed, happy with the new sheets I ordered. It wasn't easy getting a massive bed custom made. It cost a fortune, but Nataniele has given us a lot of money to start our lives with. I had to order specially sized sheets to fit the bed that's now in the apartment that used to be Nataniele's and my mom's.

Dom says he is going to work with his dad, running the college once he graduates, and will find roles for the other Devils, too, should they want them. As for me, I don't know if I'll want to work eventually, but, at first, I want to stay home with the baby. I don't want to miss those firsts. The first smile. The first steps. The first word.

One day, though, I want to do something to forge my own path because I don't want to be like Mom. I don't ever want to be reliant completely on other people. I trust my men implicitly, but I still want interests and a career of my own. I might just start it a little later than I had planned, and that's okay.

Maybe I'll start a yoga studio in the nearby town. I'd been lax with my practice before the pregnancy, but that had hardly been surprising, considering everything that had been going on. Now, though, I've found it's been great to get back on the mat with my ever-changing body, and it's been good for my mental health, too. I've rediscovered my love for yoga, and one day I'd love to share my passion with others.

"Hey, looks good."

The deep voice has me turning around to discover Tino behind me.

I smile at him and look back to assess the bed. "Do you think it's big enough?"

He laughs. "It better be, because I don't think we can fit anything bigger in this room."

We have a couple of spare rooms, too, for guests, or for if any of us just needs a bit of space. Sometimes I read in one of them, and sometimes Dom ends up sleeping in one of the spare rooms in the early hours. He has a need for alone time, and that's fine. I understand.

Tino has his time alone when he exercises. He's getting back into it these days, and I'm happy it seems to be grounding him and helping him give up the meds for good.

Kirill seems to be the only one who never wants any time alone. It's as if what happened in that basement re-triggered his old fears of the dark and being by himself, and he always seems to want to be hanging around with at least one of us. He's quieter than he used to be, too. More serious.

Or perhaps, just like all of us, he's grown up.

Tino is doing amazingly well in his recovery, and standing in front of me now, he's glowing.

The door opens, and Kirill joins the party.

He stares at the bed and raises his brows. "That's so much better. No excuse for Dom to sneak off to the spare room in the middle of the night now, claiming we're all hogging the space."

"You do hog the space," Tino grouses. "Arms and legs all over the place. I woke up with your elbow in my mouth yesterday."

Kirill snorts, and I giggle.

"Where is Dom?" I ask. "I want him to see the bed."

"Well, I mean, it's just a bed," Kirill says.

I stare at him, my eyes narrowing. "It's a custom-made bed, with custom-made sheets, and look at the throw cushions."

Tino laughs. "Sorry, Duchess, but as much as I love you, I can't get excited about throw cushions."

"It has some other special features," I say.

"Like what?" Kirill asks.

The headboard is made of metal struts, and I've had something special fitted to the middle of both the head and foot ends.

The door opens, and I know it's Dom without turning around. He still has that charismatic energy that precedes him. He fills a room with his personality alone.

"Is there a meeting I've missed?" he asks sarcastically. "Why are we all staring at a bed?"

"Oh, my God," I shout, exasperated. "It's *the* new bed. With custom sheets and throw cushions. Isn't it pretty?"

"You said it has something special? What is it?" Kirill pushes.

I walk to the foot of the bed and dig my hand down between the frame and the mattress then pull out two padded ankle restraints.

"I had these fitted to the headboard, as well."

"Nice," Dom says. "I approve of these."

"What about the cushions?" I am getting prissy now. I spent time and money getting these cushions.

"I mean, they'll look good propping up your ass." Dom chuckles. "Presenting your pussy for us. That way I can see them being useful."

"God, yes, they would, wouldn't they?" Tino growls.

"I want to see," Kirill says.

"They're not *sex* cushions," I argue, exasperated. "They're decorative."

"Baby." Dom gently turns my face toward his with the tips of his fingers. "They are so going to be sex cushions."

"We need to test the bed," Tino says seriously. "Make sure it can take all we can give it."

"Let's get our doll on the bed, tied up and propped on some cushions." Kirill's eyes light up.

Trust my men to make it all about sex. Not that I mind. My hormones are haywire right now, and I'm horny all the time. Even my dreams are absolutely filthy—which I far prefer to the nightmares that plagued me before. I've not had any sickness. Instead, I'm hungry and needy. I can't complain, but I do worry I'll end up huge if I keep eating. If having plenty of sex can stop me munching on cookies, it can only be a good thing.

Dom starts to undo the buttons of my shirt. I'm wearing a denim shirt over leggings, and he slowly shrugs it off my shoulders. My bra is just a plain white one, but he still groans when it's revealed.

"Love how big these tits are getting," he says.

Kirill moves behind me and unhooks the fastener, letting the bra fall away. He cups my breasts from behind, rolling and pulling at my sensitive nipples.

"I love how fat these nipples are already," Kirill says as he bites my earlobe gently. "When your milk comes down, I hope you'll let me taste it direct from the source."

My pussy tightens at the thought of them suckling from me. Will they fight over who gets to taste me first? There's something immoral and forbidden about the action, and of course that only gets me hotter.

"Give me one," Dom demands, and Kirill holds my tit up for Dom to suck my nipple into his mouth.

He ducks down and laves the sensitive peak with his tongue, and my eyes roll with pleasure. They've always been an erotic zone for me, but now they're off the scale. Kirill massages my breast with one hand while Dom licks and sucks and grazes his teeth over my nipple.

It makes me feel debauched.

They often treat me this way, like an object, talking about me in third person, and I find it so hot every damn time. Afterward, they always take care of me like their precious doll.

"Let's get these pants off and see if your pussy is swollen for us, too," Tino says.

Dom lets my nipple pop from his mouth and steps back to give Tino space.

I kick my shoes off, and Tino roughly pulls down my leggings. He doesn't bother to take my thong off, but just pulls it to one side. His fingers press against my pussy, finding me already wet.

"So pretty and all puffy. Is that for me?" he asks.

I swallow and nod, my ability to speak partially robbed by the way he's staring down at my pussy. He parts my folds and stares some more. God, I'm squirming with need, and he's simply looking at me.

"This is the prettiest pussy I've ever seen," he says. "Let's see if it tastes as good as it looks."

He drops to his knees in front of me and leans in close and licks me, his tongue hot and wet and firm. I jolt at the sensation. God, I'm so sensitive. I moan and spear my fingers through his thick, dark hair. He sucks my clit into his mouth and pushes two fingers inside me.

"Does she taste good?" Dom asks.

"Hhmmm," Tino murmurs against me.

I rock my hips against him, my eyes slipping shut as I fuck his face and his fingers, already lost in my building orgasm. Kirill moves in behind me again, his hands on my tits. He sweeps my hair away and kisses the side of my neck as he works my nipples, tweaking and pulling them.

"Fuck, I love seeing you all curvy like this," he says between kisses. "I can't wait until you're huge with our child. You're going to be so hot."

"Why don't we get her on the bed, all tied up for us?" Dom suggests.

I groan with loss as Tino rocks back on his heels, sliding his fingers from my body and leaving me bereft. I do like the idea of being tied up while all three of these men have their way with me, though. It was the whole reason I had the special headboard commissioned.

Kirill scoops me up.

"Hey, I'm too heavy now," I protest.

"*Kukla*, do not insult me. I will still be able to carry you when you are nine months pregnant."

He places me on the bed, so I'm on my back, my hands above my head. I'm so aware of how naked I am and how they are all still dressed. They make quick work of getting the padded cuffs in place, locking them around my wrists, and Kirill places two cushions underneath my ass.

"Spread those legs, *Kukla*," he says. "As wide as they'll go."

I'm tied to the bed, arms and legs wide apart, and my pussy raised by the cushions. Kirill moves to one side of me, and Tino slides onto the bed on the other. He kisses me, and I taste my arousal on his tongue as he pushes it into my mouth. Kirill ducks down to my tits, sucking and licking.

I lift my hips from the cushions, my pussy needing attention.

Tino notices and breaks the kiss. He reaches between my thighs, but instead of pushing his fingers inside me or rubbing my clit, he parts my pussy lips and holds them open.

"Here, taste her," Tino says to Dom.

Dom crawls onto the bed and settles between my thighs.

Still holding me apart, Tino watches as Dom flicks my clit side to side with his tongue. This is always the fastest way for them to get me off, and with me already so on edge, it's mere minutes before I'm bucking up to try to meet the flicks and get more sensation, but Dom chuckles and moves off me.

"I think Kirill should taste now," he says.

"God, someone needs to," I pant.

My entire body is alive with arousal, every nerve ending zinging with the anticipation of pleasure.

Kirill and Dom switch places. Tino still holds me parted, pulling back my pussy lips so my swollen clit pops forward.

Kirill covers my pussy with his hot mouth, and I whimper and arch my spine, pushing into him. His clever tongue works magic on me, and just when my thighs are tensing and I think I'm coming, he too stops.

I whimper. "Not fair."

Tino laughs softly. "Oh, Duchess, we're only just getting started."

He rubs my clit and pinches it before giving my pussy a playful slap.

"Let's not ignore these pretty tits," Dom says. "Look how beautiful you are all spread out like this."

He palms my breasts and squeezes them together, his thumbs rubbing over my nipples.

Tino stands and slowly undresses, watching what Dom's doing as he strips his clothes off. My gaze is glued to him. I'll never get enough of his incredible body, his abs ripped with muscles, his biceps bulging. I admire each of his tattoos—the crow, skull, clock, and a goat with a set of curly horns—and try to work out which is my favorite.

I think it's the goat, a clear symbol for the Devils.

His huge cock juts out from his body, the piercings up its length glinting in the light. He fists himself and slowly masturbates, his eyes never leaving my body.

"Pussy or mouth?" he asks Dom.

Dom grins at me. "I think I'll take her mouth for a change."

They haven't asked Kirill, and I turn to look at him, but he's already got his cock out and is slowly stroking himself.

"You can come all over her lips and tits after me," Dom says to him. "Or on her pussy."

"I'm going to paint her all over," Kirill grunts.

Jesus, he's so fucking freaky. He comes enough to do that, too.

Tino kneels on the bed, between my legs. With his cock still in his hand, he uses his other hand to work a finger inside me.

"So wet and ready for me," he murmurs. "You're so perfect, Duchess."

"I want you," I gasp. "Fill me up and fuck me."

One corner of his lips quirks in a smile. "Hush and be patient."

I almost want to sob with need.

"Wait a minute," Dom says. "I've got an idea."

"No, just fuck me already!" I cry.

I wriggle and squirm on Tino's finger, wanting more, but he refuses to give it.

Dom returns with something behind his back. With a wicked grin, he pulls it out. It's the huge dildo we bought him for his birthday.

"Let us stuff you full of this, Duchess."

This thing is huge. It's twelve inches in length and covered in ridges and veins. The head is smooth and bulbous, and a darker shade than the length.

I widen my eyes. "I'll never fit that inside me."

"You took both of us, baby," Dom says. "I want to see you stretch around it. Besides, I also have this." He pulls his other hand from behind his back.

It's a bottle of lube.

There's nothing I can do. I'm chained to the bed.

I'm so desperate to come, I'll take anything at this point. "Okay, do it. Fuck me with it."

Kirill's jaw hangs open, and he works his cock faster. "Fuck, this is hot.

Dom opens the lube and covers the head of the giant dildo. I pull against the arm restraints, but they hold me in place. Tino moves back slightly to give Dom space.

He leans over me and places the head at the entrance to my pussy. Tino and Kirill watch, rapt. Dom rubs the head around my swollen, wet pussy, and then he gently presses.

I stretch around it with a stinging pain that morphs to

pleasure. I curl my fingers into fists, and my pussy pulses.

"Oh, God. Oh, fuck," I cry, twisting my head back and forth.

"Good girl," Dom praises. "Look at how well you're taking it."

Inch by inch, he slides it inside me. My breathing has grown ragged, and I know I'm not going to last. They don't even need to pump it inside me because I'm the one doing the work, fucking the huge dildo with my inner muscles, climbing to my peak. The sensations are too much, and I shatter around it, my whole body shaking and jerking with the force of my orgasm.

I come back down, all my muscles loose as I slump onto the bed. I'm breathing hard, my heart thudding, my skin damp with sweat. I puff a loose strand of hair out of my eyes.

"Holy shit," I say on a long exhale.

"We're not done with you yet," Dom says.

He slides the giant dildo out of me, and it comes out slippery with my arousal and the lube.

Tino stares down at me with a heated gaze. "Look at your gaping pussy. All ready for my cock."

He's impossibly hard, the head dark and swollen and leaking pre-cum. He moves back between my spread legs and pushes the head of his fat cock inside me. I groan in response and drop my head back against the cushions.

Dom strips off and straddles my shoulders, his knees either side of me, as he places more pillows under my head, raising it. It's hard to focus with Tino oh-so-slowly fucking me, but then Tino holds himself deep and reaches around Dom to take hold of Dom's cock.

Dom gives a noise that's somewhere between a grunt and a growl and allows Tino to hold him. Tino's chest is pressed against Dom's back, while Tino's cock is wedged deep inside me. Tino moves his hand up and down Dom's length a couple of times, masturbating his friend, and then presses the head to my lips.

"Suck Dom hard," Tino demands.

I open my mouth, and Dom's long, thick cock slides over my tongue. The salty, musky taste of him fills my mouth.

Tino releases Dom's cock and goes back to concentrating on fucking me.

Moaning around him as Tino's piercings light me up inside, I take Dom down as best I can. Dom grabs hold of the metal bars of the headboard, the muscles of his arms and chest bunching, as he fucks my face. I choke on his cock, but I keep going, moving my head back and forth to keep up with his pace.

Soon, the room is filled with nothing but the sounds and scents of sex. The men's deep moans and my whimpers fill the air, and the rhythmic movement of Kirill's fist over his cock only adds to the debauchery.

"I'm going to come down your throat so hard, Duchess, and you're going to swallow it all for me. Don't spill one fucking drop." Dom is panting, and he's almost about to come.

His cock swells in my mouth, and he rams deep down my throat as he spills his load. I struggle to swallow it all, but I manage it, making sure not to let any dribble out of my mouth.

He pulls free and gently rubs my lips with his thumb.

"Such a good Duchess for us." His praise makes me warm inside, and he climbs off me, giving me and Tino space to finish.

Tino is hitting me deep and, when he adds a finger to rub at my clit, I spiral. I fall over the edge. It's all consuming, the intensity of my pleasure, and I buck and thrash, yanking against the cuffs as a scream escapes my lips. My pussy clamps around Tino's cock, milking him.

"Oh, fuck." Tino loses it, finding his release as his hips piston like a damned animal in heat.

We fall together, breathing hard, until he softens and slides out of me.

Kirill walks over to me, his cock obscenely jutting out of his pants, hard and angry. It's fucking throbbing right in front of my eyes, he's that needy.

He rubs the slit and watches me greedily. "Ready for me to mark you as my perfect *Kukla*?"

"Yes, please," I whisper. My voice is hoarse.

He takes Tino's place and gently wipes his finger over my pussy, and shocks me when he pushes some of Tino's cum back inside. Dipping his fingers in and out, he seems to play with Tino's semen, while touching himself. He groans as he aims his cock at me, bumping the head over my clit and rubbing it against me. Though I don't think I can come again, I'm still so sensitive, and the pressure feels incredible.

"Going to paint you, Duchess," he growls.

He works his cock with his fist, his expression intense and sexy. His jaw tightens, and he comes with a grunt, aiming right on my clit. I'm bathed with hot fluid. He's not done, though. He crawls up over me, painting my breasts too, and then aiming the last few splashes over my face.

One final, long pulse of cum dribbles out of him, and he catches it with his thumb and paints some on each nipple.

"Perfect," he says, smiling with dark satisfaction.

I'm sated, but as I come down from the high, the muscles in my arms threaten to cramp. I move a little, trying to relieve them, and wince.

"You okay, *Kukla*?" Kirill asks, all concern at my expression.

"A little sore."

"Let's get these cuffs off and clean you up."

He undoes the cuffs before Tino lifts me and carries me into the bathroom. Dom is already there, running a bath. He adds my favorite scented bath oil and tests the temperature.

Tino carefully wipes down every inch of my body with

a warm, damp cloth, and then lifts me into the warm water. They all sit around me, gently washing me, talking to me. Now and again, they kiss a shoulder, or an arm, or my cheek. I feel so damn cherished that tears threaten.

When I'm clean and dry, they rub body lotion all over me, slip my favorite, over-sized t-shirt over my head, and lead me to bed.

Something flutters low in my belly, and I snatch a breath.

"What?" Kirill asks, noticing the change in me.

I hold still, waiting to see if I feel it again. I do, and happy laughter bursts from between my lips. "I-I think I just felt the baby move."

His blue eyes light up. "You did?"

It happens again, that tiny butterfly-wings sensation.

Dom launches himself at me, pressing his hand to my stomach. "I want to feel it."

"Let me try," Tino says, pushing him away.

"It's too early yet," I tell them, "but you will."

They half-heartedly fight over who gets to be next to me, and Dom takes the spot farthest away as he's got to be up early to spend a few hours with his father, working, before he starts classes.

We lie on our ridiculously big bed, me, my three men, and our baby growing inside me.

I don't know what the future will bring, but so long as I have Dom, Tino, and Kirill with me, I'll be able to face it all.

***

Loved what you've read? Sad the Devils' and Duchess's story is over? Never fear! The Vipers are coming! Order The Vipers and Their Venom from Amazon today.

***

For a steamy bonus epilogue, which includes a baby-daddy reveal, follow this link and sign up to Marissa and Skye's newsletter at the same time - - >

https://dl.bookfunnel.com/xd0ije06cg

***

Come and join the Duchesses at Marissa and Skye's Facebook group, The Duchesses (Marissa Farrar and S.R. Jones). Be the first to hear news about the series, get your hands on exclusive swag giveaways, and hang out with the authors!

When the Vipers meet their Venom, a poisonous game begins...

They are the Vipers of Verona Falls.
Dangerous. Beautiful. Cruel.
The twins are impossible to tell apart.
The one they call Saint is anything but.
His brother Lex might act like the nice one, but it's only to hide the monster lurking beneath.
Then there's Zane: scarred and silent, and somehow ruling over them all without ever having to say a word.
They are used to meek girls. Good girls. The daughters of traditional mafia families who are seen and not heard.
I'm not that.
I come from a different kind of crime family. I'm used to fighting for what I want. Taking what I need. Saying

what I wish.

I've come to Verona Falls University to find out what happened to the sister I never met. I believe the Vipers know something, and I'll stop at nothing to learn the truth.

Our two worlds collide in a heated game of lust and sin.

But soon the fire between us turns deadly, and, in any game, there can only be one victor.

Don't miss out on book four, 'The Vipers and Their Venom, which is now available to order from Amazon!

Also by the Authors

Are you ready to play?
When I take on the job as a maid for four wealthy men on their private island, they mistake me as their plaything. Quickly, I realize they have a twisted game in mind: they want to chase me across the island and, if they catch me, they can do whatever they want.
They offer me a million dollars if I can last until the end without begging to leave, but I'm not the naïve victim they think I am. As the game unfolds, secrets are revealed and power dynamics shift.
Will there be any winners?
Or will this end in all our downfalls?
Read the complete series in **Kindle Unlimited***!*

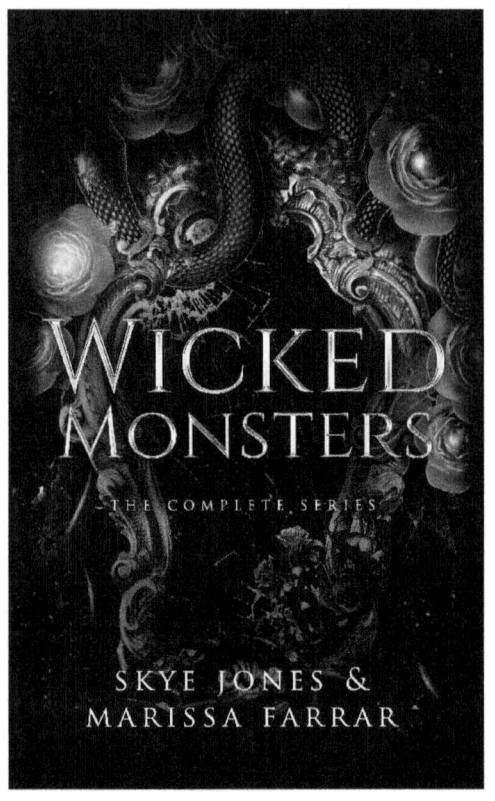

Get the complete, fast burn, Wicked Monsters series as one fantastic set. Meet Aisha's wolves, vampires, human sub, and even a demon-gargoyle in her wild harem!

One girl, five monsters, one hell of a ride.
Taken from the Pit where she was raised, Aisha believes all vampires are horrifying... Then she finds herself in Dashiell's possession.
Powerful, handsome, and charismatic, Dashiell is not what she thought her master would be.
His dark desires draw her into his world, and things heat up between them.
But with a demon gargoyle scratching at her window,

and wolves sniffing at the door, Aisha might not stay in the vampire's grasp for long.
Danger and temptation surround her on all sides, but Aisha is determined to fight them all

Read in Kindle Unlimited on Amazon!

About the Authors:
Skye Jones

Redeeming dark and dangerous heroes one book at a time.

Skye Jones is an award winning and USA Today Bestselling Author.

She writes dark mafia and contemporary romance as SR Jones, and angsty paranormal romance as Skye.

When not writing Skye can be found reading, dog herding, or watching gritty dramas on Netflix with her husband. She lives in the grey, windswept north of England, which fuels her taste for the dramatic and the gothic.

For a free read sign up for her reader club here: https://dl.bookfunnel.com/ca20ewxx71

About the Authors:
Marissa Farrar

Marissa Farrar is the author of more than fifty novels of delicious literary darkness. If you're after light and fluffy, look away now. While she mainly writes dark reverse harem romance – occasionally teetering on the taboo - she's also written mafia m/f romance, and has even dived into paranormal, fantasy and sci-fi!

When she isn't writing—which isn't often—she's taking care of her menagerie of animals, spending time with her family, or binge-watching Netflix with a sneaky gin and tonic.

If you want to know more about Marissa, then she's normally hanging out on her Instagram page, TikTok, or Facebook group. You can order signed books from marissafarrarbooks.com, or direct from her TikTok store.

https://www.instagram.com/marissafarrar/
https://www.tiktok.com/@marissafarrarwrites
https://www.facebook.com/groups/1336965479667766

Printed in Great Britain
by Amazon